OU00793413

DECAD

PAT W HENDERSEN

.

PHOENIX PUBLISHING, LONDON

FIRST EDITION

Proudly published in Great Britain by
Phoenix Publishing Ltd
PO Box 56556
London, SW18 9EP
www.phoenixpublishing.me.uk

A CIP catalogue record for this book is available from the British Library

ISBN: 978-0-9561837-0-5

Music Consultation and Publishing Clearances:
Douglas Kerrigan @ BLINDBEGGAR (Blind Beggar Ltd.)
douglas@blind-beggar.com / www.blind-beggar.com

Cover Design: Deface
Typeset in Palatino by energy typesetting
Printed in Great Britain by the MPG Books Group,
Bodmin and King's Lynn

Dedicated to those that didn't make it.

Angie, Dave, Jim, Lenny, Podge & Wullie.

Especially Wullie!

PROLOGUE

He had absolutely no idea where he'd been taken. A couple of turns out of Niddrie and he'd become completely disorientated. The big guy in the back of the car had wrapped his arms around his head. Probably not necessarily to stop him from seeing where they were going but more likely to keep him from shouting or bailing out of the door. The big guy was strong as well, his arms consisting of bone and muscle only. His face had felt like a vice was pressing against it and the back of his head was forced hard into the cushion of the headrest.

Through a slight gap in the arms he could see glints of light casting through but no way was it enough to enable him to find his bearings. He hadn't been taken far, though, when his head was released and he was dragged out of the car. He looked around the skyline and he could recognise Arthur's Seat and Salisbury Crags. He thought it looked like they were on the south side of them. Couldn't recognise any of the buildings, though. Not particularly unusual. He'd only been in Edinburgh just over a year and although it may not have been the biggest of cities he'd only managed to familiarise himself with a small part of it.

A short walk-cum-drag and he'd been pulled towards a railway line. An old railway line that clearly hadn't been used in some time. Orange-brown corrosion matting the surfaces of the track where a smooth sheen would have been if train wheels had coursed over them any time recently. Sleepers resting comfortably under grit and stone that hadn't been disturbed in some time.

It was then that he worked out for sure that this wasn't a spur-of-the-moment thing. Two pickaxe handles and one baseball bat placed neatly between the tracks. Each of the three guys from the car had prepared their weapons a long time before they managed to get him there. He'd thought as much when he was hustled out of the car.

Up 'til then only the guy behind him had spoken and he was definitely an Edinburgher. The accent was obvious. None of the deep brogue of the other Scottish city dialects. No 'fit like?', 'ehm awah' or 'awright, nawrat?' In Edinburgh, even those from the roughest parts of town managed to verbalise in a way that was all at once broad, yet somehow proper. As if to insinuate 'we're from the capital city – and you're not'.

The driver though. Once he spoke with his Manc drawl he'd began to realise that this was an organised thing. Guys brought together from different parts of the country. Probably never met before. Put together to do one job. One job that they were about to polish off with their carefully chosen tools.

They'd reached around a metre from the track when he felt the hit on the nape of his neck. He couldn't tell if it was a clenched fist or a cosh but they were probably trying something they'd seen in a movie. Like when the secret superagent hero is dunted in the back of the neck and is spark out for a couple of hours. They hadn't knocked him out though. All the strength had left his legs and his plan to make an escape along the track was now out of the window, but he was still conscious. He could hear them laughing as he slumped over on to his side.

The first hit using the weapons was sore. It landed on his left shoulder but the shock and hurt made its way all through his torso. The second hit wasn't a picnic either. It probably broke a few ribs but the muscle and flesh of his stomach had taken some of the sting out of the actual contact. This was good though. If they were working his body then it meant they probably didn't mean to kill him. The third hit, landing squarely on his left ear, was a surprise. Not so much the shock that they had now moved on to breaking his skull. He probably was expecting as much but what he wasn't expecting was that a full-on blow to the side of his head with a wooden implement would hurt so little. Surely that would be worse than the body shots but for some reason this one was mild by comparison.

Then more hits but, strangely, less pain. Some to the head but mainly around his chest and back; he could still feel the impact of the hits as they contacted with his body. Or not so much feel as hear. Dull thuds in an uneven rhythm. The pain had gone. He was over that. Past it. Just like he was past the whole situation. Had it up to here with it.

'Fuckin' deadbeat small town Scots! Fuckin' wankers. Mancunian twats! Wannabe gangsters the whole fuckin' lot of them. Ah don't need this! Don't need them! Ah'm outta here!'

OCTOBER 1989

WHAT GOES UP

1

'Twats though, are they no'?'

Martin Bridges looked out of Caskies window. Unusually interested as the conflicting tide of bag-laden bodies struggled against itself.

'Who's twats?'

Colin Nichols sat across from him. Equally intrigued, only not looking out onto the street, he was looking at the piece of paper in his hand. Nine correct results. Could happen! If it did he'd be £4,430 richer. Seemed like a pretty good way to be making money on a sunny Saturday afternoon.

'Saturday afternoon shoppers are twats man. I mean, what's that all about?'

Martin tapped his thumb against the window, pointing back out onto the street. 'These nutters spend all week working hard right? To make money! Just so's on a Saturday afternoon they can spend the time relaxing but no, no' these pillocks! They're spending their time battlin' through crowds carrying wads o' bags o' shite around that if they thought about it they could have got easily on Thursday night or something! Saturday's for relaxing man, every last man jack o' these punters should be in the pub.'

'Oh right.'

As philosophy went, this wasn't exactly Jung. Colin was able to turn his attention back to whether he thought Sheffield United would actually beat West Ham in London, this was the potential coupon buster but the one result that would really make the effort worthwhile.

'Well ah'm glad they're no' all in the pub, wouldnae leave it a very relaxing experience for the likes of us would it?'

Martin sat back in his chair and shook his head. Pitiful really. Pools coupon! *'Fuckin' waste o' time that is.'* He leaned forward to offer his explanation. Colin wasn't quite getting the point. Double doors swung open allowing a loud gasp of the outside noise to invade the bar. The commotion of the two people struggling to squeeze through completely broke his train of thought.

'Are you managing there, Nat?'

Carrie pushed forward to help Natalie with the door while she squeezed an assortment of bags through. The boys sat and watched. Said nothing. Didn't need to. The relevance of the conversation they had been having starting to hit home.

'Well just sit there eh! Dinnae worry about us we'll be fine!'

Awkwardly, they leaned towards the door.

'Bit late now guys eh, you can make yourself useful and go and get the drinks for the workers.'

Martin glanced at Colin and raised his eyebrows to suggest that workers was a well-chosen word.

'Anyway, what are you two so engrossed in that you couldnae see us struggling across Reform Street?'

'Aw, very important stuff Natalie!'

Colin was now on his feet, squeezing between two tables to get out towards the bar.

'Martin was just explaining how anyone who chooses Saturday as a good time tae go shopping probably needs their heads looking at.'

'Aye, cheers mate!'

'Y' welcome.'

'Aye whatever!'

The girls dropped their bags and took their seats. Not really paying attention to the banter.

'Not so much shopping as essential preparation anyway.'

Carrie peeked into the largest bag.

'You know what these Aberdonians are like. They just seem to think we're a bunch o' skanks from around here so we dinnae need to be giving them any ammunition. I hope you two'll be getting changed as well.'

Martin looked down at what he was wearing. Cords seemed clean enough. Shirt was less than a month old. Couldn't see a problem with them.

'Aye probably.'

He shrugged and looked towards Colin, safely at the bar.

'Anyway, better go help Colin with the drinks eh?'

The girls looked at one another and then back to Martin. Heads moving from side to side like synchronised naysayers.

'What, help wi' two drinks?'

'Aye well, you know what he's like eh.'

***

'So Col mate, what's your take on all of this Aberdeen and Fever stuff?'

A not overly enthusiastic bar girl noticed Colin's proffered fiver.

'Aye, sounds like a no' bad night likes!'

Martin wasn't looking so sure.

'Aye sounds like a crackin' night but ya know that we're no' exactly the most popular people in Aberdeen just now eh?'

Colin's attention shifted from the drinks.

'No, we're no exactly popular with the casuals but this is the raver crowd that go tae Fever, shouldnae really be a problem there eh. Anyway, doesnae matter what your or ma take on Fever is, they two are goin' and we're takin' them whether we like it or no'.'

Colin glanced back at the girls, now deep in discussion at the table.

'Havnae been able to shut her up all week about it! Apparently it's different.'

Waved his fingers in front of his face to suggest he wasn't really sure what this was supposed to mean.

'A proper rave. A lot better than anythin' happenin' in Dundee.'

'Aye mate fair do's but you know as well as ah do that casuals in Aberdeen are the same as us down here and they're goin' to Fever. Maybe no' lookin' for trouble but a couple o' sitting ducks like us might be a bit difficult to resist.'

The girl at the bar was now over and ready to serve Colin. He raised his finger. She didn't look pleased.

'Naw you're right! Just let me get the drinks in and we can get back over and explain that they won't be having the time of their lives tonight cos we've just had a sudden attack of the wullies. Cannae see a problem there!'

'Better get a couple more pints as well mate!'

Martin suddenly decided that some Dutch courage may prove useful. This was a conundrum. Colin was right. Carrie and Natalie had completely set their minds on raving in Aberdeen and it was all they could talk about.

'Jacqui Morrison is incredible likes! Best DJ in Scotland by a mile. And she's a female. Got tae see her!'

'Oh aye, that tape you gave me is the fuckin' business!'

Martin was listening, helpless to do anything about where this was going.

'Aye that's a good tape like!' he had to admit.

Colin nodded a half-grudging agreement.

'Ecstasy up there's a lot better as well. Proper tabs like!'

'Fuck aye, better than the bloody whizzbombs we're getting here.'

On this point all were more than a little curious. If they could get their hands on real ecstasy, the trip might be worthwhile. The double doors swung open. Noise from commotion outside drew all eyes towards the entrance. With an air of adopted nonchalance verging on the ridiculous, Steve McNaughton walked into Caskies. All four around the table smiled. The expressions couldn't have been much more different between the boys and girls. Colin and Martin, experienced and practiced in the art of knowing what was what, they knew how to spot a dobber. The girls smiles were more genuine. Steve noted them sitting there. Checked around the rest of the pub. Maybe there was somebody even more interesting he could talk to. Apparently not!

'Alright everyone, how the bugger are you all?'

He sat down at the end of the table.

'Not bad at all Steve.'

Natalie answered first, eager to impress.

'That's us off tae Fever tonight for the first time. Are you through tonight?'

'Fever? Tonight?'

These questions took everyone a little by surprise. Not so much the questions themselves but the way they were being asked. A strong hint that Fever might not be such a good idea tonight. A few bewildered looks ensued.

'Have you guys not got tickets for Floatation then?'

All four of Steve's audience wanted to say *'Oh aye, Floatation, forgot about that, course we have tickets, can't wait.'*

Their expressions were complete traitors to their intentions.

'I mean, Fever will be good, it always is, but I reckon that this is the kick-start for the Dundee scene tonight. These Floatation Perception guys really have put on a good night.'

Steve quickly gauged reactions. Nobody knew what he was talking about.

'Haven't you seen the posters, they're all over Dundee? Tonight's the big night! Big rave on the Frigate Unicorn down in the docks. Everyone's going!'

'Eh, we've no' really seen any posters, we're no' from Dundee eh.'

'Come to think of it,' Natalie was thinking hard, 'ah think ah did see some posters outside the Wellgate with FLOATATION written on them but ah wasnae really paying attention, eh.'

'Ah well look, fear not!'

Steve now appeared to be taking pity on the people round the table who apparently, he considered had made a huge mistake.

'I'm pretty well in with the Floatation Perception people, if I give them a call I'm sure we'll get you a few tickets.'

An almost incredibly condescending smile stretched tightly over his face.

'After all, you guys are exactly who should be going to this event.'

When everyone at the table seemed to be looking at one another in complete relief it was Carrie who reacted first.

'Aye alright, but we're kind of all set for Fever.'

'Fair do's but this sounds pretty good as well eh?'

Martin was warming to the idea of Floatation, safely in Dundee.

'Not pretty good Martin, this is the real deal.'

Steve looked around the table for reaction.

'This is the same as Fever but about twice the size. Fever is actually quite pokey. It's in Dundee so everyone we know is going and...'

He gauged the mood again, paused and leaned into the audience as if the next thing he was to say would be the most important.

'It's on water.'

Most around the table seemed impressed by this detail but again Carrie countered.

'Well aye that sounds good n' all but we've been hearing all about Fever for weeks now and we know that Jacqui Morrison is a genius. Mainly it's yourself that's been telling us that, but to be honest, we're just getting a bit pissed off wi' the shite ecstasy down here eh.'

Steve could see that all around the table were immediately brought to agreeing with this point.

'Ah'm no' trying to be cheeky, eh!' Carrie began to apologise.

Steve opened his palms in front of him in his own gesture of contrition.

'Oh hell no, that's not cheeky at all. I know exactly what you mean!' Steve lowered his hands and pulled his chair closer into the table.

'But I did say that those Floatation Perception guys knew what they were doing. I was up at a house last night where they were listening to the sounds and I'm telling you they're pumping.'

He was looking at the table now, head swaying from side to side as if remembering the music.

'Thing is as well, they have 500 Disco Biscuits to sell and well, if I'm looking a bit bedraggled today it's entirely due to them and there's one thing I can certainly assure you. They are not shite drugs!'

Everyone around the table began to get their heads round the idea that Dundee might be the place to be that night. Steve jumped into action.

'Look! Like I said, don't worry. I'll just go and make a few phone calls and I'm certain that we can get you all in and I'll make sure there's enough biccies to go round OK.'

He got up and headed towards the door, the proverbial man on a mission. Nobody had asked him to do anything. He was working to his own volition. He reached the door and turned round. Slowly he lifted his index finger to his nose, as if a sudden important issue had just struck him. He flicked the finger down to point to the people he'd left at the table.

'You guys will be here yeah? I'll just be ten minutes!'

Everyone signalled around the table. Expressions that screamed 'suppose so!' and with a wink Steve was gone. Nothing to do now but gauge one another's reaction. Martin was first to ask the question. 'Well what do we think about this Floatation thing then? Sounds no' bad like!'

Natalie and Colin nodded an enthusiastic agreement but Carrie was a little distracted. She was looking at the top of the bar where the public phone was sitting. It wasn't exactly busy.

'What d' ya think Carrie?' Natalie had clearly changed her plans and was now thinking only of the Frigate Unicorn.

'I don't know though, do you no' think Steve's a wee bit weird?'

'Naw man, Steve's well cool!'

Natalie was convinced but Martin and Colin had to think about it.

'Aye, he is cool,' Carrie admitted, 'but ah just don't know. He's just a bit strange and well, who the hell ever heard o' Disco Biscuits? What are they?'

'Aw come on, Carrie. This is gonna be the berries!' Martin was bouncing around in his seat. Trepidation never turned to anticipation so fast.

Colin stayed silent, watching Natalie and Martin try to talk Carrie round. He may have in fact been looking into excuses for not going to Aberdeen that night but had listened all week to how much Carrie wanted to go. She still wanted to go. He knew that. He also kind of agreed with her that Steve was a bit weird. Not sinister weird or in any way unacceptable but he was just a bit different and he wasn't sure that he was to be trusted. For the moment though Colin bit his tongue as the swell of opinion seemed to veer towards staying in Dundee that night. He could just tell though that Carrie was only making out to be happy with that.

2

Colin had a problem. He had to do something. Steve McNaughton had arrived back in Caskies. Although not with tickets and Disco Biscuits in hand, he had promises that they would be forthcoming. All winks and exaggerated gestures, he promised them the time of their young lives. He mentioned tricks up his sleeve and surprises still to come. All the while acting like the man with the plan. The important one. Doing his naïve country folk friends a favour.

Natalie was convinced. Happy to be in the company of someone so in-the-know and happy to entertain. Martin was just pleased that someone had entered their afternoon able to add legitimacy for a reason to stay in Dundee. But Carrie? Carrie wasn't convinced, either about Steve or Floatation, and Colin knew it. She still wanted to go to Fever.

He arrived home and sat down in the kitchen, flicked on the television and pulled out his wallet to survey the contents. Getting to Aberdeen would now be just that bit more expensive. Digs shared by four after hours was one thing. Now the cost was to be borne by Colin alone. Colin resisted going into the lounge to relax. He knew that one too many pints would probably consign him to the couch. He headed up the stairs for a shower. Warm water dressed his head and shoulders. Comfortable! It wasn't comfort he was after though, so he turned the dial down a couple of notches.

He could get the money. A few more hours at the garage. It was a busy time of year. Aye. He could afford this! Went into his bedroom to select another pair of jeans for the night. As he began to transfer the contents of his pockets into the new jeans a paper sheet fell from his back pocket and onto the floor. Colin picked up the document and studied it. He'd pretty much forgotten about it. Colin dressed and went back to the kitchen where he sorted himself out a fresh orange drink. He sat back at the kitchen table, flattened out the slip and looked up at the TV. The videprinter was bashing out results on the screen, like a little wild animal that somehow knew the score. He could see it in Dickie Davies' eyes sometimes. That wee thing scared the fuck out of him.

Colin grinned at the thought as he reached behind himself for the telephone. He dialled Carrie's number. Carrie's mother answered.

'Oh hi Colin, think she's getting ready, I'll see if I can get her!'

'Oh thanks Margaret!'

Carrie came to the phone. 'What's up?'

Colin knew exactly what to say.

'You dinnae want to go to this Floatation thing do you?'

'Eh, aye, course ah do, it sounds wicked!'

Colin left a slight pause.

'C'mon Carrie, you've been talking about Fever all week!'

'Aye but this sounds just as good like.'

'Nah Carrie, this actually sounds like yer typical Dundee tosh and this Steve McNaughton's just no' aw there is he?'

'Naaah. He's all right. Look, Colin ah wanted to go to Fever but ah know that you and Martin were a bit concerned with it being in Aberdeen so ah'm no' bothered if we go to this Floatation, honest!'

Colin paused again. Perhaps his attention was elsewhere.

'Hello, Colin are you still there?'

'Oh aye, sorry Carrie, ah was thinking of something else, nah ah think we should go to Aberdeen. Ah doubt we could talk Martin and Natalie into it now but we can still go.'

'Don't worry about it Colin, we'd have to book a room ourselves and going up on the train just the two of us would be a bit weird and…'

Colin cut Carrie short.

'Holy shit!'

'Colin, what's happened? Are you alright?'

'Bloody hell!'

'Colin, what's goin' on? Are you OK?'

'Listen Carrie.'

Colin's voice had changed. He was agitated, almost shouting.

'We're going to Aberdeen tonight don't you worry about that!'

'Nah but…'

Surprised by Colin's sudden change of expression, Carrie's own voice had now changed to a higher pitch.

'No, no, you don't understand, tonight we're going to Aberdeen, don't be worrying about the train or a room cos' ah'm just about to book a good hotel on Union Street and a taxi both ways.'

Carrie was beginning to think this was a not very funny joke.

'Oh right aye, well gie me 20 minutes and ah'll book the crown jewels to wear as well eh!'

'No Carrie ah'm serious, you dinnae understand.'

He paused again. Appeared to be doing something else.

'Look, dinnae tell Martin or Natalie about this but, well to be honest ah'm going to have to check this again, ah think ah've just won over four grand on the fixed odds!'

3

Martin and Natalie squeezed into Caskies. It was just after seven o'clock. Getting anywhere decent to stand was a struggle. They'd never seen it so busy. This Floatation thing must be as Steve had been describing. Everybody that Martin and Natalie could recognise appeared to be packed in there. All the rave crowd. A few of the casuals.

Everyone except Colin and Carrie. Carrie had told them that they were going to Aberdeen after all. There was no argument. Nothing dodgy. Natalie had thought about it and called her back anyway. 'Sorry, no Carrie you're right, we should go to Aberdeen. That's always been the plan.'

Carrie was fine though. She was cool. Just like she always was.

'Natalie listen, it's nae problem, seriously. You and Martin go to the Unicorn thing. We honestly don't mind goin' tae Aberdeen w'rsel's.'

They'd called again though, both of them. They didn't want to feel that they were letting Carrie and Colin down and if going to Aberdeen would make things better then so be it. In all reality though there was really no enthusiasm for this at all and when they talked to them they genuinely didn't seem phased to be going by themselves.

So Flotation it was. Still needed tickets though. Still needed to find Steve. Natalie spotted him. He was standing at the busiest part of the bar. Surrounded by at least six girls. He was already looking at her. In a sea of people and noise, looking right at her. She wondered why. It didn't feel comfortable but tickets were tickets. He motioned her over.

Martin was wagging his finger and shouting something to a few of his mates. They were smiling and shouting something back. None of them had a hope of hearing one another.

Natalie hoped that Steve wasn't going to get fresh with her. Martin didn't need much provocation and with the company here tonight, that could turn ugly. He probably wouldn't. Not worth the risk though! She grabbed Martin and pulled him up to the end of the bar. He was glad to be moving, hoped that they were moving to a part of the bar where he didn't have to struggle just to get his hands in his pockets.

'Hi guys, where's Carrie and ehm, the big lad?'

Steve looked pretty well on, it didn't really surprise anyone that he couldn't remember Colin's name.

'Oh, they've actually went to Fever after all!'

Steve looked as deep in thought as someone as clearly whizzing as he was could.

'Oh man, that's not much good.'

He touched Natalie on the shoulder and gestured to Martin to follow him even deeper into the back of Caskies bar.

'Scuse me ladies?'

He gestured to all he had already been speaking to.

Natalie and Martin had to push through them to follow. As he pushed through Martin noted that he only recognised one of the girls. A bit strange given that just about everyone else in the bar was familiar. The girl he knew was a regular at just about every Dundee rave he'd been to. He thought that her name was Nisha, he'd certainly been introduced before. She had a huge smile on her face, was typically smartly dressed but, unusually, she seemed to be carrying a stuffed toy bee on the end of a flexible rod. She duly flew the toy over Martin's head as he passed. Martin smiled back. He thought this was a bit strange, but cute nonetheless.

They got to the bar where they assumed Steve had taken them for a bit of privacy but where in fact was just as busy as the rest of the pub. Steve had to raise his voice to be heard.

'Can't believe there's only two of you. I managed to get four places on the guest list. Mind you…'

He peered over their heads back at the bar to the girls.

'Don't imagine it'll be to difficult finding a couple of others to impress!'

Natalie asked the obvious.

'What, you mean we're getting in for nothing?'

Steve smiled.

'It's not just getting in for nothing. What we do is we wait for the queue to build and then walk straight by in front of them. VIP style!'

Natalie was warming to this idea but Martin was thinking more practically.

'Why do we get on the guest list?'

'Well mate, I've got a bit of a deal for you!'

Steve put his arms around their shoulders and lowered his voice as much as he could while still being heard.

***

Colin and Carrie stood on Huntly Street. Looked left and right and then back at the Copthorne Hotel. It was quite a nice hotel. No idea how to get to Fever though. The taxi driver completely unable to help, being from St Andrews as he was, the concierge on the desk was able to give some instruction of how to get to Gordon Street but wasn't at all convinced that there was a nightclub there. Gordon Street however was their understanding of where Fever was. Union Street would be their best bet.

They took their time walking down. This was after all a bit of a one-night holiday for them. Not that there was much to see, mainly shops and all of them closed, but they were able to appreciate the difference between this and going out as they normally did in the familiar haunts in Dundee so they wanted to make the most of it. You could do that when money was burning a hole in your pocket.

They found Gordon Street with the concierge's directions. It wasn't too difficult but on turning on to the street they could see why he might have doubted that there would be a nightclub there. A badly lit backstreet off the main shopping area, this definitely looked like it would be more suitable for deliverymen than dancers. The one thing that gave any idea that perhaps this was the street where they had been told Scotland's most exciting nightspot was housed were the five or six youngish looking people standing outside the door of a building which looked like a warehouse.

As they approached the building it became more clear that this was Fever, with the throbbing pump of house music becoming more and more audible with every step. With no signs or lighting outside and just to be sure, before entering the door Colin felt compelled to check that they were in the right place. He made eye contact with one of the girls standing outside. She was wearing a white sheepskin type coat which Colin thought looked pretty smart but was totally unnecessary for the time of year.

Pointing at the door he asked simply 'Fever?'

The girl smiled in an exaggerated fashion and her friends paid notice as they acknowledged the Fever first-timers.

'Aye mate, Fever!'

No box office or fancy pay station and also missing from the set-up were any bouncers. Simply one man seemingly not really paying attention, sitting behind a small desk with an open cashbox and a marker pen, he relieved them of £5 each, drew an X on each of their left hands and sent them up some stairs towards the noise.

They reached the top of the stairs and could see that the party was already in full swing. Not even half past ten yet but this seemed to have been going for some time. Not that they could see that much, as most of the room was filled with fake smoke. They were just able to make out the people lining the perimeter of the club. None of them sitting down or talking to one another, but everybody moving to the music. The floor rumbled and heaved with the pressure of people bouncing on floorboards. Down some stairs again to where the main dance floor seemed to be, shrouded in smoke and flashing lights, figures could only be made out as silhouettes, hands and arms raised above the dancers' heads as one beat started to segue into another and a rhythm started to pulse which prompted an almighty scream from the dance floor as the dancers recognised another favourite.

*** *

Steve wasn't exaggerating about the main advantage of being on a guest list. He walked straight past the huge line of familiar faces, hand in hand with Nisha and another girl who had since been introduced as Hayley. All three were clearly in their element.

Martin and Natalie followed close behind. They would have been enjoying the spectacle an awful lot more but the edge had kind of been taken off of the whole situation with the nervousness of knowing that Martin had a bag full of 300 or so Disco Biscuits taped to his chest.

What hadn't occurred to Martin 'til this point was now walloping him round the head. Lording it as he marched past the queue was the last thing on his mind. If the bouncers are in on this as Steve had said and if they were the only people who definitely wouldn't be searched by them on the way in, then why had they gone to the bother of strapping them to his chest before they left Caskies?

He swallowed hard as he approached. A chill rose up his spine that had no business being in warm clothes. He could see them looking him up and down. Martin smiled and gripped Natalie's hand a little tighter. He knew it now. These guys were going to stop him. Search him. Find a bag of ecstasy and from there only one thing could happen. He went to raise his hand to his chest but stopped just in time. Steve didn't know these bouncers. He was full of shit. Martin looked at him three paces in front, swaggering with both Nisha and Hayley linked to his arms. It was all right for him to be so cocky. He was carrying nothing.

If he was busted tonight, Steve McNaughton was fuckin' getting it! Martin looked at the gap between the boat and its mooring. Around three feet of space with a dark void leading down to the dock water. Martin moved his hand into the gap between his jeans and his untucked shirt. The minute these guys said anything and the bag was being ripped from the chest and flung into the gap. Steve fuckin' McNaughton would be following them n'all.

Fuckin' dodgy bastard.

Steve approached, signalling to a few of the people waiting in the queue. He extended his hand to the first bouncer who duly reached out to shake the hand.

'Allright guys, these are my friends, they're fine!'

Steve turned around and winked. Martin's mood lifted as the bouncer reached out a hand. Not to search him but to make his acquaintance.

Steve was now talking to the second bouncer. 'You need anything tonight and this is the guy to see.'

He nodded towards Martin. Martin smiled in a way that was just short of painful. Relief much more evident than any pleasure to be meeting these men. Punting drugs was exciting. Bit of an understatement that one. Heart attack material. That was that though. Now Martin and Natalie could feel a lot more easy about the deal they had struck.

Getting from Caskies to the Frigate Unicorn was the dodgy part no doubt about that. Once inside it was just a case of sell as many as you can, any sign of trouble just get rid of them, and they would earn £2 for every pill sold. With the crowd that were coming to the boat that night and with Steve and the Floatation guys pointing them in the right direction there was no doubt that that meant all 300 or so selling with a clear £600 profit to Martin and Natalie. The bouncers were even told not to let anybody in that they didn't recognise and to let Steve know if anybody from the CID boarded the boat.

Once aboard, the Unicorn was still pretty empty. Martin and Natalie made their way to a quiet dark place on the boat and Martin removed the bag from his chest. He placed them in a comfortable place in his pocket, removing two. Yes, he would sell every last one of these pills but not these two. These were for him and Nat. They swallowed the small brownish discs and then turned to face the steadily filling event. Steve was right, this looked like it was going to be a good one.

***

Colin and Carrie had taken in the atmosphere for as long as they needed. Looking around the madness they could tell that it was more than the music that people were enjoying. Other forces were at work here and they knew exactly what these forces were. Not knowing anybody there was going to be a problem, but they needed the drugs and so people needed to be asked.

Normally people could be cagey in these circumstances, so they were surprised when the first girl that Carrie asked enthusiastically offered to take them to exactly where they needed to go. They followed her through the crowd and became more and more fused with the crowd. They nearly lost each other twice into the smoky atmosphere. The girl was pushing through like someone possessed. Somehow they managed to keep up. Found themselves being presented to a young man who nodded and came forward to meet the newcomers. Automatically knew why they were being presented to him.

'£20 each! How many you after?'

His voice was raised, so that he could be heard. Colin was about to answer 'two' but then he thought, *'Here we are, money to burn, about to buy ecstasy, who knows when we'll get the chance to do this again'*. He quickly re-calculated.

'Six.'

Colin could feel Carrie's expression, wondering if he meant to say what he had just said.

The dealer seemed to be studying Colin in some detail.

'OK, right y'are, six it is then! That'll be a hunder and twenty pounds min!'

Colin reached into his back pocket. A bunch of loose notes tickled at his fingers. He looked down as he tried to sort out the correct amount while not being noticed. The dealer also surveyed the room to ensure that they weren't attracting too much attention.

Colin handed over the notes which the dealer checked quickly before storing it in his front jeans pocket. He reached out his right hand towards Colin's but he didn't deposit any drugs. He gripped a handshake, and pulled himself closer so that he could be heard without shouting.

'Ah fuckin' ken you min!'

Colin pulled away to look him in the eyes.

'You're Dundee!'

Colin pressed his lips together and shook his head slightly. At once he considered that they had made a huge mistake coming here.

'Look mate, this is no' fair, ah'm here on my own wi' the bird. We're no looking for any trouble!'

'Nah mate, relax, relax.'

The dealer loosened his grip, smiled and met Colin's eyes with his.

'This is Fever mate. The rules are different here.'

He opened his left hand out to reveal six small white pills.

'Enjoy!'

***

Martin had to sit down. Didn't realise that selling these little pills would be so much hassle. It's not that being Mr Popular; as he certainly was tonight, was particularly problematic but he considered that he needed to get away to figure how he was feeling. A check to see what condition his condition was in. A little bit numb, a lot wound up and slightly confused. Not like acid, confused where you just had to accept what was happening. Tonight he was in control.

Seats on the frigate were at a bit of a premium. After all, it wasn't a nightclub, but basically a floating museum left as it would have been when it was a naval frigate in the 18th century and not really designed for its current purpose. Martin sat beside one of the porthole cannons and around ten customers approached him within five minutes. Word had certainly got around.

***

Within 20 minutes of taking one each of their tablets, Colin and Carrie were at the centre of Fever's dance floor, surrounded by the oscillating mass, not able to see further than ten feet in any direction. Neither of them were particularly keen dancers but what they had been told certainly seemed to be accurate. In Fever there wasn't much choice. Nobody wanted to stand still. It was clear that every last person there was there to make the most of the music and the drugs.

The effect of the pills was now pulsing with a rhythm that seemed to keep time with the music in wave after wave of euphoria. Colin looked at Carrie. She'd never looked better to him. She was dancing with complete conviction. Carrie looked at Colin and realised she'd never seen him dance before. Not like this anyway. Neither of them trying to impress anyone, just moving in the way that the situation dictated.

Carrie raised her hands to the side of her head where her hair had started to ride forward, removed all strands from her face tilted her head back and screamed for all that she was worth.

Colin looked on to this spectacle and could completely understand why she'd want to do such a thing. Seemed like the only sensible thing to do was to copy her.

***

Martin was just getting ready to rejoin the party when he realised that someone sitting next to him was talking. Whoever this was he looked out of place. Not at all smartly dressed, wearing a kind of hooded woollen poncho that Martin thought he might have made himself that very afternoon. An attempt at a beard was being made without the necessary amount of facial hair to make it a success. Plus this character was sporting the one thing that Martin considered to be a cardinal sin for anyone trying to look good; a ponytail. He might have been trying to attract Martin's attention for the past five minutes for all Martin knew, things were getting a little confused.

'Sorry mate, what are you saying?'

Scruffy boy moved back a little and drew a long breath before answering.

'I'm asking how you're getting on with the Disco Biscuits.'

Martin wasn't sure either what or why he was asking.

'Eh?'

'Well, selling plenty are you?'

A twig snapped in Martin's mind.

'Oh right, aye, sorry, you needing a pill likes are you?'

Martin reached into his pocket to serve his next customer.

'No, no that's fine, I'm not needing any Disco Biscuits!'

Martin noticed for the first time that this boy wasn't local, his accent seemed to be from Manchester and Martin was interested to find out if this was the case. Manchester pretty much being the hub of rave activity, he thought that fair enough the guy doesn't look up to much but if he's visiting from Manchester then that in itself is a bit of a feather in Dundee's cap.

'So what do you no' do the drugs like?'

Martin couldn't really think of anything else to say. The boy didn't answer, choosing to sit back and nod his head instead. After a slight snigger the boy turned back to Martin and reached into his pocket, producing two tiny pink tablets.

'What're they then?'

A grin spilled over scruffy boy's features.

'These, my mate, are pink New Yorkers. One for you and one for your lovely girlfriend.'

That made Martin wary. Bit familiar for a scruffy boy.

'No' trying to be funny *mate* but I've got a pocket stuffed full of E why would I be buying these wee things from you?'

The boy's grin didn't disappear and he looked Martin square in the eyes.

'Disco Biscuits are OK, I wouldn't have brought them here otherwise but pink New Yorkers are different. 75milligrams of pure MDMA, these little fuckers'll change your life. And I'm not selling them to you, I'm giving them to you. To say thanks for sellin' my Disco Biscuits!'

***

Colin and Carrie made their way from the dance floor. They had no real idea of how long they had been down there, by now both of them were wet through with sweat and it seemed like a good idea to get a drink at least. They climbed the stairs out of the main density of smoke and made their way to the bar. With no real need for alcohol, they both asked for a pint of water and were a little surprised when the girl behind the bar asked them for a pound each for the privilege. It wasn't really grudged though, so Colin paid the charge.

They made their way away from the bar. They could drink their drinks. Cool down a bit. Didn't need to go back to the dance floor. The whole place was moving. Carrie bumped into someone, didn't seem like an accident. She turned to see the Aberdonian drug dealer. He winked and smiled. Seemed like an affable chap. Carrie pulled on Colin's sleeve. He was in a world of his own. He turned and saw who Carrie was bringing his attention to. Both of them realised that they probably didn't look in quite the same state as they did the last time they had met him.

'Alright guys? Welcome to Aberdeen.'

The dealer spread out his arms and looked around the room.

Colin moved the short distance toward him and then wrapped his arms around his shoulders in what turned out to be a gentle bear hug. The dealer not at all surprised closed his own arms around Colin's shoulders and patted him on the back. The couple made their way to a relatively quiet part of the club.

'What was that all about?'

'What?'

'Well you're no' exactly the huggin' type, are ya?'

Colin seemed to be considering the question.

'Nah but Carrie, ah just wasnae really expecting this to be like this eh. This is just nuts!'

'Aye, it's pretty good likes!' Carrie had to agree.

'Ah've still got another four o' these.'

Colin patted his jean pocket where the rest of the pills were wrapped in cigarette packet foil.

'Oh ah don't know, Colin. Ah'm no' sure you're supposed to take two in one night eh. Anyway, would be good if we could take a few of these back eh.'

Colin smiled and leaned back against a wall. He felt his back pocket where he knew he still had some £20 notes.

'If there's as many o' these in here as ah think there are, we'll be taking quite a few back!'

***

Martin could just about make it to his feet. Slowly registering where he was again and beginning to wonder how long he'd been in a state of complete unawareness.

'Holy fuck.'

He placed his palms against his temples and brought them down over his cheeks to finally support his chin and gaping mouth. He looked around the boat but was only able to make out flickering images and flashes of light. He could recognise the music, Primal Scream's 'Loaded', but somehow it sounded different, better, much much better. Martin suddenly felt a huge swell of excitement which seemed to be making its way up through his whole body.

Like faint pins and needles in the nape of his neck. Excitement like he'd never experienced, the music was just incredible.

'He wants to get loaded and he wants to have a good time does he? Well then he wants tae fuckin' be here then!'

He regained some sort of composure and replaced the confusion with almost complete clarity of thought. He suddenly realised that he had no idea where Natalie was.

'Bloody hell, if ah'm like this, what's she gonnae be like?'

He set off towards the centre of the boat where the party was really kicking off. Everyone crammed on to the makeshift dance floor, set off what looked to be like some sort of command deck now being put to good use as a DJ console. Hands were in the air and the noise of the dancers whistling or just plain belting out their own primal scream drowning out the sound of the record. If Natalie is in amongst them, then fair enough she's having a good time. If she's not, though, Martin thought he'd better find her. He turned away from the crowd, the scene registering with him like some sort of kaleidoscopic flick show.

It was dark but he was sure that he could recognise Natalie standing just off the dance floor. At least the girl was the same size and shape and she was wearing a bustier that looked like the one Natalie had bought that afternoon. Her hair however was now in no style at all just hanging lank over her head and shoulders and her face obscured by both of her hands covering her face. Martin raced over to where she was standing. A few minutes ago he had trouble figuring out how to put a foot in front of the other, now he was experiencing a fleetness of foot as if he wasn't walking at all. He drew up and could see that it was Natalie and she appeared to be in some trouble. He placed his hands on her shoulder, hot to touch and covered in sweat.

'You okay Nat?'

Her head sprung up, her eyes bulging to meet his. She turned parallel and grabbed his elbows. Powerfully. Not like the tender way she normally touched. Her expression scared him. Usually when people didn't look right, their eyes would give the clues as to how the person was. Natalie's eyes however were searching as if to ask the question, *'who are you?'*

Martin was about to say something when suddenly the expression changed, a huge smile breaking across her almost caricatured face and her eyes lighting up.

'No' okay Martin, fuckin' magic!'

She pulled on his elbows till they both met in a tight hug. The pins and needles that had been simmering in Martin's neck suddenly surged straight up the back of his head and a feeling of euphoria overwhelmed him.

Natalie pulled away slightly so that their heads were level and she kissed him. An incredibly intense kiss, she still seemed to be grabbing him with a strength that she really ought not to have. She pulled her head away again, her smile now looking much more natural than before.

'Ah fuckin' love you man!'

Martin was just about to return the compliment when he felt a tug on the back of his shirt. He turned to find a young excited-looking man who he'd certainly never seen before, apparently out of breath, definitely out of his head, dripping with sweat and smiling broadly.

'There yi are, eh've pure been looking iverywhar! Got any mare o' thae Disco Biscuits?'

OPPOSITES ATTRACT

4

Vince Laws climbed to the upper deck, trepidation mounting, his sweat-covered palms making slippery purchase on the railings. He pulled his tie loose and undid his top button, no real idea of what was going to happen when he reached the top deck. Up until ten minutes ago, he'd been having a typical Wednesday shift, commuting between Glenrothes and St Andrews; nothing unusual, pretty busy but no excitement. Last leg to St Andrews then back to finish at Glenrothes terminal. It was about this time; as is the case every Wednesday, that Vince's mind turned to the evening. No work on Thursdays or Fridays. They gave him those days off to allow him to be on the busy Saturday and Sunday shifts. So Wednesday night usually meant a skinfull at the Golden Acorn pub, right next to Glenrothes Terminal. Couldn't be more handy. It was a good plan. Worked most weeks.

Stress had definitely entered Vince's easy day today though. Schoolkids had boarded at the Crossgates in Cupar. Little fuckers had been making a nuisance of themselves upstairs from the moment they got on. Vince wasn't a hard man, he knew that but he wasn't about to let a few tearaway teenagers take the piss out of him. He was sure he could smell dope when they boarded. He should have told them right there and then.

'No chance! You're no' getting' on here wi' wacky baccy!'

There were easily 30 of them though, so it was the easy option to let them on. He hadn't quite spotted the stitch in time. He'd been in the game long enough to know that these 'bastards' would be up to no good with their marker pens and when they started singing and jumping about with their 'Bell Baxter Barmy Army' chanting, he could see the state, ranging from disgust to blind panic, of his other passengers. There wasn't an option. He had to do something. This was his bus and he was in charge. He pulled the bus into the University playing fields, just across from the Old Course Hotel, and he climbed the stairs to face them.

'Right, youse, aff the bus, the lot of you!'

There were only schoolkids on the top deck now. Not one possible ally. All of them leaned towards the bus driver at once. Trying to look hard. Menacing. A few giggled at the idea of one man throwing them off the bus. A few thought fit to respond.

'Git tae fuck ya loser.'

'Away and shite, prick.'

'How, what are you gonnae dae, ya twat?'

Vince started to consider that possibly he'd made mistake. One more stop to St Andrews terminus then they're off anyway. Then again, why should he take any crap from these pricks?

Suddenly the Golden Acorn seemed a long way away.

'Right git aff the fuckin' bus or ehm callin' the polis.'

The threat fell on deaf ears.

One of the teenagers emerged from within the crowd. Larger than Vince and confident in manner.

'Look,' he paused. Vince took a pace backwards. He didn't want confrontation. Not on a Wednesday.

'Mate, the whole fuckin' reason for us getting on this bus is to cause mayhem.'

The boy took another step towards Vince. He was big but he was just a teenager. Vince wanted to twat him one. Teach him a lesson but he could sense the rest of the crowd rallying behind him. Go for him and he knew that the rest would get involved. He could do without this.

'We're no' particularly bothered about this bus, we'd rather cause bother when we get off, you know what I mean?'

Vince had to think now. Shouldn't have come up the stairs in the first place really. Didn't want to back off. That would be humiliating but the boy was right. Drive to the terminus, let these little wankers off and back up the road to the Acorn. That seemed like the way to go.

'Now it's up to yoursel', we can get to St Andrews and go ballistic or we can do it here on your bus.'

Vince spotted his downstairs passengers leaving through the middle door.

'Fuck this!' he thought

'Nah, look.'

Vince was talking to the big lad but not looking at him any more.

'You're no' a hard man, alright, if ya want tae go tae the terminus then fine but the only bother you'll be getting is fae the polis, ah've already called them so they'll be waitin'. The best thing you lot can dae is git aff the fuckin' bus – now!'

'Right then, fair enough.'

The big lad turned back round to face his gang. Vince suddenly felt good about himself. He'd sorted this out and in no time he'd be in the Acorn talking about his wee brush with trouble and how he sorted it out. The big lad raised his hands till his arms were outstretched parallel with the bus floor.

'Fuckin' mayhem on the bus it is then.'

'Oh for fuck's sake!' Vince thought out loud.

5

At the car park behind the bus station, Billy Fotheringham stood impatiently checking his watch and shuffling among his schoolmates.

'Where the fuck are they bastards?'

Billy shouted as opposed to simply asking this question. His way of displaying that he was in charge. Around him, a gang of his schoolmates, nervously talking among themselves. Discussing subjects such as why a thin wooden beam is better than a metal scaffold pole because you can run faster with it and bring it up quicker after you've swung it and the whole 'knives or no knives' debate.

Martin approached Billy. He had an idea. Thought Billy ought to consider it. Seriously doubted he would.

'Billy ah dinnae ken what the fuck we're daein' just waitin' fur them here. We should be in the terminus waiting for them when they get aff, it doesnae even make any sense tae let them group and find tools.'

Billy raised his eyebrows and squinted back to Martin. Clearly hinting that the suggestion wasn't exactly appreciated. Martin raised his hand to show that it was just a suggestion, no offence. All the while thinking *'you are a fuckin' Womble Fotheringham. When are ya gonnae get a grip?'* He looked around the massed ensemble. No organisation whatsoever. Looked back at Billy. He appeared to be thinking about something.

'Thinking! That's a novel approach for you ya diddy. You just dinnae understand that just because you think ya can take on anybody, doesnae mean ya dinnae have tae consider that in a gang fight, two squads of guys of similar numbers'll generally equal one another out and that it is always preferable tae hae some sort o' advantage.'

It was exactly this type of thinking that convinced Martin that Billy should pay more attention to him rather than being the autocratic leader of a gang that, for Martin's liking, ran a lot more than it fought.

'Look, Bridie.'

Billy used Martin's recently acquired nickname. Martin wasn't sure he liked it too much. 'The reason that we're no' waitin' in the bus station or ambushin' the bastards is because when ah called Scotty Henderson this mornin', this is where we arranged tae meet. Me, Henderson, top boys! It's arranged, nae fuckin' arguments.'

'Some fuckin' boy,' thought Martin. *'One of these days there's gonnae be a mutiny and ah'll be right there callin' the shots, just my luck tae be landed wi' a top boy wi' nae fuckin' sense.'*

***

Simon Gorrie walked back along Doubledyke. Back from being posted by Billy as lookout. Complete mug job that one. Billy would have to be told. *'Use somebody else for a change, ah'm gettin' a bit sick o' bein' your skivvy!'*

Total waste of time this one anyway. *'Aye, the bus arrived in the terminus. Or what used to be a bus anyway. Couldnae really count any Cupar mob off it though cos there was nae cunt on it.'*

Billy was first to see him.

'What's the fuckin' score?'

He wasn't looking or sounding too pleased.

'Fuck knows man,' Simon answered in his typically dopey drawl. 'The bus has just got in and it's fuckin' empty. Some fuckin', state it's in though, all the windaes are in…'

'HERE, FOTHERINGHAM, IS THIS PISH THE BEST YOU CAN COME UP WI'?'

The whole ensemble turned at once. Thirty odd heads swivelling in unison like startled chickens to see the 40 or so Cupar mob.

They stood around 200 yards away at the bottom of the car park. One figure stood out in front of them.

'FUCK YOU HENDERSON.'

Martin noticed a broad smile emerge on Billy's face as he answered.

'FUCKIN', MADRAS MAD SQUAD RULE YA BASS.'

Billy was in his element. Other members of his 'mad squad' displayed varying levels of enthusiasm for the impending events. Martin was at this moment indifferent to any of it, as he gauged Billy's expression. *'Ya fuckin' dopit bastard. Actually pleased that Henderson had turned up at the complete opposite direction where he was supposed to. So much for yir little 'honour among top boys' speech earlier.'*

Martin looked at the Cupar gang. Walking forward. Were they in formation? Had they practised this? *'This fuckin' Henderson's prepared this and we've no'. He's turned up in exactly the opposite direction with about 40 boys and, for all we know, he has another 40*

31

waiting anywhere we might run. This is no' a good situation. The best thing we can dae is to run right at this mob because they're bound to have cover elsewhere. Ah definitely would.'

Martin surveyed Billy's expression, now looking like he'd just won the pools.

'C'mon Billy, what are we waitin' for? Let's do it.'

Billy winked. Still grinning like the dim-witted gimp he was, as he turned to give the order to run down the hill. Henderson and his Cupar mob had broke into a slow run up towards them.

Martin felt an unfamiliar rush from what he saw coming towards him. *'Fuckin' hell this is actually goin' tae be a no' bad wee battle.'*

'Dirty bastards!'

He could hear and sense a change in Billy's mood as he turned to see what was going on. Billy was standing with his head forced forward and his arms pressed hard into his side looking now totally dejected.

As Martin continued to turn round he saw why. The gang of 30 that he had just pushed through had dwindled to around ten sorry-looking individuals, each one looked as if they were just waiting for Billy to say, *'aye you can run as well now if you want.'*

No such luck. Billy swivelled back to face the oncoming horde.

'BASTARDS, BASTARDS, OH YOU FUCKIN' BASTARDS!'

Billy was pointing both arms directly at Henderson, all of the muscles in his face seemed to be following the lead of his arms.

The Cupar mob had reached about 150 yards and were now approaching at varied speeds depending on the fitness, or perhaps importance, of gang members. Martin actually took the time to wonder which.

Billy spun again to face the remnants of his mad squad

'Right then we're doing this anyw…'

He was cut short by the sight of the backs of the final ten making their way away from the battle. Some at least turned around to give a gesture which suggested they were sorry, arms stretched low, palms towards Billy.

Only Billy and Martin remained, their attitudes to what was transpiring could not have been different. Billy, at war with the world for providing him with a set of useless bastards as an excuse for a gang, and Martin, convinced that only a fault in leadership was to blame and that culpability rested squarely at the 'twat' standing beside him.

The Cupar mob was now around 100 yards away from Martin and Billy. Bearing down. Successful invasion. No fuckin' way should this be happening. Martin was conscious of the sheer delight on the faces of the mob and the heightening volume of their chants.

'BELL BAXTER BARMY ARMY, BELL BAXTER BARMY ARMY.'

Billy must've felt like he had to say something. Didn't sound so cocky now: 'So what do you want tae dae? Do you want tae run?'

It seemed to Martin that the only sensible answer to this question was sarcasm: 'Nah Billy, ah want to stand here and have ma fuckin' head kicked in.'

'Right!'

Billy re-assumed his leadership voice as he turned and ran. Martin re-assumed his obliging soldier role and followed suit. They sprinted along Doubledyke. Football training didn't prepare you for running away from a kicking. The exertion made Martin's legs pulse. Freezing wind rushed through his hair. The one thing he could think of was that if he made the junction before any of the Cupar boys reached the top of the car park that he could make his turn without being seen. Might give the Cupar boys a bit if a dilemma as to which way to go.

Just before the junction, Martin watched Billy turning left to head toward the bus station. Martin decided to go right. There was no time to turn round and look and no way of knowing whether he had been spotted. It occurred to Martin that as Billy turned off just before him, then if anybody had been seen then it would be him. Still in the back of his mind he expected another cut-off group of Cupar waiting for runners. But then they would have been busy with the shitebags that had run first. Wouldn't they?

Martin decided to get off the street as quickly as he could. He headed up the second set of stairs leading up the closes of the student blocks, choosing not to use the first. The one most likely to be searched by the invaders. Martin burst through the back door of the block and was faced with the overgrown back garden, drying areas and sheds, so obviously not being looked after by their student custodians.

'*Lazy bastards,*' he thought as he headed towards a broken-down shed, surprised and not a little annoyed to see a padlock barring his entrance. He lodged himself between the wall facing away from the buildings and the periphery of the jungle of ferns and hogweed that decorated, well, pretty much the whole area. He thought that he'd be safe there. The gang may want to check out these closes and back greens but it's unlikely that any search would be thorough enough to discover him hidden behind the old shed. He hoped like fuck he was right. He looked at his watch. 'Quarter past five,' it was now one hour and 15 minutes since he had left school. He could hear some commotion on the other side of the block but it seemed quite a distance off. *'I'll give it half an hour here, to let everything cool down and then I'll better head home.'*

It hadn't been any great distance of a run to his hiding place, but that was as quick as he could remember ever running. Enough to produce sweat on the back of his head which had started to run down his neck and back. It was the middle of January and the chill of winter pierced the air. Martin pulled his Nike shell top closer around him as he prepared to sit it out. Thinking about how he was going to get back home. Back to the Air Force base at Leuchars. The same route as the buses back to Cupar. He'd have to walk. Even that would be tricky.

He looked across the jungle of grass and weed that was probably supposed to be a neatly mown drying green. He could see movement. Something was there. Could be a cat or some small wild animal. Possibly somebody's bunny rabbit. A baseball cap appeared over the canopy of overgrown greenery followed by the vaguely familiar face of someone slightly younger than Martin himself. Clearly the head start this guy had over Martin allowed him to hide himself pretty well up until now. His beady eyes shot over to meet Martin's and he spoke in a tone just that little bit louder than a whisper.

'Alright Bridie? That was a bit mental eh?'

Martin tilted his head back and rolled his eyes as he surveyed the sky, speaking, when he did in the same hushed tone. 'Fuck sake Fotheringham ya dos' cunt, you've even got third years callin' me it now!'

6

'Martin, where the hell have you been?' Martin's mother greeted him as he entered the house. It was just past seven o'clock.

'*Holy shit,*' Martin thought.

'What am ah, 12 again or what?'

'Well sometimes you can act like it. If you're gonnae be late you should phone. You can cook your own bleedin' tea 'n' all cos I'm no' daein' it at this time, any way your father wants to see you, he's in the kitchen.'

'Is that the wee man now?' A voice filtered from the kitchen.

'Well I suppose you'd better go and attend to whatever business you boys are getting' up tae, where have you been though?' Martin's mother looked in an almost comically quizzical way.

'Oh somethin' come up.'

'Oh right, well fair enough then, what was her name?' She was fishing.

Martin looked at his mother with a smirk-cum look of self satisfaction on his face. 'Aye whatever.'

He walked through to the kitchen. The smell of his mum's cooking still dwelt in the air, sweet and tangy. Somebody had eaten well. Martin's father stood alongside another bigger man that Martin recognised. Both men were still in uniform holding small glasses of what looked like his dad's single malt. Both men also wore the same badge of rank. Although Martin had never paid too much attention to these things, he knew that this meant they were both Warrant Officers and as such were both pretty much the bosses of their units.

'How ya doin' mate? Where have you been?' His dad quizzed.

Martin struggled to know which question to answer first. '*Why the great interest?*' he thought.

'Aye, no' bad you know.'

He pointed back in the general direction of St Andrews with his thumb.

'Just school stuff eh!'

Martin was not used to having to answer to his dad, who always pretty much trusted his son to mind himself. All these questions were becoming a bit disconcerting. He couldn't help thinking that this was all leading up to some sucker punch question. Something concerning the big guy, but he couldn't really think what he might have done to upset him.

'What's that, detention then?'

Martin senior turned to his friend and smiled.

'No, no, nothing like that dad, just football and stuff you know.'

Martin detected that his dad had had a few more glasses of his single malt than usual of a weekday.

'Any road, I want you to meet Rod.'

Martin senior turned to his colleague.

'W.O. Nichols, one of my work buddies. He's got something he wants to ask you.'

Rod Nichols moved toward Martin and offered him his hand

'How 'r' you doin'?'

He asked in a manner which seemed to merit more than a simple 'Alright!'

Martin noticed first the size of the hand of his inquisitor, they seemed to be about twice the size of his own *'this has tae be the biggest hand I've ever shook.'*

'I'm not bad thanks aye, pretty good,' Martin paused, 'Yoursel'?'

A broad tight smile emerged on Rod's face as he leaned back on the kitchen cabinet and placed his drink down. 'Yeah, I'm pretty good too.'

Curious as to what this man might want with him, the question needed to be asked. 'So, Mr Nichols, how can ah help you?'

His smile tightened still as he looked towards Martin senior, pointing at young Martin moving his hands back and forward.

'You're right,' he was talking directly to Martin senior now, 'this boy can help.'

Martin senior pursed his lips and nodded in agreement.

Rod pulled out a chair for the young man. 'Can we sit?'

Young Martin nodded and all three men sat down.

'Do you know my boy, Colin?' Rod asked.

Martin thought for a moment, realising that he did indeed know the boy, albeit not very well. Not considering they were both in the same year at Madras school, both lived in Leuchars and both usually shared the same bus in and out of St Andrews.

'Well, aye, ah do know Colin.' Martin gestured with his hand as if almost in apology. 'We were in a few classes together in first and second year but no' now though. Ah think he may be a bit more of a scholar than me, you know?'

Martin looked at his dad and offered a similar apologetic gesture.

'Oh aye, he's a bright lad, I don't doubt that,' Rod looked indifferent and not particularly pleased to be able to make such a statement. 'I'll tell you this as well.'

Martin noticed Rod becoming a little more animated. He'd hitched his sleeves up to his elbows and was leaning over the table to be better understood. This was down to business now.

'He's a big lad too, he should be able to look after himself.'

Martin made a mental picture of him in his mind and nodded in agreement.

'Never-the-less,' Rod continued, 'I think he may lack the gumption to stick up for himself, you know, all brains and no common sense.'

Martin made a pretend puzzled look while in fact he knew exactly what Rod meant.

'Anyway, consequently, I think my boy may be allowing himself to be bullied.'

Rod carried on talking as Martin sat a little straighter in his chair.

'And you know, these things can maybe lead to a lack of confidence and I don't want to think that my boy is miserable at school, that would be a shame you know…'

Martin wasn't certain if Rod had finished saying what he was saying but felt he had to interrupt. 'No, hold on man, you're gettin' the wrong idea, fair enough, ah mean, ah dinnae take any crap, ah look after myself but ah'm no' a bully.'

The two Warrant Officers looked at each other, Rod looked particularly puzzled. Martin senior was first to speak. 'No son, we know you're not bullying him, that's not what we're saying.'

'No, Christ no,' Rod interrupted, 'I'm not accusing you of anything, just saying you know, I think the lad's having a bit of trouble at school, I don't know who but I certainly don't think you.'

Rod moved his glass to one side of the kitchen table and leant towards Martin. 'I'm not suggesting it's you, in fact I'm confident it's not. What I am saying is that, well, I know you're one of the more, well, accepted or I suppose cool guys at the school, you know?'

A slight wave of self-satisfaction coursed through Martin's mind. It felt good that this assumption might be made by one of his dad's colleagues, after all how does one of the other guys on the base know about his position at school?

'Pretty cool.'

'Anyway, I just thought that you might be able to find out what's going on, these bullies are probably nothing to write home about.'

Rod seemed to know his stuff.

'Maybe you can have a quiet word with them, tell them to back off a bit, you know?'

Rod seemed to be thinking more about the matter as he spoke.

'Better still,' he grabbed his glass and began tapping it on the table. 'If you can find a way to show Colin that these boys are basically a bunch of twerps that depend on his quiet nature then he'll know not to let them bother him again.'

It was good that this man should come to Martin to handle this job. He was aware that Rod was still speaking to him about it but by now Martin was only really half listening and agreeing with him. Already Martin was working out how to help Colin. He didn't really know the boy, except for to know that he was a big ungainly type. The type that stuck in at school, a bit of a geek really, it didn't surprise Martin that maybe this guy was being bullied. Martin knew a few of the likely suspects as well. Minks and think-they're-hard types, that liked to bring attention to themselves. Not a problem for Martin. He could just politely ask them to get a fuckin' grip of themselves. Move on to somebody else. Martin didn't even have to get involved.

Rod left, escorted by a slightly the worse for wear Martin senior and young Martin set about feeding himself for the evening. It was never going to be anything fancy. His mother was refusing to cook so late and his culinary skills lacked a bit, possibly through the fact that he spent most of his time during home economics classes chatting up the girls. This was the case for most of his classes. As he sat down to his cheese and tomato toasties, he began to wonder how he was going to solve Colin's little problem. Confident of one thing; Rod had definitely come to the right man.

7

Martin jogged through pouring rain to the St Andrews bus stop. It was the type of morning that made Martin confident that it would rain heavily all day. A day already blighted by the certain prospect of the post-mortem investigation into the events of the day before. What should have been a glorious festival of organised violence had been ruined by the complete lack of organisational skills of Billy Fotheringham.

Of course, Billy's slant on events would not concur with Martin's. It seemed more likely that Billy would be hell bent on wreaking a terrible revenge on anybody deemed to have underperformed and, well, that just about included everybody. Everybody, Martin thought, other than Billy and himself.

Martin knew he'd be spared but that wasn't the point. It seemed likely that Billy's reaction to yesterday would be to issue kickings to those who he felt to blame and Martin did not doubt for a moment that that may in fact mean everybody who had ran yesterday. He knew that nobody would resist these beatings. Avoiding the inevitable and hiding would be their reaction. Giving a pasting to all gang members didn't really strike Martin as a particularly effective way to recover morale after the depressing events of the day before. But then Billy Fotheringham didn't strike him as someone who'd give a fuck.

Martin was almost certain that the idea of forming a gang from his schoolmates at Madras High School were as good as over. It was a pity because Martin knew that gangs were on the way up. In particular, organised football violence was not only becoming popular but also trendy. To be a football casual, Martin thought, was synonymous with being cool. Football casuals and St Andrews, or even the idea of St Andrews football casuals, were never really on the cards.

Possibly the most essential pre-requisite for a gang of football casuals was to have a football team with which to affiliate. That was St Andrews out then. Golf casuals maybe. Martin half fancied the chance of chasing Jack Nicklaus over the Swilken Bridge. Football was out though.

Nearest possible alternative for a gang from Madras?

Dundee.

'Dundee Utility'.

It didn't seem so unlikely to Martin that such a merger should be possible. Maybe on the proviso that the Madras boys could prove their worth. After all, the success of any casuals crew depended mainly on the strength of numbers and the bottle of its members.

Raith Rovers were the nearest Fife team and with the idea of gangs merging from all of the east Fife towns - Kirkcaldy, Glenrothes, Cupar and St Andrews - it seemed likely that a gang that could cause real damage would be possible with these resources. However, with Raith Rovers languishing in the middle of Division Two it was hardly the most glamorous of affiliations. Travelling to the likes of Stranraer, Cowdenbeath and Arbroath hardly held the promise of huge running battles. In any case, today, Martin's ambitions of becoming a football casual had never seemed less likely, with absolutely no gang credibility with which to bargain.

The bus stop was uncovered and as Martin approached, he noted five hooded figures cowering, facing away from the rain. The figures were unidentifiable in their hooded state but Martin was sure that the tallest figure, two from the front of the queue, was Colin Nichols.

Martin was keen to start to work on Rod's assignment and the sooner some contact was made with this virtual stranger the better. The tall figure boarded the bus, showed his pass and filed on to take his seat on the bottom floor around the middle of the deck. He took the driver's side, beside the window, leaving the aisle seat empty.

Martin boarded the bus, showing the driver his pass but not really paying attention. The tall figure drew back the hood of his Berghaus waterproof jacket. Martin didn't know him well but recognised him as Rod's son. He worked out if he could sit close to him. Possibly get chatting straight away.

'Aye, fair do's son, that's you, think we can get goin' now?'

Martin looked at the bus driver, impatiently signalling that the pass was fine and that perhaps he should take his seat. 'Oh right aye, sorry mate, eh.'

The bus juddered into movement and Martin bobbed down the bottom aisle of the bus behind two other younger Madras school pupils, headed for the back seat. Choosing not to take the seat directly next to Colin, he claimed the window seat directly behind him. He leaned forward in an attempt to make the next thing he said sound nonchalant, like something he would do every day.

'So, how ya doin' mate?'

Colin didn't move an inch. He may have heard what had been said but he certainly didn't realise that he was being addressed. Martin pressed into his shoulder with his hand and raised his voice slightly.

'Y' alright mate?'

Colin turned to face Martin. Slowly, deliberately, his face was completely without emotion until his eyebrows raised and his mouth turned downwards in a puzzled expression as he spoke.

'What?'

Martin sat back and moved uncomfortably in his seat, his head and neck had loosened to a kind of wobble and his eyes were pointed skyward. Any chances of this encounter seeming spontaneous were falling faster than the rain outside.

'Ah'm just saying hello man.' Martin raised his hands slightly and spread his fingers, moving his head forwards and downwards in a motion that suggested, *'it's not so unusual, you know?'*

Colin's eyebrows slowly lowered as his face regained its expressionless look. His head gave a sharp but very small upwards motion as he uttered, 'right'. He paused and then turned back to face front.

'Fuckin' hell,' thought Martin, *'what an ignorant bastard. Holy shit, this must be the only cunt in the school that doesn't seem to have any time for me. What a total fuckin' waste of time that was. No fuckin' wonder he's getting bullied. Ah ought tae twat the cunt masel'.'*

Annoyed with the attitude as he was, he was still mindful of the previous evening's chat with Rod. He was determined to help Colin but at the moment, even as much as getting a friendly word out of him was proving difficult.

8

The rain had eased slightly as the bus arrived in St Andrews, the coastal profile of the town allowing it to apparently miss the worst of the weather that still seemed to be raging further inland. The gloom of Martin's mood remained absolute. The first familiar face to greet Martin was that of Simon Gorrie. Martin, like most people, thought that Simon was a bit of a joke character. Not very bright, he always seemed to be moving uncomfortably and always had some kind of gossip, if not about who had been fighting or causing trouble with whom, then all the latest about which boys were seeing which girls. He always ready to share this information, never, it would seem, getting too involved with events himself.

This morning, Simon seemed particularly animated and excited. He was standing at the gate of the school, looking for anybody he thought may be interested in what he knew, as if on some mission to brief all relevant parties of events.

'You'll have to watch out today man!' Simon was pointing at Martin, his head drawing back and moving slightly from side to side as he drew an exaggerated breath. 'Fotheringham's on a mission after last night.'

This was a typical type of statement from Simon, thought Martin. *'Straight out of the blue, this gimp starts telling me that I need to be careful, with some side information about Billy Fotheringham, which, all things considered makes very little sense.'*

Martin made no attempt to hide his annoyance at being baffled by Simon, his eyebrows lowered, a frown spread over his face as he retorted simply, 'what?'

'Ah'm tellin' ya man, Billy's gone off on one, he's after everybody who ran last night, he's no' fuckin' happy.'

Simon had started to gesture almost uncontrollably, pointing at nothing in particular and waving his hand in pointless little circles and flaps. Martin leaned back slightly, started to rub his ear and cock his head as he looked intently at Simon.

'And this has what tae dae wi' me, exactly?'

Simon looked even more puzzled than his everyday general appearance.

'Well, you were there man.'

'Well, aye, ah was there.'

Martin started to make his case.

'But had you no' been halfway tae fuckin' Anstruther by the time the Bell Baxter mob had got anywhere near us, then you'd know that ah was the last tae run. No' fuckin' Billy Fotheringham.'

Good to get that one out. People were listening. Those that weren't there and needed to be told would see Simon at some point. And he'd let them know. Martin Bridges didnae run!

'So, Simon, maybe you have to watch out today but no' me. In fact, maybe it's me you need tae watch out for.'

Simon didn't register either Martin's displeasure or the thinly veiled threat. He started to fish for the information he craved.

'Is that right aye? What happened man?'

Martin struggled to believe Simon's reaction. It would seem that whereas Billy was somebody to be feared and not crossed, Martin was a sound guy who would be happy to talk about his disappointment. He felt a strong urge to deck Simon there and then. Let him know not to mess with him either. Then again, that would be stooping to Billy's level and Simon was just too pathetic. It would be like hitting a small child.

'Tell ya what mate.' Again, Martin was making no attempt to hide his anger. 'Maybe next time you can hang about, find out for your fuckin' self, you know what ah mean?'

Martin may have wished that this would be an end to the matter but he had the lack of fortune to be in Simon's registration class. It was now also obvious that Simon had now lost interest in informing everybody of Billy Fotheringham's mood, preferring to stay close to Martin to learn all he could of what had happened the day before.

Simon should have stayed at the gate. As he entered the main building he was greeted by the person he least wanted to see this morning in the manner he would least like to hear.

'Gorrie, you little prick. Here!' Billy Fotheringham was standing at the top of the first flight of stairs glaring directly at Simon. Momentarily he diverted his gaze from Simon to acknowledge Martin. 'Alright, Bridie?'

Martin decided at that moment that the nickname was not for him. 'Aye, no' bad,' he answered.

Billy quickly redirected his stare back to Simon. 'Fuckin' get a move on then.'

Billy was now pointing to his own feet in a gesture beckoning Simon. Simon had stopped fidgeting completely, moving only his feet as he climbed the stairs to meet his retribution. As Simon reached the top of the stairs Billy forced his right forearm into his throat pushing him backwards towards the wall. Simon moved quickly backwards, dropping his bag, finally coming to halt as his back hit the wall.

43

His eyes stayed closed for a couple of seconds before he opened them to see Billy's face around five inches away directly parallel to his own.

'Where the fuck did you go ya cunt?'

Simon said nothing. His whole body appeared to be lifeless, as though only Billy's arm was keeping him from slumping to the floor.

'Me and fuckin' Bridie could have been killed yesterday 'cos o' you cunts.'

Billy paid no attention to the sheer wretchedness of Simon's appearance.

'Well what'ave ya got tae say?'

Martin on the other hand was fully aware of how pathetic Simon was. He actually felt sorry for him. Martin cursed the fact that he felt pity for this poor excuse for a gang member but the fact was he did. Martin was just ready to ask Billy to take it easy when another party stepped in.

'Fotheringham, what the hell do you think you're doing?'

Mr Price, Martin and Simon's registration teacher, was making his way over to the top of the stairs with his usual intense look on his face. Billy let go of Simon and it seemed through necessity alone he summoned up only enough strength to stay upright.

'You'll wait,' Billy whispered. He was close enough for Simon to hear. Close enough for him to feel warm breath mixing into his chin fluff. 'I hope like fuck you dinnae think this is over.'

Simon was staring straight ahead almost mesmerised. Billy flicked his head away and moved back down the stairs.

'Yes, that's right, get to your registry class and less of this nonsense.' Mr Price was only half hoping that Billy was listening to him. He turned to Simon, not caring for his obviously stressed demeanour. 'You as well, come on, it's five to nine.'

Simon stayed pinned to the wall for around 15 seconds before finally picking up his bag and following his now departed registry teacher's advice.

***

Throughout the class, Martin was conscious of Simon's total change of character. It was obvious that to him, the experience of being in a gang had just become all too real. Simon's status as a bit-part observer had just been elevated to an active, almost leading, role. He may well have always been in his element knowing the gossip and relaying it. Knowing who was in trouble had been his motivation for being in the gang but now, knowing that he was the one in trouble would probably seem like motivation never to get involved again.

Usually Simon would be interested in the whole picture but at this moment he would have no interest in the fact that almost all of his friends were suffering the same plight. Today he would be concerned only for himself and the fact that even just being around these things can lead to involvement and that right now, there was absolutely nothing he could do about it.

For Martin, the quandary was to know how he was supposed to feel about this. On one hand, Simon was a sad, stupid bastard who deserved all that he was getting: *'if you play with fire, you know!'* On the other hand, Simon was just too pathetic a character. He wasn't supposed to be taken seriously, not even within the gang. You'd never expect to see him fighting. At best he'd stand and shout, chase when things were going well and bottle it at the slightest sign of bother. This is not a good thing in a gang, Martin knew that. In fact, it was far too common for his liking but with Simon it was accepted because, at the end of the day, he was a pap.

He wished that he didn't feel sorry for him but he did. He should be making plans with Billy to smash him but he wasn't. The opposite in fact. Simon was a dick but he was one of the gang. Useless as fuck, but still. Martin cursed himself for it but decided that, today, he would try to make things a bit more bearable for Simon.

They also shared a double physics class that afternoon and Martin thought that he would be able to find out how Simon was doing then and try to cheer him up. He didn't doubt that at the end of the day or maybe during dinner time, maybe even tomorrow or sometime later that week, Billy would do the inevitable and give Simon a going over, but in the meantime taking his mind off it seemed like the benevolent thing to do.

9

Physics was, to Martin, a complete non-starter as concerned with knowledge and information he would need to live a successful life. One of the many school subjects in which he had long since given up interest. Martin could scarcely imagine a greater waste of his time than the double period of physics he was to endure this afternoon. This double period however, was not one to be spent learning the nuances of the universal powers.

While Mrs Watson was, it would seem, dutifully if not exactly enthusiastically, droning on about Newton's wonderful discoveries. Conducting her last but one revision period, before the study leave leading up to her class's O-Grade examination prelims. An examination that Martin had already decided would not be particularly affected by his absence. Martin would be spending his time over these two hours, trying to take Simon's mind off the predicament he had found himself in. In the best way he knew he could. Taking the piss.

***

'So, Newton's first law of motion: the velocity of a moving object is unchanged when acted upon by balanced forces.'

Mrs Watson faced the blackboard and talked as she scribbled. *Law 1: velocity unchanged by balanced forces.*

'Newton's second law of motion: the velocity of a moving object is changed (i.e. it accelerates) when acted upon by unbalanced forces'. *Law 2 : velocity changes by unbalanced forces.*

'Newton's third law of motion: forces exerted by two interacting bodies on each other are equal and opposite .' *Law 3 : forces by 2 interacting equal & opposite.*

'The unit of force is the Newton (N).' *N.*

'Acceleration is the rate of change of velocity.' *Acceleration = change of velocity.*

'Acceleration depends on the mass of the object and the force applied.' *Depends on mass of object and force applied.*

The physics teacher went about her work in a diligent fashion. She had her willing disciples. The bright and shiny students lining the front two rows. They wanted her to ask questions to which they knew they had the answers. The remaining rows of pupils hung on her every word for the vital information they would need to pass the exam that they were sure would be oh-so-important to their futures.

The two characters sitting by themselves, playing with ticker-tape trolleys at the back of the lab represented the exception to this, with absolutely no interest in the proceedings.

'Simon, Martin, could you keep it down please?'

Mrs Watson was obviously exasperated at this single but constant obstacle to the task of communicating with her class. The rest of the students were looking at each other and gently shaking their heads.

'Keep what down?'

Martin drew his chin back. A puzzled look. The kind that great actors practise for the moment when it is announced that they are the year's Academy Award winners.

'Just, you know, the rest of us are trying to concentrate.'

The class murmured in obvious agreement as the teacher spoke.

'What and we're no' like?'

Simon looked on, his expression a complete traitor to Martin's sarcasm.

'Well, you know, we really need to revise Newton, he's going to be very important in your exam and this constant distraction from the back is not helping.'

'Well, there ya are ya see, there's the problem – Newton.' Eyes widened, he shook his head as he spoke.

Simon buried his face in his open hands. 'Oh jeez here we go.'

'Sir Isaac Newton is a problem?' Mrs Watson placed both hands on her desk as she leant towards the boys in obvious amazement at the statement.

'Well no, not as such, ah mean, big Isaac, he's the man, ah've nae quarrel wi' him.'

Those taking in the discourse turned back to face the teacher. No interest in what was being said. Pens dropped on to tables as they dug in for the inevitable. Eyes searching the teacher to get them back to business. To no avail. She sighed, as tired of this type of thing as anyone.

Simon grinned. This was great. He loved it when Martin went off on one.

'No, nae qualms wi' Newton at all, but all of this nonsense, ah mean, come on! No' 15 minutes ago we were shooting these daft buggies off our desks in some sort of discovery that they'll travel faster when they fall off the edge. Doesnae take Newton to work that one out. Ah mean, ah can see it now. *'If I saw further than others it was by standing at the back of the class playing wi' ticker-tape buggies.'* Ah dinnae think so. Anyway, if Newton's already discovered it why are we trying to rediscover it? Ah mean, you could just tell us, we will believe you!'

Simon was looking at Martin with his eyebrows forced toward his fringe with a look of amazement on his face.

'Jesus Christ mate,' he thought, *'ya cannae say that.'*

'So, Simon, I take it you concur with Professor Bridges' vital new theories do you?'

Simon pivoted towards his inquisitor looking as baffled as ever. 'Ah never said anything,' was the best he could muster.

'Well, might I suggest that you and your genius colleague take your advanced physics theorem somewhere that they may be more appreciated.' Mrs Watson gestured towards the door.

'What?' Simon's response was again somewhat less than imaginative.

'So what, you're kicking us out then?' Martin was hiding his delight by trying to sound shocked.

'Well, I'm just suggesting that as your physics knowledge is in advance even of that of Newton, that perhaps you are wasting your time listening to a mere preacher of his word like me.' She was making it up as she went along now. 'And that perhaps you would be better taking your vast experience somewhere else.'

'Aye but where though?' Simon was just starting to understand what was going on.

'Anywhere, Simon, just as long as it's not here.' Mrs Watson had moved to the door of the lab and was opening it. 'I'm certain that a mind like Martin's would be in demand in any number of places. Unfortunately, this is not one of them.'

Martin stood up and looked at Simon. 'Ah think that means we can go now mate.'

The two boys walked out of the door feeling pretty pleased with themselves. As the door closed they heard laughter from the class and even some applause.

'Oh well, let her have her moment,' thought Martin, *'we're outta here.'*

10

'So what 'r' we daein' now then?' Simon was still stunned by what had just happened, it's not often you're just ejected from a class and left to your own devices.

'Well ah'm thinking that seeing as how Fotheringham's gonnae be lookin' for you after school, that maybe school's no' the best place for you tae be at four o'clock.'

Simon made a pathetic-looking expression of agreement as Martin spoke.

'So d'ya fancy getting the fuck out o' here?'

'Aye, sounds good.'

Simon started to make good his escape, at least for today. They could hear a slight commotion further up the corridor. They paid no attention to it, after all there was nothing unusual about high jinks in the school corridors. Martin looked back through the reinforced glass panel of the door. He thought that he could recognise one of the figures involved in the commotion.

'Here, Simon, wait a minute mate.'

Simon turned around, already halfway down the stairs.

'C'mon tae fuck Martin eh, ehm in a bit o' a hurry, y'ken?'

'Nah wait, c'mere and see this.'

Martin was looking as if transfixed by what he saw through the window, flapping his fingers towards himself beckoning Simon. He started back up the stairs looking more than a little peeved.

'What is it?'

Simon reached the top of the stairs and Martin pointed to what he was looking at, he genuinely looked amazed. 'Fuckin' cannae believe it!'

'What?'

Simon peered through the toughened glass. He could see three boys, two of them seemed to be giving a hard time to the other. Martin had recognised the boy taking the grief. It was Colin Nichols.

'So what's the problem?' Simon wasn't concerned at all by what he saw.

Martin was. The two tormentors were much smaller than Colin and were, as far as Martin was concerned, a couple of nobodies from the top classes. Certainly nobody that Colin, at almost six foot tall, should be taking hassle from.

'Well, look, he's about twice the size o' they paps.' Martin looked at Simon, shook his head and looked back.

Simon replied, almost laughing, 'So fuck, c'mon, let's go eh!'

'Nah, ahm no' havin' it.'

Martin headed back through the door into the corridor.

Simon didn't move.

'Whoah, whoah, whoah, whut the fuck has this got tae dae wi' us?'

Martin turned to face him. 'Us? Well, it's no got anything tae dae wi' us, it's just, well, look, the boy's fae Leuchars, I just cannae…'

Martin could see that none of what he was saying was having any effect on Simon. He thought for a few seconds. 'Look, how many fags have you got?'

'Well, I've got a couple, how?'

'Well,' Martin opened out his right hand towards Simon and assumed a fake optimistic look on his face, 'how would ya like to hae more than a couple?'

'Whut the fuck has fags got tae dae wi' anything?'

Simon's brain had just about reached critical mass.

'Just follow me.' Martin continued through the door.

'Oh for fuck sake, this is mental.' Simon shrugged and followed him.

The surprise was diminishing with every step Martin took closer to the incident. He didn't really know Colin and he didn't know why he now felt anger build inside him. Who the fuck did these two think they were? They were pushing Colin about. Calling him 'freak-boy.' He heard them use the words. 'Freak-boy?' What the fuck was this all about? It didn't look like Colin was particularly phased by the whole thing. Martin was enraged now. How could this shit be meted out to someone the size of Colin, by a couple of posh dicks? Bullying itself didn't bother him. Although he'd never really been involved with it, he knew it went on but had no idea that there were people gullible enoug to let swots who think they are a little bit hard get away with it.

Martin was about 20 metres away by the time one of the two boys noticed him approaching. He tried to draw his partner's attention to the fact that they were no longer alone with their victim. Martin lifted his head and pushed his chin slightly forward as he spoke. 'Alright – how'ya doin'?'

Colin was looking still towards the ground for a second and then up to see Martin and Simon approaching. Both the tormentors were now looking sheepishly at Martin, flashing the occasional glance to one another. They'd know who Martin was. Know he had a bit of a rep. One of them piped up the courage to answer, simply, 'Alright?'

Martin stopped around five metres away from the scene, narrowing his eyes as he moved gaze between the two bullies, actually trying to look as menacing as he could. 'Now what the fuck makes you think ah'm talking tae you?'

He looked directly at the boy who had answered. The boy took a few steps back and turned as if to leave.

'Hoy!' Martin pointed at him and raised his eyebrows. 'Mate, if we don't settle this now then ah'll have to see you later, y'know?'

At this point, both boys would have known, rather than expected, that they were in trouble.

'So, what's up, Colin man?' He had to be a little more receptive than he was on the bus that morning.

Colin however wore exactly the same bemused face as he again answered only, 'What?'

'Fuckin' hell, here we go again,' thought Martin.

'Are you OK?'

Simon had arrived at the scene. 'What's the score man?'

At last, Colin managed to string more than one word together. 'Aye I'm alright, y'know?'

Martin nodded his head slightly in agreement, his eyes still narrowed, his mouth only opened slightly as he spoke. 'So what the fuck are these two cunts up tae?'

Colin looked at the two boys who had been giving him a hard time. He looked them up and down as he turned back to Martin with a look that suggested only that he didn't give a damn about them.

'To be honest, I've nae idea, why don't you ask them?'

The two boys were now looking up at Colin, saying nothing, but their faces pleading that he would take the heat off by telling Martin that everything was alright, that it was just a bit of friendly banter. Colin remained impassive and the two boys turned back to Martin and Simon.

'So what is it? What's the story? Is this a shakedown? 'Are you tryin' tae get money out o' my mate?'

Both boys were gesturing frantically with their hands. 'No… no, we're not… honest.'

'What d' ya' make o' that Simon,' Martin turned to his colleague, 'these pricks are robbin' Colin.'

Simon was, for once, somewhere near the ball as he replied in a completely dead-pan tone, his face in an obviously comical look of antipathy. 'Ah think that's fuckin' disgustin'.'

The two swots were by now a complete mess. 'No, no, you've got it wrong.'

Martin was gesturing to the boys to approach him. 'So how much have you taken from him, eh?'

'No, look… please.' The more vocal of the two moved slightly towards Martin. 'We're not stealing money were just having a laugh, that's all, no trouble.'

'A laugh? A fuckin' laugh?'

Martin considered what to say next. These boys were a clever sentence away from pissing themselves.

'You must think I'm fuckin' stupid, naebody's intae this shite for a laugh. Are you seriously trying to tell me that you boys are terrorising the corridors o' Madras High School for your own fuckin' amusement?'

Martin was now talking in a tone that left the boys in no doubt about his anger. Still Colin stood still flicking glances among all parties involved in the discussion, still looking as though he had no idea what was going on or why. Martin turned quickly to Simon, thrusting his fingers repeatedly into his own chest.

'Did y' hear that Simon'? These pricks must think I'm a right fuckin' diddy if they think I'm gonnae believe that.'

Simon looked towards the boys, shaking his head and breathing out heavily. 'You shouldnae have said that like!'

Martin moved closer to the boys, muttering. 'Ah swear tae fuck, you boys had better start gettin' a grip or ahm no gonnae be held responsible.'

One of the boys, now completely terrified offered their last word of resistance. 'No, but…'

Martin cut him off, by now he was completely exaggerating every movement and word in a successful attempt to scare them. 'But… but… fuckin' but, I'll fuckin' gi' ya but in a minute ya little bastards – now gie him his fuckin' money back.'

The two wannabe bullies looked physically sick. Martin moved closer to one of the boys. He moved away but not fast enough to stop Martin grabbing hold of his blazer lapel. Simon moved closer to the other boy, motioning with his head that he should do as Martin said.

'Fuckin' give him it back – now.'

Martin was now talking directly to the boy he was holding. The boy closest to Simon, reached into his front trouser pocket, pulled out some change and offered it to Colin. Colin waited for a few seconds before finally, awkwardly accepting the money.

'Ah knew it, ah fuckin' knew it!' Martin let go of the boy he had grabbed. 'Fuckin' thieving bastards, honestly, you're no safe anywhere these days.'

Martin pointed to the boy he had been grabbing. 'You'n' all ya cunt, give 'im his fuckin' cash back.'

The boy gave a disparaging look toward his friend, scared as he was, he was not keen to give his money away.

'DO IT!'

Martin was not giving him the choice. Reluctantly the boy reached into his pocket, pulled out some money and offered it to Colin. This time Colin accepted it a little more gracefully. With a little wry smile on his face, he was beginning to enjoy the show. Martin looked at Simon and raised two fingers to his mouth and inhaled in an imitation of smoking. Simon couldn't help giggling and Martin had to stifle his own amusement at the boys' humiliation.

'Now git tae fuck ya theivin' little bastards!' Martin pointed in the general direction of the nearest door he could see. The boys stood still, hardly daring to believe that their ordeal was over. 'Go on, fuck off!'

Martin waved his hand and the boys started to leave, accelerating as they grew closer to the door. The two failed tyrants left through the first doors they could reach, leaving Martin, Simon and Colin to review events. Martin feeling good about a job well done, Simon torn between a strong will to escape the school and an interest in the cigarette money they had just earned and Colin, completely perplexed about what had happened and how he should act now. He held out the hand in which the money rested.

'You'll be wanting this then?'

Simon moved forward to accept the gift as Martin interrupted. 'Well how much is it?'

Colin glanced quickly at the assortment of coins and notes in his hand. 'Dunno' about a fiver ah suppose.'

Martin leaned forward and started to fiddle with the money. 'One, two, three, four, three fifties, twenty, twenty, twenty, couple o' tens, load o' crap, fuck aye, that's no' bad, there's about seven quid there.'

Martin looked back towards Simon. 'What's that, about two fiftyish each?'

Simon gestured his acceptance. 'S'pose so, aye.'

Colin moved uncomfortably. 'It's no' really mine though, I mean it was you boys who earned it.'

Simon looked at Martin nodding his head. 'He's got a point eh?' Simon clearly saw no reason to cut Colin in on this money.

'Nah, nah, you're missin' the point here.' Martin had completely dismissed Simon's inference and addressed Colin directly. 'You need to take some of this money.'

Martin started to explain what had happened. 'No' just that but you have tae let these wee pricks know that you're keeping their money. There's just nae danger in the world we can allow little shitebags like that tae bother anybody fae the base. So tell them that their no' getting' their fuckin' money back and if they've got any problem wi' that, then they'll hae us all tae fuckin' deal wi'.'

Colin still looked as if he couldn't understand the whole thing, Martin moved closer to him and talked a little quieter. 'Listen man, ah've nae idea why you let little pricks like that take the piss but no more! D'ya understand? Leuchars boys stick together, alright?'

Martin turned back to Simon and raised his voice as he spoke. 'So, two fifty each right enough then?'

Simon shrugged his approval while looking over his shoulder to the doors he so much wanted to escape through. 'Aye, aye.'

Colin began to sift through the money in his hands, separating pound notes and coins and one 50p piece out for both Martin and Simon, in a conscious effort to provide the least amount of change for the other two, while he kept all the small change himself.

Martin started to wonder why Colin wasn't in a class, surely he wouldn't be bunking as well. 'So what are you up to man, how come you're no' in any classes?'

Colin momentarily diverted his gaze away from the money. 'I'm on study leave.'

'Oh right! What're ya studying for like?'

Colin again glanced up, looking a bit puzzled, checking both boys expressions to check that the question was not just a piss take. 'Well, exams, for my O-Grades.'

'Aye, obviously, I know you're studyin' for exams,' Martin rolled his eyes and dropped his arms loosely by his side. 'I didnae think ya were studying tae be a fuckin' pop star. I was just wondering what subject?'

'Oh right,' Colin pulled an exaggerated facial expression as he started to list the exams he was studying for. In the meantime Simon was wondering why they were wasting time on such a conversation when he would much rather be buying cigarettes with his newly acquired money.

'C'mon Martin eh, let's get the fuck oot o' here.' His level of patience had been reached and breached.

'Oh aye, right enough, c'mon then.' Martin realised that, of course, Simon was right and he turned to leave.

Colin stood with his mouth open but talking no more. He was only halfway through listing the exams as the boys interrupted with their plans to go, leaving him wondering why Martin had asked him about exams in the first place.

As the boys walked away, Martin turned back to face Colin. 'Are you coming then?'

Martin asked Colin the question as if, should Colin say no, it would be considered unusual.

'Coming where?'

Colin wasn't managing to figure out what was happening today. Whereas before this lad Martin had hardly ever talked to him, today he was acting like a big brother.

'Ah don't know man, anywhere, just no' here.'

Martin and Simon had almost reached the door as Martin gestured for Colin to follow.

'But I'm studying.'

Colin realised how pathetic this sounded. Martin stopped just by the door as Simon exited.

'Why, are you no' gonnae pass like?'

Colin thought for a moment. 'Well, probably aye.'

'Well then you're no' really needin' tae study then are ya? C'mon.'

Martin gestured again as he left through the door, not allowing Colin to answer.

For a moment, Colin just stood in the corridor, not knowing what he should do next. He moved forward towards the door and then stopped momentarily. *'Should ah go with them, or not'?'*

He looked around the corridor as if to check nobody was watching. He began to wonder what these two characters might get up to on an afternoon as opposed to studying or doing classwork. Eventually his curiosity got the better of him and he headed towards the door after the boys.

'Ah suppose ah would be wasting time studying and after all, what harm can it do?'

MUST COME DOWN

11

They strolled over Broughty Ferry Beach, heading towards the small dunes but to nowhere in particular. Looked out over the Tay River towards the North East Fife fishing villages and further could see over to St Andrews. It was a good distance away but on a clear day like today they could look out over the sands at Kinshaldie and even make out the shape of the abbey ruins. The North Sea stretched out to the horizon where the dark blue water met the clear light blue of the sky. Along the coast from Dundee were the lighthouses and woods of Barry Buddon, where the army had rifle ranges which, in its own way, had a picturesque quality.

They were leaving the busiest part of the beach where families were resting, their children running in and out of the tidewater and groups of youngsters sat unashamedly enjoying their carry-outs. The couple sat down on one of the dunes, sweeping aside the sharp blades of grass. Warm wind brushed their faces. Natalie slid her fingers back through her hair from her temples. She looked incredible. She always looked incredible. Martin didn't tell her that enough.

'So this is it then, you're off. Leaving me?'

'Och Martin,' Natalie looked disappointed by the statement.

'You know it's no' you ah'm leaving. Ah just have to get away from here. It's…'

She looked back towards Dundee.

'It's just no' doin' anything for me, y'know.'

Martin couldn't think of an answer, he looked back in the same direction as Natalie and winced apologetically.

'Anyway, ah've told you, the question really isnae why ah'm going to London, it's why aren't you coming wi' me? This is the time o' our lives, Martin, we're both wasting it here! Bruce would happily put both of us up and you know it.'

Martin still couldn't think of what to say. He wanted to tell her that of course she was right, he'd go home and pack his bags and they'd both be off on the next leg of their adventure tomorrow. He knew that he couldn't though and he felt like a coward for it. Why couldn't he go to London? Natalie was right, Fife and Dundee never really forced any great desire within him to stay and London would seem to be the place to go. When it came down to it he knew that it was fear of the unknown. Natalie had some money but he didn't and how could he go there without a job, uncertain of whether he would find one, and live off Natalie's money? It just didn't seem right. He looked southwards towards the direction he knew he should be going. Maybe she was pondering possibilities but in the back of her mind she also knew that he wouldn't come with her.

'There's nae blame here ya know! If you loved me enough, you wouldn't hesitate to come with me and be part of my ambition and ah reckon if ah loved you enough ah'd stay here and become the Dundee wifey for you. Face it Martin, we just want different things.'

Martin sought her eyes. Wanted her to know what he was thinking. She was wrong. He wanted to tell her how much he loved her. He did love her, he was sure of that but saying it wouldn't help much. She was right. She had to go. Wife and mother in the East of Scotland. Shopping, hanging out washing and occasionally, if she was lucky, the odd game of bingo. That just wouldn't suit her. He couldn't ask her to do it. The only option then was to follow her. He had to do it. It was that or lose her! He had to go but how could he? What would he do?

Educated to NC Level in Greenkeeping. Not the handiest qualification to take to England's capital city. No trade behind him, what was it going to be? Assistant to the deputy at a Hounslow pitch 'n' putt?

Ah'm a fuckin' coward – grow some guts ya prick!

He could sit beating himself up in his mind but he couldn't find the answer.

Natalie knew she had to say something: 'Will ya be at the station tomorrow to see me away?'

Martin looked at her. She was beautiful. Her hair shone in the sunlight behind it and her face, as always with the minimum of make up was nothing short of perfect.

'Oh aye of course, ah'll no' miss ya there.'

'What about tonight? This'll be our last night together, at least for a while.'

The words *last night* dug into Martin's heart. He could ignore the *for a while* bit as he knew that she wouldn't last in London without attracting the attention of men down there. Men more suitable than him. Especially given that he was 500 miles away. He stood up and turned towards her.

'Ah…' he drew a breath, trying hard to hide that he was struggling to keep his cool. 'Ah'm no' sure that ah can do a last night eh?'

Natalie drew her head back ad flicked her eyelids in surprise. 'What d'ya mean?'

'Ah'm just.'

Martin looked away out over the water he wasn't sure how to put it but he knew he couldn't spend the night with Natalie. He loved her but had to get away from her. This was emotional pain. Pain of loss and he knew that he'd never felt that before.

He'd never felt like it before but had been told what the best thing was for coping with it.

'Ah'm sorry Natalie, ah'll see you tomorrow but ah've just got to do other things tonight, ah'm not sure ah can handle a last night.'

He couldn't think of another thing to say. He headed over the dunes and back into Broughty Ferry leaving Natalie on the beach. Alone and shocked. He reached the high street and was suddenly hit by what he thought must have been a panic attack.

'Whoah, what the fuck am I doin here? Running from Nat. This is fuckin' mental.'

He turned and headed back towards the beach.

'Wait – what am ah heading back for? One last night. What are we going to do? Have sex? Break down and cry? Fuckin' eat a last supper? There's only one thing ah'm sure about. Ah cannae handle a last night!'

He looked across the street toward a call box and knew what to do. The number was familiar.

'Ya fucker, you'd better be in.'

The other end picked up but before there was any chance to say hello Martin was talking.

'Hello is Colin there?'

'Aye mate, it's me, how ya doin'?'

'Aw eh, no' sae good eh, can you come and pick me up? We need to go out tonight, ah need to get wasted!'

***

Martin swirled the dregs of a second pint of lager. He could do with another. In a hurry though. He looked out of the window. Looking for his transport out of there. The barmaid made her way over. She knew her job. Knew to keep the glasses full. She looked fine as well. Wasn't a day for pulling barmaids but flirting with them was expected. Wasn't it?

'You alright cowboy? Want another one of them?'

She placed both hands on the bar leaning forward to offer the best view she could. And it was a good view. It would be a bit rude to stare though. Martin's eyes were drawn to the window again. Colin's dark blue Lancia Delta HF Integrale was pulling into a gap across the street. Martin made eye contact with the barmaid as he polished off what was left in the glass.

Colin was out of the car. Wondering if he was in the correct place. There was no time to waste by allowing Colin to collect his bearings. 'Nah, you're alright doll, that's my wagon now. Catch you later eh.'

He walked out into the sunshine, immediately feeling the better for the alcohol.

'Thought you'd have been here quicker in that thing!'

Colin registered him as he crossed the road. 'Aye well, there's speed limits.'

'Well never mind the speed limits, let's see if you can break the land speed record, we've got to get up tae Downfield to pick up Stevie McNaughton. Don't spare the cuddies!'

Martin squeezed into the car.

Colin still holding his door open, probably thought that he was going into the pub for a refreshing drink. He climbed into the car where Martin sat buckled in, ready to go.

'So what's the story then? Is Nat definitely away tomorrow?'

Martin looked out on to the street to hide any emotion.

'Aye! No' really wanting to talk about that though eh!'

He turned to face Colin.

'Train's at 20 to ten tomorrow morning. Do me a favour mate.'

'Aye, nae bother.'

Martin looked out of the car again.

'Make sure ah dinnae miss her.'

12

Steve McNaughton didn't actually live in a castle but Martin could see why he'd get away with describing it as such. An apartment developed out of one quarter corner of a stately home that at one point would have been on the northwest outskirts of Dundee. Now surrounded by the newly developed part of Downfield, it still had its commanding views of the farms and fields stretching out towards the Sidlaw hills. Martin knocked the door of *'Chateau McNaughton.'*

It didn't take long for Steve to answer. They were shown through directly to the kitchen. Possibly he didn't want such ruffians in his lounge.

A familiar face sat making herself a joint. Yes, Martin knew Marianne Gellatly. And she was a good bet for scoring drugs in Dundee. They sat down around the table and the obvious question had to be asked.

'Alright Marianne got any gear th'day?'

Marianne smiled and shook her head slightly.

'Like that Martin! Nothing beats the direct approach, eh'm daein' fine beh the way, thanks for askin'.'

Martin glanced at Colin. They registered one another's unease.

'Oh aye, sorry eh,' he tried to rescue the conversation. 'Good to see ya!'

'Aye, alright Marianne?' Colin felt he had to say something.

Marianne raised her head from concentrating on roaching and looked at her tablemates.

'Aye yi've got tae watch that eh boys! Desperation for drugs. It'll sneak up on ya.'

She raised her eyebrows as she lit her joint.

'Fuck off Marianne!'

'Aye, what's the score Marianne? I need to get trolleyed tonight!'

Steve turned round from looking out of the bay windows.

'Christ mate, calm down! We've set up something with one of Marianne's contacts, we'll go and get your precious drugs presently.'

Marianne stood up from the table, took a couple of tokes from her joint and then handed it over to Steve. Something was going on there!

'Well, nae time like the present. Nae need to go over mob-handed though, if Knight Rider here can gie me a lift, we'll be back before ya ken it.'

Colin's car had earned him the nickname.

Marianne signalled to him that they should go.

Martin got up and headed to the fridge. It was a while since the pints in Broughty Ferry. There were all sorts of food in the fridge but Martin was struggling to find what he needed.

'Steve, you got any beer mate?'

'I don't have beer but I do have a couple of bottles of half decent wine.'

Martin closed the fridge door.

'You must be jokin' mate. Hey, Michael!'

Another reference to Knight Rider. Colin liked the car. He clearly wasn't so fond of the nickname.

'Fancy taking me up to the Spar, I need supplies?'

Steve moved to the table and picked up a baseball cap. 'Well, not much point in staying here by myself, we'll all go.'

Marianne took in the scene of them preparing to leave. She didn't look too happy. Looked like she was about to tell them all to get a grip.

'OK fair enough, but you boys stay in the car when eh'm in daein' the deal!'

***

Marianne had left the car with £400. The plan was to get 60 ecstasy tablets. £400 as a half payment, another £400 to pay once she'd sold them. A better deal than she thought she would be cutting today. Colin had handed over £200 to her for what he considered to be a good deal. Fifteen pills for himself. That was a surprise. A nice surprise though! This would leave Marianne with 45 to sell from an outlay of £200 now and £400 still to pay. This would boost her profit margin considerably.

Martin stood outside the car enjoying the sun and a bottle of Budweiser. Happy in the thought that Colin wasn't going to take all of those himself and even if Carrie showed up he was still confident that some would be making themselves his way. He didn't feel the slightest bit awkward about this, he wasn't after all playing the sympathy card. He hadn't mentioned Natalie since they left Broughty Ferry but he knew that Colin was aware of the state that he was in. Hadn't mentioned her but he was thinking about her. It wasn't right leaving her on the beach like that. He wanted to give her a call to see if she got home OK.

Didn't seem like there was much point to that though. This was Natalie after all, she was about to go to London by herself and everyone knew she would do well there, it was reasonable to assume that she could find her way from Broughty Ferry to St Andrews without much hassle. He thought that he should phone her, if only to apologise for leaving and assure her that he'd see her off. He ought to do it soon though. Might be pretty wasted soon. Martin looked around. They were in a car park at the bottom of a high-rise multi-storey. Looked to the stairway that Marianne had gone through. It led to a platform above from where they were standing that formed the ground floor of the building. Not exactly familiar with the part of town but he thought that he could remember that there was a telephone box on the level above them.

'Guys, ah'll be back in a couple of minutes eh!'

Colin peeked up from behind the steering wheel.

'Where ya off tae like?'

'Need to make a phone call, back in a minute.'

Steve sat in the back seat and registered the conversation but seemed more interested in the joint he was smoking.

Martin headed towards the stairway. He'd walked around ten steps before Marianne bounded out of the doorway. Chin almost tripping her up.

'Alright Marianne, how'd ya get on?'

'Fuckers havena got anything, huv they? C'mon, wi've got a few mare tae treh!"

* * *

Marianne directed movements as they drove around Dundee for the next few hours, jumping out on arrival at various housing schemes only to return each time with the same frustrated response. The sun was beginning to set out in the direction of Perth and it was beginning to look as though no deal would be made today.

Marianne turned to face a very stoned Steve in the back seat.

'Whut aboot the Digger?'

Steve took some time to realise that he was being spoken to.

'What about Digger?'

Marianne looked at the other two in the car. Colin at the wheel looking cheesed off beyond belief and Martin in the back, his carryout finished, well the worse for the combination of lager and dope.

'Well you ken'im and he's bound tae hae somethin'!'

'Yes I know him.'

Steve leaned forward in his seat.

'And you know what he's like. Just a nasty piece of work. I'd rather stay away if it's all the same.'

Martin and Colin looked at one another. They'd heard of Digger Stewart. He did have a reputation. One of Dundee's less savoury characters, he ran his little empire from Mill o' Mains. Legitimately, he sold secondhand cars but most people knew that he had a hand in protection, prostitution and many other less legal activities. Of course, part of this empire was drugs.

'Aye come on Steve, fuckin' hell. If you can get them fae the Digger then fair do's.'

Martin was clearly for the idea.

'Aye mate, ah know that this guy's a bit o' a dodgy cunt but if you've got four hundred pounds for him, he's just goin' to be businesslike, eh.'

'OK look I'll go to see him but I'm not asking to get laid on! Four hundred pounds, probably thirty E's max.'

Marianne had to think about it. Not the deal she was after but neither was she keen to get into debt with, or even meet Digger Stewart. It looked like the best she might get.

'Aye fair enough!'

13

'Right then Marianne, give me the money, I'll go in.'

Marianne handed all the money over to Steve.

Martin forced his head up to take in the conversation.

Colin slowly turned round to gauge his reaction. He was stoned but still on the ball. He screwed up his face. They both knew that this wasn't ideal.

Steve left the car and closed the door behind him.

'What are you no' going in wi' him Marianne?'

'Nah, dinnae really fancy meetin' the Digger eh!'

Martin reached for the door handle.

'Well, ah'm no' letting that dodgy cunt go by himsel'.'

He laboured out of the seat, crunching an empty can with his foot as he left.

Colin peered over at the mess on the floor that he'd left and frowned. He was about to say something but Martin closed the door and was off in pursuit.

'Hold on mate, probably shouldnae go in by yoursel', eh.'

Steve was starting to look very nervous about the whole thing.

'No Martin, bad enough that I go to his house on a Saturday night myself, I really don't think he'll appreciate two of us.'

'Rubbish man! When he sees the money it'll be sound as. Dinnae worry about it!'

Steve wasn't getting the choice.

They walked along an open aired, fence bound corridor. Steve opened a wooden gate that led to the drying area of a semi-detached house. Didn't look much like the home of an infamous gangster. They walked to the door. Steve rang the bell. An immediate reaction, there were dogs inside the house. The barking came from within as opposed to at the door.

'Probably won't be in, Saturday night and all.'

Martin thought that he looked more like he hoped this was the case than really expected it. The noise of the dogs grew louder and they could be heard scratching the door.

'Aye, he's in alright!'

Martin was keen to get a deal done. The door cracked open as far as the burglar chain would allow. The face peering round was not that of the Digger.

'Zephyr, Samson, shut the fuck up!'

The dogs fell silent.

'Right! Who the fuck are you?'

Pleasantries clearly weren't his speciality. Steve spoke first.

'It's Steve McNaughton, I'm here to see Mr Stewart.'

The doorman pulled a rolled up cigarette from his mouth and a broad smile spread across his face.

'Well, nae fuckin' shit, you're here to see Mr Stewart but am ah supposed to ken wha you are?'

'Oh but Mr…'

Steve was cut short.

'Oh but Mr This and Mr That, if you want in tae see the Digger, you fuckin' call ahead OK.'

The door slammed shut. Steve turned to leave.

Martin gestured towards the door.

'Ah thought you knew 'im.'

Steve beckoned Martin to follow him.

'Well yeah, I do know him. That is, I know the Digger, sort of, but I don't know his bloody henchman there and clearly it's him we have to get past.'

'Aye but…'

'Aye but nothing Martin, what do you want me to do now? Throw stones at his bedroom window? I don't think so somehow. We tried, now come on.'

The door opened and the doorman stood there alone, without the dogs.

'OK, Steve McNaughton, the Dig… I mean, Mr Stewart will see you now.'

He made an exaggerated sweep of his hand to usher the guests in.

Steve and Martin entered the hall and the doorman pointed towards a glass-panelled door. Rather than show them any further into the house, he sat down on the staircase, extinguished his cigarette in an ashtray on the stair and picked up a book. Martin couldn't work out exactly what it was but he could make out the author's name to be Iain M Banks.

They entered the living room to see two figures sitting on the main sofa. The Digger was relaxing prone, wearing an all-white shell suit and slippers. His hair looked immaculate for a man spending a night in watching the television, head resting on the lap of a similarly dressed girl. She also appeared to have paid an awful lot of attention to how she had made up for someone relaxing at home. Neither of them paid much attention to the two who had just walked into the room. The Digger pointed to the screen.

'Ach, come on! She looks fuck all like Kim Wilde!'

Steve and Martin looked at the screen. He was right, the girl singing 'Kids In America' didn't look much like the pop star she was trying to imitate but they couldn't help thinking that it wasn't exactly the picture they had of gangsters on a Saturday night. Sitting at home, enjoying *Stars In Their Eyes*.

'Right, turn this shite off Wendy, eh!'

The Digger sat up and looked at his guests.

'Well, if it's no' Stevie McNaughton.'

Steve raised his hand to a hip height wave and said.

'Alright?'

'So what can eh do for you mi man?'

Steve felt his back pocket. The money was there.

'We're looking for some ecstasy Digger, you able to help us out?'

'You're looking for ecstasy and you came to meh hoose?'

The Digger looked at his watch.

'It's ten past nine now, so eh'm assuming yi've been aroond the hooses before yi got here!"

Steve looked to Martin for inspiration, to no avail. Neither of them wanted to give the impression that they were there as a last resort. They weren't to know what was coming next. This wasn't their first choice but it was just a drug deal. The next thing that the Digger said sent a chill up both their spines. He pointed to a couple of easy chairs. This was just your standard family front room.

'I think you two ought tae sit doon, eh cannae imagine either o' yis realise how much trouble yi've just walked intae.'

Martin checked out Steve's face. Sure he could see his bottom lip go.

They took their seats. The Digger was looking directly into Steve's eyes now.

'You ken Henry Blake?'

Martin was just as interested to hear the answer, he had no clue what was going on.

Steve was trembling.

'I, yeah, I kind of know Henry.'

The Digger looked to Wendy open mouthed and raised eyebrows as if to ask, does this guy think I'm stupid.

'Henry wis a business partner o' yours. Was'e no'?'

'He, ehm, well, we…'

The Digger raised his voice slightly.

'He, erm, kinda fuckin' nothing. You and him worked th'gether. Quite the young entrepreneurs!'

Steve didn't feel that arguing would be a good idea. He wasn't exactly a business partner of Blake but it was true that when Blake was organising club nights, Steve would help out, handing out flyers, pasting posters and of course some less legal activities that might attract the attention of the Digger.

The Digger was now leaning forward in his chair, looking calm but quite clearly intent on straight talking.

'Now, whaur is Henry Blake now?'

Steve was able to help with an answer.

'He's emigrated to Ibiza.'

'Aye eh've heard. Lucky him! Trouble is, shortly before he went awa', your associate and me…'

Steve didn't like the way the word 'associate' was being used.

'We had a wee bit o' business. Business which, to date, is still outstandin'.'

Steve could see the hole that was being dug for him and felt he had to try to get out.

'Oh yeah but…'

The Digger had no intention of stopping the dig.

'Aye but, no but nothin'! Listen pal. Eh ken you ken nothin' of me and Blake's dealings. Nae wey on God's earth would you be here if ya did but here's the scoop. I'm owed a lot of money and whether you ken it or no', you're up to your fuckin' neck in it and that hard-neckit bastard Blake. He's in to me to the tune o' fev hunder Disco Biscuits!'

14

Steve leaned against a fence outside the Digger's garden. The Digger's words were still ringing in his ears.

'You work for me now!'

Why hadn't he just pasted him and taken the money? What does it mean that he's working for the Digger? He hadn't even taken any of the money and that had to be a bad thing. He could feel the nausea in the pit of his stomach. Martin was standing looking on with both hands on his head.

'Those Disco Biscuits. Are they the same…?'

'Yes, they're the fuckin' same alright. I can't believe that bastard Blake, fucking off and leavin' all this crap behind.'

'Nah but wait, ah met someone on the boat that said they were his.'

'Wasn't a scruffy-looking guy with a Manchester accent by any chance was he?'

'Well, aye, he was as it happens.'

'Yes Martin, that'd be Henry Blake!'

'Right, what, and you never knew they were the Digger's?'

Steve stood up straight and pointed back towards the house.

'Oh yes, of course I knew they were the Digger's. Cos I'm like that you know, always ripping off maniacs and going to their house a few months later to find out how they're doing.'

Martin felt suitably chastised.

'Listen Martin, I'm in a fucking hole here and you need to help me! I think we need to remember who actually sold those pills.'

***

'So whut makes ya want tae join the RAF?'

Marianne was keeping the conversation light as she and Colin waited for Steve and Martin to get back.

'Och, it's just to get away you know. See the world and that.'

Marianne was skinning up yet another joint and she couldn't stifle a giggle.

'And whut, so ya cannae take any mare drugs efter tonight?'

'No' really'

'Whut, iver?'

70

'Well, no, but so what, there's more to life than getting wrecked!'

Marianne looked at him displaying almost pity.

'Well ah hope the boys get somethin' cos it would be a bit shit if ya didnae git a last fling eh!'

'Well aye, ah could do wi' one last…'

Before he could finish the sentence, there was a bang on the roof and the passenger door swung open. Steve jumped into the car and screamed, 'DRIVE!'

Martin got into the back.

'C'MON COLIN LETS GET THE FUCK OUT O' HERE!'

Colin looked at Steve who was now frantically shifting in his seat and looking back in the direction they had come from.

'COME ON ¬– COLIN, WE NEED TO GET OUT OF HERE NOW!'

Colin reached for the key and then stopped himself. Steve looked directly towards him, he was rocking back and forward in the seat.

'COME OOOOON!'

Martin was getting similarly excited.

Marianne looked petrified.

Colin lifted a finger to signal to Martin that he wouldn't appreciate any interruption.

His eyes bore into Steve.

'Right!'

'NO, COLIN PLEASE, WE NEED TO GET AWAY.'

Steve was tapping the window and gesturing in the direction they had come from.

'No, Steve. You need to calm down. And you need to tell me what the fuck's going on and what the fuck's happened to your face?'

15

Martin was definitely starting to think that they had done the wrong thing in Mill o' Mains. If getting Colin out of Mill o' Mains had been tricky, then getting him to calm down now that they were in Fat Sams was proving impossible. In Mill o' Mains, after hearing Steve's events of what had happened he was intent on confronting the Digger to get his money back. A tricky little situation for Martin and Steve, because the fact was that the Digger didn't have any of the money. Steve had kept it. A situation that Colin had already hinted that he suspected.

'Listen Martin, if that cunt McNaughton's trying to rip off Marianne then that's one thing but he'd better not be trying it on with me.'

Martin had pulled him to one side when he had threatened to go and find the Digger and *'fuckin' kill the cunt.'*

'Holy shit Colin, what do you think is happening here? I was in there with him. The Digger just went mental. Set his dogs on us and his minder pulled Steve into the kitchen and done him. I couldnae dae anything!'

Even as he said it Martin doubted Colin would believe a word of it. Couldn't believe also that he was in on Steve's plan to take his money from him. Steve had made a convincing case though. He was certainly in a lot of bother. Martin could agree with that. He couldn't work out how keeping the money would help but he knew that he had to help somehow. By ripping money off his friends though? It didn't seem right. Now that he had had time to think about it, it wasn't right. He knew he shouldn't have done it but he had and not because he wanted to help out Steve. Neither was it Steve's insistence that he didn't really owe Colin much loyalty.

'He's going away to the RAF in two weeks anyway and he's fucking getting money from somewhere, you're not telling me that a part-time mechanic can afford a car like that and still have two hundred pound to bandy about on a Saturday night.'

That wasn't why Martin went along with the plan. It was the basic survival instincts brought to him by knowing that he was implicated in the Digger problem and wanted to buy Steve's silence on that. This was plain and simple. He'd sold his mate out to get himself out of trouble. So Martin would give Steve a couple of punches to make it look like he'd been filled in and then they'd hit the car running, get out of Mill o' Mains quickly and explain how the deal went sour. How Steve had been involved with the Digger's sister and the Digger wasn't pleased.

At the time it seemed plausible but now that they were away from the scene it just seemed insane. Not only insane but a very dangerous game to play. Colin had insisted that they still go out to Fat Sams and that they would score the drugs anyway. If they wondered at the time how he planned to do that they certainly knew now. Brute force if necessary. Find someone selling the Digger's drugs.

'There's bound tae be somebody.'

Then simply take their drugs from them. Easy! Not a great prospect for Martin, he could see how that would end. Back in the Digger's house in a couple of month's time.

'You ken Colin Nichols? Business pertner of yours ah believe! Oh, off tae the RAF is he? Lucky him. Owes me a lot of drugs though – now you work for me.'

16

Tonight Fat Sams was as Fat Sams always was. A heaving mass of sweaty bodies and as always there were plenty of people punting ecstasy if you were willing to pay nightclub prices. Tonight though, Colin was far from willing to pay that price. Two hundred pounds down and with nothing to show for it. He couldn't believe that he'd let Martin talk him into leaving Mill o' Mains.

'No Colin, you cannae go in there! He's no' like the casuals mate, this is a proper gangster and he'll be armed.'

Couldn't believe that he'd just let Steve McNaughton go home. Something was telling him that the whole thing wasn't right and that Steve had been behind something. Martin wouldn't lie to him but something happened in that house that stank of Steve McNaughton being shifty.

For now though, he knew what he was looking for. People in Fat Sams who sold drugs for the Digger tended to stand out like sore thumbs. Everyone else wearing Kickers, Timberlands and designer jeans and them with their Sambas, Levis and Fred Perrys. He'd already pulled up a couple of people, asked where the E's were and been led to some obviously flying dealers, just there enjoying the experience. He had decided that those guys could rest easy.

Colin walked through to the dining area. Dancers on the seats, dancers on the tables, bouncers half-heartedly trying to get them down but knowing that that was just the way the place was. He headed upstairs past the dining area bar. There was a relatively quiet area behind there but no dodgy characters. He walked into the gents toilet. There was a door to the dining area and through the other end the door to the main hall. He walked through and opened the door to get through to the occurring madness. The noise hit him, the heat hit him, the lights and smoke all barraged his senses but he was able to largely ignore them as he could see his target standing at the end of the back bar.

Four or five people had mounted the bar and were dancing with their hands in the air and the staff behind the bar were trying to work around their oscillating legs. Yet there at the end of all this chaos were three men apparently oblivious to the whole thing. Colin knew that there were two opposite ends of the spectrum of people who came to these nights that stood out so readily. Police and pushers. He knew these were not police only because he recognised one of them. He knew him by nickname only, 'Fitchy', but he knew that he sold drugs and it was likely that he was *working* for the Digger.

Colin approached, Fitchy and his pals dressed exactly as expected, they didn't notice Colin until he was right up against them. Fitchy was a small five foot six and wiry to Colin's six foot and broad. The two henchmen were tall and well built but they had goatee beards and that told Colin all he needed to know. If you want to walk about looking like a hard man, you grew a goatee beard. This was sweets-from-a-child time.

'Fitchy, you sellin' tonight?'

Nothing untoward about the question, Fitchy registered the possible customer.

'Aye, mate, how many ya efter?'

Colin checked out Fitchy's two minders.

'Ah need to speak to you!'

'What's that mate? Speak up, eh cannae hear ya.'

The music was loud and Fitchy was probably just used to just having fingers held up as an indicator of quantity required.

'Ah said, ah need to speak to you. In the toilet.'

Colin signalled towards the toilet with his head.

'What's that mate, how many? Ah cannae hear ya!'

Colin pointed towards the toilet with one hand and batted his thumb against his fingers with the other. One hand signalling toilet, the other talk. Fitchy understood and as Colin walked away he decided to follow but not before he signalled for his cohorts to follow. The toilet was full. The urinals being used and the cubicles closed. Cigarette smoke hung in the air. The noise of the music died down as the door swung closed and then quickly amplified when Fitchy opened it again. Colin positioned himself beside the sinks. Fitchy walked in with his minders following behind like lap dogs.

'What's going on man?'

'You work for the Digger?'

Fitchy looked around then straight back to Colin.

'Whut the fuck's that got tae dae wi' you?'

Colin was taking this as a yes.

'He owes me!'

Fitchy paused, the out-of-place meeting was attracting the attention of some people at the urinals.

'You're mental!'

Fitchy decided he'd had enough of this and turned to leave.

'Dinnae turn your back on me ya prick!'

Fitchy turned quickly and thrust his finger up close to Colin's face.

'What the fuck do you think…'

Colin didn't wait for the whole question. He whipped his left hand up to remove Fitchy's finger from his face and his right hand came up to grip his neck as he thrust him backwards through his shocked minders and back into the urinals area. After two paces, Fitchy lost his balance and he fell backwards, his fall coming to a stop only when his head connected with the steel of the urinals. Immediately, the two minders were on Colin. The remaining occupants of the room finished what they were doing and hurriedly left the room. The minders seemed more interested in getting Colin away from Fitchy than inflicting any damage.

This was a mistake.

Colin could see that Fitchy was probably not going to be much more of a problem so he turned to face the other two. For the first time, one of them tried to meet force with force and threw a punch that landed pretty squarely on the side of Colin's head. Painful but not debilitating. Colin grabbed him by the collar of his jacket and pushed him to arm's length; the attacker was now unable to do anything.

The other minder had now decided that he should get involved and moved forward to attack but before he could connect with anything Colin thrust his clenched free hand into his throat. The result was a gasping and quivering goatee-bearded wreck on the toilet floor. Colin looked at the other attacker still in his left hand. He'd clearly now lost much of the will to fight. Colin pushed him towards the door that he had come in and then let him go.

'Ah think that you should get goin' pal.'

He took his cue to leave. Colin turned towards Fitchy, still on the floor by the urinals but getting up to his feet.

'You dinnae ken what you've jist done.'

Colin moved forward and Fitchy shrunk back into the urinal.

'It's no what ah've done that you should be worried about, it's what ah'm about tae dae!'

The doors flung open and in poured three of Fat Sams bouncers. Colin turned to face them. Readied himself for a fight. He drew his hand back to throw a punch but already they were too close to make it effective. Three bouncers, who had probably been working out all week and spiking with steroids to be ready for just such an encounter, managed to grab a hold of him. They were good at their job and had him so that he couldn't move within seconds.

'Bastards!'

They knew the techniques.

Colin had strength to match any of them but they were carrying him out of the toilet in a way that didn't allow him to move at all.

'Get the fuck off me you bastards, ah'll fuckin . . .'

One of the bouncers looked him in the eye, the irony of him having a goatee beard wasn't lost on Colin.

'OK pal, you shut up now eh.'

The bouncer brought up a clenched fist and brought it down on Colin's nose with a force that sent the pain all the way up through the head, temples and down the back of his neck. The rest of the trip out of the club was a more sedate affair. Blood had begun filling into Colin's eyes. The bouncer had done well. It was a good hit.

At the bottom of the stairs they reached a short tunnel to the door. Colin began to find his feet again and on the final push out of the door he had gathered the strength to fight on. He grabbed the hand of one of the bouncers who clearly didn't expect it judging by the ease that Colin managed to pull him out of the door, across the road and into the mesh fence opposite the club. Colin couldn't have known who he'd managed to grab. So it was good to see the goatee-bearded doorman bounce off the fence like in a wrestling ring. Momentum was on Colin's side and when his hand collided with the bouncer's nose, he could just tell that he wasn't getting up any time soon. *'Fuckin' touché, ya cunt.'*

Colin turned to face the door. Three more bouncers making their way over the road. Colin felt that this was more in his favour though. Not a grapple with some overly pumped up bears in a confined space. Here he had room to fight. The closest bouncer had both hands in front of his face, martial arts style, but as Colin moved in, he drew away and another bouncer moved in past his shoulder. The punch was thrown but Colin could see it coming and managed to dodge it completely. The bouncer had made his move and was now completely open to Colin. He decided to get rid in the quickest fashion. He brought up his foot and drove it into the inside of the bouncer's knee, his foot's contact with the ground providing the necessary leverage to ensure the break.

Some of the shocked people, still standing in the queue to get in, winced and even screamed at the sound of the bones shattering. The martial artist kept retreating as the next bouncer made his move. These big lads could grab a hold of you without much trouble and punching a nose when you're bound up poses little trouble to them but when it comes to stand-up fist-fighting, they just lacked the necessary speed.

Colin didn't wait for the punch, he just brought his own hand down over the bridge of the nose of the next attacker and again, although this one didn't go straight down, he knew the fight was out of him. To make sure, Colin kicked him, pushing the hands that were covering his face back into his head and through, sending him on to his back.

The remaining doorman now had his hands slightly lowered and fingers held upwards in an apparent attempt to mollify the situation.

'Look mate, just go alright, you've done enough.'

Colin, however, hadn't finished inside Fat Sams. He stared into the bouncer's eyes. The kung-fu stance was reinstated. Colin walked straight towards him and again he backed off.

'Ah'm going back in there mate. Ah'm no' finished.'

'Dinnae think so pal.'

The bouncer now stood his ground. Colin could see the bouncer's eyes move to one side and the signs of recognition in them. He knew that someone was getting ready to attack from behind him. He spun to meet the attacker. As he brought his hand up to connect with the jaw he could make out the black and white checked band on the cap. Too late to do anything about it, the punch landed. The face going one way, the police cap the other.

17

Martin took the call early on Sunday morning. Carrie had been Colin's one phone call and she'd been told to make sure that Martin knew.

'He's in Bell Street police cells, fighting outside Fat Sams. Serious assault, GBH, police assault, they're throwing the book at him.'

Martin got the earliest bus he could get over. He'd heard that you couldn't visit but you could bring things in for the prisoners. He knew that Colin would be there until Monday and knew that he'd want something to read at least, picking up a Sunday Mail and a book. 'Ian Rankin - Tooth & Nail. An Inspector Rebus novel.' Back cover notes mentioned a wolfman in Edinburgh. Sounded quite good, so he bought himself a copy as well. He bought a couple of filled rolls. Visions of bread and cheese in the cells. Thought that his mate should probably have better than that. The desk sergeant looked at what Martin had brought in.

'Oh filled rolls is it? PC Burns will you break out the silver salver please? His Majesty the police beater is to be served breakfast.'

Martin could tell that Colin's time in these cells was not going to be made easy. The sergeant pushed the food back over the desk.

'You can keep these pal, we'll make sure he gets the rest.'

Martin stood outside and could feel the morning sun begin to burn. He thought over the events of the previous day. Where it all started to go wrong. Lying to Colin was what sent him over the top. Martin knew what he was like when he felt he was being ripped off and, more importantly, he knew what he was capable of when he was angry. He could wave aside all of these feelings that he should have been looking after him once they got to Fat Sams. Yes, maybe he should have known better than to let him go there. Try harder to placate him. He could have convinced him that the plan to just steal drugs was scarily bizarre. He knew he could have stopped him but at the time he felt he shouldn't. He'd just helped to rip off his best mate and was then just agreeing with whatever he was saying. However stupid the ideas were, he just thought, *'go along with it, don't upset him any more.'*

Why hadn't he looked for him after he had gone missing inside Fat Sams? Not that that would have done much good really. The point was that he was actually avoiding contact with Colin, having lied to him. The fact was as clear as the day's blue sky. He shouldn't have lied to Colin. Martin looked out around the back car park of the police station. Cars belonging to the officers working inside, separated from the street by a low wall with an entrance just large enough to fit two cars through at a time, with a sign either side stating, "TAYSIDE POLICE. HEADQUARTERS & CENTRAL STATION."

Just then the word hit him.

'Holy shit! STATION.'

He began running down the small flight of stairs.

***

Martin burst into Dundee train station just after quarter to ten that Sunday morning. He sprinted down the main stairway in some vain attempt to be there on time.

'Maybe the trains'll be runnin' late. Ah hope like fuck the trains are runnin' late.'

Some five minutes after Natalie's train had departed.

THREE FIRSTS FOR COLIN NICHOLS

18

'Okay then 5L, if I can just have your attention please. Thank you. For anyone who doesn't know me, my name is Miss Watson.'

The class looked around each other trying to determine who the unfamiliar ones were. Those who had encountered her before actually felt some pride in this fact.

'And I will be your registration teacher for your time in 5L. However long that may be. This time, you'll be glad to know, will not be spent in the usual class lessons type format; rather, your time here until you leave will be spent adapting and preparing for the day when you leave. Careers advice and work experience will be the order of the day.'

Martin fidgeted in his seat, looking around as he sat with his friends in the last place in the world he wanted to be. Colin sat directly behind him and Billy by the window, a row in front. It was a curious quirk of fate which brought upon these boys the necessity to return to school that year and indeed, the same quirk which would bring them to be in the same registration class. This class was named 5L. The figure five obviously signified the fifth year but the suffix L may have stood for Leavers, Leaving, Leaving early or even Lost in space, as far as the three boys and the rest of the pupils in the class were concerned. At the end of fourth year most pupils faced the choice between leaving school or staying for one or two more years of scholastic achievement. For the pupils of 5L, this choice, at least in part, was not theirs to make. They could stay on for further years but they couldn't leave. Their problem being that each of these pupils were still aged only 15 and did not have a birthday before the legal cut-off day in September that year.

This being the case, although none of them felt it necessary to further their academic careers, they were not allowed to leave school, at least until they reached 16 years. Legally not allowed either to enter full-time employment or claim benefit, they had no choice but to return to the place they would least want to be. 5L was a kind of purgatory in schooling terms. They could not enjoy the freedom afforded to most of their classmates of the previous term, released at the end of fourth year, yet neither would it be any use for them to endure lessons of any type, as these would not be tested at any point and in any case, would not likely be listened to.

That morning, an attempted explanation of their remaining time at Madras was offered by their unfortunate registration teacher, form mistress and careers counsellor for their time in 5L, Miss Watson. A task for which she felt even less genuine enthusiasm than the pupils she was looking after and with only forced conviction. Miss Watson moved from behind her desk, assuming a semi-seated position on the edge of it.

'The few lessons that you do have will focus on success in this area for when you finally do leave. This session will also provide a chance for day release to Elmwood College in Cupar, for a beginners' level City & Guilds course in work-related subjects, such as farming, land-keeping, animal care and the like.'

A few of the pupils perked up a little as this idea was announced.

'Of course this will involve more of an obligation to stay on until the course finishes, as opposed to just staying until you turn 16.'

The same pupils slumped back in their chairs. Miss Watson noticed the reactions and her heart sank even further as she continued.

'Perhaps the most helpful part of this time will be spent on work experience. We will encourage all of you to approach local businesses, to gain work experience with them. Although the school will help in every way to assist you to gain such placements, the onus really is on yourselves, not only to decide the type of work experience you would like but also to approach these businesses.'

All through this little speech, Martin was busy thinking of a witty reply. Although there was never any real love lost between he and Miss Watson, he always thought that they enjoyed the harmless banter which was only ever occasionally allowed to get out of hand. It occurred to Martin to hint at the accusation that the school was turning its back on them or highlight the absolute pointlessness of the situation. Both of these options seemed a little harsh this early in the session however and he decided that his old friend sarcasm would be more apt.

'Miss Watson?'

Martin raised his hand slightly, interrupting Miss Watson as she found her flow. The teacher visibly slumped, frowning slightly as she acknowledged her pupil.

'Yes Martin, what is it?'

Martin sat straight in his chair, cocked his head and smiled.

'Ah bet you were well chuffed when you heard you had us this year, eh?'

The majority of the class found this amusing.

'Ah Martin, the laureate of disenfranchised youth.'

She felt that there were points to be scored by stating that which would not be understood.

'Thank you for that wonderful piece of free thinking. Free thinking of course, is something we will positively be encouraging in 5L.'

Miss Watson gestured with both hands to include the whole class.

'After all, who is it going to distract?'

Most of the class were clearly bewildered by what was being said. Martin knew it was some sort of insult. He just knew by the tone of voice. He looked around his classmates to see a collection of blank faces, as confused as his own. The only exception was Colin, looking directly at him shaking his head with a broad smile.

'Aye, you've got your work cut out for you there!'

Billy Fotheringham had been busy scribing his name on a classmate's bag. He stopped momentarily to listen to the brief exchange between Martin and the teacher.

'Aye Bridie, shut yir puss eh!'

With this, he went back to completing his mention on the bag.

Martin sat bolt upright in his chair and looked around his classmates. Everybody was looking at Martin other than Billy himself who now seemed completely engrossed with the bag. It didn't particularly surprise Martin that Billy would just say such a thing but it always bothered him that he thought he should just get away with it. Martin stretched out both hands, completely open in the direction of Billy, shaking his head, mouthing the words 'what the fuck?'

19

Miss Watson moved through the rows of seats placing a single sheet of lined paper on the desks in front of each pupil.

'OK, so have a think about what you want to do. You're not in 5L for long, so pretty soon you'll be out there looking for jobs. Your choices? Take the first job you can get and spend your days, miserably waiting for the clock to strike five, or use your time now to work out what you want to do. What kind of job you'd enjoy. And crucially, what can you do in the next five months to get such a job?'

She squeezed herself between Martin's desk and the pupil in front, placing the paper on the desk. They made minimal eye contact and Martin smiled in a way he hoped she'd find charming. Her return glance was nothing less than challenging.

'You'll have to do better than that young un.'

She couldn't avoid pressing against the desk, revealing firm thighs. As she passed he could see the shape of her lithe buttocks filling her tight tweed skirt.

Miss Watson. Not married then. Not old though, probably not even in her thirties yet. Her upper body was covered completely in a plain white blouse and deep red long-sleeved cardigan. Martin could tell though. She could dress as dowdily as she liked but below the clothes there was a tiger. He'd seen enough porn to know that it's always the ones you'd least expect.

He pressed his pen to the paper.

Things he'd like to achieve while in 5L.

Number one. *'I'd like to get Miss Watson's top off.'*

The pen slid over the paper and he began to write. *1. Get work experience, somewhere outdoors.*

He looked down at what he'd written. Whispering his response.

'Fuck me, that's lame!'

He looked around the room. No one really seemed overly interested in the task.

No one other than Colin, that was.

Martin watched him scribble his thoughts on the subject, his curiosity as to why Colin would choose to stay in 5L getting the better of him.

'So how come you're no' staying on tae do any Highers then Colin?'

Colin stopped writing and looked up at Martin, saying only 'eh?'

Martin picked up a pencil with his right hand and drummed it between the thumb and index finger of his left.

'Well would you no' be better off stayin' for the whole term and getting' some Highers?'

Colin squinted as if to ask, why the great interest? He looked around the room. Some of the class showed no interest in the question. Colin felt a little uneasy. Half of the class seemed interested in the conversation and it felt to him that any answer to the question would seem almost like an announcement to that audience.

'Ah just dinnae need any… y'know?'

He talked in a way that made him seem unsure of what he was saying.

'Aye but they might be useful though, eh?'

Martin considered that if you worked as hard as Colin had in fourth year, gaining eight O-Grades, and you must stay on for fifth year, you might as well continue in that vein.

'Help you get a job and that.'

Colin again scanned the class. More and more people were becoming interested.

'Well – ah've already got more than ah need for the job ah want.'

He was halfway through saying this before realising that it would invite further questioning. Billy had been monitoring this conversation and had obviously felt that it was time that he got involved.

'How, what's that then?'

Colin knew the rest of the class were listening now. Billy was the hard nut. If he was interested, they were all interested. How could he nip it in the bud? He probably couldn't. So let's get it over with.

'Ah'm gonnae join the RAF.'

Colin surveyed the faces of his fellow 5L pupils, trying to gauge their reaction.

'Like my old man,' he added.

Again he scanned the class for reaction. Most of the class clearly couldn't care less about this revelation but it did seem to cause a stir with two of the girls sitting together towards the back of the class. The girls whispered something to one another and smiled.

'Ya gonnae fly jets like?'

The prettier of the two girls started off their banter.

'Aye Top Gun Nichols eh!'

Her neighbour carried it on. They both giggled.

Colin was immediately struck by two things. Firstly, the looks of the girl who spoke first. He'd seen her in passing before but only now, looking directly at her smiling face was he totally aware of how good she looked. Also, he was surprised that these girls knew his surname. He felt that these girls were just people in the passing before and didn't know why they would know him.

'Mind you, ah think you're mare o' an Ice Man than a Maverick.'

'What do ya think Manda?'

She gave away the name of her friend but in reality this was just background information.

'Aye.'

Manda talked in a hushed tone but Colin could still hear what she said.

'But he can be ma wing man any time, y' ken what ah mean Carrie?'

Now at least he knew the first name of this girl. He watched as both girls broke into fits of giggles.

Martin also watched this exchange and it was obvious to him what was going on. He caught Colin's eye, raised his eyebrows, pressed his lips together and gestured towards Manda and Carrie.

Colin hurried to look away from Martin and what he was suggesting. He sat facing the front wondering what was going on. He considered that he may be being chatted up but if this was the case, he was being chatted up more by the one he was less interested in. Colin began to dismiss this anyway, thinking that it was more likely that the girls were just taking the piss. Colin was used to being slagged off but was not happy that these girls were ribbing him about his plans for the RAF. After all, that was his future. He turned to face the girls. They had calmed down a little bit but were still a little rowdy.

'Nah, ahm no' gonnae be a pilot, you need to be an officer to be a pilot.'

Another member of the class had been quietly listening to the whole conversation. Decided he'd held his peace long enough and had to intervene.

'Surely that's mair o' an argument for you to take Highers then.'

Colin looked at him, almost revolted by the suggestion.

'What, so ah can go to university and apply to be a commissioned officer.'

He could see from his reaction that Colin wasn't sold on the idea.

'Well aye, ah suppose if you need to become a pilot, ah mean that would have to be the best job in the RAF.'

His name was Gordon McGovern but nobody called him that. Most people didn't even know his name. For as long as he could remember everyone had called him Goof. In the school anyway. Maybe not so much at home although it had started creeping in there as well. For all intents and purposes, in Madras at least, that was his name. Goof. He was well known in the school. A couple of years ago he had been involved with Billy and Martin in the school gang scene but everybody knew that he spent most of his time playing football. He'd even gained a place with Dundee Football Club, in their youth set-up.

Colin thought about what Goof was saying and of course it shouldn't seem strange that to him, given the effort he was now putting into football that Colin should aim high. Colin however didn't feel that joining the RAF as a ground crew man was not ambitious. Both his father and grandfather before him had done just that and both of them went on to become senior non-commissioned officers.

'Nah Goof, you dinnae understand.'

Even Colin used Gordon's nickname. Not really through choice, he had no idea what he was actually called.

'I doubt if my dad would ever speak to me again if ah became a Rupert.'

'That's daft.'

Carrie was still smiling but no longer making fun.

'Ah think your dad would be pretty chuffed if you become a pilot, that's what it's all about is it no'?'

Colin felt a slight rush of excitement. She was speaking to him. The rest of the class melted into insignificance. She was genuinely interested in what he had to say. She looked incredible. He had to say something cool now. Something that would impress her. He began to think that there were great advantages of being in a lower class. All the way from first to fourth year, he had never felt that he was doing as well as he was doing now with a girl he liked.

'Aye you're probably right Carrie.'

It felt good to be on first name terms with her.

'But ah'm not gonnae achieve as much as he did by cheatin' at the start. Bein' an officer's a different life, you know? It's just no' me.'

Carrie looked at her friend Manda who now had the same pleased-at-nothing look on her face.

'Suppose that's cool.'

Carrie was half suggesting and half asking Manda.

'Oh aye, suppose so,' was her answer.

Martin felt a little awkward interrupting what he recognised as being sexual advances but he thought *'well there's two of them, there may as well be two of us.'*

'Ah think your mental wantin' tae join the Air Force. There's nae way I'm following in my dad's footsteps, I mean, it's no' exactly a family business is it?'

*** *

By mid-morning the class had been dismissed. Sent away to make their approaches to local businesses. Eager youngsters willing to give their time for free to employers for some oh-so-important experience. An important and exciting time for the pupils of 5L, there was no time to waste. Possibly it could wait till tomorrow though, it was such a nice day. They were off to the playing fields for a game of football that was more to do with being entertained by Goof, than any competitive competition. Martin spent the lion's share of the short trip telling Colin what he knew about Manda and Carrie, convinced that they were 'in there'.

Colin tried to make out that he didn't know why Martin was telling him these details but in fact was listening to all he had to say about Carrie. Her second name was Brown and Martin seemed to pay an awful lot of attention to the fact that she had a younger brother Danny in fourth year. It didn't surprise him that Martin paid so much attention to this, as 'Broonie,' he explained, *'fancied himself as a bit of a hard man.'*

Colin wasn't certain that he liked all the details provided about Carrie. She had a bit of a history going out with boys at the school. Okay, so this was good as it probably gave Colin more chance with her but the implication that she was a bit loose didn't impress him. What impressed him even less was the news that she had 'a bit of a carry on' with Billy earlier in the year.

Didn't really make sense. Of all of the people in 5L, Billy was probably the one person that Colin couldn't imagine getting on well with. Billy was a loudmouth and someone who used his notorious reputation in exactly the opposite way from Martin. Whereas with Martin it seemed that other people were important and always included in his jokes and stories, Billy was conceited and selfish. Everything he did seemed to centre around him and the fact that he was, as he would always remind everybody at every opportunity, 'Top Boy.' What could she have seen in him?

Colin checked to see if Carrie was following on. He couldn't help it. Needed to know. They turned onto a narrow street leading down to the University playing fields. He turned around to see if she was following the group. If he kept it nonchalant she need never know he was looking for her. She turned on to the street and their eyes met. Carrie smiled. Colin pivoted forwards. *'Oh no, what am I doin'? Keep eye contact. Smile back. Jesus, she must think I'm a right gimp.'*

He went to turn around again but was gripped by anxiety.

'Was it even me she was smiling at? People do just smile though. If ah turn around now ah'll freak her out. Oh no but she'll think ah'm ignoring her. What's happenin' here?'

Martin was saying something to him but he couldn't really make it out. He had to work out what was going on and what he was supposed to do about it. An hour ago, Carrie Brown had just been a good-looking girl that had landed in the same registration class as him. Now, he couldn't think straight because she was walking along a road behind him. She was beautiful. Looking into her eyes when she was quizzing him had been exciting and terrifying all at the same time. The idea that she may be interested in him caused him to gasp.

'Oh come on here, she's just a girl, I hardly know her.'

He wanted to turn round again but physically couldn't do it. Another smile would make his day. His week. His year. Anything other than a smile though. A quizzical frown *'Why d'ya keep lookin'? Ya want a picture? It'll last longer!'* That would be hell. The risk was too great. The main thing was, she was following. Keep it nonchalant. *'You'll get your chance!'*

As much as some of the information about Carrie disappointed Colin, he was certain that a connection was made that morning. He wasn't sure how to go about it but he just had to get talking with her. Once talking he could better gauge her interest. Could be tricky though. Signs were confusing when there was so much at stake. If the signs were good, though, he would have to get together with her.

Where to take her though? What to do? He knew none of it and she, apparently, all. It wouldn't do to be bumbling around not knowing how to act and where to go. He had to make a good impression. Women like a man who's assertive. He was sure he'd seen that in one of his mum's magazines while he was flipping through the underwear adverts. Underwear adverts were in the past for Colin now though. He was going to be quite the charming and sophisticated gentleman. Passionate lover!

He had to learn fast. Know what women want. Know how to please them. Know how to treat Carrie right. It seemed to him that a good way to achieve this would be to use the help of Martin again. Martin not only seemed keen to help with this but Colin considered that he would be much better at it and more experienced than himself.

20

Yet another day in 5L, Colin stood at the edge of a Madras playing field football pitch. *To hell with running the line.* Waiting for a pass that just wasn't going to happen, *be damned.*

Around five weeks into their time in 5L few of the class had succeeded in gaining work placements, around half of them had enrolled in Elmwood College's school leaver course and most of the boys had been given ample opportunity to improve their football skills, football games being a very regular occurrence in their timetables, albeit that they were actually being played when their actual timetables were telling them they should be elsewhere.

During these frequent games of football played during Colin's time in 5L, he just knew that not enough balls were passed to him. Okay, so he wasn't among the best players in the class but it was a bit much that he was more or less left out of these games by the total lack of passes in his direction. It was definitely happening though. The only time he had the ball, he'd had to win it himself. Sure, he lacked skill but he was strong and quite fast and made, he thought, some useful passes. Yet passes never seemed to be made back to him.

He was standing on the side of the makeshift pitch, wondering whether there was any point in his being there. Martin had just dribbled from a ball passed out to him by the goalkeeper into trouble inside the centre of the pitch. It was like he knew what Colin was thinking. He turned and deliberately pushed the ball into an area in front of where Colin was standing and issued the order, 'Right then, take it for a run, Col'!'

As well as the general lack of passing in his direction, there also seemed to be a lack of attention paid to him by opposing players. This in itself was a little insulting but at least it gave him a chance to do something with the ball. As the ball trundled in front of Colin, a few of the other side had begun to amble over towards him without any great urgency. Colin looked up and could see that the side of the pitch that he was on had nobody really challenging between him and the goal. *'Fuck it!'* he thought, *'Ah'm scorin'.'*

He approached the ball and touched it in front of him as he began to accelerate towards the goalposts. The plan was simple. Use his pace to take the ball through the space, as close to goal as he could get without being challenged and then just fucking wallop the thing toward one of the sides of the goal. Opposing team members began to jog towards the area that Colin was headed for but clearly no great effort made. The exception to this, as usual, was Goof; who, spotting the threat of having Colin speeding towards goal, exerted his customary conviction to the cause and general enthusiasm for the game, to start to make his way over to stop him.

Colin was around 20 yards from goal, still encountering no resistance, confident of at least making the shot, even deciding which side to put it. Goof appeared, halfway between him and the goal. He emerged from behind the less concerned defenders, sprinting for all he was worth, looking completely intent on tackling the incoming striker. He arrived directly in between Colin and the goal and stopped. Colin knew that the original plan was now defunct but made up his mind that he would make up the ground between himself and Goof, push the ball inside him and from around that ten-yard range, take his shot. It could be done. After all, Goof was the only barrier to this plan and well, yes he was good, but this time he was beaten.

He looked directly at Goof, trying to gauge his intentions. It occurred to him that possibly it should be Goof trying to make eye contact to determine what way he would go but Goof stared steadily at the ball. Maybe he should use some sort of distracting movement to fool Goof as to what he was about to do. Goof began to make his own distracting movements. Skipping a little as if performing some kind of dance, he pushed his legs out first left and then right, his body almost completely still, all the while his eyes tracking the ball, without distraction.

Colin reached around two yards from Goof and then moved his left foot inside the ball to push it wide of Goof. The last defender. Goof's legs had been moving the whole time, short sharp jumps and sprints on the spot. Colin made his move to push the ball wide. Goof dropped his stance slightly and begun to move forward, his eyes still fixed on the movement of the ball. He placed his foot on top of the moving ball and gently pulled it out from Colin's intended route of travel. Goof had placed half of his body directly into the path of the sprinting 13-stone frame of Colin. He then spun around completely, the momentum of Colin instead of clattering in to him, as seemed would happen, only made a slight impact on the turning Goof, if anything, assisting the spin.

Once around, Goof again placed his foot on the ball, this time to stop it and bring it under his control. Colin's momentum carried him on five or six more paces almost falling as he turned around to see Goof, as calm as you like, beginning his run towards the other goal. Not so much a tackle, as a complete robbery of the ball. Colin felt like a child who had just had his lollipop stolen, totally without hope to stop the crime. Colin steadied himself. Goof was now around ten yards away running in the opposite direction.

In contrast to Colin's run, Goof seemed to be taking things much more slowly, deliberately, weighing his options as he moved up field. Colin looked up the pitch. That the lack of bodies on that side which had led to him believing in his opportunity, now represented a clear cut chance for Goof. He was going to run the whole length of the pitch and score one of his trademark controlled, well placed goals.

Colin needed to save some face now. Had to do something! Goof wasn't exactly motoring up the wing. He began sprinting in the attempt to catch up. The easy thing would be to get behind him and take a swipe but immediately Colin decided that this would be bad form. He decided to cut inside him to make the tackle from the side.

The best part of the pitch had been run but eventually he drew level just inside him as he made his way in from the right hand side. By this time bearing down on the goalkeeper who had probably accepted the inevitable, that Goof was about to score.

Colin thought about the previous tackle by Goof and kept his eyes directly on the ball as he stuck out his right leg. His intention, simply to check the run, anything after that would be a bonus. Colin lunged with his right foot. Goof, just in time, brought his left foot inside and just under the ball and lifted it slightly upwards and to the left. The ball just made it over Colin's leg as his body slumped to the ground underneath it.

Goof hurdled over the falling defender, waited for the ball to bounce and just as it began to make its way down for a second bounce, whacked it with his left foot. He'd caught it just right of centre, slicing the ball enough to produce a curve which brought it just inside the goalkeepers left hand post. The goalkeeper only made a token gesture to move to that side to save it.

'Fuckin' goal mate.'

'Ya beauty.'

A chorus of approval rung out from both sides of players. Goof just turned around, smiled, made an appreciative gesture for the plaudits and walked back up the pitch. It didn't occur to him, even to acknowledge Colin, lying just behind where he had taken his shot.

Colin lay on the ground and assessed his general appearance. The right leg of his grey trousers had risen up to just above his knee and as he rolled it back down he revealed a large green stripe of grass stains.

'Oh for fuck's sake!'

He struggled back on to his feet, realising that he would have to walk around with dirty trousers all afternoon. The rest of the players were making their way from the field. With Goof's solo wonder goal and Colin's humiliation, the game had clearly drawn to a close.

At the side of the pitch Carrie and some of the other 5L girls, who had been sitting paying scant attention to the game were talking to the boys trooping off. Colin would have to go that way. There was consolation that they probably wouldn't have been watching what happened. They'd notice his trousers though. Excellent! Another opportunity to look like a gimp in front of Carrie Brown. Colin stood up, looked around just to check that nobody was watching his actions with too much attention, shook his head, shrugged and followed his classmates.

21

The whole school had been enjoying their lunch break in the early September sunshine. Most were now thinking of returning. Some of them diligent, others could not be bothered but it was school. It was important. It's what they did!

Unless you were in 5L. The weather was unusually bright and warm and, for the class of 5L, heading back to Madras from the school playing fields, the thought of attending the afternoon session seemed pointless. Lessons for them never really amounted to much and most of the time involved whatever spare teacher there was, imparting pointless information which was generally of no use to the pupils. The general consensus of opinion amongst them was that the only reason that they couldn't just bunk off en masse, was that this might be noticed by the teachers. That is to say, that if the class was completely missing, the teachers might get a bit annoyed and it might cause a bit of trouble.

Billy, Martin and Goof and a few of the other boys had, however, decided to carry on their afternoon football session whatever the rest of the class were doing. The only reason that they were leaving the playing fields was the idea that it was a bit cheeky playing truant on school property. So they headed to the university pitches.

Colin didn't particularly want to go back to school that afternoon but in all honesty had no desire to carry on playing football. As he reached the edge of the pitch, Carrie, who had just finished picking up her things from where she had been lying sunbathing, was standing shaking her head.

'What the fuck happened to you?'

She was pointing at Colin's trouser leg but remarking on his appearance in general.

'Aw well, just, football, fell over, y'know.'

Normally he would have leapt at the chance to talk to Carrie. Had the circumstances not quite been as they were.

'Christ, what a mess you're in.'

Carrie began to giggle and Colin just wished he was somewhere else. Humiliation was beginning to overwhelm him. Carrie grabbed his arm and linked it with her own. And then, just at that moment, things didn't seem so bad.

'Honestly, ah think you boys just need a bit o' lookin' after sometimes.'

She was now looking towards the ground, still shaking her head with a broad smile on her face. The group heading for the game of football at the public playing field had now started to break away from the main group. Martin turned round to face the group, mainly of girls walking towards the school building and noticed Colin and Carrie linked like an old married couple.

'Oh aye.'

A wry smile stretched over his face.

'What'r' you daein Col', comin' for a game o' fitba or what?'

Colin, numbed by the feeling of complete elation to be walking along linking arms with Carrie was suddenly struck by embarrassment. He shouldn't really be doing this. Carrie was still looking towards the ground, seemingly not paying attention to much but Colin was sure he could feel her grip tighten on his arm. He looked at Martin, skewed his mouth and held out his free hand in an indication that he didn't know what was going on.

'Nah Martin, ah think that some o' us should go in this afternoon eh.'

Billy turned around to notice Colin's position within the group heading back towards the school. Clearly disgusted that Colin would, as it seemed, prefer to go back to school with Carrie than play football in the sun.

'C'mon tae fuck Bridie eh.'

Billy grabbed the ball from Martin as he addressed him, still using the nickname that he must have been aware that only he used.

'If that pap would rather go back there wi' a bunch o' birds than come wi' us then that's his fuckin' problem. He's fuckin' shite at fitba anyway.'

Billy turned round and continued to walk away. It was clear that as far as he was concerned that matter was closed.

'Right well, aye, fair enough then, see ya later.'

Martin gestured a kind of dismissive wave with his hand, then turned and followed the footballers. Colin gestured back, too late to be noticed by any of the defecting group. He felt like he may have let Martin down. They were starting to get on well and Colin was aware of Martin's attempts to teach him to be a bit less of a geek. Giving up an afternoon in the sun playing football to go back to school, just because a pretty girl had grabbed his arm, was a bit of a dodgy thing to be doing.

Carrie turned to Colin as they walked. She looked concerned.

'Ah wouldnae let Billy bother you.'

'What d'ya mean?'

'Well, him havin' a go at you like that.'

Carrie was looking over at Billy, clearly unimpressed.

'He's just being a prick.'

Colin hadn't really realised that Billy was having a go at him but he realised then that Carrie was right and that Billy was, as usual, out of order. Before then, he had actually felt quite pleased that Billy had all but validated his reason for not playing football.

'Aw no, ah dinnae worry about him.'

Credibility needed now after not even realising he had been so badly insulted.

'Well neither ya should. He's no' as big a man as he thinks he is, you know what I mean?'

Colin immediately picked up on the innuendo of the statement.

'Aye! Is that right?'

He was satisfied to learn this.

22

'Some day th'day though eh?'

Carrie looked skywards as she walked back towards school.

Colin followed her eyes to the sky, thankful of the direction after a few minutes of not knowing where he should be looking.

'Aye it's nice likes.'

She looked down again and sighed.

'Pity to waste it at school likes, eh?'

Colin could feel hairs prickle on the nape of his neck. He knew what this was. He'd fantasised about it for weeks. Carrie and him, together, away from school. His chance to take control. He could just grab her and tell her how it was going to be. *You and me babe – how about it?*

Now, though, she needed to be asked. No way did she want to be going back to school. She'd just said as much, hadn't she? So this is it. Turn towards her and ask her. *You're right Carrie. School's shite. You come wi' me. Ah'll show ya a good time.*

He turned to face her and she tilted her head to meet his eyes. He opened his mouth and went to speak but stopped. Momentary doubt. *Can I do this? I've got to do this.*

They kept walking. Kept looking into one another's eyes. It should have been an uncomfortable silence but it wasn't. Colin closed his mouth after a deep exhale. He couldn't ask her. He just kept staring, transfixed. She stopped suddenly and let go of his arm.

'Oh no! What've ah done? I've freaked her out.'

Colin took a slight step backwards, convinced she was about to tell him to get a grip.

She smiled. The sexiest most roguish smile he'd ever seen from any woman.

'Jesus Colin, they breeks are in some fuckin' state.'

She was looking down at Colin's legs, exaggerating as she shook her head. Colin looked down at himself to check the extent of the mess of his trousers, muttering only, 'eh?'.

He looked back up to see Carrie looking back at him with a broad contented smile.

'Ya cannae go tae school lookin' like that.'

Colin looked around himself and then back at his legs, raising both eyebrows and nodding in agreement.

'Aye fair enough but it's no' like ah can just go home and get changed.'

He looked back at Carrie who was still smiling but this time rolling her eyes a little. Actually trying to look mischievous. She carried this look off rather well.

'Well, why don't we just lie low for the afternoon?'

As she spoke Colin's nerves began to get the better of him. He stood there convinced that he was giving off the impression that he was petrified, desperate to look like he was used to this sort of thing.

'We could just go for a wander or something, down the beach or...'

Colin didn't allow her to finish her sentence, blurting out, 'aye, OK, sounds good,' as he moved uncomfortably on the spot, fidgeting with his bag.

Carrie grabbed his arm, linking in again as they began to break off from the group heading back to school.

'Aye it does eh?'

She smiled and looked towards the ground again as they walked.

***

The pair walked through St Andrews in the direction of the beach, their ties taken off in a completely failed attempt not to look like school pupils. They reached the sand and Carrie remarked at the lack of people on the beach.

'Where the hell is everybody?'

It was a Monday afternoon in September and, as such, it wasn't that unusual that the beach would not be busy, but as a resident of St Andrews, she couldn't remember seeing the beach so empty on a sunny day. There were a couple of people walking their dogs and further up, one man being pulled around on a beach buggy with a parachute, kite-type contraption.

'Look at the state o' that guy!'

Carrie was in no mood to let the matter lie.

'Aye, bit dodgy eh?'

Colin was in no other mood than to agree.

Halfway up the beach, just opposite The Old Course, the couple settled down in one of the grassy dunes.

'Some day though eh? For September like.'

Colin was looking up at the blue sky as he spoke.

'Oh aye... crackin'.'

Carrie seemed a little less interested in the weather as she started to rummage through her bag. After a small search, She pulled out a worn-looking 20 pack of cigarettes. She flicked open the lid, pulled out one of the cigarettes, an even more worn packet of rolling papers and then turned the pack upside down, shaking it until a small white wrapped bundle fell out into the sandy grass.

'Shite!'

Carrie looked annoyed with herself as she searched for the wrap on the ground.

She muttered a little, spread out some grass blades and Colin moved over to assist the search. Not really sure of what he was looking for.

She found the white bundle and unwrapped it to reveal a small dark brown chunk.

'What is that, hash?'

'Aye,' Carrie answered as she thrust her hand back into her bag eventually producing a plastic lighter.

'D'ya smoke the dope like?'

Carrie looked up to see Colin's slightly shocked expression. He didn't want to appear like a total square but at the same time thought that lying wouldn't be too clever. He thought that if he just said 'Aye, all the time,' that he'd look really stupid coughing and spluttering when he tried some.

'Nah, no' really.'

He looked at her, his expression that of exaggerated worry.

'Oh, right, sorry man.'

Carrie began to rewrap the chunk preparing to put it away again.

'No, no, it's alright, ah'm no' bothered.'

Colin didn't want to spoil her afternoon by stopping her from getting a bit stoned.

'You sure?'

'Of course, aye, no problem.'

Colin paused and thought for a bit.

'In fact, if it's alright, ah wouldnae mind trying it, eh.'

Carrie's face reassumed the mischievous contented look.

'Aye?'

She began to giggle to herself as she started to build her joint.

'That's no problem man, no problem at all.'

She began to build a joint with Colin the keen spectator.

He didn't know what his favourite Carrie expression was but the one of concentration she was wearing now had to be among her best. The sun shone through her hair casting shadows over the parts of her face that it covered. Where the light hit her skin, the shine intensified as it bounced from its perfect texture.

It took her a couple of minutes to finish all the different little processes with Colin looking on quite oblivious to what she was doing. Simply watching her. A chilling thrill ran all the way through his body every time she raised papers to her mouth to lick them.

Carrie raised the rolled joint to her mouth, lit it and took a couple of shallow draws. She looked over at Colin who was looking a little bit coy but still managing a smile. Then she handed it to him. As she stretched out her hand towards him, she faced up towards the clear sky and exhaled.

Colin was glad that she wasn't looking at him as he took the joint from her. Conscious that he must look like a complete amateur sitting there with a joint in his hand for the first time. He positioned it in his hand in the way he perceived to be correct, placed it to his mouth, closed his lips and drew through the joint. A long deep breath. As he inhaled he could taste the smoky sweet flavour of the drug. The rear of his mouth and throat began to tickle towards the end of the breath. He took the joint away from his mouth as the tickling sensation intensified, holding his breath for a short time before he began to exhale.

As he breathed out, the feeling in the back of his throat became such that he gave an involuntary cough. With this, it seemed that his lungs and throat, all at once, rejected the smoke within it. He began to cough violently his throat in particular felt as though it had caught fire. After a few seconds the coughing developed into a choking, gargling heave from within his lungs. Drool that seemed to come from deep within his chest started to build up in the front of his mouth and he spat it out as he looked up towards Carrie. He knew she would be laughing at him. Knew she'd want to take the piss out of this. But she wasn't. She didn't! Instead she looked concerned.

'Jesus Christ Colin, you dinnae have to Hoover the thing.'

She moved over and struck his back with her open hand.

'You alright?'

She looked into his eyes as he looked up finally regaining some semblance of composure. He swallowed, which seemed to help slightly. At least he was able to speak.

'Oh aye.'

He swallowed again.

'Never better.'

He started to laugh for a second and then continued coughing, slightly less violently than before.

Carrie removed the joint from his hand, placed it on the ground then delved back into her bag, producing this time a carton of Ribena.

'Here, this'll help.'

She offered the carton to Colin who duly accepted the gift, ceasing coughing momentarily to thank her.

He drew hard through the straw and the smooth liquid began to cool the walls of his burning windpipe. He drew a clenched fist over his closed lips, removing as he did so the remnant of drool and bile.

Carrie smiled and shook her head. She wasn't being mean though. She probably knew all about first-timers. Probably used to it. She was so cool. She lifted the joint out of the sand and began to teach how to smoke dope properly.

'Look man, just short tokes, nae need to burn you lungs out.' And she began to teach Colin how to smoke dope.

By the time Colin felt halfway fit again, he had finished half of the Ribena and Carrie had smoked more than half of the joint.

'You ready to try again?'

Carrie half stretched her hand out towards Colin, not certain that he would accept. Colin paused for a moment before accepting it again.

'So just short draws like?'

He looked at her smiling face as he accepted it.

'Aye mister, short draws win the day.'

He took her advice and began to take smaller controlled draws of the joint. Once or twice he felt his throat going again but he remembered how the Ribena helped and took small gulps that seemed to quell the feeling.

'Aye, that's better eh?'

Carrie lowered her head to get a good look at Colin's reaction. He looked back directly into her eyes and thinking that talking may affect his throat, nodded in agreement. As Colin finished what was left of the first joint, Carrie began to skin up again.

Colin began to think about how he was feeling, or indeed how the drugs were making him feel. He looked out across the North Sea, watching the waves as they trundled up the water line on the beach. He noticed parachute buggy man and thought about how right Carrie and he were, that this guy must be a complete twat to spend Monday afternoons whizzing around a beach on a silly little cart, going just as fast as the wind would allow. He could feel the same warmth from the sun that he had earlier but somehow, now, it was more comfortable. Then he looked back at Carrie, busily burning and sprinkling the hash into the papers and he thought at that moment.

'This is exactly where I should be. No place else in the world would be preferable to this, at this moment in time.'

Carrie finished rolling the second joint but this time, rather than lighting it herself, she offered both it and the lighter to Colin.

'Remember, just the short tokes today mister.'

The expression that Carrie seemed to be wearing a lot today had, Colin considered, changed from being an attractive, mischievous look, to become just the perfect picture of beauty.

Colin duly accepted the gift, lit the end and continued with the controlled, short draw smoking of the joint, conscious of the lack of Ribena, should anything go wrong. He smoked around a third of the way down the joint and encountered no real problem. Colin handed the joint back to Carrie. She looked eager to receive.

'So how ya feelin' mate? Wee bit stoned?'

Carrie was looking into Colin's eyes, trying to gauge his state as she raised the joint to her mouth. Colin considered again how he was feeling.

'Aye, a wee bit.'

He looked out again at the North Sea, checked on the progress of buggy boy, who seemed to be zipping away quite nicely, then all at once thought, *'how the fuck can they call this a soft drug?'*.

Everything looked the same but felt different. It occurred to him how comfortable it was just sitting there on that beach. Not weird at all, slightly strange but very comfortable. He thought that if somebody came now and told him he'd have to move he'd probably just tell them to bolt. Whereas before he'd likely be up and away as soon as asked, right now he wouldn't bother and this was the point. He just did not bother, about anything. Anything other than, of course, the fact that he was sitting on a beach with a girl that he just wanted to grab and ravish.

The thought crossed his mind as he watched her finish the rest of the joint. An idea grew in his head that something might happen. Colin leaned back until he was prone, looking upwards at the blue sky. For the next few minutes nothing happened. He lay there looking up into the sky, analysing how he felt, getting lost in his thoughts and drifting away into his own world. Suddenly the sky seemed to darken as a black silhouetted mass moved in front of his face. He moved his head directly underneath the object to completely block out the sun. As his eyes moved into the shade and he managed to focus, he could see that it was Carrie's face in front of his.

'You alright mate, still with us?'

She had moved over to be directly beside him and was looking into his eyes. She was still wearing the same naughty look, which Colin now thought to be even more attractive. Without any thought or fear that what he was doing might not be right he lifted his head so that his lips met hers. Carrie moved her head back only slightly, not allowing Colin to kiss her but only allowing a few centimetres between their lips. She smiled and Colin could feel her warm breath on his lips as she spoke.

'Ooh, good god.'

She had adopted a parodying comical accent.

'So, Colin's getting a bit frisky, is that it?'

Colin again moved closer and yet again she drew her head back, maintaining the same distance. Again she smiled, looked as if she was thinking about something else to say, before deciding not to bother and finally pressing her lips to Colin's.

From this point, she took over. She knew that Colin had never done this before and she thrust him backwards and began to teach Colin what to do and where to touch. After a while of moving his lips to where she wanted them, cajoling him into position and manoeuvring his hands, one of which was now on her back, the other wedged into the top of one of her stockings. She raised her head, bit her bottom lip lightly and looked down at Colin. He looked completely overcome. Breathing heavily, looking directly into her eyes, an expression of complete intensity.

'Ah think maybe we should go somewhere a bit more private, eh?'

She looked around and although only buggy boy and one dog walker were visible, she considered them to be unwanted possible spectators.

'C'mon, ah know where we can go.'

She grabbed Colin's hand who, seemingly reluctantly, gave up his lying position and struggled to his feet. The couple started to walk back across the beach in the direction they had come from, Carrie leading Colin by the hand, heading somewhere private to complete the seduction of her target.

23

For Martin, Billy, Goof and the majority of the rest of the boys from 5L, the afternoon was spent playing football in the sunshine, skinning up and generally having a good laugh. It was now a quarter past four and Martin set off with Billy from the university playing fields. They headed in the general direction of the bus station. The after-school bus to Leuchars left at half past four. Billy didn't need a bus to get home. It wasn't even his way. But Billy was a strange one and it didn't really do to ask him what he was up to. So they walked to the station together.

The road branching left towards the station had been closed for road works but at that time that afternoon it seemed that work had finished for the day. Billy decided as Billy always did that they would cut through the roadworks site. This would save them from going a long way round. Billy spotted someone else on one of the side streets. Also making his way towards the road under repair. He was obviously planning to cut through the road works as well but, more importantly, not from the direction of Madras school.

'Here Bridie, there's that daft fuckin' mate o' yours.'

Colin looked lost, as he squeezed into the works site from another side street.

'Ah'll tell ya, there's nae fuckin' danger he's been tae school this afternoon!'

Billy started off towards the side street clambering over a pile of loose mortar sand.

'Oi! Baw-heid, where the fuck have you been?'

Colin looked up to where Billy was standing. He spotted Martin standing behind him then gestured an acknowledgement to the two boys but didn't answer Billy's question. He started to walk towards them. Billy glanced down at Martin, clearly annoyed at the lack of attention paid to the question. He looked back at Colin jutted his head forward and made clear his insistence on an answer.

'Here! Ah asked you a fuckin' question.'

Colin stopped and looked up at Billy standing on his little hill of sand.

'What?' he said, like he actually cared.

Again Billy checked back with Martin.

Martin wasn't liking it. He could see things kicking off. He shrugged as if to suggest that there wasn't a problem.

Billy was visibly not impressed. He scowled and nodded his head. Like he'd just made an important decision.

Martin knew what he'd decided on. He'd seen that look before.

Billy started to move down from his elevated position towards Colin, his arms slightly pushed out from his side, trying to look threatening as he spoke in sharp choppy sentences.

'What – the fuck – is the matter – wi you?– ya cunt – ah asked ya where the fuck ya've been.'

Colin didn't answer, raising his hand to his forehead and shaking his head.

Martin shook his head as well. He wanted to signal to Colin. Tell him this was a bad situation. Buck up his ideas. People didn't just talk to Billy that way. He just wasn't used to it. Didn't Colin know that? Didn't he know that this would antagonise Him? What was the mater with him? He started to move over to the sand pile. He willed Colin to answer the question and sort out his attitude.

'Aye Col, where've ya been mate?'

He started to climb over the rubble. Get closer over to make it more like they were all just having a chat. Billy was squaring up to Colin and he didn't even know it.

Colin turned in to look at him. This was the worst thing he could do. He was basically allowing him a clean shot. Get some distance. Bring him back on side. Just answer the question, for fuck's sake. Colin did none of these. He just stood looking at him. He looked annoyed but not particularly aggravated.

Billy was going to hit him. Martin could see it happening. Billy didn't hit him though. Was he intimidated by the fact that Colin wasn't backing down? Nah, not Billy. Martin had never seen him back off before. He didn't get intimidated. He basically hadn't the sense. Billy began to snigger. A nasal wheeze and a snort from deep in his throat.

'Hold up, ah know what the fuckin' score is here, Bridie.'

Billy turned back towards Martin, a broad smile on his face his hand pointing at Colin.

'Your daft mate's been wi' Carrie. Ah fuckin' seen them slopin' off th'gether at dinnertime, eh.'

Martin looked towards Colin. Looking for a sign that Billy was right. Colin stayed staring at Billy. He wasn't giving anything away but Martin just knew that Billy was right. He couldn't stop a smile forming.

Billy faced Colin again.

'See that fuckin' lassie, fuckin' dirty cow, ch. Hope you got a good blow job off 'er.'

Colin's hands dropped by his side and his head shot up to look straight at Billy.

Colin took abuse most of the time. Martin knew that. He didn't know why but most of the time he just took it. He'd been trying to tell him not to but that was just Colin. But there were times when you didn't take crap and well, there were times when you did. If Martin was making the decisions now, this would be a time to take it. Just ride it out. You didn't have to like it. Just get it out the way. But Martin wasn't making the decisions now. Colin was. And it looked like he'd picked a hell of a time to stop taking it.

'What?'

This time Colin's 'what?' wasn't a calm dismissal of what he perceived to be a crap question. It was a challenge to Billy's statement and Billy recognised this.

'Ah'll fuckin' what ya'.'

Billy moved slightly towards Colin, again assuming his threatening posture and tone.

'Dinnae get aw fuckin' high and mighty 'cos ya just got yer hole aff the school bike, alright?'

Colin's face seemed to tighten. Martin hadn't seen him like this before but he knew the look. Anger was building. He said nothing, just standing allowing his rage to grow. Martin watched on. *'Keep the head mate. Dinnae fuckin' lose it now.'*

'Let me tell you somethin'.'

Billy carried on. His tone every bit as threatening.

'You're no' alone. Most of us have already been there. She's nothin' fuckin' special but she does give a no' bad blow job, so, get yourself one o' them, then get fuckin' rid o' her and then stop bein' such a prick!'

Billy turned around and started to walk towards Martin, mumbling quietly, 'ya fuckin', mong.'

This was good. Billy was turning away. All Colin had to do now was accept the slagging and it would all be over. But Martin didn't like the way he was looking. Colin's face now started to contort as he moved a couple of steps towards Billy and stopped.

'Can I tell you somethin'?'

His voice had changed to nothing, certainly that Martin had heard from him before. His eyes had narrowed and his mouth now seemed to be pressed as tightly shut as possible. Billy turned round to face him and was obviously disconcerted by Colin's appearance. He got over it quickly though. He stretched out his hands and began to bounce slightly on the spot, as if to ready himself for some action.

'What is it? What have ya' got tae say like?'

Martin clambered over the sand and made his way over to them.

'C'mon tae fuck boys eh, there's nae need for any…'

Martin's involvement was cut short by a quick look and shake of the head by Colin. The look suggested both that he knew what he was doing and at that point he did not appreciate Martin's intervention. Martin stopped dead halfway down the pile of rubble in the road. He had never seen Colin act like this before. Confident and composed but clearly very angry, he seemed to have no fear of either Billy or the situation. But this was wrong. Martin knew that. This couldn't go well for Colin.

Colin looked back towards Billy. He didn't protect himself. Didn't adopt a defensive stance. He was smiling and shaking his head. There was something though and Martin could see it. Something in the eyes. A coldness. Something that told Martin that Billy might just have a problem here. The smile turned into a revolted sneer.

'You must be about the most pathetic excuse for a fuckin' tosser that there is.'

Martin's eyes half closed and his mouth winced as Billy moved towards Colin.

'Fuckin' tosser aye? Fuckin' tosser is it?'

Billy reached about a metre away from Colin and jumped slightly upwards but more forward in Colin's direction. At the same time, his right arm drew back very slightly and he swung a punch downwards at Colin's face. The speed of the punch took Colin by surprise but he managed to react just in time, his head moving backwards and the rest of his body turning away from the impact. There wasn't enough time to move completely out of the way and Billy's fist scraped the bottom of Colin's chin, eventually landing more firmly on his shoulder.

Colin spun and his left arm came up and instinctively hit Billy on the back as he followed through. Not a particularly damaging blow but the impact of this hit, given Colin's size and strength, knocked Billy off balance giving Colin time to steady himself before Billy managed to regain his fighting posture. Billy turned back towards him

'Ya dirty fucker.'

He again launched into a speedy aerial attack but this time Colin could read what was happening. He quickly darted his own right hand in the direction of Billy's face, with all of the weight of his body following. Billy had no time to react to this and Colin's hit impacted, not on Billy's face but between his throat and chin. Billy's feet had no contact with the ground. His whole body began to turn in the air and he fell to the ground, his shoulders hitting first and his legs following above. Colin had thrown everything into the punch and no longer had the balance to stay on his feet.

He landed on top of the legs of the grounded Billy.

Martin considered whether he should do anything but after these first two attacks and the outcome, he began to think better of it. Both bodies landed around half a metre away from the ditch that had been cut into the road. Colin raised slightly on to his hands and knees. Billy seemed to be in some distress. He was making gurgling noises but not much else. Colin drew level face to face with Billy who had now lost all of his previous cock-suredness. He looked towards a small pile of loose cobbles and then looked back towards Billy.

Colin reached for one of the cobbles, picked it up with his right hand. He moved Billy on to his back with his left hand and straddled to sit on his chest, pinning Billy's arms in with his knees.

'No' sae fuckin' smart now though, are ye'?'

He brought the boulder across his left shoulder and held it there for a couple of seconds. He was breathing heavily. A single sliver of drool slid out of his mouth and dropped onto Billy's chin. Billy coughed once more. He was looking deep into Colin's eyes now. What could he see in there? Whatever it was he looked freaked. Not scared, but he knew he was in trouble. He wasn't saying anything but his expression screamed, *'Go on then. Ah fuckin' dare ya!'*

It was as though years of taking crap from just about everybody was eradicated in one sweep of Colin's arm. Like some sort of sexual ecstasy, a grunt through bared gritted teeth. He lifted the rock as far as he could and then swung it down across Billy's face. It was like watching in slow motion. Martin couldn't quite believe what he was seeing.

The force of this blow spun Billy's head around 90 or so degrees, spraying blood and gunk from his nose and mouth over his left shoulder and on to the road. As the cobble made contact, there was a cracking noise which made Martin feel almost sick. He took a couple of steps back and brought his hand up to his face.

'Oh for fuck's sake!'

He looked round to see if anybody was looking but the street was deserted. He looked back to see Colin, now standing, pushing Billy with his feet into the ditch. Billy was motionless, apart from the movement caused by Colin's feet.

'What the fuck've you done?'

Martin now started to walk towards Colin. Colin didn't answer. He finished pushing Billy into the ditch and then just stood there for a few moments, only saying one word before setting off in the direction of the bus station.

'Prick!'

Martin ran towards the ditch and looked down at Billy. He wasn't moving.

'Billy, Billy, you alright Billy?'

Colin stopped momentarily to check what Martin was doing. Martin checked up to see him standing there, the same look on his face as before the fight.

'Fuckin' leave him!'

Martin was struck by an almost unreal sense of fear. He'd never seen anything like this, especially not from Colin. For all he knew Billy was now lying dead in the ditch but he didn't know what he could possibly do about it. In any case, Colin was now *ordering* him away. He stood and wondered for about 30 seconds. Colin had now clearly washed his hands of the incident and was squeezing himself between two bollards to get out of the work site. Martin again looked down at the motionless Billy. He looked around to see if anybody was looking and then, realising that nobody had seen the fight, was hit by the recognition that he had to get away from there.

24

The bus ride home that afternoon was tense. Both boys sat quietly together, not uttering a word to one another for the whole journey. Martin's mind was racing. First he thought that probably Billy would be alright. This began to seem unlikely though. He replayed the fight in his head. Watched the stone spin Billy's head again. Remembered the sound. That had to be a skull cracking. Could that be enough to? He didn't want to think about it. Couldn't really avoid it though, because if he wasn't already dead, he was definitely out the game and it would be very unlikely that anybody would find him until morning. By then anything could have happened.

Should he call an ambulance once he got back to Leuchars? Then he would have to tell the police what happened. It even occurred to him to lie to the police about them being attacked together and him escaping but then how would he know that Billy had been hurt and where he was and why would he wait to get home before alerting anyone? Was it a big mistake to have left the scene? He just could not get to an acceptable train of thought as to how he was now to act.

Colin was much calmer. He was also quiet but did not fidget or look at all nervous. Just taking in the scenery of the bus ride home. Scenery he had seen thousands of times before. They bus reached Leuchars and they started to walk the path to the base married quarters.

It was still too warm. But Martin knew that it wasn't the sweat caused by the football that he needed to wash off in a shower. He was still engaged in an all-embracing wrestle with his conscience when Colin began to talk in a manner, so ordinary, that following the events of the last hour, seemed completely callous.

'Been some day today though!'

He looked at Martin, registered the look of disbelief on his face but did not react.

'Ah was on the beach wi' Carrie after we left you and we had a couple of joints. That's the first drugs ah've ever had like.'

Martin said nothing as he continued to listen in disbelief. He noticed blood on the sleeve of Colin's shirt and this chilled him even more.

'Then later on, well, me and her, we… em…'

Colin looked at Martin and made suggestive motions with his eyes and eyebrows as he continued.

'You know what ah mean, eh. Ah've never done that before today either. Then, obviously you seen that wi' Billy, eh.'

Again Colin made no great outwardly emotional display as he talked. Martin stopped dead as Colin turned to talk, looking directly at him.

'Ah've never done that before either.'

Martin could now no longer hold his silence.

'Never done that before?'

He blew out hard and shook his head.

'Never done it before, eh?'

He looked around to make sure nobody was listening to him.

'Never done what before Colin? What is it you think you've just done there?'

'Well, got in a fight.'

'Got in a fight, got – in – a – fight. Well, now ah'm kinda hopin' that you smoked a pound o' hash and shot a fuckin' porno movie, 'cos ya certainly didnae dae the got-in-a-fight bit by halves, did ya? You've fucked Billy right over. Jesus Christ mate, you've just bloody whacked his skull wi' a brick. For all we know he could be fuckin'…'

Martin didn't continue what he was going to say. At this point he just didn't want to consider it.

'Fuckin' what?'

Colin now looked as he did just before the fight.

'What's your problem anyway, eh? What is Billy yer fuckin' pal like? Eh? Fuckin' Bridie.'

To Martin's knowledge, Colin had never used that nickname before and was aware that he didn't like it. Billy in fact, was the only person to use this name and it was obvious the point that Colin was making.

'Ah didnae fuckin' kill him, alright?'

Colin suddenly didn't look so sure.

'Well, at least ah dinnae think so but he got what he's been asking for, simple as that.'

Martin was now looking at Colin, listening to what he was saying, still worried but now less worried about Billy and more about Colin.

'What the fuck's happened to you today man?'

Colin looked to one side and laughed for a couple of second before turning back.

'What do ya mean? Nothing's happened to me mate. Anyway, you're the one that's always telling me to look after myself, stick up for myself.'

Martin started to giggle as well but it was a more nervous, stifled laugh.

'Jesus Christ though, there's a difference between stickin' up for yourself and knockin' fuck out o' the hardest cunt in the school though, eh.'

'Aye but he's no' the hardest cunt in the school though is he? He's just a prick, maybe you'll realise that now.'

Martin thought about what Colin was saying. Half engrossed in what he was being told, half amazed by the total change in Colin, for the moment not thinking too much about Billy's state of health. Colin interrupted his thoughts.

'To be honest though, ah might not come into school tomorrow. It's no' because ah'm scared but you know what Billy's like, he's bound to do something. Ah'd probably better leave it 'til next week.'

Martin was reminded of Billy.

'Honestly Col, ah really dinnae see Billy being back at school tomorrow, or for that matter, giving you any grief for a while.'

25

Colin used the evening after the event to convince his parents that his time would be better spent the next day looking for work experience in Dundee and in the morning his mother drove him in, leaving him with enough money to make his own way back when he was done. After around four hours of visiting construction firm offices, becoming more and more exasperated at the fact that nobody seemed to be able to help him, even though he was offering his services for free, he decided to head home.

On arriving, his first instinct was to head to the fridge for sandwich material but noticing the blinking light on the answerphone he first pushed the button to listen to messages. There was a lot of activity on the telephone that morning but all the messages were short silences and then hang-up tones. After listening to around three of these, he decided that the sandwiches could no longer wait and he made for the kitchen. Just before he reached the kitchen door however a voice emitted from the machine.

'Col it's me.'

It was Martin's voice, sounding a little less confident than usual. The thought suddenly struck Colin that maybe there was trouble from yesterday.

'Look, ah'll call you later man, we need to talk.'

With this, Martin hung up again and the answer machine returned to quick silent calls being hung up. Colin made his way to the fridge, now a little worried by Martin's call. The very fact that Martin had been trying to call him all morning and the sound of his voice was a little off putting. However, not enough to put him off his sandwiches. He reached the fridge and the phone rang again. Colin considered that possibly, at this time, Martin's news could be important. As he answered the phone he could hear Martin, his voice still a little unsure.

'Hi Col, is that you?'

'Aye Martin, how ya doin'?'

Colin was trying to keep the conversation natural but was expecting some very bad news.

'Col mate, Billy's in the hospital, they've been operatin' on him all night, he's in intensive care and it doesnae look too good, ch. The police have been round the school, they want me tae go to the station tonight, to rule me out o' their enquiries like but naebody's mentioned you, eh.'

Colin was surprised by Martin's tone and the fast pace of his words. It was obvious he was panicking.

'Well, there's nae reason why ah should be mentioned is there?'

'Well, this is the thing mate.'

Martin began to explain how he saw things developing, he seemed to calm down as he spoke.

'Fae what the police have been sayin', they seem tae think that it was a Cupar thing. They've been askin' about Scotty Henderson and that.'

'Aye, that makes sense.'

Colin was now trying to work out how the police would approach this and wondered if Martin would be in the frame.

'They dinnae think that maybe it was you do they? You bein' the last person seen with him like.'

'Eh, ehm, no! I'm no' sure but I dinnae think so, they said they wanted to rule me out o' their enquiries, so I'm hopin' that they dinnae think, no, I'm no really, I dinnae think…'

Colin stepped in to stop Martin from rambling, it seemed like he would go on forever, seemingly talking himself in and out of the frame.

'Look man, you're right, there's nae reason why they should think it was you. They'll know that you're mates and there's nae motive, eh.'

Colin didn't want to worry him but there were things that occurred to him that could land Martin in trouble.

'The thing is mate, you'll have tae get rid o' the shoes you were wearin' yesterday.'

Martin was quiet for a few seconds.

'How come?'

His voice seemed more nervous than ever. Colin wanted to reassure him but was more concerned with the one thing that may lead Martin into getting the blame.

'Well, because we walked over that wee hill of sand, eh. That's probably the best clue the police will be looking at. Well let's face it mate, that'll be their only clue and it points tae you. If you go walkin' intae there station wi' them on, then we're both fucked.'

Martin was shocked that Colin was able to think of this. He had been worrying about this all morning and at no point had it occurred to him that he had been talking to police, wearing a pair of shoes that placed him right at the place where Billy had been found.

'Are you throwin' your shoes out as well then?'

Martin was now relying on Colin to have all the answers to get them out of trouble.

'Well, probably no'.'

Colin began to explain how he saw things, hoping that this would calm Martin down.

'The thing is, once you've got rid of the shoes, the police'll rule you out and me; well, they have absolutely no reason to suspect me. Once they shoes are away, neither have they any reason to suspect you, then that's it, we're in the clear.'

Thirty seconds passed. Both boys stayed on the line, neither saying a word. Martin was astonished that Colin could think so clearly and was coming round to be convinced that he was right. That Colin would get away with it no matter what.

Colin started to think about Billy. At the moment all he knew was that he was in intensive care but not really how bad it was.

'So what is the full story wi' Billy like? How bad is it?'

'Oh fuck, no' good like. Seemingly if he does pull through, it's likely he'll have brain damage.'

'Is that right?'

Colin interrupted.

'Brain damage aye? Well, it's no' like his brain was in that great nick anyway, was it?'

'Fuckin' hell man. There's a good chance that he'll fuckin' die.'

'No, you're right man, Sorry man, no, hopefully he'll be alright eh, I dinnae suppose he deserves all this.'

Again there was a short silence over the telephone as both boys considered what to say next.

'Actually, Martin.'

Again Colin was first to break the silence.

'Can you do me a wee favour?'

'Aye, what is it?'

'The thing is.'

Colin's voice now seemed to show nerves, which momentarily gave Martin cause for concern.

'Do you think you could get Carrie's phone number for me? Thing is though, I'm no' gonnae be able to see her till next Monday, and that's a wee bit hard necked, eh, no phonin' and that, eh.'

There was another silence on the line broken this time by a stunned Martin.

'Aye, aye, nae bother man, I'll let you know, eh. See you later man.'

Martin hung up the telephone, walked to the outside of the public telephone he had been using and leaned against it to reflect on the conversation he had just had. It was almost too much for him to believe that Colin, the quiet geeky bloke that only really he seemed to get on with was capable of such a conversation. It seemed unbelievable that such a person could be so calm about such a situation. Not only could he think with perfect clarity about how to distance himself from trouble and possible blame but at the same time, was more worried about getting together with a girl, than the fact that he had nearly killed someone.

After the initial shock however, Martin's thoughts began to clarify. Here was somebody who not only had taken Billy on but had beat him, beaten him badly and done so in a matter of seconds. More impressive however was the complete lack of egotism. The arrogance usually displayed by Billy was replaced by calculation and almost cunning to ensure the best result after the event. It occurred to Martin that Colin would be a much better partner then Billy in matters gang-related. That to combine his know-how and wisdom of the gang scene with Colin's cool calculation and ability to fight when angry, this would be a much better lead than Billy's gung-ho approach.

Martin had now put the problems of Billy's injuries and their connection with the incident to the back of his mind. If he could somehow manage to get Colin interested in this scene, then they had a real chance of causing some bother.

JULY 1991

INSIDE

26

'Colin Charles Nichols. You plead guilty to all charges of serious aggravated assault and grievous bodily harm and it may be argued that this is to your credit. Your council have also lodged a plea for leniency based on the fact that you have already experienced some punishment through the fact that you have missed out on your planned future career choice. A career in the Royal Air Force has now been rendered as a choice that you no longer have following your arrest.

'I myself served as an officer in this country's Royal Air Force and although I can laud your decision to attempt a career in the service I'm not certain that I can regret that circumstances have barred it. Regardless of what you may think, the military is not a place where mindless violence aimed against authority figures can be made welcome.'

Lord Justice David Greig pushed his glasses further up his nose as he turned and faced the dock, meeting Colin's eyes for the first time since beginning sentencing.

'You made a decision to launch a vicious attack on all members of recognised authority, stopping only when they could muster enough numbers to render you unable. The question being left by your guilty plea is why? No plea of self defence. No mitigating circumstances. Nothing to explain these senseless acts of violence.

'It is part of the job of the judiciary to protect those employed in the maintenance of public order, be they privately employed, as is the case with the nightclub security and certainly those employed in the civil service as police officers of the law.

'The punishment meted out for such crimes should not only be severe enough to match the gravity of the crime but they must also send out a clear message that such crimes will be dealt with in the strictest possible way. Only then will people realise that when you strike with violence against the authorities, the authorities, *will* strike back. You will go to prison for 90 days.'

The judge brought the gavel down. Colin's neck stiffened as a rush of blood and adrenaline coursed its way upwards struggling to contain him from an outburst. A simple 'What?' quietly escaping form his mouth, he looked over to the viewing gallery where most wore a similarly dumbfounded expression to his own. He knew that jail was a possibility but in actual fact had almost discounted it as a likely outcome. His solicitor explaining over and over and at length how a first offence like this would not be likely to lead to a prison sentence. Yet here they all stood, wondering whether to expect the judge to say something else or to excuse himself, he'd just made a bit of a mistake, but slowly coming to the realisation that the gavel was down and the decision had been made.

Martin and Carrie were standing side by side when the sentence was passed. Carrie's hands had shot up in front of her mouth in what looked like an attempt to stifle a scream. Martin was static for a few seconds, with the exception of his head scanning to take in the scene of the whole room, finally resting on the sight of Carrie's shocked expression. He swivelled to face her and placed his hand on her shoulder and with this she shrunk three or four inches and turned to him, opening her arms and hugging him. Almost fully collapsing. Martin could feel all of her weight transferring into the hug.

The expression of Colin's parents seemed a little more resigned than everyone else. No shaking of the heads or looking at one another and shrugging, they appeared to have simply accepted that their son was now to go to jail but Colin was sure that he could make out their underlying emotion. An emotion that he was quite sure that, before the last couple of months he had never really caused his parents to feel. Now confident that they would probably always carry to a certain degree. They were ashamed of him.

Colin could feel the two security guards who had been flanking him moving closer. Inexperienced in this situation, he may have expected them to have been ready to gloat and give him a hard time and so was surprised by their actions. The taller of the two, on his left hand side gently touched his elbow and asked with what seemed to be genuine concern: 'You OK mate?'

'I'm, eh, no, don't know!'

The other man made contact with the small of his back.

'OK, look we're going to have to put these on.'

He showed Colin a pair of solid-looking handcuffs.

'Don't have to do it here with everybody watchin' though!'

He motioned down the small flight of stairs behind the dock. Colin looked back towards the viewing gallery. Martin and Carrie were still in their clinch. His parents had sat down now, also beginning to hug, his father with his teeth tightly clenched as his mother looked ready to begin crying.

Colin started down the stairs unsure of when he would see any of them again. With little experience of how these things worked, he fully expected to be whisked off to start his sentence straight away.

27

Colin faced the jumping crowd. He was elevated above them on some sort of podium. Orbital's 'Chime' pumped from the speakers behind him. Weird but wonderful. He didn't actually know where he was or how he'd got there but this must've been some sort of super-club. There were easily two thousand revellers on the dance floor below him.

Carrie was walking up a small flight of steps towards him. Walking slowly, seductively, staring him in the eyes. A wicked smile stretched over her face. The kind of smile she always had when she knew he was going to please her. When she knew that he was going to send her into sexual ecstasy. This hardly seemed the time or place though. Colin moved down the stairs towards her but as he walked he could feel a dull ache in the back of his right calf.

The music grew louder. Carrie was around five feet away now. She looked disappointed and began to shake her head. The pain in the leg intensified. Colin hurried down the stairs. Something was wrong. He began to hobble. Carrie looked away towards the crowd. What had he done? Had he upset her? He reached her and held her by the shoulders. She began to turn round. The music was too loud now. He couldn't make it out, it was just a wailing noise.

The pain in his leg was unbearable now. He bent over to hold where the pain was centred. Closed his eyes and then opened them again and he was prone crouched on a bed. The pain was intense and he muttered a groan through clenched teeth. Colin looked around. Four bare cream coloured walls and he was alone. No music. No Carrie. No excited crowd. Just four bare walls, a bed that was too small for him, a sparse collection of very basic furniture and a slatted barred window that offered a view of the sky outside. Grey sky.

The pain in his leg subsided and Colin quickly realised that he couldn't have been further away from super-clubs or clinches with Carrie. Not the first time he'd woken up on the past two weeks holding his legs from having to sleep in an unusual position. Perth Prison was now his personal dungeon, where he knew he had many more nights to spend, with only the hope of further dreams acting as respite. Certainly no hotel but not the image of Victorian suffering that he had feared. From the few people that he had talked to that had spent some time in the remand C hall before conviction, he was told that the wing was in fact 'a palace' by comparison.

Colin couldn't decide whether he was lucky or unlucky to have been given a cell by himself but certainly the cell he was in was not his perception of what a jail cell should be. His experience amounted to watching Fletcher and Godber on the television so that was fair enough. It was small but carpeted and clean with brightly painted walls. A window, barred and clearly reinforced, offered a view of a high wall around 20 metres away topped with curls of barbed wire, above which the sky was visible, albeit in the two weeks since he had arrived it appeared to Colin, a very grey sky. Not exactly a picturesque view but then Colin considered that for those spending longer than 90 days, which, he was aware was almost everybody, it might really be quite cruel to provide a constant reminder of what they were missing.

Within the cell, a bed with footlocker and a chest of three drawers. No television or ability to cook or brew hot drinks but clearly the most important omission for the period when the doors were locked was a flushing toilet. Instead a large chamber pot for slopping-out purposes. Not ideal, but Colin kept in mind the sharp and succinct statement that he had heard a few times since his arrival.

'If ya cannae dae the time!'

If not knowing anyone who had been to prison had proven problematic with regard to gaining advice as to what the living conditions would be like, then prior to his arrival it seemed as if it would prove no hindrance to people wishing to advise him on how he was to behave during his time behind bars.

'Keep your head down and do your time.'

'Don't make any enemies.'

'Remember, everybody's in the same boat.'

Colin was surprised that on the day of his sentencing he was released and ordered to return in three weeks to begin the sentence. In that time everyone seemed willing to help with the same information about keeping himself to himself and it was 'only' three months, regardless of the fact that most of them hadn't even come as close as police custody to having been incarcerated.

There had even been a night out planned for the last Friday before he went down, which he was sure would be full of well-meaning people offering advice, all completely without substance. Colin had decided not to turn up to the night out and at the end of his three weeks' wait, he was actively avoiding people and in some perverse way, looking forward to going to jail so that he could begin to get the whole thing over with.

For the moment though, he was in prison and although the advice was in no way expert it seemed sensible enough and in fact there wasn't really an alternative other than to try to just get through it with the minimum fuss. It wasn't as though Colin had any notion about trying to make his mark on the wing to ensure he wasn't messed with. Just, talk when you're talked to, don't be rude, don't upset anyone and try not to be noticed. Like being back at school really, except he knew there was no bell at four o'clock.

He'd been asked a few times the standard question 'what are you in for?' and had considered that telling people that he laid out a few policemen may bring some kudos but that just wasn't in line with the keeping the head down principle. Even telling people serious assault and GBH seemed a bit like making himself out to be a bit of a hard man but then, there was no point in lying.

Colin sat eating his breakfast, clearly aimed at nutrition above any attempt at flavour or variety. Listening to the conversation, it appeared that the banter was pretty much the same as at the garage where he worked. Mainly football, with the Old Firm fans unable to agree, at the half season point of the league, with positions too close to call, whether Rangers would extend their League championship to five in a row. The non-Old Firm fans expressing their derision, Colin; had he been at the garage, would have joined in with the Old Firm baiting but considering where he was, this seemed a little bit like poking his head over the parapet.

Colin made his way back to his room, he had almost an hour before work started and a good book in his locker so this morning was dealt with and if everything stayed the same then just another 75 days and he was out but then, counting the days wasn't such a good idea. Colin walked the stairs back to his cell. He couldn't help looking behind himself. Something wasn't quite right. Something told him that that he was being followed. He always tried to ignore anything that seemed like paranoia.

Something this morning though was different. People were staring at him. Discussing him. Not everyone. He singled it down to two other prisoners. He watched them as they were talking about him at the breakfast table. Didn't try to hide the fact when Colin looked directly at them and now as he climbed the metal stairs, the same two guys were on his tail. The feeling was exacerbated by the feeling that one of them looked vaguely familiar but then Colin managed to shrug it off.

'You're imagining it, you don't know anyone here, no one knows you, it's a coincidence.'

Colin left the stairs and turned left on to the corridor to his cell, confident that his imagined pursuers would continue up the stairs. As he approached his cell, he was certain that he was still being followed. Colin turned into his cell. He didn't want to appear flustered by looking properly but he had to look. He had to check it out and sure enough, the two men were following him along the corridor. He sat on his bed and waited for what he was now sure would be a visit from these two prisoners. Seconds passed, nothing happened, no one entered the cell but neither did anyone walk past. They were loitering outside.

Waiting for a good time to make a move? Looking out for guards? Colin sat wondering what was happening. Who were these people? What did they want with him? Had he done something to attract their attention? He didn't think so. Were they just at it? A couple of chancers who thought they might have spotted a weakling. The same as the bullies at school?

If this was the case then he was sure he could deal with it. A nonchalant point of the finger back towards the door and an exclamation that he 'really couldnae be bothered wi' their pish' delivered with enough enthusiasm would be enough. Martin had taught him that much.

Sitting there on his bed, though, Colin could feel his pulse quicken and tension rising in his chest, he suspected that this was something far more sinister. A few more moments passed. Colin breathed out heavily, tightening his lips together into a blow as he finished. The two men entered the room. No knock, no permission asked or granted, they strode in and looked at Colin. Colin first flicked a glance at both of them and then reached over to nonchalantly store his mug away in his locker. As if their presence there wasn't overly troubling him.

The larger of the two looked oafish as he stood slightly behind his colleague. Colin didn't know why but some people, even when wearing prison uniform seemed to be particularly badly dressed. In bad need of a haircut, Colin considered that he had the look of the people who ordinarily opted to shave the hair off of the top of their head and compensate with a goatee beard on his rounded chin. Not this fellow though, his hair was clearly receding but he kept it at about six inches length and apparently uncombed for months. As he stood in the room, clearly trying to look menacing the one thing that Colin knew about this one was that he had never seen him before.

The other one was much neater and better presented. Colin knew that this man was vaguely familiar but just couldn't place his features, had he seen that face before? The ears, the mouth, the general gait of how the man was standing he didn't know but the eyes were familiar. Colin not only knew that he had looked into these eyes before but was sure that he had stared deep into them on an occasion when the two of them had been involved with something that he should remember. For the life of him though he couldn't remember when and where and in a strange way had the feeling that they had never actually met. Colin placed his hands on the bed and leaned back slightly. This would either be over with very quickly or maybe, just maybe the next few minutes would define the rest of Colin's stay at Perth Prison.

'Can ah help you boys?'

Colin kept it chatty. The familiar one sniggered.

'You dinnae recognese me di yi?'

Colin now knew that his instinct had been correct. He should know who this was but he didn't. He should probably know why he was there in his cell. Again, he had no idea but the way that he had asked the question convinced Colin that this wasn't a social call. He decided to keep it non-committal, even apologising just in case he should really know who it was.

'Ah'm sorry mate, but have we met?'

With this, the man moved closer to Colin.

'Nah mate, we've niver met!'

It suddenly struck Colin. Those eyes. He had seen them before. He had stared deep into them at a crucial time. In fact, the last time he had looked into these eyes, the person was trying to struggle off of the floor beside the urinals in Fat Sams toilet. Colin had looked in his eyes. Fitchy's eyes. The same look of defiance as in the man now confronting him. Colin had meant to deal a final blow to render Fitchy helpless. The man now in the cell, though, was not Fitchy. This was not the same man that he had knocked for six in those toilets. He was older but the features roughly the same. The man was now a couple of feet away from Colin stooping to bring his face down almost level with Colin's.

'But eh thought yi might've recognesed is anywey.'

127

Colin's body tensed, he wasn't sure whether to expect an immediate attack. He focused intently on the man in front of him but his wits were still aware of what the other man might be doing.

'You're Fitchy's brother?'

Accepting that he had now been recognised, the man stood up straight, still looking down at Colin's seated figure.

'Eh mate, eh'm Fitchy's brither.'

He took a step back and checked with his colleague.

'Eh'm Fitchy's big fuckin' brither.'

Colin felt that he was going to be attacked right there and then. He flicked his eyes looking for a weapon, either in Fitchy's brother's hand or in those of his goon but could see none. Colin looked up into the contorted face of the man feet away from him, a face displaying nothing but hate now. Sitting down was not a good option for Colin an he prepared to spring from his bed to meet the attack head on.

A dark figure appeared at the door.

'Right what the fuck's the scoop in here then?'

All three men faced the cell door where stood the officer they knew as Gibson.

'Och nothin' boss.'

It was the goon that spoke first.

'We're just haein' a crack wi' Colin eh. Aw mates and that!'

They knew his name.

'Right well, social club's finished.'

Gibson was a switched on screw and was in no mood to just let things carry on.

'C'mon' Ecky, back to your own floor. You n'all Fitchy, get motorin'.'

He shared a nickname with his brother. Both men went to leave but before he went, Fitchy delivered his message to Colin, a quiet whisper in his ear.

'You got lucky in Fatty's mate but yir luck ran oot the minute you landed here. Cos you're no' leavin' here in any fit state!'

Gibson interrupted.

'Fitchy, am I talking in ancient fuckin' Greek or something? Get back to your own fuckin' floor!'

Fitchy went to leave the room but had one parting shot, audible to everybody but delivered in a way meant to sound convivial

'Right well, look efter yoursel' eh Colin, lot o' nutters aroond in here eh!'

Colin stayed in a tense nervous posture on his bed. The removal of his visitors had done nothing to relieve his anxiety. The last few minutes were probably the last thing that Colin would have wanted. All of his fears about prison had just become a reality. It wasn't that Fitchy's brother was particularly frightening.

After all, big brothers would be much of a muchness with their younger siblings and probably just as easy to deal with but now, here was Colin. Alone in a completely inhospitable place, where the only person he vaguely knew had a genuine and serious vendetta against him. Not only that but as much as he knew that he was alone here, he was sure that Fitchy was right at home.
Already he knew of one thug willing to help but he was sure there would be more.

Fitchy was at home in Perth Prison and Colin couldn't be further. Five minutes ago he'd been gaining confidence that prison wasn't going to be too bad but now and for the first time since he arrived, he sensed real danger.

28

Colin woke with his start, his legs draped over a wooden beam on the bottom of the bunk, his feet hung over the edge but no cramp this morning. Probably due to the fact that he hadn't had enough sleep to allow one to develop. As he prepared to leave his cell he was completely at a loss as to how to look after himself now. Convinced that at some point soon, someone would try something.

Trouble had made its way into Colin's time in Perth Prison. It was inevitable. Going to happen. But so many questions. Where would it happen? When would they make a move? Who would it be? It needn't be Fitchy himself and Colin considered that it probably wouldn't be. He knew that some prisoners would do anything for a gram of heroin and was aware that that's how most hits were organised. Not like in the movies where professionals were hired and hits meticulously planned, it was just a case of giving some strung-out loser their wrap, asking them to do something awful and knowing that their desperation would keep them on course.

Colin didn't doubt that Fitchy could facilitate this. If his brother worked for the Digger then he would surely have connections there as well. For all Colin knew, and he certainly considered the fact, perhaps it was the Digger that was pulling the strings. It didn't really do to have his dealer done over in Fat Sams. If the Digger was behind it then anything was possible.

Colin spent the whole day looking over his shoulder, avoiding being isolated and if he could, always staying within sight of a guard. As the day went on the tension didn't fade. It was not as if Colin could consider that the longer things went on the safer he might be.

The meal queue was the worst time. Everyone huddled together in one large throng, it would be quite easy for someone to quietly slip something sharp into his side as he waited and make their getaway into the crowd without being noticed. Breakfast passed, nothing, dinner passed, nothing, tea meal passed and nothing had happened, perhaps the attack was not to take place today. Colin made his way up the stairs and turned left towards his cell. As usual after mealtimes there were people milling around outside their cells. Colin moved past them avoiding eye contact and concentrating on whether anyone appeared to have anything in their hands that they shouldn't. Three doors from his cell he heard someone standing just beside him.

'You Colin Nichols?'

Somebody had been waiting there for him. Colin spun to look at him. Movement quickened by the adrenaline. The man was clearly not armed. He had nothing in his left hand and was lifting a rolled cigarette to his mouth with the right. He was only slightly smaller than Colin and not as broad. One on one, Colin thought that he could handle this guy and get away, except he wasn't exactly alone on the landing and anybody else here could be an accomplice. He had a shaved head and his facial features all seemed to be crunched into the smallest possible area in the centre of his face. He appeared to be looking Colin up and down as Colin stood with his back hard up against the landing rail.

'Well are yi?'

'I'm Colin, aye. Why?'

'Mr Gordon wants a word.'

Mr Gordon sounded official but Colin didn't know who it was.

'Who's Mr Gordon?'

'Well, if you don't know now you're about to find out eh?'

***

Instructions had been issued how to find the mysterious Mr Gordon's cell and Colin was dispatched with advice that it didn't do to keep him waiting. He knew this was a trap though. It had to be. There was no Mr Gordon. Just a few hard-arsed bastards waiting in the relative secrecy of the ground floor cell that he was being sent to. Colin considered just not going but in a way he was glad. Pre-warned was pre-armed and now Colin knew when and where it was going to happen. A sight better, he considered, than simply knowing that it was going to happen. He wasn't kidding himself that this was going to be something he could fight his way out of. He approached the door with the attitude *'right then, let's get this over with – it might hurt but then again, if you can't do the time!'*

He rushed through the cell door expecting immediate contact from a blunt instrument or a sack to be pulled over his head. Only to see a single figure relaxing on his bed. The man was medium height and slim. Well presented but certainly perturbed by the almost violent entrance Colin made to his cell. Colin began to apologise for the intrusion but the cell's occupant spoke first.

'You alright mate?'

The man began to get up from his bed. He seemed mid-thirties and spoke in an almost hushed tone. Brown slightly receding hair, kept short and well combed. His face clean shaven and tanned with the beginnings of lines to mark his age. His eyes were piercing and gave him the look of someone very serious. A professional.

Mr Gordon.

What did it mean that his cohort called him Mr? Was he once a lawyer, accountant, forces officer even, he just had that look of authority about him.

'Are you Colin Nichols?'

Colin composed himself, this didn't seem so much like a trap anymore.

'I am, aye.'

Mr Gordon moved towards him and thrust out his hand. Colin, no longer feeling particularly threatened, took the hand and began to shake. Mr Gordon's grip was vice- like.

'I'm Lawrie Gordon.'

The name rung a bell. In fact, you couldn't live around St Andrews without having heard that name. Not a place renowned for the number of hardened criminals living there but one name was known by all that really needed to know that the person was not to be crossed or messed with. That name was Lawrie Gordon.

'You have enemies Mr Nichols!'

Colin thought about asking him to tell him something he didn't know but smart comments somehow didn't seem appropriate.

'Nasty little bleeders. Dundonians.'

He almost spat out the word.

'They'll have you within a week, mark my words.'

Gordon positioned himself back on the bed.

'You're from St Andrews right?'

Colin could see obvious advantages with being from the same town as Gordon but none in lying.

'Leuchars,' he corrected.

'Leuchars, St Andrews, same thing really. This is why you're here. See, I've sanctioned this attack. It really doesn't do for me to seem partial in any way but given that you and I are near neighbours, I did think it community-spirited to at least give you the heads up.'

'OK, thanks!'

Colin was keen to leave and even though he knew that this man was probably now his only ally, albeit a rather tenuous one, he really did want to leave the cell, thinking that perhaps at some point he would say the wrong thing or get on Gordon's wrong side.

Gordon seemed to sense the tension and motioned towards a single dining chair at the foot of his bed, an obvious invitation for Colin to sit.

'Can I give you some advice?'

Colin sat but didn't speak, choosing to nod his acceptance.

'The advice you got before coming here, keep your head down, don't attract attention, right?'

Colin shrugged but Gordon knew that he understood.

'No! Wrong! In fact, that's the reason why you're here man. You're a rotweiler!'

Colin's puzzled expression was obvious.

'Eh?'

'Well, you know what a rotweiler is?'

'The dog?'

'Aye mate, the dog! Probably the most dangerous dog you'll get, maybe next to those Japanese ones!'

Colin thought that maybe Gordon had been smoking dope, the conversation just made no sense.

'Aye, rotweilers are dangerous.'

He just agreed.

Gordon looked at Colin and all of a sudden seemed very serious.

'Aye, but most of the time they're just docile dopey looking things. They just don't look like they'd harm a fly. I've seen five-year-old kids practicing their karate moves on rotweilers and the dog just sits there and takes it. So your kids are oblivious to the fact that the animal could take their arm or, just as easy, their fragile little lives away from them at any point. And then, every so often, that's what they do. They just explode and think, NO, I'm no' takin' any more of this, and that, well, that's when people get hurt.'

Gordon paused slightly

'And the dog gets put down. You see my point?'

Colin was thinking hard, he thought that there may be some sense here but couldn't really get it. Gordon could sense the doubt.

'Y'see, that's you! You'll take everybody's nonsense and not lift a finger. So they grow in confidence and you get more nonsense.'

Gordon was getting more animated.

'This goes on till you've just had enough and at that point; and you have to trust me on this, people will die. And you…'

Gordon pointed directly at Colin.

'You go to jail. Christ, I reckon even the judge saw it, *this guy's a rotweiler. I can do what I want with him.*'

All at once Colin could make sense of what he was being told. It was true. All of the trouble he was in was being encouraged by his own behaviour. He invited it and unless he changed, he always would.

Gordon seemed to calm down.

'You can't be like that man! You've got to be an obviously dangerous dog, pitbull, akita, something along those lines. You know not to mess with those dogs and it's good. Because when people know where they stand, they don't put themselves in danger. With you mate. People don't know where they stand and they just think, no bother, and walk right into your way and it's no' good for them but, more importantly, it's no' good for you!'

Colin could hardly believe what he was hearing. So profound yet at the same time, so obvious. Why hadn't he worked this out for himself?

'If I were you, in the same position you're in and with the ability you've got, I'd be a pitbull and I'd make a Billy Fotheringham out if this guy Fitchy. Then you can enjoy the rest of your stay at the request of Her Majesty.'

The mention of Billy Fotheringham rocked Colin to his core. How could Gordon know about Billy? Did he know about Billy? He would have known about his condition but did he know that it was Colin that caused it? He must have though or why would he use him as an example?

29

Colin sat now back in his own cell thinking about the day's events, what Lawrie Gordon had said and how it all made sense. Avoiding trouble and being the person he was seemed to be the root of all his problems. He had to face it, if he openly carried the threat around with him that he knew he possessed he just wouldn't be there. People should be scared of him and if they were, there just wouldn't be the same amount of bother.

He thought about Billy, now vegetating at his parents' home and for the first time felt a twinge of guilt. He'd always just shrugged it off. Billy deserved it. Billy was a prick! Now he realised that Billy didn't deserve that. In fact it was him that had encouraged Billy. Billy was just stupid, reacting to the obvious stimulus. He had no idea that Colin could attack like that and why would he?

With what he'd done to Billy he was basically lucky he hadn't gone to jail sooner. It's only the fact that neither could the police have expected that the docile rotweiler that was Colin Nichols could have been responsible. As he sat alone in his cell, he realised now what he should have realised a long time ago.

'I'm dangerous and I'm responsible for that and if I don't start to realise that people need to know how dangerous, then things are only going to get worse.'

**

Colin had requested another meeting with Lawrie Gordon. He'd remembered what he had said and knew for sure that he had to clear what he was to do next with him. If he was pleased that the meeting had been granted then he was overwhelmed with what he'd achieved by attending the meeting. Gordon not only sanctioned the attacks but was happy to lend advice on how to proceed and had even provided some very handy items of contraband to assist. In all he had been in the room for over an hour and when he left he knew two things. First, that he could affect the plans that he had made, free of the threat of reprisals. Second, once the job was done he would no longer be alone in Perth Prison. Not as long as Lawrie Gordon was there.

30

Colin stood on the landing looking up at the open cell door. He could feel his pulse race with a mixture of fear and excitement. He'd hurt people before but never like this. Never planned. This was new territory. He looked around and all seemed quiet enough. Colin started up the stairs, his eyes everywhere. It just took one screw to see him on a landing where he didn't belong and the plan was bust. He reached the level and hurried along the landing. There were prisoners outside their cells but that wasn't a problem, there always were, and Gordon had assured them that nobody would come forward as a witness. No guards saw his approach to the door. He entered and looked at the two occupants, sitting at a flimsy table and playing, of all things, dominoes. Fitchy was seated facing the door. Already Colin could see the early signs of fear in his eyes. He'd saw it in his brother's some months ago and now he knew that the older Fitchy ought to be frightened.

'Whut the fuck dae you want?'

Fitchy tried to overcome the fear.

Colin ordered one word, not loud enough to be heard throughout the jail but with enough menace to provoke compliance.

'UP!'

Fitchy stayed seated but his playing partner began to rise. Poor guy had nothing to do with it but he had to be hurt to make the plan a success. Before he could turn to see the cell's intruder Colin placed a hand on the back of his head and accelerated it towards the cell wall. The head collided with the solid wall with a dull thump and Colin began to worry that the commotion would definitely be noticed.

Fitchy's cellmate stumbled to the floor and lay motionless. Fitchy was rooted to his chair but had begun to push backwards away from the assault. Colin pulled a lock knife out of his pocket, opened it and then drew the blade over the prisoner's face. The blade slid over his prone victim's chin, slit his mouth and caught his nose as Colin drew it back, careful to avoid the eyes. That may be going a little too far. The blade had the slightest hint of blood smeared on it as he turned to look at Fitchy who was now pushing himself out of his seat. Fitchy looked at his cellmate on the floor and for a second, no blood appeared on his face then suddenly the whole gash seemed to burst as the blood began to flow steadily from it. He looked back at Colin who was now approaching him. All at once he began to regret entering Colin's cell the previous morning. He should have realised that someone capable of causing so much damage at Fat Sams would carry a level of threat but had no idea that he would be as cold as to slash someone while they were unconscious on the ground.

Colin looked serious but composed. Fitchy was now hard against the back wall of his cell as Colin drew up to striking distance. Fitchy whimpered something in the broadest Dundonian accent Colin had ever heard as Colin raised the knife. Fitchy looked down to see that the knife, rather than having the blade pointing towards him was the exact other way round and Colin appeared to be offering it to him.

'Here Fitchy, you'll need this.'

Fitchy looked back into Colin's eyes, struck with fear he had no idea what was happening but considered that accepting the weapon may prove to be one chance of a way out. He didn't notice that the hand holding the knife was gloved. Fitchy reached down to take the knife to prepare to defend himself with it.

'Stupid cunt.'

Colin couldn't believe how easy Fitchy was making it.

Fitchy looked up allowing himself to think that he had gained a little bit more advantage by now having the knife when the impact of Colin's punch pressed through his shattering nose. His head whipped back, connecting with the wall and his body began to slump to the floor. Colin looked down at him. He could have hurt him much more but the job was done. He hurried out the cell and removed the glove immediately, checking the rest of his clothes for blood he appeared to be clean. He made his way past the prisoners standing on the landings and down the stairs. They now appeared to be making the effort to get out of his way.

***

The other intruder from Colin's room yesterday morning was lying on his bed reading a book. As Colin entered, he removed the book from the reading position, clearly flustered and annoyed at the interruption.

'Whut di you want?'

Colin put both his hands up in a signal of contrition.

'Hey, Ecky, you and me, remember, we're good mates from back in Dundee eh? Remember, even that screw Gibson knows that. So that's what we've been doing tonight eh? Catchin' up on old times eh.'

Ecky stood up from his bed.

'Whut the fuck are you on aboot?'

'Ah'll tell ya what ah'm on about!'

Colin moved further into the cell.

'Ah'll tell you your story of what you've been doing tonight and if you cannae stick to it then you'll end up in worse nick than your shitebag mate Fitchy. Understand?'

An alarm was raised outside and all hell broke loose. Ecky was clearly interested in what was happening outside but Colin looked directly at Ecky and a broad smile broke out over his face.

'C'mon Ecky mate, ah think we ought tae go outside to see what's happenin'!'

Out on the landing they could see the commotion, as guards appeared to be everywhere, prisoners ushered back into their cells and medical attention being called for directly outside Fitchy's cell. Ecky asked the obvious question.

'What's goin' on there like?'

Colin grabbed and spun him so that they were face to face. He looked directly into his eyes but Ecky couldn't keep the contact. Colin put his hand to Ecky's chin, to ensure that he was looking at him. Ecky flinched and drew back his head slightly before regaining eye contact.

'Well, you know what it's like Ecky. Dangerous fuckin' game that dominoes eh?'

Colin knew it wouldn't make much sense but couldn't help himself from saying it anyway.

'Ah'm no' a fuckin' rotweiler Ecky. Ah'm a pitbull!'

OCTOBER 1985

REPUTATIONS

31

Martin and Colin walked from the Cross in Cupar's town centre to Elmwood College on the Western exit of town. Not a long walk but not exactly made pleasant by the biting October wind, chilling their skin and blowing dried leaves into their faces.

The college was okay though, basically just a load of similarly aged people practising the rites of those in the throes of adolescence. Eyeing up one another. *'Ah could take him.' 'Ah'd give her one.'* This is what being a student there was all about.

Arriving early, the two boys opted to collect the overall bin from the motor vehicle workshop they had been working in the day before. From there take them up to the second floor where they were due to have a lecture on computing. Not a class that deemed overalls necessary but they were to take those overalls with them everywhere to avoid them being stolen.

Before picking up the overalls Martin and Colin stopped to share a joint outside the workshops. Not getting wrecked but just preparing themselves to take the edge off the mind-numbingness of using BBC computers for three hours. Goof and three of the Bell Baxter members of the class walked in together. Heads bowed in slim defence against the chill wind, they noticed Martin and Colin at the last minute. Goof had no interest in the joint that the boys were smoking, fitness fanatic that he was becoming; by contrast, the three from Bell Baxter, once they realised, were hanging on the hope that Colin or Martin would leave them a few tokes. Martin could see anticipation in their eyes. He took a last long toke, surveyed what was really now not much more than a roach before handing it over to an eager recipient.

'Enjoy!'

The word escaped with a billow of smoke that he thought they'd probably be better off trying to inhale.

'Right we'll go and get the overalls then eh.'

Martin signalled for Goof and Colin to follow as the other three gathered around the tiny morsel of spliff that none could hope to get a stone from. The motor vehicle workshop was open with nobody there. The overall bin tucked neatly behind the door, the walls adorned with tools on shadow boards. They collected the bin looking around the shop. On another day and if occasion merited it a few of the tools might have been placed in the bin. Another day!

They headed along the corridor, to the main reception and began to climb the stairs to the second floor. No great exertion but not helped by the weight of the overalls and their slightly stoned condition. Goof could see that they weren't quite at the races and grabbed the bin, slinging it behind his shoulders and bounding up the rest of the distance. Colin and Martin stopped momentarily and shared a look of appreciation.

They may have felt like taking the lift but this was not allowed. The fact that something wasn't allowed was rarely a barrier to these boys but the nature and origin of this rule contributed to its general acceptance. A couple of years earlier, some of the female hairdressing and art students from the top floor had complained of sexual harassment and assault in the lifts. This had actually led to criminal convictions. As a result of this the only people allowed in the lifts were the females going to and from the top floor and staff. Because of the sexual nature of these crimes, nobody sought to break these rules for fear of the pervert label.

Colin and Martin pushed through the double swing doors slightly after Goof to see him standing next to but not really acknowledging another Bell Baxter pupil already waiting outside the computing room. This boy was considered pretty much the class's dopey git and was regularly picked on and slagged, mainly by the Bell Baxter pupils he had come with. Stick-thin, ungainly and dressed with apparently no consideration for current fashions, his name was Mark Etchels but he carried from school the nickname of Des or Dessie. Some time earlier Goof had asked why he had a nickname that bore no relation to his actual name. The Madras pupils were amused by the accuracy of this name once it was explained. Dessie was short for Desert Lighthouse, on account of the fact that he may be bright but he was absolutely no use to anyone.

The three Bell Baxter pupils, who had been having a full and frank discussion on whether or not they were 'feeling it' after their few tokes, began their ribbing the moment they reached the top of the stairs and saw Dessie there waiting.

'Aaawwlrigghtee there Dessie boy?'

'How's it goin'?'

Derek Lester, one of the other Bell Baxter pupils was the first to greet him, moving over towards him and performing some fake boxing body shots, without actually making any contact. Dessie adopted a pathetic-looking defence posture, as if to protect himself from the blows which, in fact, only ever landed on thin air. Seeing this, the other two rushed over, patting him on the back.

'Wahay Dessie boy, ya daft bastard.'

'Dessie, Dessie, Dessie, Dessie.'

The Bell Baxter boys revelled in Dessie's humiliation, leaving Martin, Colin and Goof standing, looking at one another, smiling and shaking their heads.

'Fahk off goys, will you?'

Dessie's accent was a bit of an anomaly to everybody else. All rolling r's and swapped-around vowels. Although to their knowledge he'd lived all of his life in Cupar, his accent seemed to be drawn from all around the English-speaking world. A juxtaposition it seemed of Australian, American, South African and possibly Cornish.

'Maybe that's how they speak English on Mars,' Goof once remarked; a comment not only on the unusual accent but the general all-round strangeness of the boy.

Derek backed off a little into the main crowd of his mates.

'Jeeesus mate, ah'm just tryin' tae be friendly like and you're tellin' me tae fuck off.'

Derek was portraying someone deeply hurt by Dessie's reaction.

'Honestly, ya' try tae be nice and ya' just get a mouthful o' abuse.'

Dessie came out of his defensive stance and faced his schoolmates, standing shaking their head, tutting and playing along with Derek's little pantomime.

'No baht you're tehking the pehss though, you're always tehking the pehss out of me.'

'Aw, dinnae be like that.'

Again Derek tried his best to look despondent at Dessie's reaction.

'We're no' takin' the piss out o' you. We wouldnae dae that. You're a great guy, we're aw mates, eh.'

Derek raised his hands in line with his hips, clenched his hands and started to move them up and down quickly in some sort of display of enthusiasm. Like someone trying to drum up support for a good idea.

'Come on Dessie boy!'

Des raised his left hand to his face as if deep in thought and then removed it back to his side and elevated his head to suggest that he had just thought of something clever.

'Not taking the pehss, hmm, that's interesting.'

He moved towards the bin full of overalls which had been unceremoniously dumped at the top of the stairs beside the entrance to the lift. All of the other students were now spectators, actually quite interested in Des's movements.

'Darak!'

Des turned to his audience as he reached the bin.

'What's my name?'

The boys looked at one another, laughed and to a man realised that they had forgotten his actual Christian name. Derek struggled a reply through giggling.

'What?'

Des started to poke around in the bin with his hand.

'Do you thenk my name is Dasmond? It's not!'

Des now began to rummage with a little more purpose in the bin as he spoke.

'For enstance, what do you thenk the name on my overall is?'

It was clear that Des's overall was not near the top of the bin as he began to dig deeper to find it.

'Do you think it says Das or Dassie? Because it doesn't! No, my name is naht Des, it's Mark! Now, where the blahdy hell ehs this thing?'

Des had half emptied the bin and was bent over double, scratching around the bottom looking for his overall.

'Here Dessie, let us gie ya' a hand, eh.'

Derek moved towards Des and the bin tapping one of his friends on the chest and motioning for everybody to follow him. When he arrived at the bin he removed a few more of the overalls.

'Can ya' find it?'

Around half of Des's torso was now inside the bin.

'No, eht's not in here I must have already have tehken the fahker out.'

Derek placed his hand firmly on his shoulder.

'Nah mate ya havnea, it's no' out here.'

Derek whispered to his mates.

'Get his legs!'

Des tried to remove himself from the bin but Derek strengthened his hold on his shoulder.

'Aw cahm on goys, what are you doing?'

With this, the rest of the boys picked up his feet and stuffed him head-first into the now almost empty bin.

'Aaaah.' Des whimpered a bit and then began to shout something that nobody could make out.

The Bell Baxter boys found this hilarious, while Colin, Goof and Martin looked on. Des, forced downwards by the weight of his whole body on his shoulders and head and with his arms trapped inside the bin was stuck, with no way of either freeing himself or toppling the bin, set steadily on the floor. The laughter began to die down but the Bell Baxter boys continued to jump around it, kicking it lightly and generally wondering what to do next. Dessie's ranting could now just be made out from inside the bin.

'C'mon to fahk goys, let me out will yahs.'

The Bell Baxter boys were now looking at one another hoping that someone would come up with something bright to do. Martin walked over.

'Can he no' get out o' there like?'

Two of them answered at once.

'Nah man, he's well stuck.'

'Aye, nae chance he's getting' out o' there.'

Martin smiled.

'Well, get him in the lift then.'

'Nah mate, you cannae dae that, eh.'

Martin looked at Derek in disappointment.

'How no'? That would be well cool if he arrived at the top floor wi' just his legs pokin' out the top o' the bin.'

The Bell Baxter boys shifted some worried glances between one another as Goof interrupted.

'Aye and like, the rules are only that you're no allowed in the lifts yourselves. Doesnae mean you cannae throw a bin full o' somebody else in it.'

This was a typical statement from Goof. It didn't really make any sense but it certainly got the Bell Baxter boys moving. Their enthusiasm jarred, they pushed the lift button and manoeuvred the bin into place outside it. When the lift stopped on the floor the boys were relieved to see it empty. They moved the bin into the lift with Des inside screaming all sorts of obscenities, which could only barely be understood. They stood and watched as the lift reached the top floor, giggling and congratulating one another.

Once the lift had arrived at the top floor, the boys watched the light indicating the lift level. For a while nothing happened with the lift staying at the top floor. One of the boys then pressed the button to bring the lift and, of course, Dessie back. They were still all hugely excited by the whole thing. The lift arrived back and the door opened but to the surprise of the boys, Des and the bin were both missing.

Everybody looked at one another with puzzled looks.

'Daft fucker must have got out, eh.'

One of the Bell Baxter boys pointed out that which was markedly obvious.

'Nah, y' think?' came the sarcastic reply from Derek.

There was a moment's pause. A few shared puzzled looks. They could hear some commotion on the stairway. A few of the boys made their way around the lift shaft structure to look up the stairs.

'That's them thehr, blahdy idiots.'

Martin, Goof and Colin could hear the shouting from the stair well and recognised Des's voice. The Bell Baxter boys moved back from the stairs and after a few seconds Dessie appeared with a flustered-looking older man who they assumed to be a lecturer.

'Right then, you little morons, you know this lift is out of bounds and he could have suffocated in there. Who the hell are you, because I'm not havin' this. Something's goin' to have to be...'

Martin quietly interrupted the lecturer's ranting just loudly enough to get the attention of Goof and Colin. 'Ehm, time tae get the fuck out o' here ah think.'

With this they started to make their way sharply towards the stairs. The lecturer noticed their attempt to escape. 'You stop right there, don't you think you're getting away.'

The boys stopped at the top of the stairs leading downwards just long enough for Martin's simple response.

'See ya!'

The moment these words were exclaimed, all three started their sprint down the stairs away from the scene. Laughing all the way, out of the front swing doors and onto the car park. They stayed together sprinting all the way to the little garden at the college front gate before turning round to assess whether they were being chased.

The doors crashed open once again with the three Bell Baxter boys making an equally hasty exit, also laughing as hard as they were sprinting fast. As they reached the car park, the Bell Baxter boys noticed Colin, Martin and Goof standing at the college gates and made their way over.

All six boys stopped and collected their thoughts. Nothing was said, no plans relayed, no consensus sought. All six of them turned towards the gate and walked towards it. The occasional giggle as they went, they headed back towards Cupar to find somewhere private enough to continue getting stoned.

32

Eight pupils from 5L at Madras school had decided to take up the City & Guilds course at Elmwood College with another ten making up their group from Bell Baxter High School in Cupar. All of this class were boys and indeed the main thrust of this course was aimed at the generally accepted male careers of construction, mechanics and farming.

Initially there had been a divide between these two sets of pupils and in particular, Billy had instigated a lot of the trouble between the opposite members of the group. Now however, as the eight originally from Madras shrunk to seven with the absence of Billy, the pupils from Madras and Bell Baxter had started to get along better.

Billy's absence was due to the fact that two months after his run-in with Colin, he was still in hospital. Nobody other than family had been allowed to visit him. Apparently his injuries were so severe that it was thought that he would never fully recover from them, rumour even having it that he had died twice on an operating table. Not a confirmed rumour but everybody was aware that Billy was in a bad way and were sure he would never be the same again.

Fife Constabulary, for their part, seemed no closer to finding out who had dealt these terrible injuries. Martin had been to see the police a few times. They may well have suspected him for a while but their questioning on most occasions suggested that they believed, not that he was the perpetrator; rather, he was an unwilling witness who could help them with their enquiries, if he wasn't so scared of doing so. These lines of questioning had stopped however for some time and the longer Martin spent away from the police station the more confident he became that the police would now leave him alone.

The Cupar connection had also been investigated and for a while. Scott Henderson was in the frame as an identified enemy of Billy's. He however only appeared once in front of the police and was able to provide corroborated evidence that he was not at the scene. He was in fact, coincidentally, at Elmwood College himself that afternoon, attending one of the opening lectures of his HNC/D course. The fact that he was studying Art & Design had raised a few laughs among the St Andrews youngsters, who considered this to be a little bit 'poncey' or indeed 'poofy' for the considered top man of Cupar's young gang scene.

In any case, the students of the class of school leavers from both schools had now started to mix better and were now beginning to talk, share jokes and generally have a bit of a laugh together. All of these students had long given up the idea that this course was anything other than a bit of a carry on. Whereas all the other students were either working towards higher education or forced to attend as part of their youth training schemes, these students had no such ties and as such, had no real fear of any reprisals should their behaviour be deemed by college staff to be out of hand. The result was a class which much of the time ran amok, completely ignoring any rules set down by the college. Fire appliances and alarms had become a particular favourite, with many false fire drills having been performed lately and most of the corridors suffering drenchings from misuse of fire hoses.

The best thing about this, to the class, was that they had never been caught for anything they had done, always making a successful getaway. The college management were probably well aware of who the perpetrators of these high jinks were, knowing that these were the only students attending with no real aim or purpose to their course. Nothing however could be done about this and the school leavers' course was something that the college was obliged to offer under current education policy.

**

The errant students returned to Elmwood, slightly stoned, at around 12 o'clock for the afternoon's machining lecture but, more importantly, for the lunch break in the canteen. The lunch break in Elmwood canteen was not only useful for the cheap cooked food for those with the munchies but also, in itself, possibly the best opportunity for a good laugh at the other students' expense.

The dopey looking students, of which there were many, were slagged to death and every girl who entered the canteen, many of whom by now had nicknames attributed to them by the boys, were either torn to shreds or talked up depending on their looks. Girls would be marked out of ten and either be ridiculed completely for their unattractive appearance, or sexual fantasies would be described in great detail relating to those who were deemed to be 'shaggable'. All of this discourse was of course kept between the boys.

Colin, Goof and Martin were making their way steadily down the queue to the servers with their mechanic overalls already on. Extremely hungry and full of the joys, they were in their element. The way they always were when stoned at Elmwood College. Martin was on the lookout. It must have been four hours since he last slagged somebody off properly. He could take his pick in this canteen though. Nerds wasn't quite the word.

Where to start though? The people in front of him in the queue? The people sitting close by? The staff? That was it! The staff. They were employed by the college and as such, shouldn't expect any better. Then, what with the fact that each and every one of them seemed to be of a slack-jawed disposition it was difficult to resist really.

Martin moved down and decided that the lasagne looked the choice of the menu. Not particularly due to the richness of béchamel sauce or firmness of the pasta, much more the appearance of the poor unfortunate serving it. Jet black hair at just about shoulder length, this boy looked like the last time he'd seen a comb he probably tried to clean his teeth with it. Looking half decent should have been made easy by the fact that he'd been given a uniform but this guy still appeared not to have a pound hanging the right way. Martin was thinking now, didn't kitchen staff call their clothes 'whites'? If they did then this lad was pushing it a bit. Possibly bright grey at a push. It looked like perhaps he was doling the food out at a ratio of two to the plate, one down the front of his tunic. Martin drew opposite, held out his plate, looked into his eyes and kept his expression deadpan.

'Here mate, you know a lot about dirty clothes, do ya' think ah'll get another week out o' these overalls?'

The server looked him up and down, oblivious to the implications of what he was being asked. No clue as to why the three boys in the queue were doubled over with laughter. Goof wasn't stoned but his natural childlike sense of humour allowed him to understand the stoner wit. His competitive character meant that he had to join in. If Martin was cracking jokes then he had to be on that ball as well.

The boys made their way over to a table next to where the Derek Lester and Bell Baxter lads were already sitting. The canteen was busy and a middle-aged woman of generous proportions was clearing the table for the next occupants. As she wiped the table with her damp cloth, the boys eased into the seats with their laden trays. Goof thanked the woman and smiled. A smile meant to charm her into some level of allure before he spoke.

'Here are the wages here alright for what you're doin' or do you just like get paid in lard and sausages?'

For that, in fact, he did get a rather dirty look but by adopting an innocent expression he escaped any more repercussion than a simple shake of the head and an unintelligible mumble. As the boys sat victimising all and sundry for their own amusement, Scott Henderson walked in with a couple of girls from his art class. The talking all but stopped as he entered with Martin, instinctively knowing that everybody would have noticed him saying only 'fuck aye, they're alright,' expressing his views on Scott's female companions only, as if Scott himself didn't matter.

For Martin, Goof and the Bell Baxter boys, who were, of course, interested in gang related things and paid attention to reputations and talk, Scott was definitely worthy of respect, and this was duly granted. Stories of how he had handled people at school who were two years his senior, to become the school's considered top boy by third year and how he had never run away from any of the many gang fights he was reputed to have attended, had elevated him to a position of esteem even greater than that of Billy Fotheringham's, before his demise.

For Colin, however, this reputation was met by indifference. Scott was not like Billy. He had never bothered him and for that reason he didn't really care about the stories. He had of course heard plenty about Scott from Martin and had considered some of what he heard as impressive. It was not that Colin, after seeing off Billy, now believed that he was in any sort of position of comparison with such people. He just felt that he was not at all involved with these matters. To the surprise of everyone at the table, rather than joining the girls for lunch, Scott made his excuses to them, made his way over and actually asked Martin if he could join them. Martin tried to act as unconcerned as he could as he answered.

'Aye, nae problem man.'

Although in reality he was more than a little curious regarding his motive for coming over. Scott pulled out a chair and sat facing Martin with Colin sitting beside him to the left. Goof was sitting directly beside Martin and the Bell Baxter boys were scattered in no particular order around the table. Scott looked directly at Martin as he spoke.

'Listen man, ah know what you're thinking but ah had nothing tae dae wi' what happened to Billy Fotheringham.'

Martin sat listening, conscious of the fact that he was being addressed personally on a one-to-one basis about this. Scott looked around the table and for the first time acknowledged his former Bell Baxter colleagues.

'Anyway, it was nothing to do wi' anybody fae Cupar.'

Scott continued to explain things as he saw it.

'Or like, naebody's said anything about it tae me, eh.'

Martin considered what to say next. Obviously he didn't want to give anything away but did want to convey the fact that he wasn't completely in the dark about these matters.

'That's alright mate,' Martin nodded in reassurance.'We know you never had anythin' tae dae wi' it.'

Colin, who until now, was paying only lip service to this conversation sat upright in his chair and started to glare at him. Martin paid no attention to Colin's change of mood, lost in what he perceived to be a high level meeting between two gang heads. Scott also sat a little straighter in his chair as he came to realise that maybe Martin knew something about it.

'So, what, d'you guys know what happened like?'

Martin sat back in his chair.

'Put it this way. Billy wasnae' just a problem to you guys. We were all getting' a wee bit sick o'…'

Martin's little explanation was cut short by the intervention of Colin who, Martin now noticed, was leaning between the pair looking directly at him.

'Billy,' Colin now diverted his gaze to Scott, 'was a prick!'

Colin paused for a few seconds, sat back in his chair and looked back towards Martin. 'And he's no' worth talking about.'

Martin realised what he had been saying and why Colin would be upset by this. He looked towards Scott, raised his hands slightly above the table, closed his eyelids slightly, saying only, 'Aye.'

It was obvious to Scott that Colin had just corrected Martin from the mistake he was making. By stopping Martin rambling, Colin had meant to protect himself from any possible suspicion but in fact had achieved the opposite. Scott Henderson was now aware that he was sitting next to someone who knew something about the incident with Billy but was not keen to say anything about it. It was also now clear that this person was able to impose some sort of authority over Martin, at least as far as details of this incident were concerned.

Scott however had no idea who this person was. For the other people around the table, there was a little consternation at Colin's statement and demeanour but nobody else had any idea why he would act like this. Scott looked back towards Martin, pointing with a flat hand towards Colin. A gesture that perhaps he should know who he was. Martin did the honours.

'Right, Scott.' He gestured towards Colin. 'That's Colin Nichols, he's fae the base in Leuchars where ah live, eh.'

He then looked towards Colin, who by now was sitting looking a little less concerned but still angry. 'That's Scott Henderson.'

Martin paused as he wondered how to describe Scott, eventually saying only, 'Cupar, eh.'

Scott offered his hand and Colin duly accepted the gesture. 'Alright? Sorry about bein' nosey, eh.'

Colin visibly relaxed as he answered, even managing a smile. 'Nah, that's alright man.'

During this time, Martin sat a little peeved that the thrust of Scott's attention had moved away from him towards Colin. He tried to remember if Scott, or anybody of such standing for that matter had ever offered to shake his hand but he couldn't. Just as Martin almost began to lose himself in his own self pity he realised that Scott was talking to him again.

'Look, Martin mate.'

Martin raised his eyebrows to look attentive as Scott spoke.

'This is a wee bit daft, us chasin' yous and yous chasin' us every wee while.'

Scott was referring to the infrequent skirmishes between Cupar and St Andrews.

'See, a few o' us Cupar boys have been goin' intae Dundee on Saturdays, to the games and that. If you boys could get a bit o' a mob together then we could probably join up, hae a bit o' a carry on eh.'

Scott now gestured to everybody around the table.

'What do ya' think? You up for it?'

Through the surprise of what had been said, Martin could not have been more pleased. Here were basically his own ideas being suggested by somebody else. Not just somebody else but probably the main person other than himself with enough influence to encourage people. Scott Henderson, it had now become obvious, did not suffer from the same dogmatic views on these matters as Billy did. The fact that Billy was now out of the way seemed in fact to be the falling of the last barrier to this kind of amalgamation. Martin was aware that different gangs in Dundee had been coming together to form the Utility and could never understand why Fife couldn't be the same. It had now become obvious that the answer was Billy. But Billy didn't matter now. Not any more!

ZULU DAWN

33

'Did ya watch that fuckin' *Zulu Dawn* on the telly last night?'

'Aye, ah did aye. No' a bad film that, eh.'

Natalie Carter and Carrie looked first at their respective boyfriends sitting on the upstairs back seat of the bus and then shifted a disbelieving look at one another. Martin and Colin didn't notice their disgust at their film taste and continued.

'Aye, Burt Lancaster and they English boys. What was their names again?'

Martin paused to think about Denholm Elliot, Bob Hoskins and what their names were.

'Doesnae matter who the English were, it was the Zulus that were the stars o' that show. Zulu, Zulu!'

Colin motioned with his hands in the air, mimicking the beating of spears against shields as he chanted their war cry, emphatically but not particularly loudly.

'They boys had it well sorted. Put the shitters right up His Majesty's finest.'

'Oh aye! Right set o' mad bastards, eh.'

Colin seemed to be every bit as enthusiastic as Martin.

'See that's what you boys need to be like.'

Colin referred to Martin and his gang antics, still not including himself in the reference.

Although he now went around with them and to a certain extent joined in, he still was not comfortable with considering himself a gang member.

'Making all that noise and everything. Can you imagine them running down the Hilltoon at ya?'

Natalie could hold her silence no longer. 'What are you two on at all? Total bleeding rubbish that movie.'

'Aye, maybe you two want tae try getting' a grip, eh,' Carrie agreed.

The two boys looked at them with injured expressions. It was Saturday afternoon and all four were on the St Andrews to Dundee bus. Colin had been seeing Carrie steadily since school and Martin had got together with Natalie Carter recently. She'd been in the year below them at school but was only about a month younger than Martin. However, she seemed and acted the most grown-up of the group. If you could consider a hierarchy at school that regarded trendiness, looks and popularity, then Natalie would definitely have been the girl in charge.

Although Martin considered that he couldn't really go out with a girl in the year below him at school, albeit that she was only slightly younger, he had always had an eye on her. It wasn't just that she had model looks but her confidence which saw her carry herself with an uncommon grace. Her wits and street-wisdom propelled her into a class of her own. She never failed to look good, dress well or say the right things at the right time and of course, she was always with the right people and at this point in time, for a North East Fife girl of her age, Martin was the right man.

After the short course at Elmwood in 5L, Martin had decided that he quite liked the student life, young people marshalled together in not quite as regimented a fashion as school. Not that he had ever paid that much attention to school rules. Elmwood College was also where he had managed to get together with Natalie and had got to know his new cohort, Scott Henderson. If Natalie Carter was considered one of the coolest girls at the college, then Martin Bridges and Scott Henderson were definitely the coolest boys. Between them they didn't so much have friends as command a following. It seemed like scores of people from all classes in the college seemed to learn where these three would be during their spare time and just arrange to be there. The same could be said at nights and especially at weekends.

Natalie and Martin had both just finished their HNC year, Natalie in art & design and Martin studying golf course green-keeping. A course at Elmwood which was actually in some demand. The college's close proximity to St Andrews and the experience of the lecturers making it a highly regarded course. At weekends and on spare days Martin worked as a green-keeping assistant at the St Andrews Courses, spending quite a bit of his time working on the Old Course. As he put it, *'if you're gonnae be working on a gowf course, you might as well work on the most famous one in the world, eh.'*

Scott, who had just finished the HND; also in Art & Design and was waiting for word back from Duncan of Jordanstone School of Art in Dundee, for a second year start on their highly sought after degree course. He was hopeful and had put together quite an impressive portfolio of work while at college. It would seem that he was not only just a tough nut but also it would seem a talented artist. He never considered this a contradiction even if others did.

Colin decided not to stay on at college even though of all the 5L students, he achieved highest results. Instead he went to work as a sort of assistant-cum-apprentice at a small car repair garage in Ceres, just south of Cupar. Colin particularly liked the motor vehicle repair lectures at Elmwood but considered that the experience he could gain in the garage would be more useful when he joined the RAF. Colin's dad had arranged this placement himself as, even though Ceres was some distance from Leuchars and he himself was no slouch with a spanner and socket set, any large repairs or services to his cars were always done at this garage. Here he knew he was getting a good job at a fair price. He had been going there for years and was pleased to learn, when he had asked on the off chance, that the owner would be happy to give Colin some work. Not great pay, but he'd be kept busy and get some good experience.

Even though Colin didn't go to Elmwood, he and Carrie would still be with Martin, Natalie and Scott in their spare time. Of the people who were trying so hard to be part of this 'in' crowd, there were questions as to where Colin fitted in. To Martin though, there was never any question that either Carrie or Colin were much cooler than most of these people. Colin wasn't a hanger-on like most of the others were. He had a mind of his own and spoke to everybody as an equal. He may not have been considered the same as these three by everybody and indeed, many were jealous that he could be such close friends with them. After all, he wasn't as trendy as them. He had never tried to be. He was also less enthusiastic about the gang scene, which, to many, made him a bit of an outsider.

However Martin knew who he would rather be with in a gang fight and it wasn't his followers. It was the one that he quietly gave the credit to for the formation of the North East Fife collaboration. The one that had solved the Billy Fotheringham situation.

34

'So, tell me again Zulu warrior, what's the story with this Posh People's Collective?'

Natalie was teasing Martin. Normally this would be a bad thing but with Natalie it was different. As Carrie and Colin sniggered below their breath Martin played along with Natalie's little game.

He looked deep into her eyes. Everything he liked was there. A blend of charm, sophistication, mischief and, most of all, beauty. Had they not been sitting at the back of a crowded bus he would have grabbed her right there and then and done terrible things to her. But she could make sex out of conversation. For Martin, even flirting with her was exciting.

'The Posh People's Collective, Natalie, is our plan for domination of Dundee.'

Martin gestured towards Colin and Carrie, who looked at one another as if to ask *'is he talking about us?'*

'This little merger could see us goin' number one.'

'Little merger?'

'Aye Natalie, little merger. It's what small organisations do to become large organisations.'

'Aye, Martin, I know what a merger is but your plan is merge wi' the Broughty Ferry, eh.'

'Aye, Broughty Ferry. What's a matter wi' that likes?'

'Well, er, nothing wrong wi' Broughty Ferry. It's a wonderful place. Really nice in the summer 'n'all. Especially if you're a Dundonian. It's where they aw go when they become a wee bit upwardly mobile, to develop a keen denial of ever having been a Dundee schemie.'

Natalie was adopting a television presenter's tone for effect. Martin was loving it.

'The problem for you boys is that, Broughty Ferry, crackin' place that it is, doesnae actually have a gang. Or at least, no enough to take on any o' the Dundee gangs.'

Martin pushed both of his index fingers against his lips in an obvious caricature of intellect.

'Yes, Natalie, I can see your point but, and here's the thing!'

He began to wave one of his fingers in front of him.

'Neither do we. Hence the need for a merger.'

He adopted the most patronising tone he could muster.

'Do you see now?'

Natalie smiled and Martin winced a little. He knew he couldn't keep her on the back foot for long. She was way too smart for that.

'And your title for this merged ensemble. The Posh People's Collective? Very much a working title, I assume?'

Natalie hit right on the button. It was a stupid gang name and Martin knew it.

'Aye, well, we've got to call it somethin' though, eh.'

'Well, aye, ah suppose you do, but the Posh People's Collective? Come on! What the fuck were you on?'

Carry and Colin couldn't stifle their amusement at that one. Had it been anyone else Martin would have felt uncomfortable at the obvious ribbing but with Natalie it just felt good. Hilarious and charming.

'Natalie. It's ironic. Well, ah think it's ironic, it might be facetious. I'm no' William Shakespeare but if we're gonnae call oursel's something it might as well point out the advantages we have over the Dundee gadjes. Modesty basically forbids me to tell you how good we look and, you know, your Broughty Ferry punters, they know how to kit themselves out, eh. And well it might have escaped your notice but your typical Dundee schemie is a bit o' a fizzy drink. Ah mean look at us! El Charro, Lacoste, Timberland, Replay for goodness sake and what are they walking about in? Whatever they can get a five-fingered discount for in Next, that's what!'

'That's aw well and good Martin but you're no' gonnae be Dundee's number one cos you're dressed better and you need to face facts, when they Broughty Ferry punters smell the first bit o' trouble they'll be putting' their Timberland moccasins to good effect getting' the hell out o' there.'

'Naw, naw, no' them aw' Natalie, Michael Duff's been getting a bit o' a rep and ah think we have to face facts. We've got a few runners w'rsels, eh.'

Colin felt a little awkward interrupting but he felt he ought to say something.

'Aye, Mike Duff is a bit tidy likes. It was him that flew in about they Motherwell the other week there. He was doin' alright 'n'all.'

'Oh aye, dinnae worry about that Col. Ah dinnae actually think ah ken anybody that likes fightin' as much as him. He'll no' run away, eh.'

The bus pulled into the terminus in Dundee's Seagate and Natalie leant forward to place the back of her hand on Martin's face and gently stroked his face. A mixture of goose pimples and pins and needles made their way throughout his entire body.

'Well you take care o' y'rsel' cos ah don't know much about Zulu Dawns or Posh

People's Collectives but you're definitely right about one thing. You do look the business!'

**

Whether it was the good weather or the fact that schools, colleges and most peoples' works were on holiday, Martin was delighted to see a much higher turnout at the bus stop waiting for them than usual. About double in fact. On disembarking from the bus however he was a little disconcerted to see that very few of the party standing waiting were from Fife.

Scott Henderson himself was sitting on a bench with, among others, Michael Duff. He looked an unlikely leader, small and not particularly well built. He had a complexion which would suggest mixed race or at least continental decadency, with thick black matt hair, heavy eyebrows and strong square features finishing off the foreigner look. Michael was considered head of Broughty Ferry for good reason though. Of all of Dundee's young casuals, he was one of the most respected. No, he wasn't well built but he could certainly fight and never really liked to let an opportunity slip to prove this.

The talk in the bus stop that afternoon among those already assembled concentrated very heavily on one subject. Michael had arranged with one of the gang members from Mill o' Mains, to meet for a battle in Dundee's Caird Park later that afternoon. This was what it was all about. Organised gang violence.

35

Around 30 members of the combined force of the Posh People's Collective assembled in Caird Park that afternoon for their arranged showdown with the Mill o' Mains. Thirty people, large as it was relative to the kind of gangs the individual factions could normally bring together on a Saturday afternoon, need not have been considered a large force to take to another Dundee scheme. Nevertheless, Martin Scott and Michael were confident that this force would be sufficient to take on one of the smaller Dundee schemes.

This was an accurate way of considering Mill o' Mains. On the northern fringe of central Dundee; to the north side farmland, the south side Caird Park itself. Flanked on both sides by the considerably larger schemes of Fintry to the east and Kirkton and Trottick to the west, Mill o' Mains was indeed one of the smaller of Dundee's housing schemes. In total the population probably was no greater than 1,500 and given this, an assumption was made by the leadership of the PPC that they would probably not be able to bring together any more than 30 members of a gang at any one time. Added to this, neither Martin, Scott, Michael nor any other member of the PPC could bring to mind any individual Mill o' Mains resident that they should either respect or fear. Admittedly, they didn't really know anybody from that scheme, but with their recent involvement with the gang scene of Dundee and the soccer casuals, they would think that if there were anybody of any consequence from Mill o' Mains, they would have known about them.

However, if the suspicion that Mill o' Mains would not be able to raise a sizeable force and the perception that they had no real talismanic figure in their ranks served to encourage the PPC, then the fact that this was, in effect, an away tie for the joint Fife and Broughty Ferry mob did have some members a little worried. The idea that you could travel to an organised confrontation in a park directly adjacent from any Dundee scheme with a mob of only 30 people put the idea of a massacre in many people's mind. Colin, for his part, attending in what he saw as a spectator role, may not have considered this a massacre waiting to happen but he certainly was thinking that it may not go as well as some people seemed to be expecting.

The gang had assembled in a children's play park on the northern tip of Caird Park.

Just a thin line of trees, a gradual downward slope of grassy land and the main road between Fintry and Kirkton separated them from the scheme of Mill o' Mains. As Colin watched the mob prepare for battle, he could see levels of bravado rising with every new swig of super strength lager. This of course was the main preparation for the impending mêlée.

Prior to congregating in the park, the group had split up to allow smaller groups to arrange the purchases of their underage carry-outs. Everybody had been successful in gaining their Dutch courage although many had arrived later at the park than others, signifying that they had a little more trouble in securing their booze. Difficulties aside however, all of the people who were assembled in the bus terminal earlier had now made it to Caird Park and were now enjoying the late afternoon sun with their intoxicating substances.

Colin sat between Michael and Martin with a joint in one hand and a can of strong Kestrel in the other. He had been charged with the task of buying their carry out, his size and appearance had always been considered an advantage for this task and as usual, he was quickly successful, with himself Martin and Michael arriving earliest to the park after completing the task. Carrie and Natalie had been left in the town to be met up with later and thirty minutes before the action was due to start the three boys had already been in location for around an hour.

With increasing intoxication and with every new arrival, Colin had found himself growing in anticipation of the events to follow. Much as he was fearful of the idea that their mob may be heavily outnumbered, he had over the last hour became more enthusiastic about what he perceived might happen. He had even accompanied Martin over to where he foreseen the action taking place, Martin checking out the area for his forecasted appreciation of the skirmish to come.

Colin was surprised to find that while Martin was doing this, he himself was conducting a similar appreciation. He couldn't consider his thoughts as particularly well thought out tactics however; rather, his mind flashed back to the film he had watched on the television the previous night.

Whether it was the lager or the hash, Colin considered how cool it would be if the mob could emerge from the trees, like Zulu braves in a single line chanting and building up pace, just 'putting the shitters right up Mill o' Mains finest.'

Probably the hash!

Since the formation of this idea however, Colin had found his own enthusiasm for the plan growing and he had even begun suggesting this idea to others, pleased and surprised at their seemingly warm reception of the idea. It was not an overstatement that Colin was getting a little fed up with what he saw as being the typical gang confrontation. Mainly this involved nothing more than the smaller less prepared gang running away from the larger force with never two gangs coming within 100 metres of one another. Just once he thought it would be good to see what happened if two forces hit each other at full pelt.

36

The arrangement between Michael and his Mill o' Mains contact was to meet at four o'clock on the slope just behind the trees where the PPC now sat. At around quarter to four, Martin began to mobilise the force with the tactics that he decided. Before he did this he had one last word with his Leuchars compatriot.

'Colin, you're a fuckin' genius mate. *Zulu Dawn*, bastards won't know what hit them.'

A broad smile emerged on Colin's face.

'Fuckin' aye.'

Martin marched over to the tree line keeping his little army in tow. He physically positioned each member beside separate trees, each one at around five to seven metres spacing, issuing last minute orders to each member.

'Right then, as soon as we see any of them, we start chantin', right, 'Zulu, Zulu!' loud as we fuckin' can – then, the minute, and I mean the fuckin' minute they get over that road, we fuckin', charge them, OK?'

Each gang member seemed to swallow the plan with complete enthusiasm. Replies ranging from 'aye, let's do it' to 'oh man, this is gonnae be fuckin' great' rang in his ears as he positioned himself in the middle. Scott and Michael were already standing there, looking very pleased with themselves. Martin tipped Colin a wink as he took up position. It seemed that all the main players were assembled in the one place and Martin considered Colin to be within that group.

For around ten minutes, nothing happened. Everyone stood beside their trees in anticipation, drinking, smoking, passing whispers to their nearest neighbours, some even taking the opportunity to skin up a celebratory joint, to be smoked after the event.

Looking down on Mill o' Mains from their vantage point, there was around 150 metres of grassy slope leading to the road bordering Caird Park from Mill o Mains. A single road broke away from this main thoroughfare leading into the scheme itself, forming a bridge over a small burn. Small though this burn was, the banks leading down to it and the rough weeded landscape on either side meant that the bridge was the only sensible route in and out of Mill o' Mains on foot. Slightly further north of the bridge, the road split into two, the junction sending one road around the west outskirts and the other east, treading into the heart of the estate, disappearing where blocks of tenements began to obscure it.

The chant was suddenly raised by one single member positioned at the furthest west tree in the line. 'ZULU, ZULU!'

'What the fuck's goin' on here?'

Michael walked back from the group to investigate why one person had started singing. Looking along the line he saw the end man; one of his Broughty Ferry was, jumping on the spot and pointing. 'There they are man, they're comin'.'

Every other gang member had become focused on this one person.

'Where are they man?' The question of most.

'How many?' The standard query of the more nervous.

Martin and Scott were in no mood for questions, their eyes fixed on the likely route out for the defending mob. Scott was the first of the two to see them and started to chant the moment he clapped eyes on them.

'ZULU, ZULU! ZULU, ZULU!'

Half of the PPC were now chanting. The Mill o' Mains gang were not yet in full view but glances of them were being made through gaps in the tenement blocks. By the time the first members of the gang emerged from the last tenement on the east routed road, all of the PPC were belting it out.

'ZULU, ZULU!'

The sound was impressive standing there in the trees but Martin wasn't happy with it. Yes, it was loud standing there but Martin considered that to the gang still a distance away it would sound like exactly what it was. Thirty boys, standing in the trees, chanting. He wanted it to sound like one hundred and thirty.

'COME ON, LOUDER!'

He ran along the back of the group, drumming up enthusiasm. The volume did rise as a result, probably to as loud as thirty boys could manage. As they chanted and the other gang advanced the answer to the 'how many?' question was answered. Ten or so boys appeared and no sign of numbers letting up. Thirty of them emerged; a force to match the PPC, and still no sign of diminishing. The Zulu chanting audibly quietened. Forty, fifty, it was becoming clear that the combined Fife and Broughty Ferry gang was not the only amalgamation on parade today. By the time all of this gang had cleared the last tenement, suspicion was high that this wasn't just Mill o' Mains. There were around 100 members, now approaching the bridge out of the estate. The chanting had now all but stopped and looking along the line Colin could see people already backing away from their trees.

Martin's forehead dropped to his waiting flatted palm. Rubbing his temples, his head rocked back and forth, his mouth clearly repeating below his breath the word 'fuck!'

To Colin it was now obvious that the whole of the PPC had now lost the will to be there. It was now only a matter of time before they turned and headed back to the city centre at pace. This time however, Colin had no intention of retreating. For the past ninety minutes his anticipation had been building and he did not want to run now. Not again. Before this moment Colin had been the only person in the trees not chanting. As the Mill o' Mains mob reached the centre of the bridge he himself raised his hands to his mouth and began to chant.

'ZULU, ZULU!'

Other members of the gang looked at him, their heads shaking. It was clear that chanting alone would not be sufficient to drum up the support he needed.

'Fuck it,' he thought. *'What's the worst that can happen?'*

He was determined that the newly formed PPC would not be embarrassed on their debut. He made his way to around ten metres in front of the tree line and repeated his chant.

'ZULU, ZULU!'

Looking back into the trees he could see the gang, almost to a man, still in place but beckoning him back. The gang on the bridge were pointing towards him, drawing each another's attention to that which was pointedly obvious. The advancing gang had by now almost cleared the bridge.

Colin knew the plan but also knew that if this gang managed to get to his side of the road and make it into any sort of formation the PPC were doomed. Every other member believed they were doomed already and were waiting for the first person to run. Nobody ever wanted to be the first.

Colin looked down the hill and took a deep breath. Something was going to happen today. Even if it was only him taking out a couple of the unfortunate first people he came into contact with, he was not for running. He began to pace down the hill. Convinced that he was about to be dealt a beating, he cursed everybody standing behind him in the trees. Focusing on the gang standing on the bridge he could see the initial reaction, displayed by only a few of the forward members, by this time leaving the bridge. They seemed to stop momentarily leaning back and just generally looking amazed.

As Colin approached the road, some of these front members had sped up a little, not running but walking at pace towards the road. Colin continued shouting. Continued towards them. He broke into a run. This was it. He knew that the next few minutes wouldn't be fun but he was prepared for the beating. Prepared to take it. Somebody had to do something or the whole day was a waste.

This new gang, the PPC. He wasn't one of them. Not really. Was he? Not important really. The fact was, he was there and he wasn't prepared to be embarrassed by running away. So his choices were limited anyway. Stand still and take a beating or run forward for the same result. So he ran forward. He was now sprinting and less than 50 metres separated him from the mass of bodies all waiting for today's single victim.

Then, suddenly, the mood seemed to change among the larger gang. The front men were looking back towards the main body, who by now, seemed to be making their way back off the bridge towards Mill o' Mains. The front runners shot furious looks towards Colin and then back up the Caird Park hill before they themselves turned and ran back over the bridge.

'What the fuck's goin' on here?'

Colin was half asking himself the question, half shouting at the retreating mob. Things quietened at the road and his adrenalin settled. Colin could hear the 'ZULU!' chant behind him. He turned round to see the cause of the Mill o' Mains retreat. Thirty members of the PPC, halfway down the grassy slope, sprinting, perfectly spaced, making all the noise of 130, smiles broadening with every pace.

The main body met with Colin as he stood on the south side of the road, watching them continue over the road, past the bridge and into the housing estate itself. Colin remained rooted for around a minute. As he watched the last of the invading troops disappear into the mass of houses, he himself crossed the road walking at a brisk pace into the scheme. He could feel now why his friends wanted to be hooligans. This was great. Not a gang fight. Not really, in as much as there would probably be no fighting, but this was not the same as usual.

166

There may not be contact and yes, all that was happening was one gang chasing another, but this was different. The small gang was chasing the bigger one. Not only that but they were invading their scheme. And why did they have the gall to do this? Because he had shown them that if you've got the bottle, you won't be stopped. At this moment he felt like the hero. He'd never before even felt like part of the group. Perhaps he'd been convincing himself that he wasn't interested. Today, however, he'd proved to himself that he was.

37

Colin still had the ability to surprise. Today Martin stood watching in virtual awe of his friend as he extolled his will on the growing collective. A gang of Broughty Ferry, Fife, assorted casuals and hangers-on who seemed to be joining the group. A little bit drunk, a little bit stoned, a lot pumped up from the afternoon's victory in Mill o' Mains, Colin had turned into a different person altogether.

As for the gang, grown now to about 80, two factions were evident. Those who had been there in the afternoon, recalled with vigour and added arms and legs their part in the victory, always giving credit to the fearless nutter who was prepared to take the whole hundred on himself. Others who did not attend, who were not necessarily from either Fife or Broughty Ferry; rather, the usual limpet types who hung around wherever they deemed appropriate, listened intently to the gross exaggerations being told. Happy to be part of the successful gang. Occasionally pointing out today's icon: 'Aye, there he is there, right mad bastard, eh.' Recalling other times – sheer works of fiction – when they had been in attendance and Colin had done something similar: 'Oh aye, that boy's no' faird o' nae cunt.'

As that gang strolled, bounced, swaggered and paraded around the main streets of Dundee's city centre. A gang comprising mainly of people who would normally be terrified at the prospect of populating these streets. Not on a Saturday night. Not for fear of the usual gang gatherings. Taking advantage, it would seem, of the fact that a lot of the gangs seemed to be depleted, their members off on holiday, most likely. There had been some small gang presence in the town when they arrived but the buoyant PPC, encouraged by their earlier success, relieved of their usual trepidation, had managed to disperse them quickly. No violence, just the usual 'chase me' games. Intrigue provided more by the wonder of what would happen if one of the pursued were actually caught, than the actual act of interception. Tonight, this gang ran the show.

Many of these factors acted as irritants to Colin. He knew that most of this mob would flee at the first sign of trouble. He wondered who they were, where they had been that afternoon when he had been putting his neck on the line. From time to time he even wondered why these people felt they had the right to be there walking, celebrating, chanting with the Posh People's Collective.

Not however letting these feelings get to him. For tonight they were not the Posh People's Collective. Colin neither felt nor wanted to be considered posh. Tonight the chant was the war cry of Colin's choosing. As this gang marauded around Dundee waiting for the inevitable interception of Tayside Police; possibly the only thing that could stop them, they chanted their anthem.'ZULU, ZULU! ZULU, ZULU!'

THE COSMOS CENTRE

38

Martin was late. Should have been in Caskies on St Andrews High Street 20 minutes ago. Colin was out of prison. Released two days earlier but had spent all of that time with his parents and Carrie. It was Friday now though and time for a night out. Martin actually hadn't seen his friend for about two months. Although in the first couple of weeks he had visited frequently, there quickly became an undiscussed agreement between them that Martin's visits should stop. No falling out, Colin had intimated that there wasn't much to talk about during his visits and Martin had taken it that Colin would have preferred just to wait until he was out. Said that he wanted to keep all visits for Carrie and particularly his parents. He really had to straighten things out with them.

In actual fact, Martin had been glad for the excuse. He'd found the whole atmosphere of going to visit in Perth awkward. Both of them understood that chatting over a bare prison visitors' room table just wasn't much fun. So, now he was out and waiting in Caskies. For some reason though, Martin couldn't just go along to see Colin without first having a couple of joints and a few vodkas. He didn't know why but he just had a few butterflies in the stomach and felt strangely nervous about meeting him again.

Martin had heard a few murmurs about Colin's time in prison and wondered if the experience would have changed him dramatically. Throughout the time the two boys had known one another, Colin had certainly changed. Attitude, confidence and manner were all definitely different since they had first met but Martin always considered himself to know his friend well. Now though, he considered that the last three months may have caused changes that may even change that familiarity. Having a drink and skinning up joints in his flat may have made Martin late but it was needed.

When Martin walked into Caskies it was still early in the evening and the bar was quiet. Colin was sitting on the comfortable sofa at the back of the bar and not alone. Scott Henderson was sitting directly opposite and Martin cursed himself for letting Scotty get there first. Carrie was there and another man that Colin recognised but hadn't met. All at once, Martin realised that the stories he had heard about Colin in prison were probably true.

Martin wished that he could have another drink before going over. If he was nervous about meeting Colin then meeting the company he was in knotted his stomach. It was time to turn on the charm and Martin knew he could do that but recently, he'd felt that turning on the charm was a lot more effective and easy, once he'd had a few good drinks. No time to stop at the bar though as his friend that he hadn't seen for months was sitting waiting for him and sitting directly opposite was a man that Martin knew it didn't do to keep waiting. Lawrie Gordon.

Martin walked over to the back of the bar. It was Colin who was first to notice him. Colin stood and greeted his friend by walking over the short remaining distance to give him a hug. 'Martin mate, good tae see ya, where have you been man?'

The question may have seemed inquisitive but the tone, completely convivial and loud enough so that everyone could hear. This was just a friendly greeting and Martin could tell straight away that nothing much had changed between them over the last two months.

Carrie also looked happy to see him. 'Alright Martin?'

'Aye Carrie, no' bad!'

Everything seemed to be back to normal, except of course the presence of the man sitting opposite them at the table. Colin gestured toward Gordon.

'Martin mate, there's somebody you should meet. This is Lawrie Gordon, he…' Colin paused as if to get the next thing he said exactly correct. 'He helped me out when ah was in the jail, eh?'

'Aye Colin, ah know who Lawrie Gordon is!'

Martin couldn't stifle his grin as he offered his hand out to Gordon. Gordon gripped his hand and got up just a little into a neat crouch as he acknowledged him. Martin sat down and immediately noticed that the 20 minutes that his colleagues had already had waiting on him had allowed them to almost finish their drinks. This was all the excuse he needed to buy them and, more importantly, himself a drink.

'Right will ah get them in then?'

'No, not for me Martin, ah'm not about to get in the way of the lads' night out!'

Carrie turned to Colin and kissed him clearly without any regard to anyone watching, such seemed her relief that she was now able to. As she got up she turned to Gordon. 'Aw, it was really nice to meet you Lawrie.'

She extended her hand to accept a shake and Martin strongly doubted that he would grip her delicate hand the way he did his, still slightly throbbing as it was. She placed her hand on Martin's shoulder. 'See ya later Martin mate, try to look after him tonight eh?'

As she left, she looked back at Colin the smile on her face displaying all the signs of a girl who hadn't spent a minute away from her love for the last two days and couldn't wait until they were united again.

Martin thought of Natalie. If he'd gone to London with her, would he now be in a pub looking at her and not needing a drink to be able to relax with her? She must have hated it that he hadn't even said goodbye to her at the station. In all the time since she hadn't contacted him and he didn't have the nerve to contact her. The last time they had seen one another Martin had been walking away from her on Broughty Ferry beach. He doubted that could ever happen to Carrie and Colin. If she'd decided to go to the end of the earth, Colin would follow and similarly if Colin had decided the move.

'Martin, mate!'

Martin snapped out of the dope-induced fug that he had slipped into to see Colin trying to attract his attention. He didn't doubt that he had probably missed his first attempts.

'Oh aye, Colin mate, sorry about that, away in a wee world of my own there. So, what are we having?'

39

The Cosmos Centre was a one-storey, modern white building that looked completely out of place close to the traditional centre of St Andrews. Flanked on one side by the grounds of the ancient abbey ruins, the other by the 18th-century university buildings and historic shopping precinct, it just didn't seem to blend in. A community centre, it was the venue normally used for activities for the old and disabled. Job clubs for the town's unemployed and youth clubs for the town's soon-to-be-adults. It played host to occasions such as whist drives and jumble sales.

It might have been considered a strange place to hold St Andrew's first organised house music club night outside of the university union, but not to Lara Borland. To Lara, the fact that it had a large hall with a stage and importantly, a licensed bar made it ideal. Lara was an enterprising type. She was in on most deals it would seem and for those who asked, was usually able to get most things for a price. Be they knock-off or narcotic. Usually on Fridays, the small but tight knit group of house music and ecstasy devotees based in St Andrews would turn to Lara to provide them with tickets for the popular Rhumba Club, but this weekend Lara was taking advantage of the fact that the club had recently lost its venue. The organisers had fallen out with the management of the Perth club that they were using. A temporary halt to the festivities, she was sure, but in the absence of the Rhumba, Lara was sure that not only Fife but the whole area including Dundee, Perthshire, Angus and beyond would be full of young people looking for an alternative.

In the Cosmos, she thought she had the answer. Even the name seemed right. She hadn't had much time, only learning last week about the Rhumba management's troubles in Perth but the short lead time wasn't to perturb her. She knew the DJs. Any number of people who would have her arm off for a chance of playing to a crowd on a Friday night. No money needed. She could get the PA, needn't cost much either. The hire of the Cosmos and bar staff, hardly a dent to her expected earnings. Couple of bouncers for the door? She knew just the two people to ask. Getting the crowd? A little too late to be printing tickets and flyers so she considered the old-fashioned method of word of mouth to be just as effective, if not better.

Lara began early in the week telling all that she knew to pass on the message and wasn't surprised near the end of the week when people were approaching her in the students' union to tell her about what was happening at the Cosmos on

Friday. The crowd was coming, now one more essential element. The drugs. No chance was she taking any in herself but she could contact those likely to be interested in punting them inside.

Martin took the call on the Wednesday. Clearly Martin and Lara were going to know one another. So very different yet so much the same, they had both been at Madras together. In the same year, but from around the second year had seldom been in the same class. Lara was a high academic achiever, she had eight high O-Grade passes at the time Martin was joining 5L. Not for her though; Lara stayed on and after two more years at school had six Highers, only two below the A mark. This was enough to see her accepted to the engineering course at St Andrews University. She'd breezed through that course. She'd now returned from her year off travelling the world and was into her Masters year, spending most of her time there helping the undergraduates understand the nuances of mathematics and physics.

She may have had different ideas from Martin with regard to ambition and academia but they certainly shared some traits when it came to social skills. Always popular, Lara had the confidence and cock-suredness that made her stand out in any crowd. A natural entrepreneur, she also seemed always to be at the heart of any deals that were being done and wasn't afraid to embrace the less-than-legal activities of dealing drugs and fencing goods. Although always, it would seem, a slight distance away from the actual hands-on activities. Not from one of the more wealthy families from within St Andrews, she simply did whatever she could to get through her education with a level of comfort.

It was the way that she carried herself made her attractive. She was a little overweight but she was OK with that. She wasn't fat, after all, and she was pretty. Although the company she kept both at university and in the clubs may have been more classically beautiful, it was her that people seemed to be drawn to. She had delicate features and the rare combination of clear smooth skin and dark red hair that whether worn up, down, straight or curly always seemed to suit her look.

Tonight she stood outside the Cosmos centre defending herself from the December chill in a three-quarter-length gents Valentino coat, greeting all those that she considered her guests. Albeit that most of these guests were paying her to be there. Not however the four characters now entering the car park, Colin, Martin, Scott Henderson and another slightly older man that she wasn't familiar with who were now making their way into the Cosmos. They wouldn't be paying though. These guys certainly were guests and Lara made a beeline straight for them.

'Martin, Colin, Scott, how are you?'

Lara greeted Colin and Scott and was introduced to the man called Lawrie with equal warmth but was clearly now elated to be in the company of Martin.

'Alright sex god?'

Lara moved close and embraced Martin in a way that was clearly more sexual than convivial. The two were not playing their cards close to their chests.

'You got the necessary?'

Her eyes were full of the usual hope of people expecting ecstasy.

Martin nodded towards Scott.

'Oh yeah! Anyone asks you, you send them straight to Scott.'

Martin smiled and looked deep into Lara's eyes. He'd clearly sampled the goods.

'For now though, you'll be needin' these!'

Martin reached down, opened out her hand and placed a couple of tiny white discs in her palm. Lara let out a slight whimper of delight.

'Ooh, I could get used to this!'

She looked round to see the large queue of familiar faces filing into the Cosmos Centre with Martin still holding onto her hand and she knew she was right. She could get used to this.

40

By nine o'clock the Cosmos was full to capacity and it was unfortunate that the bouncers had to start turning people away at the door. Lara was certain though that everybody that should be there was there and, with the majority of the 400 or so having paid £7 entry, she knew this would be a profitable night.

The crowd were every bit as up for it as they usually were for the more organised club nights, the music was good, the PA loud and everyone bouncing in time. The dance floor was mobbed. The walkways were moving with people dancing. Getting from one place to another was difficult. There were screams when the music merited them. Sweat-covered and smile-wearing people were dancing for all their worth. Had there been rafters, people would have been hanging from them.

Chris Ellis was glad he had arrived early. This night was going to be profitable for him as well. Chris was one of Dundee's well recognised wide boys. A jovial and chirpy sort, he seemed always to be present at any club night worth mentioning. He had hung around with the casuals but had always been one of the ones that did it for the fashion rather than fighting and was glad that the club scene was giving him more of an opportunity to get involved. In his early twenties, he was already sporting the paunch and receding hairline of someone ten years older but masked the look by always wearing the trendiest clothes and a cap to hide his baldness.

Chris had come to the Cosmos that night with his best of allies, Bob Storrie. Chris and Bob always seemed to be seen together and sharing a similar look as they did could have passed for brothers. Until they spoke that was. Whereas Chris spoke in an excited manner barely ever falling below almost shouting volume, jokey and welcoming, Bob talked in an almost monotone rhythm and hardly ever appeared to have any enthusiasm for what he said. Many heard Bob talk and drew the conclusion that he was a bit slow or stupid. Chris knew that Bob wasn't stupid though. Capable of droll quick wit at the drop of a hat, he seemed to be able to humiliate anyone that he felt needed to with one throwaway remark. Whether that was behind their back or to their face.

Bob was also not afraid of violence like Chris was. When they were both casuals Bob was always a lot more willing to run into any opposing mob while Chris would generally be looking for a way to get out of it. This was one of the main attractions for Chris. Bob could protect him were protection needed, and on a night like this protection may indeed be required.

***

Scott Henderson had a money change bag full of ecstasy in which Gordon had assured him were 300 pills. On a night like tonight with around 400 revellers, all with the same thing in mind, he was sure that he could sell them all. He'd sold them before but never so many. Then never had the plan of attack been so well thought out. Every time he sold around ten he was to take the money to either Martin and Colin and give it to them. Under no circumstances were they to carry any large quantities of the drug.

Scott was also told to keep them in the bag until sold and not to have any loose in his pockets. If anyone slightly irregular asked for anything they were to be told to sling their hook. The bag was also to be kept relatively loose and easy to access so that at the moment when either the hall was raided or someone identified themselves as police, he would get rid of it straight away. Simply by dropping the bag on the floor he was assured he'd get away with it. Only if he had loose pills or large amounts of cash would the police have anything substantial and Gordon assured him that even if caught, then as long as he claimed that a bag found on the floor had nothing to do with him, then the police could do nothing. Gordon certainly seemed to know what he was talking about. The plan was sound, however, Scott's reckoning on the demand he would have was a little less sure.

After around an hour Gordon checked with Scott Henderson. 'How are we doing, are they all away yet?'

Scott looked out over the crowd, his disappointment clearly evident. 'Well, naw, ah reckon ah've only sold around 50.'

They looked around the hall. Hands were in the air, sweat matting the hair and clothes of everyone moving on the dance floor, those populating the fringes either hugging one another or cooling themselves down with bottles of water.

'Well, somebody's sellin' them,' he gave a shrug of the shoulders that was both understanding and apologetic.

'Nah look, it's no' your fault Scott. It's not like you can advertise, is it?'

***

Chris Ellis was jumping around the Cosmos centre enjoying the music and clearly enjoying the effects of his drugs. His ample frame bouncing off everyone surrounding him but no one cared about that. In fact it would seem that every three or four people he bumped into one of them had the question for him: 'Got any E mate?'

Of course he had! Plenty of them and oh my god they were good. Pink New Yorkers in fact were Chris's recommendation of the best ecstasy money could buy. He had walked into the Cosmos that night with 500 of them secreted about his person and, save the ones he and Andy had taken complete ownership of, were selling like the proverbial still warm sweet baked products.

Sure he'd got them from probably the most dangerous person he knew but given that that person only asked for £15 back per tablet, Chris knew that all night he could sell every last one of them for £20. Unless of course to a girl that he thought he liked the look of because, let's face it, tonight he could afford to be Mr Generous to a whole assortment of beauties and one or two going away gratis wouldn't break the bank. Right at this point with a change bag half full of ecstasy and a bumbag stuffed with cash, Chris felt unbeatable.

***

'That's yer man there!' Martin pointed out Chris Ellis to Lawrie Gordon. He felt kind of bad about it. 'Ah think it's Pink New Yorkers he's punting. Cannae really compete wi' them!' Gordon looked at Martin and made no real attempt to hide his annoyance at that statement.

So Martin had led Gordon to him. He felt bad about it. He knew Chris from hanging around in Dundee. He knew that Chris was basically harmless and a real fish out of water when it come to the likes of Lawrie Gordon asking about him. He knew that Gordon wasn't happy losing business to someone like Chris, especially on what should be considered his territory. But then when someone like Gordon asks you to find out who's behind it when clearly there's an awful lot of ecstasy being sold then you don't want to say you don't know. Sure he felt bad about it, particularly given that he himself had bought a couple for him and Lara earlier in the night. He had to do that though because, well, he was right, you can't compete with Pink New Yorkers. He *did* feel bad but when it came to it there really was a limit of how bad you could feel about something when you're as high as can be expected so for now, he was happy to let the feeling pass.

'Maybe you should chill out mate, get over there tender your twenty pounds, get yourself sorted, have a good time.'

A huge grin broke out on Martin's face. Amused at the idea of Lawrie Gordon relaxing from his image and embracing rave culture but mainly just glad that he had managed to just think that and not say it out loud.

* * *

Lara cruised around the club feeling like temporary royalty. Everyone in the room seemed to know who she was and were quick to express their gratitude for putting on the night for them. She could for the moment, readily disregard the fact that that she was making a lot of money in the process. The important thing was the feeling of complete popularity. So many people hugging her and wishing her well, it took her a few seconds to realise that the figure now holding her was Martin. She looked into his eyes and as recognition hit her she smiled broadly. 'You OK Martin, enjoying yourself?'

Martin surveyed her face. A little dishevelled maybe, certainly the hair and make up were not in the same state of care they were when they'd met in the car park but when she smiled like that, good god she was cute.

'Ah'm doin' fine Lara.' Martin paused and crooked his own smile, deliberately in a way that he thought would match Lara's cuteness but introduce a bit of rough to his look. 'You're fuckin' amazing, you know that?'

'Well, ah try my best!'

Martin laughed a little and then, not for the first time that night he kissed her. This time though at the height of another ecstasy rush the serotonin seemed to swell in just the right place and the feeling of complete exhilaration filled him. Martin pulled Lara's body in closer to him and felt as if the two were almost beginning to merge. He pushed his right leg in between Lara's knees and thrust his hips inwards as he pulled her close. He could feel her crotch rub against the top of his leg as his now solid prick pressed hard against her hip.

They broke off the kiss and looked at one another with equal intensity breathing out hard as they did so. The problem with having an insatiable horn in such a public place was clear in both their expressions. Martin surveyed her face again and watched as the look of complete frustrated intensity seemed to slowly morph into one of mischievous delight.

'You know Martin, there is a staff office here.' She reached into her purse, pulled out a key and dangled it in front of Martin's face. 'Shall we?'

41

It was bitterly cold outside the Cosmos Centre. A fact being largely ignored by the crowd now leaving, as they congregated in the car park. Still high as kites wondering where they could go to finish off the night with a few joints. Of course Lara knew just the place and was busy inviting her select few people back to a students' residence. She knew the party would extend long into Saturday morning. Chief amongst her prospective guests of course was Martin and his friends. Well, Martin would just have to be there and wouldn't it just be a bonus if Scott still had pills left. She had approached them at the opening to the car park and with her usual chirpiness and bolstered by the enthusiasm of her hit she invited them along in a manner that suggested that they had no choice.

But for Lawrie Gordon, there was still business to look after. He began to issue his orders. 'Scott, can you make your way straight to Lara's place. From what she says there should really be quite a few people there and some opportunity to get rid of some more pills but don't whatever you do, sell anything while outdoors, you understand?'

'No problem Lawrie!' Scott was actually enjoying the role of salesman.

'Martin, I need you to create a diversion.'

Martin looked puzzled and not simply because of the amount of drugs he'd taken. 'A diversion?'

'A diversion,' Gordon put his hand on Martin's shoulder and moved a little closer to be better understood. 'Martin, you have what we call the gift of the gab and you're resourceful. Which makes you the most valuable person here right now.'

Martin could feel another rush of serotonin.

'What we need you to do is to attract the attention o' the police away from what Colin and me are doing. Not sure how but ah think you'll find a way.'

He turned to Colin. 'Colin, you come with me, we're the muscle end of the business I'm afraid. Does everybody know what they're doing?'

Everyone answered yes but in actual fact Martin had no idea how he was going to keep the police busy in one place without getting arrested.

42

Shaun Maliburn was, Martin thought, a bit of a strange character. Martin knew him from the club nights that he always seemed to be at. He lived in Edinburgh but was at every Rhumba Club that Martin could remember. Martin noticed Shaun, looking lost among the crowd. What could he do to create his diversion? Shaun looked weird. Maybe he could help.

He bounded over in the strange way that Shaun tended to bound: 'You alright Martin? Any parties on?

The thing about Shaun Maliburn was that if he was at the club, Martin would remember. Not just because of his outlandish appearance. Whereas most at the clubs would sport designer gear, Shaun designed, made and wore his own clothes for club nights. Far from rags however, these were stylish garments mainly in black leather with metal decorations, which he branded as 'Mally Clothing'.

Girls' clothing mainly but a lot of the club scene had begun to cotton on to Mally's clothes and even that night, a few of the girls were wearing Mally Clothing bustiers, leather trousers or hotpants.

Martin noticed these things. Natalie used to love Mally Clothing. Mally was alright! He was one of the gang. Martin couldn't really see how he could help now though.

'Don't know Mally, mate. Bound to be something. Ah'll let you know.'

He probably would take Mally with him to the party but for now he had business to tend to. Other than those led away by Lara, everyone seemed to be at a loss as to where to go next. This was the usual. A crowd would always hang around after such events hoping to be invited to some party or another. Looking after this crowd, there appeared to be only two flustered looking policemen standing beside their van. Usually the police would wait a little while waiting for most of the crowd to disperse before strongly encouraging the remaining stragglers to follow suit.

Tonight, however, only two police in the area and a complete lack of will among people to leave seemed to make that plan unworkable. The older of the two policemen talked into his shoulder receiver, calling for backup but seemed frustrated. Martin took this to mean that his request was not being granted. This didn't help Martin much as what he wanted was to attract as much police attention to the area as possible.

Starting a fight might work but he just felt too good to be tussling with anybody and knew that any possible arrest and a night in the cells would not be the end of the night he was looking for. Martin considered another approach. He walked over to the younger policeman, pulling out a cigarette from a packet as he approached.

'Got a light mate?'

The policeman took a few seconds to register that Martin was talking to him.

'What, eh, no!'

The policeman's attention returned to the crowd. Martin held up the packet and offered the policeman a cigarette.

'Want one?'

The policeman looked at Martin holding out his cigarettes and screwed up his face.

'What are you talkin' about? Ah'm no' here to be smoking fags wi' you, ah'm kind o' busy.'

Martin nodded his head, turned back to look at the crowd and nonchalantly leaned on the van. 'Aye, ah can see that!'

The policeman looked Martin up and down, lost in concentration for a few moments. 'Sir, can you please stop leaning on the van, it is police property!'

Martin snatched one hand away from the van and raised the other in an apologetic gesture.

'Oh Jeez aye, sorry man no offence like!' Martin smiled. 'What am ah like, eh? No offence he says.'

Martin paused and pulled a mocked worried expression. 'It's no' an offence like is it?'

The policeman shook his head in despair. He knew when somebody was as high as the empire state.

'No sir, it's not an offence, now I think you should get off home now!'

'Aw mate nah, dinnae be like that! Ah'm just tryin tae be friendly and aw that, eh?' Martin thrust out his right hand.

'Ah'm Martin, nice tae meet ya.'

The older officer pushed past. He wore three stripes on his shoulder and looked decidedly more serious than his colleague.

'Right son, what do you want?'

'Well, ah dinnae want anything mate, just saying hello, eh?'

The older policeman raised a gloved hand and pointed up the street away from the Cosmos Centre.

'Right pal, you've made your point now get up the fuckin' road!'

'Whoah, hey soldier, calm down.'

Martin raised his voice slightly to attract the attention of the people close to him.

'What's with the attitude man? Ah never swore at you.'

The older policeman pushed his younger colleague aside.

'Listen prick, either get up the fuckin' road or you're goin' in the back of the van – comprende?'

There was a murmur from the crowd, Martin knew he was attracting attention.

'Oh hey, wait a minute, what's the story here? You're threatenin' tae lift me for saying hello. Out o' order like! What's the charge exactly? Possession o' a positive attitude with intent to use it? Being sociable without due care and attention?'

Martin could hear a section of the onlookers laughing. More and more people seemed to be drawn to the commotion.

The police sergeant probably realised that arresting Martin might not be such a good idea.

As the policeman wavered, Martin grew in confidence. Lawrie Gordon was right. He did have the gift for the gab and tonight he was on the ball like never before. What was more he was doing the job. Causing a scene.

'This is typical man! All these people work hard all week. Paying taxes, you know.'

The police sergeant winced. He'd obviously had the 'we pay your wages' speech before. Martin decided to steer clear of that one. He waved his hand behind him to draw attention to the crowd.

'These people deserve to enjoy themselves at the weekend and far from trying to stop them, you guys should be serving them and protecting their right tae dae that.'

A thought then jumped into Martin's racing mind and even though he knew it was corny and wasn't at all sure that he knew it off by heart he decided to recite a familiar passage.

'Just what is it that you think we want to do? We wanna be free to do what we wanna do and we wanna get loaded and we wanna have a good time.'

Martin was sure that he saw the younger officer smile. Maybe he knew what Martin was talking about. The sergeant certainly had no idea. 'Look pal...' but Martin didn't let him continue, he could hear the whole crowd behind him egging him on. Martin raised his voice.

'That's what we're gonna do, we're gonna have a good time. We're gonna have a party!'

Martin heard a vaguely familiar sound and turned round to see Shaun Maliburn standing on the Cosmos Centre car park wall. Yes. You'd always remember if Mally was at the club. The main reason that you would remember Mally being at a club night was not however his strange appearance; rather, that he would always bring along his saxophone and when the music stopped at the end of the night, Mally would begin to play, giving the partygoers a few minutes of live sax music to wind down to. As far as Martin could remember though, Mally had only ever done this within the venue but tonight it was obvious that he had picked up on the party vibe outside the Cosmos and he was giving it some on the car park perimeter dyke.

All at once a cheer went up as everyone turned around to face the bizarre character playing his saxophone on the wall. Hands went up, feet started moving and not a person was ready to move from outside the Cosmos Centre. The young policeman looked on aghast at the sight of 200 or so young and clearly high partygoers jumping and whooping on the ancient street as the saxophonist whipped them into a frenzy. The sergeant was clearly less surprised or for that matter impressed. He leaned over to the radio attached just below his shoulder.

'Charlie Echo Two to control, we need a little more assistance outside the Cosmos Centre, public disturbance in progress.'

Martin looked around and considered that it might be fun to stay and join in. He looked at the police officers and had overheard the radio message. He knew his job was done here and that within minutes all beat police attention would be concentrated in this area. It might be fun to join in but Martin was curious about something else. Exactly what was the muscle side of the business?

43

Colin and Lawrie Gordon had followed Chris Ellis and Bob Storrie around to St Andrews High Street apparently un-noticed by either of them. Gordon checked up and down the street. At this time on Saturday morning it appeared to be deserted. It was important that no one was around in case something more serious than a warning needed to be meted out to Ellis and Storrie. They were just about to get into their car when Gordon decided to stop them

'Here mate hold on a minute!'

Ellis turned his attention away from the car lock to study the two men approaching.

'Aye, can ah help like?'

Ellis noted that the two men were trendily dressed and thought he knew how he could help them.

'Alright boys you after a few pills like?'

Gordon and Colin shared a quick glance at one another and stopped a matter of yards away from Ellis.

Gordon answered simply, 'No!'

Ellis stood up straight and looked at Gordon and Colin. They were dressed trendily but seemed a little bit older, more straight-laced and certainly more serious than your typical ecstasy users.

There was a silence as all parties just looked around one another. Ellis began to panic, he now knew exactly what this was. He looked down at the car lock. The key was there, the fob dangling beside the door. Ellis began to consider whether he could get into the car, get it started and get away before the men could grab him. It seemed unlikely but he knew he had to get away. He looked over to Bob who had a similarly intense look in his eyes. Both Colin and Lawrie Gordon could see the panic in Chris's movement.

'Mate, look at me!' Gordon attempted to attract Chris's attention. Chris turned slowly to look at Gordon, he now looked completely terrified and Gordon knew why. 'It's alright mate, we're not police.'

The panic appeared to die immediately from Chris's demeanour. His hand raised to his chest and he shook his head slightly.

'Fuckin' hell mate, whut are you trein' tae dae tae me? Fuckin' shat mysel' there.'

Chris looked over at his friend a little surprised to see that he still looked like he was in fight or flight mode. He looked back at Colin and Lawrie Gordon. 'Well, eh'm no' trein' tae be cheeky like but who the fuck are ya?'

Gordon answered first, he knew that Colin would understand that his name would have more relevance. 'Ah'm Lawrie Gordon, have you heard o' me mate?'

Gordon was surprised to see a large grin appear on Chris's face.

'Aye mate, you're Lawrie Gordon. Quite a coincidence really cos' ah'm fuckin' Flash Gordon!'

Chris turned to see Bob's reaction, he felt sure he would appreciate that one. Bob's eyes widened and he shook his head. Chris couldn't work out why his friend looked so concerned because he knew this couldn't be Lawrie Gordon he was speaking to. He turned back to Gordon.

'Nah mate, Lawrie Gordon's in jail eh? Everybody kens that!'

Gordon smirked as he appeared to consider what Chris was saying. Chris thought that he had just made the checkmate move. Gordon didn't feel the need to explain himself.

'Chris, mate this is serious!'

He may have been baffled by Gordon knowing his name but Chris had already decided that this was getting boring and turned to get in his car. Bob still stood rigid at the other door, still shaking his head, he seemed more concerned then ever.

'Chris, that is Lawrie Gordon, eh?'

Chris realised that Bob would be right. He looked completely panicked by the situation and he tended to know these things. Chris's heart sank into the pit of his stomach, the complete high of the ecstasy he had taken disappeared to be replaced by sheer terror. If he was frightened earlier by the idea that he had been stopped by the police then the fact that Lawrie Gordon was now standing behind him filled him with dread. What could he want? Why was he interested in him? It had to be the drugs but Chris had one major concern worrying him. What the fuck was he thinking about taking the piss out of his name? Chris looked at Gordon and the other man that had stopped them. They looked completely untroubled by the situation.

'Ah'm really sorry man, ah thought you were in jail, eh? Ah honestly didnae mean to be cheeky. Ah thought you were some joker trein' tae pull a fast one.'

Gordon and Colin said nothing. Chris's mind was racing as he began to consider whether he was saying the right thing or not. There was a short silence before

Gordon decided to get down to business.

'No' really bothered about you being cheeky, I'm a bit more concerned about you thinking you can just come to St Andrews and sell your drugs without any sort of say-so.'

Chris swallowed hard, he was beginning to think of the option of the key in the car door but Gordon wasn't finished.

'What are ya, trying tae take advantage because you thought I was in jail?'

'Naw, naw, eh wasnae thinking that. Eh just didnae really think there wis a problem, eh?'

Chris was panicking as the seriousness of the situation began to sink in. Lawrie Gordon was known as someone who was capable of brutality to get his way and who was the other guy he was with?

Huge big guy who hadn't spoke yet, he clearly wasn't brought along to enhance the conversation.

Lawrie Gordon moved closer to Chris Ellis. Chris flinched backwards but there was nowhere to go.

'Somebody has been taking advantage of you, mate.'

Chris tried to consider what Gordon meant but his drug-addled state wasn't helping.

Gordon was within feet now of Chris. He lowered his voice. 'Who are you here for?'

'What?' Chris had no idea what he was being asked.

'You thought I was in jail mate but I'm guessin' that whoever sent you through here wi' the drugs knew fine that I was out. Who was it?'

Chris considered what he was being asked. Crossing Digger Stewart wasn't a great option but the Digger wasn't here and Lawrie Gordon was. Chris thought that there may be a way out of this but he would have to play his cards right.

'What d'ya mean?'

'I'm no' stupid mate, when somebody like you turns up and is able to supply a whole club with ecstasy, you're clearly not working off your own back.'

'No, ah'm no'.'

'No, I know you're not but what I want to know is who you're here for?'

Chris looked around everybody and decided that appearing pathetic may be the best tack to employ. 'Ah'm no' eh just, ah cannae really tell, like it's no' that easy.'

Gordon raised his hand in an indication that Chris should be quiet. 'This is no' really a choice matter here. You either tell me who you're working for or…'

Gordon paused, looked Chris Ellis up and down and then looked over to Colin, using his prop to maximum effect. 'Pity help ya!'

Chris could feel his knees begin to weaken. He had no idea what would happen either now or when he got back to Dundee but he was sure that it couldn't be much worse than the harm that the big quiet lad was about to inflict. 'It's Digger Stewart!'

Gordon smiled when he heard the name. This was just too easy. The reaction of Colin however was more of a surprise to Chris Ellis. Colin leaned forward and blurted out the name in laughter. 'The Digger? Holy shit mate, that's perfect.' Time for a little payback he thought.

Gordon considered Colin's reaction and could tell what he was thinking. He placed his hand on Chris's shoulder. Chris flinched even though he saw that Gordon was backing off a little. 'Tell ya what mate, Colin here has a bit of business with Digger Stewart so I'll let you two talk.'

Colin assumed the interrogator position. 'Right then Chris, how many pills do you hae left there?'

Chris felt the bag in his pocket, he didn't feel like messing Colin around. 'No' that many, why?' Chris immediately regretted asking the question.

'Ah'll tell you why mate, because if they're the Digger's then they belong to me now!' Colin held out his hand to accept the content of Chris's pocket.

'Oh no, no you cannae dae that!'

Colin was sure he could now see tears begin to well up in Chris Ellis' eyes.

44

Martin walked around on to the High Street and stopped when he saw what was happening. Colin was talking to Chris Ellis with Lawrie Gordon apparently just looking on as a spectator. He wondered who out of the pair was in charge and then thought back to Lawrie Gordon issuing orders outside of the Cosmos. Martin walked over to get closer. He wanted to hear what Colin was saying.

'The money as well mate!'

Chris Ellis hesitated. No way could he go back to the Digger with nothing.

Colin leaned forward and stooped so that he was level with Chris. 'You dinnae know how much that fucker owes me, now give me his fuckin' money!'

Chris Ellis spluttered and bubbled for a while before finally detaching his bumbag belt and handing it over. The severity of what was happening wasn't lost on him and he was crying like a baby.

'There's a way out for you Chris, you know that?'

Chris looked up, it was obvious that he knew what would happen when the Digger found out. 'No… no.'

'Oh aye Chris, there is.' Colin tried to use a comforting tone. 'Ah'm assumin' you dinnae hae money to pay him back right?'

'No.'

'If you try to run from him, your life will be shite and then he'll get you. You know that don't ya?'

'Eh think… eh'

'Then all you need to do is go back and tell him what happened. You'll owe him some money for a while but you'll find it eh?'

'Eh could… maybe.'

'If you tell him that Colin Nichols took it all from you then it'll be me in trouble and no' you eh?'

'No, eh… eh dunno.'

'Trust me Chris, this is your way out. You blame me and you'll be alright.'

Colin doubted that Chris would be alright but he considered that he probably would be stupid enough to go back to the Digger and tell him what had happened and that was the important thing. He wanted the Digger to know that he'd stole his money back, with interest, and he wanted him to know that he wasn't afraid to do so.

Chris Ellis got back into his car and Colin wasn't sure that he hadn't pissed himself before he got in. Bob Storrie at least shared a glance with Colin and Lawrie Gordon that suggested that he wasn't happy. Hinted that he didn't consider it over. He had a bit more balls than his friend but it was just for show. Colin knew that.

They were allowed to leave empty handed but unhurt. Gordon again took over and had a quick conference with Colin. Gordon placed a bag, which looked like it contained around 50 small pink disks in Martin's hand.

'OK, you go back to Lara's party and give these to Scott Henderson. He'll know what to do. Oh, and remember the rule, you see the police, you drop them and deny all knowledge. How much money have you got?'

Martin felt in his pocket but before he could answer, Gordon was on his case. 'Give it to Colin and don't worry, your pay tonight's a good deal.'

Gordon turned to leave and beckoned over Colin. After a few steps he seemed to think of something else and turned back to Martin. 'You were supposed to be causing a diversion.'

Martin pointed back towards the Cosmos. 'Oh aye but…'

Gordon cut him off short. 'No buts Martin! If I tell you to do something then I need you to do it, OK?'

Martin wanted to explain but it was kind of a long story and Gordon didn't hang around to hear it.

Colin came over to take Martin's money.

'Colin mate, ah did the diversion, eh?'

Colin withdrew slightly. He was surprised that Martin would feel the need to explain to him.

'Ah know you did mate! Ah know that.'

***

The trip to where the party was took Gordon's car back past the Cosmos Centre. There were no drugs in the car so there was no problem going back that way. Gordon hoped that Martin wouldn't be stupid and go back the same way. Colin knew he wouldn't.

The car turned on to the road leading past the Cosmos Centre. The scene was pandemonium. All of the crowd that had been in the Centre now appeared to be in the car park jigging along to Mally's saxophone playing. There were two police vans parked on the road outside lights flashing, with around 12 officers gathered in a conference apparently working out how to handle the situation.

Gordon was clearly amused by the sight. 'What the hell is this?'

Colin smiled, he knew exactly what this was. 'This'll be Martin's diversion!'

193

STREET FIGHTING YEARS

45

'Eh mind o' that day up in fuckin' Mill o' Mains though man! That wiz fuckin' mental aye? Tellin ya' couldnae've been mare than, whut thirty fehv o' whu? We pure fuckin' ran aboot fuckin', a hunner in thirty o they Mill o' Mains cunts though aye? We pure just ran doon the brae though eh? No thinking likes. See when eh got right intae there though, we ah pure split up eh? Eh runs inta this couple o' wideos. Must've fancied thir chances eh, pure wahks up tae us thinkin' thi wir gonnae do us. Fuckin' wirnae really payin' attention that eh hud a fuckin' pole ahent ma back. Only managed tae git the one o' thum likes but fucked him right ower the head wi' it.'

Colin raised his hand to his forehead. An involuntary physical reaction as he tried hard not to show his true feelings about what he was hearing. He didn't know if he'd ever met him before but the shell-suit-clad teenage reprobate that was telling the story didn't look like anybody he remembered rushing past him over the road into Mill o' Mains on that day.

He caught Martin's eye. Clearly Martin was readying himself for some sort of reaction. He raised his eyebrows and pouted towards the guy doing all the talking. Colin knew the look. Knew what it meant.

'Ah heard about that, were you there that day? What was it you were callin' that mob, Posh People's Assembly or somethin' like that eh?'

'Eh, that's right, Posh People's Assembly, fuckin' mental cases iviry one o' thum.'

The storyteller didn't seem quite so confident but he was sticking to his guns. He rubbed a sweaty palm down his chest.

'Where was it that mob was from? Was it no' Fife and Monifieth?'

'Eh, ih think it wuz like eh.'

'Where are you fae then?'

Colin even winced a bit when Martin asked the question, he knew this was about to get uncomfortable for their new tinker friend.

'Eh'm fae Drehburgh aye but eh met thum up there.'

He bounced on the spot looking around. An excuse to get away would've just done him fine.

'What, you're fae Dryburgh but you were just waiting about in Caird Park in case anybody from Fife and Monifieth had just happened to put together a mob that you could join?'

Martin smirked just a little.

'Naw mate.' The youngster was flapping. Thinking fast but he knew a way out of this. 'Eh'm pure in wi' the top boys fae that firm. Met thum in the toon earlier that morning.'

He looked around gauging reactions pulling an expression to indicate that this explanation should really suffice. He nervously looked over towards the bar. Colin could see he was looking to get away now. It was Colin's turn now though.

'Wait a minute, ah heard about that boy that got the pole over his head, was he no' related to the Mill o' Mains top boy? What's his name again?'

One of the audience who had no real idea what the conversation was about answered. He certainly knew who the main criminal in Mill o' Mains was. 'Aye, Digger Stewart's the top boy up there.'

'Oh aye, that's the boy, Digger Stewart.' Colin was glad of the intrusion, now he could dig the knife in. 'That boy that got the pole over his head was his cousin or somethin'. Did he no end up in a coma for a wee while? Digger Stewart's apparently after the guy who did it. Was that you? Fuck me! You are mental. Ah think ah'll get you a drink!'

The storyteller backed off from Colin, he really wanted away now. 'Nah, that wuznae Digger Stewart's cousin that eh done. Nah, nae chance, cos eh ken um aye. Nah, he's no related tae the Digger. Ken, cos eh, niver really hit um that hard anyway. Wuznae him like!'

Martin shook his head as he watched him disappear, gibbering like a loon into the Houlihan's crowd: 'Honestly Col mate, you can be a right sick bastard at times.'

Colin brought both palms up level with his shoulders and mocked innocence: 'Who, me?'

***

Colin loved the stories told by casuals as they waited for things to happen. They weren't just exaggeration. No mere fabrication. They were imagination of the most impressive variety. Colin thought that they were great just because they were so bad. He would listen intently as arms and legs would be added almost visibly to his eyes through the storytellers' body language. Stories of mounting ridiculousness, he often wondered whether in fact the people telling them either expected their audience to believe them or whether in fact they had come to believe them themselves. Either of these possibilities to Colin seemed incredible but often these stories would be told by more than one party, singing it would seem, from the same hymn sheet, agreeing with one another's version of events.

Colin reckoned that football casuals seemed to have come to some sort of unwritten agreement that their stories just had to be interesting and nothing else. The truth; that was for other people. Exaggeration and down right fiction were just the casuals' way of describing things. Everybody was in on it and everybody was OK with that. Some were definitely worse than others but it seemed that nobody was immune. Should somebody tell you that they were in a fight with around eight boys the night before, you could basically read that they had shouted some abuse at some poor innocent by-standers and scarpered, just in case their victims could actually fight.

Colin couldn't get enough of these stories. He recognised them for exactly what they were. Sometimes after a few drinks he would even tell them himself. When he told them however, they would generally become so outlandish that it was obvious to all listening that he was just ridiculing them and their own efforts. This, of course, was the point.

Most amusing to Colin, was some people's use of the description of facial hair as an indicator of toughness or ability to fight. On countless occasions he had listened to casuals excusing some underperformance during scuffles on the fact that the opposition *'had beards'*. It may just have been that the significance of saying that somebody had a beard simply meant that they were older than the typical Dundee casual. Colin knew this but he also knew that to anybody overhearing this, without the knowledge of the accepted terminology, it really did sound as though the beard was the determining factor. It was almost as though the beard itself was a feared weapon in these situations.

'We heard that your mob ran fae ten Motherwell last week.'

Not an unusual accusation to be levelled.

'Fuckin' right we did! They ah' had beards man!'

Certainly not an unusual retort. This was just the way that they spoke and nobody really found it that strange, other of course than Colin. He was getting into it though. He got a laugh out of it. This was what Saturdays were getting to be all about. Colin and Martin. Getting drunk with the casuals, interested to see what was going to happen. Every Saturday started the same way. Waiting in a pub, wondering how many people would appear.

Today was no different. The late Saturday morning bus ride over to Dundee from Leuchars. On to Houlihan's, the city centre pub, accepted by everybody to be the casuals' local. The two boys waited, anxious to know the strength of today's squad, enjoying the banter, listening to the stories.

46

Nobody was talking about anything other than plans and tactics for taking on Hibs casuals. Today, however, Colin and Martin were actually interested in the game. Hibs were in town to play Dundee and usually this would not be an important detail to the two boys. However, on this day, they had been told that Gordon McGovern was due to start the game on the Dundee subs bench.

Goof had been making his way towards the fringes of the squad for some time now but this was his first time in an actual first squad on a Saturday. They had been trying to drum up some interest among the others but only very few of the people in Houlihan's were Fifers and none of them were at Madras and in particular in 5L with Goof, when watching him play football was pretty much what they did all day. To everybody else he was just some new guy, warming the bench with little chance of coming on but to Martin and Colin, he was a magician with a football.

They and the rest of Dundee's casuals waited in anticipation of the day's events. Houlihan's had never seemed so full. The gang was definitely growing in strength. Talking, laughing, jokes being told, people being slagged off and slagging off straight back. Casual banter tainted with an edge of excitement and fear in almost equal measure.

Busy; very busy. Busy and loud, the music of the video jukebox audible among the constant arena of noise. Simple Minds making an almost vain attempt to entertain as Jim Kerr began to sing their latest offering.

When my love said to me, meet me down by the gallow tree.

Colin stood up to walk to the bar. Getting a round today would not be as easy as usual. Not only would getting served take time with the bar being so crowded but actually making his way back to the table with drinks would be difficult, squeezing past everybody. Thankfully the round was only three drinks. A couple of pints of lager for Martin and himself and vodka and lemonade for the limpet type that seemed to have attached himself to them. As Colin stood waiting at the bar, Jim Kerr was doing his best to drum up some emotion within the crowd.

Brothers, sisters, where are you now? As I look for you right through the crowd.

Colin looked at the drinks lined on the bar. Two pint glasses and a tall glass. Not a huge problem normally but with everyone so closely huddled together it would be tricky. He clasped both hands around the glasses, turned and began to negotiate the crowd. Shuffled paces to keep the drinks steady while people slowly and reluctantly let him through. He reached the top of a small but precarious flight of stairs. He checked the stairs. Four of them, relatively clear and then lifted his head to survey the people standing below them.

There was a gathering of people who all seemed to be trying to attract the attention of one young man among them. He was clearly being regaled by all with their stories of valour and facial hair. He wasn't paying attention to them. Instead he was looking up at Colin. Looking and smiling. Colin didn't know him well but he knew who he was. Colin walked down the stairs towards him.

The girls are crying, it's been oh so long. And your father's calling, come on home. Won't you come on home, won't you come on home?

He slapped Colin firmly on the shoulder, spilling the top contents of the pints. He didn't seem to notice that.

'You alright big man?'

Everybody acknowledged Colin. It was clear that any friend of his was a friend of theirs.

All the girls are crying but all's not lost.

Bruce Dunne was probably accepted as the leader of Dundee's casuals. He had just returned that week from London and his absence had done nothing to tarnish his reputation. He had told everyone that he had gone to work in London but with all the stories that had circulated while he was away there wouldn't have been time for work, with everything else he was rumoured to have done. More tall stories of course.

Come back people, you've been gone a while, and the war is raging through the Emerald Isle.

Bruce himself on the other hand was not a tall storyteller. It seemed as though every body else did it for him. He was about the same size, both in height and build as Colin. The two boys stood out among the people gathered.

Bruce looked however a little bit more rough. Not that he wasn't well dressed: El Charro jeans, Replay shirt, Ciao jacket and Timberland moccasins. The staple wear of the Dundee Utility. Bruce however had that coarse look that could only really be finished off with medium length tousled ginger hair.

Colin always felt a little awkward around Bruce and probably would have preferred not to have bumped into him as he held court. Whereas with everybody else, Colin could feel accepted and in many ways superior, Bruce represented somebody that even Colin had some respect for. Not a bullshitter, not just a daft laddie but a leader and, by all accounts, a very handy fighter.

The streets are empty, the streets are cold.

'Alright Bruce? Good to see ya man. I'd shake your hand but...'

Colin gestured towards his drinks and wetted hands.

'Oh, nae bother man. Wha' are ye wi' th' day, is Martin here?'

'Aye, I'm just away back to the table now, eh.'

Colin gestured towards Martin who was sitting listening to his new friend, nodding but looking as though he'd probably prefer to be just about anywhere else.

Bruce glanced over and spotted him sitting there.

'Alright, well I'll come over and see you in a minute, eh.'

The streets are empty.

If nobody else was getting overexcited, Jim Kerr certainly was.

Life goes on.

The door opened and somebody made their way through the crowd, obviously aiming for Bruce. The character to emerge from the crowd was Adam Bailey. One of the gang's, and indeed life's, hangers-on, Adam was proof, if proof were needed, that just because you had made the life decision to mix with violent people, there was no real need to be violent yourself. Thin, generally ungainly and hair already badly receding at 24 years old, without the expensive clothes he would certainly have not looked out of place among the city's homeless but he could tell a good story, was fully conversant with casual lingo and, as such, fitted in quite well.

One day we'll return here, when the Belfast Child sings again.

Adam stopped in front of Bruce, made a pained expression, blew out hard and pointed back towards the door. 'Hibs are makin' their way in frae the city centre. Must hae got aff the train.'

He stopped, composed himself, looked around and raised his voice as he continued, his face now stern like the stereotype of someone assuming some authority. 'Fuckin' loads o' thum.'

When the Belfast Child sings again.

Bruce turned towards the bar and placed his drink down readying himself to move. All around Houlihan's the mood seemed to have changed from anticipation to action, as people began to grab their coats and quickly finish their drinks. Simple Minds seemed to be doing their bit as well, getting all atmospheric.

When the Belfast Child sings again.

Adam Bailey stood amid all of this preparation, clearly satisfied with his informant role. Colin approached him. This was too good an opportunity to miss.

'So did you see them then?'

'See who?'

Colin looked around in exasperation.

'The Hibs mate, did you see the Hibs?'

Adams face showed signs of registering.

'Aye, eh saw thum aw right. In the city centre, heading this wey. Fuckin' loads o' thum.'

'Loads o' them aye?'

Colin pushed out his bottom lip and slowly moved his head up and down. Adam said nothing, he narrowed his eyes and smiled in a knowing look, meant to signal the affirmative. Colin matched the facial expression to assure him that they were on the same wavelength.

'So ehm... did ehm,' he paused slightly, 'did any of them hae beards?'

Adam didn't look at all surprised to be asked this question. He looked pleased. In fact, to Colin, he looked as if he'd just been asked the most pertinent and important question he could have been asked.

Conscious now that his answer was being waited for not only by Colin but several of the crowd, he took a couple of steps backward, looked back in the direction of the city centre and began nodding his head as he turned back to Colin, looked him directly in the eyes and with absolute conviction answered.

'Aye mate, a few of them do.'

The streets are empty, the streets are cold. Won't you come on home?

Nobody had even left Houlihan's as the first window crashed in. Moments before the table beside the window had had several people sitting enjoying a drink. Luckily for them they had moved away from the window into the saloon area, preparing to leave. A whole house brick was launched from the street outside and landed, followed by thousands of fragments of broken glass on to the floor.

And the war is raging through the Emerald Isle.

A second window was smashed in the same way. Martin was standing closest to this window. He darted out of the way of the missile. Through the gap of light in the darkened window he could see the invaders manoeuvring outside. He was able to bend down to pick up the half house brick without stepping towards it. With a single movement he drew back his left hand and thrust the projectile as hard as he could back from the direction it came, watching as it cleared the gap in the window and connected with the hip of one of the outside mob.

Won't you come on home, won't you come on home?

Looking back into the lounge of Houlihan's, the atmosphere was now one of disarray. No real en-masse movement had been made towards the exit to meet the threat, although some had made a move towards the door. Bar staff were taking cover somewhere out of sight but the majority of people had began to move away from the dangers of windows and doors, the glass of which continued to crumble under the onslaught of missiles from outside.

The streets are empty, and your mother's gone.

First to the door was Bruce Dunne. The doors themselves had taken quite a battering by the time he had got there but none of the Hibs casuals had entered Houlihan's yet. When Bruce reached the doors there were people there to meet him and he began to lash out at them. A hail of bottles and glasses began to land around the doors and through the windows, the majority of which were now crashed open. Other than Bruce, however, nobody seemed interested in meeting the force at the door.

Come back people, you've been gone a while.

As Martin looked around he noticed two things. First, the bar seemed to be emptying of people. There certainly seemed to be less there than there were a few minutes ago. Second, the bottles and glasses being thrown at the door seemed to pose much more of a danger to Bruce than to any of the Hibs casuals, safely outside the bar.

That's flesh and blood man, that's flesh and blood.

From the mob inside the bar, which now seemed somehow to be dwindling, Martin spotted Colin moving over towards him. He placed the drinks on the table.

'C'mon tae fuck Martin eh, Bruce is gettin' a doin' there.'

Colin motioned towards the door and then stopped abruptly.

All the girls are crying but all's not lost.

Glass projectiles were still streaming towards the door but Bruce had gone.

'Where the fuck is he?"

Martin shrugged. The only expression he could think of.

'Don't know mate.'

Martin looked around the bar.

'Where the fuck is anybody?'

Colin turned to look as well. Martin had a point. Things were getting much quieter in the bar and there were only around half of the people that there were five minutes previously. Colin started up a small flight of stairs behind him. From there he could see the back door open. The only fighting the people using this door would be doing would be the fight to get out of it and Colin was under no illusion that this meant everybody.

'Dirty fuckers are bailing oot the back door.' He turned back to see Martin rubbing his forehead in exasperation.

'Shit, shit, shit.' Martin's head and upper torso started to rock in time with this expletive rant.

Come back people.

Colin moved back down the stairs his eyes fixed on the front door where Bruce had left. Only a few people were left in the bar. Of those evacuating, some gestured over to the two boys signalling that it was time to leave. Colin picked up his pint of lager and drained almost half of the glass.

'Ah'm away to see what's happenin' wi' Bruce.'

He started to move towards the door. Martin stretched out to place his palm on his chest. Colin wasn't sure whether it was fear or concern he saw in his eyes as he spoke.

'Nah mate, that's fuckin' suicide, eh.'

Martin's eyes averted reluctantly towards the back door.

'Ah think maybe we should get out o' here.'

Colin said nothing. He registered that going to the front door would be stupid but he was in no mood to turn tail and run.

And the war is raging.

Everything in Houlihan's had gone quiet. Nobody remained at the back door and it seemed that the initial onslaught of the outside of the pub had ended. The front door was also eerily silent. Colin lifted a beer mat from the table he had been sitting at and began to sweep glass from the chair. He walked over to collect his and Martin's drinks and sat down.

The streets are empty.

'Fuckin' shambles that was then, eh.'

He looked up at Martin. His expression was only shock. Martin looked around at the quiet devastation that was Houlihan's and then started to consider that maybe it had all finished as quickly as it began. He quickly brushed off a seat opposite Colin and sat down blowing out hard through pressed together jaws. He took a drink of his lager as he assessed the situation.

'Drink up Col mate, ah really dinnae fancy bein' here when the filth arrive, eh.'

Colin also took a gulp from his pint.

'Aye, nae probs Martin.'

Martin had convinced himself that the assault was over. Didn't know where the Dundee casuals were. Probably chasing one another outside, but it did look like they'd all left Houlihan's. He allowed himself to think that they were safe now. Then the doors swung open and a group of five boys poured through. Martin was facing directly towards the door and recognised none of them.

'Fuck!'

Colin could see Martin's mood change instantly. He had obviously heard the noise but not turned around, preferring instead to gauge what was happening from Martin's reaction. Martin lifted his right hand to his face, nervous as he spoke. 'It's Hibs mate.'

Colin sat back in his seat and sighed. 'That's no' sae good is it?'

Martin's heart was racing, palms sweating, his mind a mess of ideas of how to get out of this, he didn't appreciate Colin being so facetious in the face of obvious trouble.

'Colin mate, we cannae fight the whole fuckin' Hibs w'rselves.'

Colin turned round to see a constant stream of people entering through the wrecked doorway. 'Ah know that mate, ah know.'

He placed his drink back on the table. Still he looked as though nothing particularly untoward was happening. Martin half rose to his feet still crouching, his hands on the table as though he was hoping that nobody had spotted him there yet.

'C'mon then mate, we need tae go now.'

Now, however, was too late. At first the invading hoard never noticed the two remaining punters in a bar they had assumed to have emptied. Suddenly however, almost all at once, the raiders became aware that they were not alone in Houlihan's. For a while nothing happened. The Hibs casuals seemed to be wary of the two people left in the bar.

Come back people, you've been gone a while.

Martin was eyeing the window as a possible escape route. Colin was studying his pint, now only quarter of a glass full, flicking the occasional glance towards Martin, as if to gauge his frame of mind. Martin fingered his own pint, almost full.

'Col mate, the police will be here any minute mate, eh.'

In the back of his mind he was hoping they would arrive now to give him a legitimate excuse to get away.

Won't you come on home…

Colin looked unperturbed, save a little wince towards his friend, his way of showing that he wasn't exactly enjoying the prospect of the next few minutes either.

Won't you come on home?

Both boys knew that the gang from Edinburgh didn't mess around. Stories of kneecappings, stabbings, axe attacks and all sorts were well known about them, but for Colin this was about pride. Foolish pride, he knew it himself, but he had never run away from a fight before and was compelled beyond all logical reason to stay now. Even in school, before he knew anything about gangs, the bullies could have pestered him for hours and he wouldn't budge. The only difference was that in school he didn't care, now he did. In school he'd take it because of indifference to the situation, now he readied himself for the worst because he couldn't run away like everybody else. They ran because they were weak. Crap casuals.

Bruce had hit the door without hesitation. Colin wished he had followed. He couldn't be fake like those who left through the back door. To him, at that moment, they weren't even people any more. Just sheep. Only worse than that, sheep were supposed to run scared, casuals were not. Sheep had an excuse and more importantly, sheep wouldn't be making up stories about it that night, making out that throwing bottles that were only hitting Bruce, was in some way heroic. He was glad that Martin had stayed. Part of him wanted him to leave. He was well aware of how he would be feeling but it was good that he was here too. He wasn't one of the flock.

As the Hibs casuals approached the table, Jim Kerr reached his epic conclusion.

The streets are empty, life goes on.

'Well ah dinnae ken aboot the streets bein' empty but this place seems tae have gone dead aw o' a sudden.'

The first of the Hibs casuals reached the table, brushed down a seat and sat beside Martin and Colin.

One day we'll return here, when the Belfast Child sings again.

The rest of the gang in tow, Martin noted with interest that nobody else sat, preferring to stand and look ominous. The seated Edinburger wasn't tall for an apparent leader of men. Pretty in fact, with meticulously styled fair hair, which suited his light blue eyes and unspoiled features. Casuals didn't vary much with regard to their clothes and this one, like his friends, dressed much the same as Martin, Colin and indeed everybody who had just felt fit to leave in such a hurry. This boy seemed to suit the look a little better.

'So what the fuck are you boys still daein' here?'

Colin thought that it was easy for him to act the hard man when the chips were stacked so heavily in his favour. He didn't feel like letting him get completely his own way.

'So, should you boys no' have ran away wi' aw your wee pals?'

Pretty boy leaned back confidently towards his mob who were clearly amused by his wit.

'Nah mate, ah've just got the drinks in, we're no' goin' anywhere!'

Colin, who had been flashing glances and stares among the collective of raiders only realised the pointlessness of his statement as he looked back at his glass. Drained as it was of any liquid, save the dregs of a pint of lager.

So much excitement, thirsty work.

47

After pushing through the first few people attacking the door, Bruce Dunne found much easier work making his way through the rampaging crowd to get away from Houlihan's. A few people had squared up to him on his way through. The first received a fully swung right hook from possibly a shorter distance than Bruce would have liked. Nonetheless it was pretty effective, sending the victim straight over on to his back and giving some of the others food for thought as they started to back off. As he reached the rear ranks of the mob he was again confronted.

'Fuckin' come on then ya prick!'

Bruce stopped and exaggerated his look at his aggressor. He was not overly impressed with what he saw. Bouncing on the spot without actually ever leaving the ground, his face stretched into a menacing contortion, hands held out in front, fingers pointing upwards, spread out and waggling 'playing the upside down piano'. All of this effort so obviously aimed at impressing his friends, Bruce could see that this was just a daft little boy. After all, he wasn't at the back for no reason. Bruce shook his head slightly and rubbed his forehead. The crap casual continued his little war dance and his colleagues converged beginning to mimic, obviously growing in confidence, convinced they had found a victim they could deliver a pasting to.

Bruce removed his hand from his forehead, placed them by his side and stood up straight, looking directly into the little dancer's eyes as he spoke.'Look pal, awa' ye go before you get hurt eh!'

Bruce turned away with no intention of paying any more attention to any of this mob. To Bruce it seemed much more damaging to snub these people than to swat a few of them and watch the rest back off, as was his other option. No, much better to attack their pride and leave them feeling foolish, safe in the knowledge that they were not likely to do anything about it. In any case, he now had an appointment to keep.

Bruce had known about the planned attack on the pub. He was in on it but was asked to keep it quiet. It was always planned to be a spontaneous attack but Bruce was told. Bruce had to know, as the beginning of the attack was his signal to make his way to the meeting. The venue in fact specified by Bruce as a wide open space where it would be unlikely he would be attacked. It may have crossed his mind that the meeting was a trap but it seemed unlikely. He after all was hardly a prize target, although he was aware that points would be scored for luring the top boy from the Utility into an ambush.

The manner of the setting up of this meeting had convinced him otherwise and far from frightened he felt honoured to have been asked along. It was during his stay in London, spending some time with West Ham United's Inter City Firm, that he was made aware of these plans. One of the ICF who already had contacts with Hibs casuals was keen to speak to Bruce and the Edinburgh contacts together, to set out arrangements and ground rules for Scottish casuals.

As it had been explained to Bruce, there was a national network being set up which was to include Scotland. The idea being that contacts would be shared among all of the team's gangs and arrangements made for fights to be set up away from the usual terraces and near stadia venues. The police after all were becoming wise to these sorts of battles and far too many arrests were being made for some people's liking. It seemed to Bruce that his pastime was becoming more and more business-like and in Dundee he had been selected as the manager of the business.

***

Saturday afternoon and the car park behind the Seagate ABC cinema was full and busy with people to-ing and fro-ing from their cars. More cars circling for spaces. Bruce cursed his decision. It suddenly struck him how naïve his choice of venue was. In picking this place he had pictured it as he generally always saw it. At night, a barren open and unused space. He hadn't considered the fact that on Saturdays it was completely the opposite.

He looked for the people he was due to meet, angry with himself, convinced that either he would never find them in this mess or that when he did they would consider him a complete amateur for picking such a space. He walked the length of a row of cars before spotting a recognisable face. Three others were standing beside and together they stood out like a sore thumb. Not busy, not going anywhere but obviously there for a reason. Bruce made his way over, preparing his apology as he walked.

The single familiar figure noticed him coming, smiled and winked in recognition. Bruce felt worse for this. Friendly faces making light of his mistake, he took this to be a clearly patronising gesture. The only one of the four people that he knew that he had met before was Christian Breen. He couldn't be sure who anybody else was but had met Christian a few times in London and knew that he belonged to the top ranks of the ICF. He held apart his hands as he prepared to make his excuses but was cut short, Breen close to shouting in his Cockney accent.

'Tell ya what mate, you're not stupid are ya?'

Stunned by this statement, Bruce stopped in his tracks as Christian approached and offered his hand to shake.

'Choosin' Dundee's answer to Piccadilly fuckin' Circus for a meet.'

Breen looked Bruce directly in the eye, nodded and winked again in an apparent gesture of approval. Bruce forced a smile and nodded back, trying his hardest but not at all convincing himself that he was looking cool about things. Christian placed a hand on Bruce's shoulder.

'But don't worry man! There's no trap, it's just a meeting, OK.'

Bruce clicked. Of course, this is the smart move. Only a complete gimp would meet these people in a quiet place. He quickly regained composure. Thought about what to say next. 'Ah know Chris, ah know but you can never be too careful, can ya?'

All four men looked at one another and nodded their agreement. Bruce was thinking fast now, feeling in the zone. Fair enough a fair bit of serendipity may have played its part in making him look like he knew what he was doing but now it had to be followed up with a bit of guile to continue the illusion. He had to think of a quiet place to continue discussions nearby and he was sure he knew the place.

The Wine Gardens was the name used by most Dundonians for the small landscaped area at the foot of the Tay Bridge. A last bastion of quiet on the outskirts of Dundee's city centre on busy shopping days, in actual fact the only people who ever congregated there to appreciate the skills of the city council's gardeners were the homeless drunks. Hence of course, the name. This location was perfect. Fair enough, there may be a slight interruption from the winos begging for change but Bruce knew that generally a quick 'fuck off' delivered with enough verve was enough to silence them and send them back to their quiet stupor.

***

Christian Breen was heavy set, not particularly tall but not fat either. Built in a way that people would know he spent a lot of time in the gym, the only question would be whether he was on steroids or not. Casual style clothing never looked good on people built like this, in the same way as any overweight figure seemed not to suit the style. Supposed to be loose fitting or sporty, on larger set people it always looked clingy. These people probably thanked God every night that Farah slacks had died a death as a casual fashion item.

As with a lot of bodybuilders it wasn't just the muscles that were worked on in an attempt to look good. Christian's hair was immaculately styled with Brylcreme or some other shiny hair product and his skin tanned, obviously not from the less than glorious sunshine in East London. He was a good bit older than Bruce, in his early thirties probably and it occurred to Bruce that he was older than any of the attendees of this meeting, all of whom he gauged to be around about his own age.

Breen began introductions to Bruce. He could tell that everybody else had been introduced. There was one other Londoner, introduced only as Robbie. He hardly spoke at all, preferring instead to stand posing, looking a little menacing, breaking the image only ever to laugh at the jokes. Bruce guessed that he had probably only made the trip north to keep Breen company.

The other two were Scottish, both from Edinburgh. Their involvement at the meeting was as enthusiastic as it could be and they were both desperate to know how their boys had got on at Houlihan's. Bruce of course couldn't really help them as he hadn't hung about to see the outcome. The introductions only included first names so Bruce only knew that he was talking to Andy and Scott.

Bruce sat on a slatted wooden bench, joined by the two Edinburghers. Christian Breen had positioned himself sitting on the grass while Robbie stood looking out towards the extended lawn leading to the Tay. He clearly had little interest in what was to be discussed. Other than this little committee meeting, the wine gardens were empty. Fifty metres from the chaos of Dundee's city centre shopping precinct, it was bizarrely quiet. Birds could be heard in the trees with only the intermittent swoop of cars coursing their way around the circular ramp taking them on to the bridge and over to Fife.

Breen sat up straight. The sun shone from behind him and mirrored on his treacle-gloss hair.

'Okay, so it's important that you realise that I'm not here to tell you what's what.'

He held up a finger. Not pointing but displaying that he had a point to put across. 'There ain't a plan.'

Dropped his finger again. Possibly felt that this was a little like him assuming chair status.

'The plan'll come from you guys. You make the ground rules. You make the decisions.'

Andy and Scott looked at one another, nodded with every ounce of enthusiasm they owned and said their piece together, verbatim and in time.

'Aye, sounds no' bad likes.'

These people from Edinburgh may have been rival gang members to Bruce but this was not an angry exchange. All parties were in agreement on all issues and it seemed that the aims were the greater good of the complete movement, rather than of the individual factions. Like friends discussing work on a day off. Complaining about this and that but never of each other. Suggesting and listening to suggestions agreeing that there had to be a better way and coming to agreements of how things would be done in the future.

The boys talked seriously about their issues, they cracked jokes, shared anecdotes and compared experiences. Scott and Andy seemed like cool guys to Bruce. He liked them. He was certain that had they been Dundonians they would be friends. Thinking about the future, though, and considering what was being said, he couldn't help notice the irony of casually and affably discussing occasions to come when they would become bitter enemies. That was weird.

It was a little before three o'clock when discussions started to draw to a close. Both Scott and Andy had mentioned the fact that they were going to be late for the game and had suggested that any further discussions could be done either on the way or inside Dens Park. Andy turned to Bruce and looking a little unsure extended one further invitation.

'Look, Bruce mate. We're in kind of an,' he paused and looked skyward as if to try to remember the word he was looking for, 'amnesty-type situation here, at least fir th'day anyway.'

He didn't look at all convinced that amnesty was the word he was looking for.

'Anywey, what I'm sayin' is, if you come into the away end th'day, we'll guarantee yir safety.'

Bruce considered the invitation. The talks were cordial and he did not in fact perceive there to be any danger from being in the Hibs end. So why not? This was what being in charge was all about. Mingling with the enemy under the protection of their leaders. This was authority. And, as an added bonus, he'd probably get to see the one he had sent flying outside Houlihan's to check on the damage and, even better, really put the wind up the little twats at the back who had given him grief.

* * *

Dundee city centre was heaving and getting up to Dens Park took a little longer certainly than Scott and Andy would have liked. They arrived with Bruce and the Londoners a little less than 15 minutes after the kick-off. Scott and Andy were growing more and more anxious to get into the ground, obviously dying to know the score and what was going on. Christian and Robbie seemed a great deal less interested. Possibly the prospect of a low- to mid-table Scottish Premier game held little allure for two East London boys.

Even less bothered at the lack of punctuality was Bruce. Not overly interested in football, if he was to express a preference for a team, it would have to be the team he supported as a boy, going to the games with his father. The team 'across the road', Dundee United. Dens however was to provide something today that he would find pretty interesting. A surprise he was not expecting. As he reached the back of the Provost Road Stand he was looking for his two victims from earlier that day to see if he could provoke a reaction, hoping to see them squirm. But it was not these two that he spotted first, it was two people he would never have expected to have seen, here of all places, at this time.

Martin and Colin were sitting among the Hibs casuals, looking no more daunted than had they been sitting among long-time friends. Martin noticed Bruce coming up the centre isle first. He stood up and pointed towards him.

'Fuckin' hell, Bruce. What are you daein' here?'

Martin was standing with a smile on his face shaking his head. Colin then noticed Bruce and adopted the same bemused look common on all three faces.

'Wow man, this just gets madder and madder.'

Martin appeared to regain his composure first and then pointed to the pitch. He started to blurt out, stifling his enthusiasm for what he was saying.

'Fuckin' one nil Bruce.'

He looked around to see that he wasn't upsetting anyone too much. To anybody else it probably looked as if he was but he continued anyway.

214

'Goof scored the fuckin' goal, he's playin' fuckin' brilliant.'

Bruce surveyed the crowd around the two people looking so out of place. None of them looked particularly happy with this outburst but only one reacted. Sitting directly beside Colin, not tall for an apparent leader of men, pretty in fact, with meticulously styled fair hair, which suited his light blue eyes and unspoiled features.

'Martin, yir mate Goof's pish and so's your hale fuckin' team!'

AUGUST 1992

MANCHESTER

48

Goof had long since made his peace with the booze. Sure there had been years when he was able to blame alcohol for his present situation but how could you stay mad for any length of time with something so willing to help?

There was a time when he wouldn't have touched the stuff. A time when playing football, winning tackles, making runs and scoring goals were all the inebriation needed. A time when all Goof needed to feel like he was on top of the world was the sound of his fans cheering him on. And there was a time when Goof had plenty of that…

***

After two successful years at Dundee FC, the second season finishing the top scorer by a street, young Gordon McGovern was attracting plenty of attention from the press amongst others. A frequent back page feature, the good-looking goal machine always seemed able to provide an interesting sound bite after a good performance. Pundits were predicting a call up to the full national squad before long but, more importantly, scouts from some major teams were now appearing at Dens Park to have a look at him.

At the end of the season 1990-91 Goof was ready for a move. He still had two years of a contract to run at Dundee and some were advising that if he stuck it out there, playing like he was, he could start to call the shots on a move to almost anywhere.

'Get an agent, they'll see you're alright!'

Much of this talk was about money but for Goof, money wasn't important. He just wanted to be playing a higher level of football and he was impatient to get it. Offers came in from both sides of the Old Firm and the salary was attractive but again, money was not the important thing. He'd seen too many promising youngsters go there and be used as bench-warmers for the growing number of foreign 'stars' playing at those clubs. Not that this was overly important. Goof knew he could give most of these respected names a good game but at the end of it all, he hated both sides of the Old Firm. For Goof, the only good result of an Old Firm derby would be for the ground to open up and everyone to fall down it. Players, officials, fans, the lot.

There was a buzz about the English First Division. There was talk of re-branding it into an English Premier League. Money was being thrown at it from the television revenue and an influx of great foreign players seemed to be making their way to England. Real superstars though. Not like the jokers plying their trade in Glasgow.

Of the offers coming in, the best by far was with Tottenham Hotspur. They played in London and offered more than a liveable wage for living in England's capital. It wouldn't be easy earning a starting place but Goof wasn't short of confidence so he thought he could make it, and making it might mean forming a strike partnership with current Scotland international, Gordon Durie. If those two could get it together at club level then this could catapult him into the international frame. So Goof was off to North London.

Pre-season went well but Goof was under no illusions. He would need to play a few reserve games. Maybe come on as a sub a few times before he could carve his niche. Five games into the season though, the team were due to travel to Manchester to face City and Goof was named in the squad to travel. Now, for the squad, such a promotion for the young lad was reason enough to celebrate and on the Thursday night some of the squad decided to take young Goof out for a celebratory drink. Goof wasn't a drinker but with the squad that were there it would just have been rude to not partake and there was two days till the game so what would the harm be?

Next day, Goof turned up at the club to prepare for the trip. Light training but just as well as Goof was not at all well. The managers were concerned and asked Goof if he was OK for the trip but there was only ever going to be one answer to that. Some of the stars were ribbing him about the state he got in but he couldn't remember much of that. What he could remember was the laugh they all had.

On the day of the game, Goof boarded the bus feeling ten times better but he knew he wasn't 100 percent. How could he be so stupid to start drinking just two days before possibly the biggest game of his life? His only real lifeline was that his name probably wouldn't be on the team sheet. Get it together, never be so stupid again and wait for the next game to be able to show them what he could do but of course his name was on the list.

He was starting.

Twenty-five minutes into the game, nil-nil, both defences were dominant and doing their jobs. Not great news for Tottenham's bright young hope. He was already feeling the pace. He shouldn't have been. He knew that. Knew it was the lingering remnants of a hangover that rendered him a quarter yard from match fitness and he vowed at that point never to be so stupid again.

The job was to put in every effort he could but he knew he was having a bad game. Pace was letting him down. Maybe he could run it off. The ball broke and Tottenham started to move forward. A near perfect ball made its way past the City defensive midfield to the danger area, just outside the right hand side of their box. Goof had been keeping line with the last City defender and now it was basically him against this big lump of a man.

This should be easy. Beat the defender who he should certainly have for pace and then finish. Pundits talked ad nauseam about brilliantly skilful finishes but for Goof this was bread and butter. Once past the defender, he knew he'd score. He just had the knack for it.

Goof raced towards the ball. He was quicker than the defender, he knew that, but he hadn't shown him the clean heels he normally would have. He lunged his right foot forward. First touch was everything. Get the ball out of the defender's area and kill the pace to allow the shot. Sure enough, his foot made contact first but the defender was just there behind him and clipped his heel. Nothing malicious and only the slightest of touches and Goof could ride it with the minimum of disturbance to his run.

The ball was positioned perfectly, the defender now behind him. Compose, pick the spot, eye on the ball, beat the keeper, celebrate. He'd done this thousands of times before. His right heel struck the ground, one more pace to address the ball and then the shot but Goof could feel a slight twinge in his knee, the contact had twisted something. No pain but certainly a strange feeling.

The keeper was now just off his line, panic etched in his features. Goof planted his left foot for support and lifted his right for the shot and then the pain. It was bearable but something wasn't right. As he contacted the ball, the pain heightened just that little bit. Just enough to affect the shot. The ball lacked the pace to make certain, the keeper lunged and almost made contact, he was unlucky. The ball though wasn't as accurate as it needed to be.

Goof, tumbling to the ground looked on in shock.

'It's hitting the post, I've missed a sitter'

The ball bounded off the post and trundled back towards the keeper. The keeper reached to grab the ball but faffed at it and directed it back towards the goal. Goof watched as the keeper vainly tried to stop it crossing the line. A section of support in

Maine Road went wild. Goof was now prone on his back but thrust both arms skyward.

'Ya fucker, ah've scored ma first goal!'

Just then the rest of the squad, including some of his heroes jumped on top of him. Amid the celebration he was ignoring the rising pain in his right leg. He could run that off no problem.

***

The goal at Maine Road was the last ball Gordon McGovern ever kicked competitively for Tottenham Hotspur.

Three minutes later during the game he had to be substituted and was met by delighted players and staff on the bench but a very concerned trainer. It was the next day and back at the hospital in North London when he learned that the slight contact by the defender had caused a small tear in his cruciate ligament. This would keep him out for three months at least, what with the repair, then the physio and training back to match fitness. He couldn't help thinking that the contact would not have been made had he been totally match fit. He was finished with drink. Never would he let that happen again.

Three months turned to six months turned to nine. The club was great. Operations were needed and they were more than willing to foot the bill while paying his salary but there was a limit that a club would stretch to for a player who couldn't play. The fans were fantastic. For a while. They remembered the hero at Maine Road that day, how he got injured for the cause but then, by the end of the season with results to worry about he got less and less recognition. A committed servant of the club for only 25 minutes after all in their eyes.

With very little else in his life constituting any joy, at the end of season 91-92, Goof decided to go out with some of the fringe players for a drink. Now he knew it couldn't do him any harm. He certainly wasn't starting this Saturday. The season had ended and two months had passed when Goof turned up for pre-season training. Training for the first Premier League season. The most exciting time imaginable for a young Tottenham Hotspur player. Training? That was a laugh. Pre-season doing of odd jobs and generally getting messed around.

Two weeks later, still an employee of Tottenham Hotspur, Goof decided he was going home. He knew he wouldn't be missed at White Hart Lane.

49

Goof had been sitting in Caskies for around two hours when Martin Bridges walked in. The Jack Daniels was just beginning to do its job. In fact Goof had been in the bar most days of the week sitting in pretty much the same place. It was now Friday and this was really the first familiar face he'd seen.

'Alright Martin, How you doin'?'

'Alright Goof, no' bad mate, what about yersel?'

'No' bad Martin, good tae see ya mate.'

Goof held up a slim glass of JD and Coke.

'You want a drink mate?'

Martin thought about it, he could murder one but knew it would lead to more.

'Naw, no thanks bud, busy today, eh.'

'How, what you up tae likes?'

'Me and Colin are away doon tae Manchester on a bit o' business mate.'

Martin surveyed Goof, clearly on the beginning of getting drunk. Martin could feel for him. Everyone knew his story.

'We are makin' a wee holiday o' it though, got a hired car, booked intae a room, should be good likes. Room for one more, nae problem there.'

Goof smiled. He didn't appear to realise that he was being invited.

'What do you think then, fancy it?'

Goof looked pensive for just a moment and then smirked.

'Manchester?'

He almost shouted the word.

'Oh aye, ah just fuckin' love that place.'

He raised his glass

'Here's to Manchester!'

He looked into the glass and signalled to the barman that it needed refilling.

'If it's aw the same to you ah'll gie it a miss, ah'm fine where ah am likes. Sure you dinnae want one?'

Martin thought about it. Goof cut a pathetic figure sitting drinking by himself. He probably hadn't kicked a ball in about two years and for someone who's life revolved around doing just that, he showed all the signs of someone torn from a passion. Around two stones overweight, unshaven and clearly dressed without the help of either Daz or Morphy Richards, he cut the exact figure of someone in need of a drinking partner and hell could Martin use a drink.

He'd had a couple of hefty lines of cocaine before he'd left the house. Lara didn't half like her lines big. He had another couple of grams in his pocket but coke was basically shite without a drink. He knew that Colin wouldn't be overly pleased if Martin announced that he needed to drive down to Manchester because he'd been drinking. He did have another hour or so to wait for him finishing work and, well, it would be alright if he offered to drive back next week. It would be fine.

'Aye mate, of course ah'll hae a drink wi' ya!'

50

Lawrie Gordon knew somebody whose single task as a favour was to hire cars with a forged driver's licence. Not a difficult task, Colin would have thought, but today, on a day that he really needed to get moving, the car hirer was late. By the time Colin got into Caskies it was after five o'clock. He had actually planned to be at Gordon's flat by now.

This didn't particularly concern him as, after all, it was Gordon's contact that fucked up with the hire of the vehicle. Being late however had given Martin the chance to have a few drinks and a couple of lines with Goof and this was more of a concern.

Colin parked the red Rover 216; not a car he would have picked himself, on Warrender Park Road in Edinburgh. Directly across from Lawrie Gordon's flat. It was now almost half past eight and they still had to get to Manchester. Still had to book into their hotel.

'You alright now?'

'My alright about what?'

'Well, have you sobered up yet?'

'Colin seriously, ah'm fine, eh. Look, ah'll take another line if it makes you feel any better!'

'Naw ah'm no' sure that's such a good idea.'

Martin shook his head just slightly.

'Honest to god Colin, it's no' the headmaster we're away to see, it's Lawrie Gordon. He'll be cool.'

'Aye, ah know, ah know but you know what it's like with him. Business is business.'

Martin relaxed in the Rover's passenger seat.

'C'mon Colin, this is no' like you. Relax mate remember, we're on holiday. Here have a line!'

Martin offered the wrap of cocaine.

Colin hesitated a little before realising that Martin was right. He knew that Gordon needed them to do some things while they were in Manchester and also knew that the car would be carrying drugs when they come back but mainly, the next week for Colin and Martin was exactly that. A holiday.

***

Lawrie Gordon's flat was massive. It had three bedrooms, a large sitting room with bay windows, a ceiling that was easily 15 foot in height and a kitchen that Martin thought you could probably have a half decent game of five-a-sides in. The decoration and furniture were what would probably be described as minimalist and the whole flat had a bright, airy and uncluttered feel.

Martin's favourite feature though was the bar room between the sitting room and the kitchen. This didn't seem like an afterthought stuck away in the corner of a room but genuinely an integral part of the flat's design. How cool was it to have a bar in your house? Martin and Colin had been talking about moving into just such a flat in Edinburgh and if what was going to happen next week was to lead to anything then this possibility might be close to realisation.

'So you boys are running a wee bit late are you not?'

Gordon led them into the sitting room.

'Aye, no' really our fault though. Your man didnae turn up until after five. You want to see the bucket he got us!'

'Aye, I'm startin' to worry about him. Right guys have a seat. You want a drink before you set off?'

'Ehm, maybe no' such a good idea, eh.' Colin pointed out towards the road. 'Drivin', you know.'

Gordon started to fill his own glass. 'You guys ever been to Salford before?'

'No!' they answered at the same time.

'It's about four hours from here.'

Martin and Colin shared a glance.

'Then you guys are goin' to check into a Marriott hotel, once you've found the place at about, well, after 12.'

They realised the specious nature of this situation.

'Aye, well, like ah say. Your man, eh!'

'Look, don't worry about it.'

Gordon placed another two glasses on the bar.

'You've got all week in Manchester and you don't have to meet the Anwars until tomorrow. We've got a lot to go through, so relax, have a few drinks and you'll be good to go in the morning. Now, Martin, I'm assuming it's you that's got the couple of you buzzing so if you've got any Charlie left maybe you can get it on the go!'

Martin sat on the cream leather sofa and reached into his pocket, flicking a glance toward Colin which he knew to mean *'See that! I told you he was cool about it!'*

***

The conversation ranged between serious instructions about how to conduct themselves in Manchester to childish wind-ups. Cocaine was like that.

225

Martin walked over to the bay windows and looked out onto the street. The street lights and the windows of the Earl of Marchmont pub cast a hue orange glow onto the street, where crowds of people, men in short sleeves and women in summer dresses were busily making their way either to or from some festival attraction. Eleven o'clock on a Friday night in a residential area and it looked as busy and as exciting as any time he could think of in St Andrews but then North East Fife and rush hour were never phrases that particularly sprung to mind together.

It was clear to him that he was now outgrowing St Andrews. He thought about Goof and how he had landed back in St Andrews. Completely embittered by his experience of trying to get away. Probably hammered now in Caskies, alcohol his new best friend and nothing to look forward to. That wasn't the life for Martin and the sooner he could engineer the move to Edinburgh the better.

Should have been London though. He knew that now. Should have went with Natalie. Should have had the guts. Lara was alright and he knew she was set on a move to Edinburgh but if it was bright lights and a beautiful girl he wanted then London with Natalie was where he ought to be. Too late now though. Natalie was gone and sure as the cocaine he was taking was causing him to ponder, she'd not be alone.

Then an explosion rocked Marchmont.

'What the fuck?'

Streams of blue sparkles were rushing through the sky, more sparks, this time orange casting a larger circle than the blue ones. Another explosion, not just heard this time but the vibrations felt. Martin turned back into the room to see the obvious amusement of the other two.

'Ha, Martin, you fuckin' shat yourself!'

Colin had to put his drink down to avoid spilling it.

'Aye, well ah wasnae expectin' that like.'

Martin looked back out the window, the sky now filled with four or five colours.

'What's aw this about like?'

'That's the Tattoo ending. It's like that every night!'

Gordon came over to the window to get a better view.

'What so you get a fireworks display every night?'

'For the month that the festival's on, yeah.'

'Man, that is cool as fuck, eh.'

'Well, aye, I suppose.'

Gordon turned to take his seat again, he'd clearly seen enough, what with having seen the same display for almost a month now.

'It's no' that cool on a Wednesday night when you're just dozing off to sleep though!'

51

Nazim and Parveas Anwar were surveying the Rover car that Martin had parked in front of their sales lot. The cars for sale in their yard were generally your nearly new top-end executive models.

'Ah yes, this car is perfect,' Nazim nodded agreement to his brother.

Martin glanced at Colin . *'Easy for him to say.'*

'OK, so you two will need a car to get around in during the week. Look around the yard, we'll basically let you have your choice.'

Colin had already had a look around the yard though. 'Well, does that include the 911 Turbo?'

Parveas smiled as he considered the choice. 'Ah yes, that's a good…'

His brother cut him off. He looked a little awkward: 'Oh no, I'm sorry, not the Porsche. Any car is fine but you will need a car with a boot.'

Colin and Martin looked a little lost. Why would they need a boot? Nazim clearly understood.

'Yes, of course, we actually have a four-year-old Mercedes S Class, perhaps you will be more comfortable in it.'

This didn't seem like a bad compromise.

'Aye, fair do's.'

'OK come inside then, we have a lot to discuss.'

Colin and Martin had been well briefed on the Anwar brothers. They looked every bit the successful businessmen that Gordon had told them. Immaculately dressed in tailored designer suits and starched white shirts without ties. The brothers ran their many businesses for their now retired father. Not just car sales, but fruit markets, fabric warehouses and designer label shops among others.

Of course, on the back of these, they also had a hand in drugs (the reason why Colin and Martin were there). Not the internal tomfoolery of Manchester's drug supply network, where guns were just as necessary as scales. They were more involved in the smuggling networks that brought the goods into the country. Like all parties who were successful in such ventures, they never got close to the supply. Everything was done by third or fourth parties that they could trust and the profits filtered back through their legitimate ventures.

'So, friends of Mr Gordon. How is he?'

'Oh aye, Lawrie's fine!' Martin assumed the meeting spokesman role.

'Would you like coffee. It's very good, filtered and fresh.'

'Oh aye, thanks!'

Nazim pressed a button on an intercom: 'Henry, can you come in now, if you can bring some coffee this will be fine.'

'While you're here, Mr Gordon would have mentioned that we have some light work for you.'

'He did aye, that's not a problem!'

'I think you will enjoy it.'

Both brothers smiled and Parveas added. 'Don't worry, it's not to do with drugs and nothing that can land you in trouble.'

Lawrie Gordon had intimated as such before they left Edinburgh.

'We have many clients and customers, many debtors, you know and sometimes such people are not so keen to pay.'

Nazim took over.

'These are not drug debts, such people always know to pay and the seriousness of running up large debts but you know, it's the other people, traders and so-called legitimate businessmen who don't seem so keen to pay. This is where you two come in. When our clients meet you, they will know they have to pay.'

'So we're collecting debt?'

'Well, no, not really, you won't actually handle any money. You see, the people that you will see, they won't have any money for you. As I've said, they do not want to pay.'

The office door opened and a man walked in that Colin and Martin assumed to be Henry, with a tray of cups and jar of coffee.

'Ah just in time, gentlemen, I'd like you to meet Henry.'

Henry placed the tray on the table and Martin and Colin got out of their seats to shake his hand.

'Henry is your secret weapon. When these people see you two with your Scottish accents, they'll wonder who you are and whether they should pay or not but when they see Henry, they will know that they have to pay!'

This last statement seemed to be highly amusing to both Anwars.

Colin and Martin shook Henry's hand thinking that this must be a real Manchester villain. A proper hard man, if people were going to pay long-standing debts just at the sight of him. Colin exchanged the usual pleasantries but when Henry gripped Martin's hand he held the shake for a few moments.

'I know you!'

'Naw, ah doubt that mate!'

Clearly he was mistaken. Martin had never been to Manchester before.

'No, I do, I've met you before, now where was it?'

This was all Martin needed, a Manchester nutter mistaking him for someone else. Suddenly a light seemed to go on behind his eyes. Martin could see it now, this guy mistaking him for someone he was due a pounding to but no, Henry started smiling.

'No, I remember, I lived in Dundee for a while a few years back. You were on that boat in Dundee 'arbour. Floatation!'

Martin smiled back and pointed at Henry, his eyes now also wide with recognition.

'Oh aye… New Yorkers!' The first thing that popped into his head. 'Wait a minute, you're Henry Blake!'

Henry smiled. Quizzical. Obviously wondering how Martin would know his surname. Martin stopped himself from blurting out all sorts of questions. Questions about Disco Biscuits. About Ibiza and, of course, about the Digger. Questions that should Colin have any knowledge about, would change everything. Martin needed to play dumb. Henry had to be just someone he'd met on the Frigate Unicorn. Anything more he actually knew about him would have to be kept to himself. It was just too dangerous.

52

Henry had asked them where they'd like to go to sample Manchester nightlife. He seemed keen to play the hospitable host. There was only ever going to be one answer, The Hacienda. Henry told them that there were plenty more and better clubs on a Saturday night but Martin was caught up with the whole history of the Factory Records club. It was, as far as he was concerned, the original UK house music club and he just had to see what it was like.

'OK, I'll get you in but when you're there, don't try any wheelin' or dealin'. Give me a shout and I'll get you what you need.'

And so with Henry's warnings still ringing in their ears, they set off for the legendary club. The Hacienda was exactly as they expected, the main hall being a good bit larger than any other clubs they had experienced. Stowed to the rafters, mainly with people freely expressing their delight at the music on the dance floor and as far as Martin and Colin were concerned, a worrying amount of people lining the fringes and bars trying to look important. Villains, dealers, wannabe musicians, DJs or perhaps just people too up their own arses to get involved in what people who come to house music clubs were supposed to. There was probably a mix of all of these types of characters here.

Martin had been noticing that all house nights that he was going to were starting to fill up with such people. Only a year earlier, he could remember nights at the Rhumba Club in Perth and then in Dundee where the whole club just shook to the beat of the music. New people would turn up at the Rhumba to see what the fuss was and Martin thought it hilarious to see them looking around the club, completely astonished for the first half an hour or so only to be totally involved with the madness halfway through. Even funnier when Martin knew them. Guys who were completely straight-laced and appearing out of curiosity alone. A number of times, they'd even asked Martin what the hell was going on when they got there and then meeting up outside at the end and hugging their sweat-soaked bodies.

Even the Rhumba, now in Dundee's Fat Sams, was going a little like the rest, with people who had no interest in letting loose, coming along with their own agendas. Not just the drug dealers but the think-they're-hard casuals and general poseurs who turned up simply because they'd heard that this was the trendy thing to do. He knew a few of them and, fair enough, they were good guys but they just didn't belong there.

Martin had convinced himself that the Hacienda would be a throwback to the crazy days, everyone there for one reason. Within 20 minutes, he knew he was to be disappointed. So much so that he was actually able to sit down at a table with Colin and Henry to spark up a conversation. Probably not such a bad thing, because Henry intrigued him.

'So, what's the crack with the Anwar brothers?'

'Wha' d'ya mean?'

'Well, they're a bit strange, eh. Big time drug smugglers that look a bit like your friendly corner shop magnates. No' exactly your gangster types, eh?'

'Yeah mate, don't be fooled by what they look like. Those two are gangsters alright. Their dad was worse. Apparently came to Britain without two pennies to rub together. Knew how to get gear in though, flew below the radar for years. I'm telling you, you don't make the amount of money that he's done in Manchester unless you know how to handle yourself. Parveas and Nazim as well. Seem like thoroughly decent sorts. It's them that have set up all the legit stuff. Your other dealers around here though, they know not to mess with the Anwars. You stay around long enough, you'll get to hear the stories. Not like these fuckers we're going after. These guys don't know the half of it. Put it this way, these fuckers don't pay after we've been to see them and they'll probably end up being tortured on a fruit processing table. Not nice.'

'Aye but they'll pay when they see you though, eh?'

Martin was fishing to find out why the Anwar's thought this.

Henry took a drink of some god awful looking cocktail and sniggered. 'Yeah they will, you're right!'

Colin and Martin checked one another's expression. This guy must be the real deal. A slow, synthesised orchestral movement segued its way through the song being faded out by the DJ. The beat changed to a deep house rhythm that complemented the almost classical music. Henry jumped to his feet.

'Ya fucker, this is a total tune man!'

Henry squeezed past and made his way on to the huge dance floor to join the mass of thrusting and screaming bodies assembled there, his wiry frame jerking in an uneasy alliance to the beat.

Colin and Martin watched him disappear into the throng thinking the same thing. Can this guy actually put the fear of death into the people they were going to see the next day?

'What do you make o' Henry then?' Colin needed to know if Martin was on the same wavelength.

What could Martin say though?

'Henry's a dodgy bastard, no way should we trust him. Fucked off wi' thousands o' pounds fae Digger Stewart and went tae Ibiza. Steve McNaughton got the blame and I helped him to rip you off to try to clean up Henry's mess. Remember? You done three months because of it?'

No, definitely best to play the cards closer to the chest. 'Dunno mate, bit strange eh.'

'Well, aye, strange is one way to put it. Ah just cannae imagine why the Anwars think anybody'll be intimidated by him.'

'Well these are the guys that know what they're doing and Henry there has the plan so let's just see what he comes up wi', eh.'

53

Martin drove the shiny silver Mercedes up to the Portakabin with a Naylor Construction sign displayed on the gable end. The Portakabin was in the site of the latest Naylor Construction contract and this was basically no place for a Mercedes S Class to be driven. Martin might have considered leaving it outside the yard but the S Class was a big part of the plan.

Martin and Colin exited the car. Builders relaxed their tools and peered over at them. Everyone on the site seemed interested in who they were. This was a little inconvenient as they didn't really want to attract too much attention. Thankfully, by the time they got to the Portakabin door the bricklayers were back to work, probably assuming that, with a car like that, the owners of the building work had just turned up.

They kept up the façade of looking like they owned the place by simply walking into the makeshift office without knocking. The walls of the office were covered in plans and a harried-looking man in his early fifties was sitting behind a desk, a telephone receiver pressed to his head with one hand and the other hand flicking through an open folder. Colin and Martin stood watching him for around ten seconds before deciding that he was probably not going to acknowledge them. Colin walked over and pressed down on the phone hang-up catches.

'What the…?'

'Are you Arnold Naylor?' Colin interrupted.

'Eh, who the fuck? What the hell do you think you're doing?'

Martin approached the desk. 'Arnold Naylor?'

'Wait, hold on, you can't just come barging in here fuckin' hanging up my call. Never mind who I am, who the fuck are you?'

Martin went into character as the leader of the Portakabin intruders.

'OK look, you'll hae to excuse my partner, he's no' exactly subtle and he'll never get intae the Guinness Book as the world's most patient man but we really need to find Arnold Naylor, is that you?'

Arnold Naylor sat back in his chair to better survey his Scottish invaders.

'Yes, I'm Arnold Naylor. This is my office and outside is my building site, now in the spirit of *glasnost* that I've just initiated would you mind, please, if it's not to much trouble, telling me who the fuck you are, barging into my office.'

'No' really important who we are pal.'

Martin was using his best Scottish hard-case accent, which included, rather strangely Colin thought, a slight Glaswegian twang.

'Important thing is we're here on behalf o' the Anwar brothers who we're told you owe some cash to.'

'Oh.' Naylor moved a little less easy in his chair. 'Look as I've told Naz and, er whatsisname er, Parveas, isn't it, I will be able to pay in full but not until this contract is over.'

'So what, we've been sent here for a laugh, is that it? We've been told that you should have the money ready.'

'Ah, fir fuck sake, ah could dae wi'oot this!' Colin began his side of the double act. 'So you say you're no' fuckin' payin'?'

'Well lads c'mon, I'm not saying that, it's just not so easy you know. I'll pay. Of course I'll pay, just not right now.'

'Aw well, this is jist fuckin' great eh. Well, you'll have to sign the paperwork to say you've refused, eh. Colin, gie him the paperwork.'

'Eh, ah've no' got the paperwork.'

'Well, how no'?'

'Eh, well, this fucker was supposed to have the money, eh.'

'Colin, mate, it doesnae matter if he pays or no', he's still got to sign the paperwork. Where is it?'

'It's in the strongbox in the boot.'

'Right well, we'll better go and get it, eh.'

Colin and Martin made for the door. Naylor stayed in his seat. Martin turned towards him and smirked.

'Well, are you fuckin' comin' or no'?'

'Oh, right you need me to come as well, sorry!'

Naylor got up and followed them outside. He was led around the back of the car and the boot was opened but Naylor's attention was clearly elsewhere.

'Look at that idiot without his hat on, honestly if I've told him once! OI CHRIS!' Naylor pointed to his head. 'P.P.E. CHRIS, P.P.E., KIND OF IMPORTANT YOU KNOW.'

Naylor turned back to look into the boot. Colin was pulling out a clipboard.

'OK, I'll just have to write on it that you're no payin' the now and you'll hae tae sign it here, eh.'

But Naylor's attention was drawn to the other contents of the boot. Inside he could see the pathetic figure of an emaciated Henry, tightly bound and gagged, his eyeballs almost popping out of his head in an expression that screamed *'PLEASE HELP ME!'*

Martin noticed that Naylor had seen this and then closed the boot quickly flicking an embarrassed and apologetic smile to Naylor. Henry had done his job.

'Right OK, just sign here please.'

Colin kept his expression businesslike. Most of the colour had disappeared from Naylor's face. He looked at Colin and Martin in turn. Colin still with the expectant expression of someone going about his business, Martin looked a little more like he knew what was going on.

'What… what was that?'

'What was what?' Colin kept the game going.

'That, in the boot?'

Martin took over. 'Oh aye sorry mate, kind of forgot about him, eh. Don't worry about him, nothing to do with you.'

'Oh aye, him.' The penny had appeared to drop with Colin.

'Yes, but you've got a man tied…'

Colin interrupted. 'Aye, OK fair do's, we've got a guy, fair enough. Sorry, you werenae supposed to see that, benefit of hindsight and all that but you know this is no' really anything to do with what we're doin' so can you please sign this, we've got kind of a lot on today, y'ken?'

54

Martin drew up to the Anwars' lot. The Rover was parked a slight distance up the street ready for them to be collected.

'Pity,' he thought, as he was just about getting used to lording it in the Mercedes.

Martin and Colin both went up to the sales office, they thought there may be some instructions for the trip back. Nazim looked pleased to see them as they entered.

'Ah it's our Scottish connection, how are you? Take a seat!'

Colin and Martin positioned themselves in the office chairs.

'We have somebody here who wants to meet you!'

After the bizarre week of driving around under the charade of being mafia hitmen types it wouldn't have surprised them if Jeremy Beadle come bursting into the office. Instead, from the private quarters behind the sales office Parveas appeared followed closely by an older Asian gentleman, with completely grey hair and a suit even sharper than Naz and Parveas's.

'Good afternoon, gentlemen. I am Tariq Anwar.'

Colin and Martin knew immediately that this was Naz and Parveas's father even though they had not heard his name before. He was slightly smaller than the brothers, but the look and gait was definitely the same. There were a few wrinkles but other than the grey hair and spectacles perched on his nose he didn't look much older than his sons. Martin and Colin rose from their seats to greet him and he was smiling broadly when they shook his hand. There were two chairs. Tariq assumed a seat but his sons positioned themselves behind him, obviously preferring to stand.

'Did you know that the outstanding debtors that our organisation now has totals only two people, both of whom are now promising us their cheques by the end of the weekend?'

'Some of these people have owed us money for six months or more,' Naz added.

'Oh aye well, it was all Henry's plan and he did all the work really!'

'Ah yes, Henry is a clever man! None the less, thanks very much for what you have done and I hope we will see you back here soon. You're welcome any time.'

Tariq rose from his seat to shake their hands again.

'Now, I don't want to keep you, I know you have a long drive so I'll let you get away. Is there anything you need? Anything we can do before you leave?'

'Aye, you could let us keep the Merc.'

'Yes, we could do that!' Tariq turned to leave the room with a wry smile on his face. 'We won't though!'

55

Martin and Colin eventually arrived at the club in Edinburgh. They had driven around the Grassmarket and Cowgate for about a half an hour before conceding defeat to ask someone where Grindlay Street was. The club was called the Citrus, a ground floor section of a block that appeared to have tenement flats above it. It didn't look like a particularly well looked after building. Pretty shabby really, in sharp contrast with the impressive and new looking Royal Lyceum Theatre directly over the street from it.

The street was full of cars but there was one space directly in front of the club where two yellow traffic cones had been placed. As the car drew close the doormen seemed to recognise it and walked from the door to remove the cones. This was all part of Gordon's instruction. Martin and Colin left the car with all of their luggage still in it and handed the keys to the doormen. They were late but there were still around 50 people queuing for entry. Colin and Martin walked straight past them adopting the usual air of indifference of people on the guest list.

The first thing to hit them was the heat. On entry they took a right turn and were in the bar, separate from any dance floor or main club body. It was still early in the night but the scene was near mayhem. The bar staff were struggling to serve people through the legs of others dancing on the bar. Seats opposite the bar were crammed with people who were clearly reaching their narcotic limit.

They were surprised by the amount of familiar faces. Just about everyone sitting cabbaged in the seats were the regular attenders at the Rhumba Club. Daniel Brown came bounding into the bar from the main club area.

'Alright there, how, you doin'? How was Manchester?'

'Aye, a good laugh Danny.'

Colin looked puzzled.

'What'you doin here? Is Carrie here?'

'Oh aye, Carrie's here, Lara's here, we all came together, eh. In fact everybody's here'

'What's goin on likes?'

'Oh right, you boys'll no' have heard, eh. The Rhumba's landed in Edinburgh.'
Suddenly it started to make sense.

'Oh right, so this is the Rhumba Club?'

'Aye Martin, this is the Rhumba and that, playin' through there is Alistair Cooke.'

'Well, who's Alistair Cooke like?'

Daniel pulled a faux surprised expression. 'Nah Martin. Not who's Alistair Cooke! The question is what is Alistair Cooke? He's a fuckin' genius!'

This wasn't like Daniel to get so worked up about a DJ but Martin and Colin peered through to the main part of the club and it did look like the DJ was causing chaos. Daniel reached into a pocket and pulled out a money change bag from which he picked out four little white balls. They looked like miniature bon-bons. He thrust them out towards Martin and Colin. Chances were that these were ecstasy but they didn't look anything like ecstasy they'd seen before. They were almost completely round and about three times the size of normal pills.

'What the fuck are they?' Daniel was acting pretty strangely and Martin wondered why he would be keeping sweets in a money change bag.

'These are Snowballs.'

'Right well, what are we supposed to do, swallow them or throw them at one another?'

Daniel grinned, his chin was quavering and his eyes all over the place. 'Mate, these little bitches are the future, ah'm tellin' ya.'

Martin picked two out of Daniel's hand and popped them both in his mouth.

Colin looked around the bar and thought that if Snowballs were the reason why everyone was in a state then two at a time mightn't be the best idea. In for a penny though. Colin grabbed the two remaining pills and swallowed them.

'Danny mate, where's your sister?'

Daniel pointed into the main club. 'Last time ah saw her she was at the top o' the stairs at the fire exit.'

Colin and Martin walked through the doorway to the main dance floor. It was pandemonium.

The place itself was about half the size of Fat Sams, but there were none of the frills to get in the way. It was all dance floor except a small raised area and walkway on one side and a very scant and basic placement of seating at the other side.

The décor was at best industrial, but not in the clichéd way of the Hacienda, with genuine scaffolding poles taking the place of where rails and rests would normally be.

The seating was mainly being used by people to stand on to gain some elevation over the bouncing crowd all of whom, to a person, appeared to be lost in the music.

The DJ console was in the opposite corner from the bar door. There was a small collection of people in the console that Colin recognised as the Rhumba organisers.

They were watching the DJ and looking at one another, nodding in acceptance. The music, the standard low bass thump of underground dance music, loud and immediate with the size of the club. Completely appreciated by the crowd. The lighting low with the occasional lasers darting around the room.

Colin looked to his right, up a small flight of stairs to see Carrie making her way down towards him. They came together and she hugged him tightly.

'How's my man? Did you get on alright in Manchester?'

Colin drew back slightly so that he could see her face, her chin was wobbling and her eyes half closed as she looked directly back.

'Aye, it was a good laugh, eh. You enjoying yourself tonight then?'

Carrie spread out her arms.

'Oh god aye! Love this place. Little P-shaped dungeon that it is.'

Carrie thrust her hips in towards Colin's. She moaned as she had a look of thrill in her eyes. She leant forward and kissed Colin, long and deep, holding on for around ten seconds.

'C'mon are you comin' for a dance?'

The question wasn't put in a way that hinted at choice. Colin followed Carrie on to the dance floor. He had to stop occasionally for a hug from the many familiar faces all with the same look. Half-closed eyes and a chin that appeared to have the consistency of setting jelly. Colin was happy to dance for a while looking at Carrie. So sexy when her inhibitions were lost like this, flashing the occasional glance at Colin, the message so easy to decipher.

'You're gonnae get it later pal!'

The music was good as well. Colin could get the deep underground house. Trance type music that never hinted at the over-exuberance of what the lesser clued-up clubbers were now beginning to call dance anthems. Alistair Cooke certainly didn't seem to be the type to rely on these 'classics' to get the crowd onside. Colin looked over towards the seating to see another familiar face, a frame swaying to the music in a very unfamiliar way.

'Carrie, just have to go and see someone OK?'

Carrie looked completely blissful. 'Well, you hurry back soldier!'

Colin pushed past the crowd and sat down. 'You alright Lawrie?'

Lawrie Gordon looked over and seemed to take a few seconds to register who it was. 'Oh, alright Colin, how d'ya get on?'

'Aye pretty good, eh.'

Gordon faced forwards and resumed shaking his head in time to the music. Colin had never seen him like this before.

'The Anwars reckon you two played a star turn. You did well.'

Gordon put an arm around Colin's shoulders. He was clearly away with it. Colin could feel the hairs on the back of his neck begin to prickle. His hit was on its way.

'You give the car keys to the bouncers?'

'Aye, we did that, nae bother, everything's done.'

'Ah, you're a good man Colin. The car'll be waiting outside when you leave and don't worry, it'll be clean by then.'

Colin and Martin hadn't known what was secreted in the car on their way back from Manchester, they agreed that not knowing was probably a good thing. If they were stopped they wouldn't particularly know what they were hiding or where it was. If any policeman found it then it would obviously be because they knew what they were looking for so there wasn't much that could have been done.

The deep house thump began to fade to be replaced with the easy strain of an off-beat reggae rhythm. A mysterious sounding lady began to sing and the thrill of ecstasy's hit surged in Colin's neck. The woman was singing about a far away place and exotic people. Colin looked back to the dancefloor. Back towards Carrie, Lara and Martin. All still dancing but looking quite astonished at the music being played.

Colin stood up and felt like he'd continue to the ceiling. The reggae now had a tingly electronic tune segueing into it that matched the sensations all through Colin's body. All at once his jaw dropped and he took a long inward breath. This was easily as powerful as any hit he'd had before. Exhilaration flooded all of his senses and he began to walk towards Carrie. The woman kept singing but now he could hear a familiar voice recite a passage that he knew very well.

'Let us not wallow in the valley of despair, I say to you today, my friends. And so even though we face the difficulties of today and tomorrow, I still have a dream.'

He stopped and listened as Dr Martin Luther King extolled his obvious wisdom on the out-of-it crowd accompanied by the singing of clearly the most exotic woman on earth. The music and voices reverberated around the room and Colin could do nothing but stand and allow the whole thing to wash through him.

'I have a dream that one day every valley shall be exalted, and every hill and mountain shall be made low, the rough places will be made plain, and the crooked places will be made straight; "and the glory of the Lord shall be revealed and all flesh shall see it together.'

He was rooted to the spot. The woman still sang and the electronic tingle grew more and more intense as it fused with the power of the words.

'Let freedom ring from the mighty mountains of New York. Let freedom ring from the heightening Alleghenies of Pennsylvania. Let freedom ring from the snow-capped Rockies of Colorado. Let freedom ring from the curvaceous slopes of California.'

And now he was in the Rhumba Club proper. Not just a place to listen to music and be with friends. It was a drug addled paradise where men developed super powers and their women grew even more beautiful.

'But not only that.'

Clearly at this time a bastion venue of American Civil Rights.

'Let freedom ring from Stone Mountain of Georgia. Let freedom ring from Lookout Mountain of Tennessee. Let freedom ring from every hill and molehill of Mississippi. From every mountainside, let freedom ring.'

Carrie was now looking directly at him. A hand out in front of her face, she beckoned Colin over with one finger and Colin summoned the ability to walk towards her. The music stopped but Dr King continued to the background noise of the excited crowd.

'And when this happens, when we allow freedom ring, when we let it ring from every village and every hamlet, from every state and every city, we will be able to speed up that day when all of God's children, black men and white men, Jews and Gentiles, Protestants and Catholics, will be able to join hands and sing in the words of the old Negro spiritual.'

Colin and Carrie merged together. They kissed. The DJ started the atmospheric intro to another new and wonderful house record as the reverend shouted his closing call to action.

'FREE AT LAST FREE AT LAST,'

The music built and intensified.

'THANK GOD ALMIGHTY… WE'RE FREE AT LAST!'

And at that very moment the beat surged and a bass scooped around the club sending every last one of the revellers into uncontrollable frenzy.

Two people stood still. Colin looked Carrie directly in the eyes.

'Carrie, I'm completely and wi'out limit in love with you.'

He breathed in again and his chin shuddered. The ecstasy was still growing.

'I want to be with you forever.'

The music continued to throb and the crowd jostled them but they stood and kept staring deep into one another. Carrie smiled, cute and seductive at the same time and Colin knew that she was about to say something deeply moving. But she didn't. She pushed her arms around his back and pulled him till they met together tightly and when she kissed him this time, he knew, without words that he'd get his wish.

DECEMBER 1993

HOGMANAY

56

Martin crept his car over the Friarton Bridge. He'd been over the bridge a thousand times and had never felt so nervous before. A gale was blowing sleet sideways across the bridge which seemed a couple of times to have been entirely capable of lifting the car from the road and depositing it in the River Tay some 200 metres below. It was not even six o'clock in the evening and the sky around him was completely dark. Driving was difficult.

The view from the window was an occasional beam of light into the howling sleet when the wipers managed to move the water from the screen. A gust of wind caught the car square on the side and it lulled and sidled towards the bridge crash barriers. Martin looked at the speed dial and quickly decided that 40 mph would be a bit better than 50 mph as he eased his foot off the gas. After all, it was not as though anybody should ever really be in too much a hurry to get to Dundee, New Year or not.

Martin didn't know exactly where he was going once he got to Dundee but remembered the last time he was there that Morgan's on North Lindsay Street had the required amount of ne'r-do-wells to make the procurement of drugs a possibility. Even if he couldn't get them there he was sure that he could meet someone who could get them somewhere.

Travelling to Dundee on New Year's Eve for the purpose of getting drugs was probably the last thing that Martin wanted to be doing but he was coming to the obvious conclusion that, at the moment, in Edinburgh, if Lawrie Gordon didn't have drugs then none of them did. All down to some completely outrageous whimsical notion that the Anwars had that they were being watched. Not really relevant, Martin thought to what they were doing in Edinburgh, but this wasn't a view shared by Gordon. He wanted total avoidance of them and what Gordon wanted, he got.

It was all right for everybody else. Colin and Carrie were now almost complete owners of the garage in Ceres. Colin was hardly there any more but it seemed the less he turned up the more money it made for them. Even when times were good, they seemed to have more money than Martin. Maybe something to do with all the nights he'd been spending in the Links Bar but *'fuck it, a man's gotta live.'*

Danny Brown was in the smallest room in the flat they were now all sharing in Edinburgh's Bruntsfield. He worked out of an office in Livingston, which clearly paid enough for him to get along. Martin had no doubt that Lara was the highest earner in the flat with her position as an engineer in the city's planning and building standards department. He could probably live off her quite comfortably until they were back on their feet dealing again but couldn't bring himself to do that. No, Martin needed something for himself. A little deal that could get him some money for the festivities. Otherwise, this Hogmanay was due to be a washout for him.

Martin made it off the bridge on to the relative safety of the A90 heading east past Walnut Grove. He considered that he'd maybe drive back through Fife. Still the Tay Bridge to cross but ten times safer than the Friarton Bridge in this weather. He reached over to the passenger seat and picked up his flask, now half full of Talisker. Martin had learned that unless you were driving like a prick, the police hardly ever stopped you and that a little dram didn't really put him off.

No driving tomorrow though. January the first being the police's annual festive catch a drink driver day. He opened the lid and took a couple of deep gulps. Some single malt for the trip wouldn't hurt. Anyway he might need something to get him to a state where he could walk into Morgan's to face all the dodgy punters in there.

***

He battled through the driving sleet from the car park just across the road from Morgan's. It was just a little after six but it was busy. New Year always had the pubs filling up early. Out of the cold, he continued up the stairs to the main bar. Morgan's had a small bar downstairs and the upstairs formed a balcony which circled above the downstairs lounge type area. Across from the balcony was a large bar and further raised area. Right at the top of the stair was the DJ console where some large ugly geek with a ponytail was playing some cheesy festive nonsense.

Martin made his way to the bar. First thing was first and Martin needed a pint of lager. He waited around five minutes at the bar, competing with scores of people all waiting to be served by bar staff who clearly hadn't wanted to be working that night and then made his way back to the balcony with a flat pint of lager-cum-water.

He surveyed downstairs in the lower bar and around the balcony to check whether he could recognise anybody and his spirits were lifted ever so slightly at one person that he knew. Albeit a bit of a fuck-up of a familiar person, Martin thought that he might be able to help. Martin made his way to the other side of the balcony pushing his way past all manner of drunks, poseurs and underage tarts.

'Alright Steve?'

Steve McNaughton looked up slowly and registered who was talking to him.

'Oh, man, Martin Bridges, how are you doing mate?'

Steve stood up to shake Martin's hand, his movements laboured and clumsy.

'I've not seen you for ages.'

Steve was surrounded by four girls. This wasn't unusual for him but these girls lacked the class of the girls Martin was used to seeing him with.

'Here man, have a seat.'

Steve still had the middle-class accent but his words were slow and seemed to tail off at the end. It didn't matter if they were the broadest-speaking person in the world or a member of minor royalty, you could always tell when someone was on downers when they spoke.

'So what have you been up to man?'

'Ah, we're living in Edinburgh now, eh.'

Steve flicked a glance among his female companions.

'What you're living in Edinburgh and decided to come to Dundee for Hogmanay?'

Steve was referring to the world famous street party on Edinburgh's Princes Street which most people in Dundee would consider to be what Hogmanay was all about but in which Martin had no interest, especially on a vile night like this.

'Nah well ah'll be heading back to Edinburgh later but believe it or no' we're experiencing a bit o' a drought the now, so ah thought ah'd maybe try Dundee for some gear. Any ideas where ah can get anythin'? Ah'd have to get a lay on like but you know ah'm good for it. E's or coke, maybe even sulph?'

Martin thought he ought to be specific to avoid being taken up to some shooting alley for a couple of grams of heroin.

Steve sat back, smiled and then mumbled, 'Aye, mate, course I can do that for you. No bother.'

Steve left to make the necessary phone calls leaving Martin to endure the small talk of the girls around him. Steve arriving back with the thumbs-up sign couldn't come quickly enough.

'Right then girls we won't be long. OK Martin mate, let's get going.'

Martin wondered where they were going but it was just small talk really. Didn't matter too much.

'So where are we off to Steve?'

'Ah, we're going up to Mill o' Mains, the Digger will sort you out.'

Martin's mind flashed back to around two years earlier going up to Mill o' Mains to see the Digger and what an almighty fuck-up that had been. More importantly he thought back to just over a year ago when Colin had taken around six grand of the Digger's money on St Andrews High Street. He knew nothing had been done about this. Not yet. But if he was supposed to go up to Mill o' Mains to cut a deal now surely the Digger would be able to put two and two together. Suddenly panic filled his mind.

'What the fuck am I doin' here? What am I fuckin' thinking about? I cannae be doin' deals with Digger Stewart and look at the dodgy cunt I'm trying to team up with.'

The cold air outside Morgan's hit him at the same time as the obvious realisation that he was making a mistake and needed to get out of there.

57

Martin sat in the Earl of Marchmont, cursing his decision to try Dundee for drugs. Anywhere would have been a better choice than that. The Earl wasn't exactly known for its drug-taking clientele but some of the older guys actually had some good grass from time to time and he figured that New Year would probably be just such a time.

A familiar tone played from his jacket pocket. He fished out his mobile telephone and looked at the screen. The name scrolled across the LCD screen. LARA B.

'Oh wonderful!'

The phone had been a gift from Lara on his birthday and although he thought it was great at the time it was now a bit embarrassing to have his girlfriend pay his phone for him and it only really ever got used for her to check up on him. He looked around the phone for a button to hang up or a dial to make it quieter but not finding such a button, he placed the phone back in his jacket pocket.

'No one important then?'

Martin looked up to see a man about his own age looking down at him.

'What?'

'Your phone, it's still ringing.'

The man seemed to have a deep South Eastern American accent.

'*Brilliant,*' thought Martin, '*a bloody tourist.*'

The man took a seat.

'Not going to answer it?'

What was this all about?

'Well, no, as it happens.'

The telephone stopped ringing but the man didn't move away.

'Sorry mate, can ah help you wi' somethin'.'

'Maybe!'

He leaned forward in an apparent attempt not to be heard by the rest of the pub.

'I recognise you from the Citrus Club. You...' he checked around. 'Well, you sell drugs, right?'

'No' in the Earl o' Marchmont ah don't, no!'

'Nothin' doin' then?'

This was bizarre, being asked about drugs in the Earl from a Yank but Martin wanted to know if this would lead to something.

'No, ah didnae say that, what you after like?'

'Just a bit of blow, not much!'

'How much?'

'Well, an ounce.'

'An ounce, fuck me, that's a fair chunk o' dope.'

'Yeah, sure, but I'm off to London tomorrow so I may not get a chance for a while.'

'Aye sure mate, it's fine, ah'm no' needin' your life story, eh.'

Martin was starting to think about options now. This guy was American and, as such, probably stupid. He wasn't exactly sure how but he was sure there was some money to be made. Just relieve this poor sap of some of his Yankee dollars, then down to the Subway on Lothian Road. That place would be sailing with drugs, he knew that. It would be those dodgy Hibs casuals but any place in a thunderstorm. New Year might just be saved.

'Look mate, ah'm no' really involved wi' dope but ah know a few people who could probably cut that amount off for you. You'll have to come with me though, the guys in here would string me up if they thought ah was using the Earl for dodgy dealing, you know?'

Outside the Earl of Marchmont the weather was dreadful. Sleet had turned to driving rain and was blowing sideways along Warrender Park Road. Martin didn't want to use his car. Didn't really want this idiot knowing anything about him.

'How you getting tae London? Takin' the train?'

'No sir, I got me a car so I'll be drivin'.'

'Oh right cool, you got your car with you, cos we've got a bit of a distance to go, eh.'

'Yeah sure, follow me.'

***

As Martin expected the American twit knew nothing about the area and had to be directed to the street with a series of 'turn left here' and 'take the next right.' They parked on Leven Terrace. Just a block away from Bruntsfield. This would be perfect.

The flats were six to a block with a back green through the back leading to other six block flats. On the other side, Leven Street, then a short walk down to Lothian Road and, hey presto, you were five minutes walk to the Subway.

Perfect.

'Right then here we are. Right, ounce o' dope. Mate, ah'm no even sure how much that'd cost. What do you normally pay?'

'Well, I don't know, I don't normally.'

'Oh right ah see, well look, you give me £150 and ah'm sure ah'll bring back change.'

'Oh no, I ain't letting you go up by yourself.'

'Well mate look, no choice, eh. Ah go up there with an unknown American and ah'll be the one getting bounced off the wall. These people are pretty paranoid about the Old Bill, eh. Hold on, you're no' Old Bill are you?'

'Old who? What're you talking about?'

'The police, are you a fuckin' policeman?'

Martin opened the door as if to prepare to leave in a hurry.

'That's crazy, of course I'm not police. OK look, I'll give you the cash but don't try to rip me off OK. I'll know.'

Martin breathed out and shook his head.

'Well, that's fuckin' great, eh, ah'm doin' this for you as a favour. Havnae even asked you for any money mysel'.'

'OK, yeah, you're right. Sorry.'

The American looked genuinely apologetic as Martin stepped out of his car. Martin walked into the first close, looking up to make it seem like he was checking for lights at the windows. The inside of the close was dimly lit but certainly brighter than outside and a whole lot drier and less windy. There was a flight of just three stairs leading towards the back door out to the greens.

Martin checked that he wasn't being watched and walked down to the backdoor. It was a wooden slatted door, badly in need of replacement with dark brown paint flaking from it. He checked the handle but the door was jammed shut. Just below he could see a black attachment which he checked to find a padlocked bolt.

'Bastard!'

He shook it and it didn't seem too well attached to the wood. A good kick would probably do it but he had to think about the noise. What to do?

Martin walked back into the close and looked up the first flight of stairs. There was an old fashioned panelled slide window which was currently being pelted by the driving rain. Martin climbed the stairs and after some effort managed to open the window, wide enough for him to fit out and the sleet to howl in.

'Cannae believe ah'm doin' this!'

Martin squeezed through the window, battered by the weather, where there was ten foot drop into total blackness. He manoeuvred himself so that he could hold on to the window sill and extend so that the jump would only be around four foot or so but the wetness of the window sill made it impossible to hold on and he began to hurtle towards the ground.

His fall was broken as his feet collided with a metal bin, sending the bin clattering one way against the wall and Martin the other way into thick grass, soaking wet nettles and hogweed. The bin made an almighty crash as it emptied its contents, mainly it would seem of beer bottles on to the green's perimeter path.

Martin picked himself up and composed himself. The right side of his body was now completely soaked, the rest of him catching up rapidly. He could hear shouting from inside the close. Seconds later the door was rattling.

'You fucking Scottish bastard. I'll fucking kill you!'

'Oh shite!'

Martin could hear the latch of the door being pulled and rattled. He headed off across the green towards the flats on the other side. The grass must have been around two feet high with weeds twining themselves around one another making progress slow.

All of this undergrowth was soaked and within seconds Martin's jeans were completely wet through.

'What the fuck am ah doin' here? This is nuts.'

The close door swung open, casting a dim glow long over the green but just missing where Martin was standing.

'You dirty bastard, where are you?'

The American came storming through the door. Martin looked across at the flats opposite. He couldn't see an open door. The American was now jumping around, muttering all sorts of obscenities.

Martin crept over to a blackened silhouette of a building that he assumed to be a dilapidated garden shed and crouched against it. Surely the American wouldn't search the green. Not in this weather. Martin thought about what he was doing there. The sleet cascading from above had now almost completely soaked all of his clothes. No way could he walk into the Subway like this. This was hair-brained from the start.

'What the fuck was ah thinking about?'

The American was now standing up to his knees in the weeds. He could only have been around 20 feet from where Martin was hiding but his enthusiasm for the chase seemed to be waning. He was now muttering instead of shouting.

'Dirty Scottish bastard. How could I have been so fucking dumb?'

He turned back to the open door and it would appear that the search was over. The American started to walk back.

'Thank fuck, away and get a grip you dopey Yank fuck!'

He had taken around three laboured steps when a familiar tone leapt out across the green from Martin's jacket pocket.

'Oh no, Lara, no' now for fuck sake.'

The American swivelled to the direction of the telephone ringing.

'Ha, you Scottish bastard, I've got you now!'

Martin stood up as the American came steadily towards him, both of them were now standing drenched with the sleet still pouring on top of them. The phone was still ringing allowing the American to home in. This was ridiculous, all for £150.

'OK mate, let's no' get stupid, eh. Ah'll give you your money back.'

'Oh no friend, you're way past that now.'

He was around five feet away now and Martin could just see him making out karate shapes with his hands.

'Oh for fuck's sake!' *'OK, if this dodgy Yank wants a rumble then fuck him, I'll just keep the money.'*

Martin heard a quick yelp 'hooy' as he felt what seemed like an open hand connect directly on his mouth, making him stumble backwards.

'Aaaye.'

This time there was no doubt, a foot had connected to the side of his head and stunned, Martin tumbled headwards back towards the shed and landed on the soaking undergrowth.

'Right then you Scottish bastard, I'm going to teach you a lesson!'

'OK, OK, ah think we've established that ah'm Scottish and ah'm a bit of a cunt but this is getting a bit…'

'Yaaaah!'

Martin wasn't allowed to finish his sentence as he felt the full force of the American's foot thrust into his chest.

'Oh fuck!'

The kick hurt. He could feel his whole stomach constrict. The pain stretched out across his chest into his back and across his shoulders. No way was he winning this fight now. Martin reached out above him to grab on to what he could, he needed to get away now and crawling seemed the only option left. His hand connected with a wooden shaft. A shovel, rake, hoe, in the darkness it was impossible to tell what it was but it was something he could use to repel the attack. He picked it up and pointed it towards the American as he strode forward for another hit.

'Hooy.'

The American made another advance unaware of the implement being held up by Martin. There was no contact this time though as the American let out a loud gasp followed by a gurgle. The shaft became heavy, thrust its way behind Martin and lodged into the ground. A few seconds passed and the American appeared to slump onto the shaft making it impossible for Martin to hold up. It slowly tumbled to the side and the gurgling sound suddenly stopped.

'Mate, you alright?'

There was no answer.

Martin slid his hand up the shaft and the water on the handle became thicker and sticky. Martin could feel a cold metal attachment at the end of the shaft. The attachment wasn't a shovel, it formed into four prongs.

'Oh no!'

Martin slid his fingers further up one of the prongs but his progress was halted after a couple of inches by the American's clothed chest. A spurt of warm liquid enveloped his hand. Martin lifted his hand to the relative light of the sky. He could make out the drips of blood falling from his fingers.

'Oh, no. Christ all fuckin' mighty, no!'

58

Lara was now the only one in the flat whose partner wasn't there. Pretty embarrassing considering he lived there. Colin and Carrie had obviously been there all day. Scott Henderson arrived with his girlfriend Cheryl at around nine o'clock and Daniel's new boyfriend, Jim, had just arrived around quarter of an hour ago.

Daniel had been nervous about introducing a boyfriend to his sister but was pleased when Carrie and Jim had seemed to genuinely hit it off. Daniel was a bit nervous still, as he'd considered that Martin would probably be the one that would take the most getting used to it, and being that he wasn't there yet, he still couldn't relax knowing that the night would be entirely comfortable. He was genuinely interested to know how Martin would react as he gauged that Martin's reaction would be similar to his parents when they found out, blissfully unaware as they were of their son's sexuality.

Lara looked at her phone and considered calling again but it was embarrassing enough that he wasn't there without everyone realising that he was ignoring her calls as well. Then suddenly as if willing it to do so was working, the mobile rang. She checked and as she'd hoped the screen showed simply – 'M'. She answered the phone trying not to sound as angry as she was.

'Martin, where are you? Where have ya been?'

There was a short pause.

'Lara, listen ah really need to talk to Colin, can you put him on?'

'Oh come on Martin, I've no' spoke to you all day, are you comin' home now?'

Another short pause.

'Lara, please, ah'll be back soon enough, ah really need to speak to Colin though.'

She could tell that all wasn't well.

'What's wrong Martin?'

'Lara!'

Something in his voice told her that she should do as he was asking. She held out the phone.

'Colin, it's Martin. Something's no' quite right.'

Colin surveyed the room as he took Lara's mobile. He wasn't used to using them and held the phone awkwardly against his face.

'Alright Martin, what you up to mate, everybody's here, where are you?'

'Ah'm downstairs.'

'Well, what's the story mate, are you coming up?'

Colin made a quizzical gesture to everyone in the room.

'Naw mate, ah need you to come down. By yoursel' though, eh. Oh. And bring a drink.'

***

Colin walked to the bottom of the stairs still in a festive mood until he saw the state of Martin, sitting at the bottom of the stairs.

'Fuckin' hell Martin, what the fuck happened to you?'

Martin sat there completely drenched, his top lip was burst at the left side and he had an open cut just above the left eye. Colin sat down beside him. Martin raised both hands to his face and dragged them down, breathing hard out of his open mouth.

'You bring that drink mate?'

'Aye,' Colin handed him a three quarter full bottle of Talisker. 'What happened, you been fightin'?'

Martin removed the lid and took a long swig of the whisky, wincing when the spirit hit the back of his throat. He looked Colin in the eyes.

'Ah just killed somebody.'

'Come again?'

Martin took another drink. He struggled to stay looking at Colin as he reinforced that he'd heard correctly.

'Ah just killed somebody!'

'Right, do you think ah can hae a drink of that now?'

Colin took the bottle, now down to around half full and took a swig.

'Who?'

'Just some fuckin' nutter!'

'Well, which fuckin' nutter? What have you been doin'?'

Martin reached out his hand to accept the bottle back.

'This fuckin' American tourist. Stops me in the Earl and asks if I can get him some blow. I'm like, eh, no' really mate, eh. Then he tells me he's off to London tomorrow, then stupid fuckin' me' eh. Ah'm startin to think, maybe ah'll just rip the cunt off. So we jump in his car, ah take 'im tae some fuckin' stupid address ah've never been tae before. Takes his money, goes to do the runner and he catches me.'

Martin paused for another drink.

'We get in a fight and, this fucker's like Mr Miyagi or something, so ah reach out, pick up the first thing ah can get my hand on and the next thing ah know, the cunt's fuckin' impaled on a pitchfork.'

Colin looked around the close his mouth now open in amazement.

'Martin what the fuck are you on? This isnae April the first, you cannae be serious right!'

'Look Colin, ah've been a stupid cunt, eh.'

'Nae fuckin' shit. Wait, how do you know he's dead?'

'Well if ah was listin' the main reasons ah'd probably say the top three were that he's lying in the rain no' movin', ah checked his pulse and there was nothin' and, oh aye, the fact that that he's got a huge fuckoff pitchfork sticking out of his chest probably has something' tae dae wi' it.'

The bottle changed hands again.

'Well, where the fuck did you find a pitchfork?'

'We were in the back greens off of Leven Terrace.'

'What, down at the Meadows?'

'Aye.'

'In the back green?'

'Back green, aye.'

'Fuck were you doin' in there? Actually… no, doesn't matter. Anybody see yous?'

'Nut!'

'Well does anybody know he's there?'

'No' unless somebody's had a sudden Alan-Titchmarsh-inspired urge tae go and look after their garden in the pitch black pishing rain, ah wouldnae have thought so, no.'

Colin handed back the bottle without being asked.

'Did anybody see him wi' ya?'

'Nah, no' really, couple o' punters in the Earl but they werenae payin' any attention likes.'

'Quiet down that part of the Meadows just now ah would have thought, eh. Is his car parked near to the backies that he's in?'

'Aye, right up against the close, eh. Why?'

Martin could sense that Colin was thinking about something.

'Right, ah'm away to get my coat, we're goin' down there.'

'Why what are we gonnae do like?'

Expectation was now chiselled into Martin's expression.

Colin took the bottle from him placed it on the ground and put his hands on Martin's shoulders.

'Look mate, you need to sober up a wee bit. This guy. American tourist. Here probably just for Hogmanay. Away to London tomorrow you said.'

'Well no' now he's no'!'

A shiver went down his spine that he could be so flippant at a time like this.

'Aye well look, as long as he's no' found in that garden, then you might get out o' this.'

'So what are we gonnae' do like?'

'Well, you were in his car, so he should have the keys still on 'im. We pile him in the boot, and then, look mate, you'll have to drive him up here. You think you can manage that?'

'Aye, aye, nae probs, eh.'

'You'll hae to speak to Lara when you get back, make up some shite about what happened to your face and ah'll speak to Daniel and Scotty and we'll work out how we're gonnae get rid o' him and his car tomorrow.'

'Whoah, whoa Colin mate come on.'

Martin grabbed hold of Colin to stop him making his way back up the stairs.

'Come on Colin, we've got to get rid of the body, the car an' aw, now. We cannae wait until tomorrow. There's gotta be somewhere where we can get rid o' 'im tonight in Edinburgh, eh.'

'Nah mate, you dinnae understand. We're no' getting' rid o' 'im in Edinburgh, we're getting rid o' 'im in London.'

MAY 1994

DARK

59

The Links was nearly full. Friday, not even noon yet, but then the student regular crowd weren't exactly known for their diligent approach to studying on sunny Fridays. Martin sat at the back of the bar by the pool tables. This was his regular spot. He wasn't much of a pool player and, sure, it was still students but those that played pool seemed to talk less about socio-economic politics and the like than the pretentious crowd that peopled the rest of the place. He was even beginning to get to know a few of them. Hardly surprising, given that he was possibly the most regular client they had. He had just nipped out for 'a message' but couldn't really resist the lure of the place.

Another trip to Manchester was on the cards for today. He hadn't been for a while but there was no great hurry, if they left at one o'clock then they could easily be there by five. Perfect timing really. So for now he could afford some pints and chasers and a bit of banter with his clever student buddies.

***

'OK, just give him this for me Colin will you?'

'Aye, no probs Lara. He'll be back soon like you know that, eh?'

Colin checked his watch.

'Probably better if ah'm no' here when he gets here though, don't you think?'

'Dunno Lara. Maybe.'

Lara picked up a suitcase of her things and turned towards the door.

'You'll be alright Lara, aye?'

Lara turned back into the hall put her case down and hugged Colin.

'Ah'll be fine Colin. Ah'll be fine.'

She pulled back and looked at him.

'You'll make sure Martin's alright though, won't you?'

She could see him wince slightly.

'He'll be alright!'

Lara didn't look at all convinced as she turned round and picked up her case.

'Ah'll see you later Colin.'

'Aye Lara, keep in touch, eh.'

Lara closed the door and she was gone. Colin walked into the lounge. Daniel was sitting by himself. He put concisely into one sentence exactly what Colin was thinking.

'He'll no' like that, eh?'

Colin frowned.

'No, he'll no' like that? Wait until he hears what we've got tae tell him!'

***

Martin walked over Bruntsfield Links towards the flat with slightly less preying on his mind than usual. A trip to The Links could do that for him. Lara had been in a funny mood that morning. Martin hated silent treatment. Anything was better. If she was shouting at him at least he'd know what the problem was but when she said nothing, it just made him wonder. Is this just your normal-type female issues or had she something on her mind? Fair enough, he'd been drinking a bit lately and if he was honest not exactly bringing sufficient money to fund it but she knew that today was the day that he would start putting that right.

Or, maybe she knew about the American. He could play on Martin's mind. He'd have to get a newspaper from a shop to see if anything had been printed yet. Get some snacks for the trip as well. Gotta get the paper though. That American must have been a right loner. Hasn't even been reported as missing yet. Well, not in the Scottish papers anyway.

***

Martin fumbled with his key at the lock for a few seconds before Colin opened it.

'Y'all right mate, we ready to get goin'? Ah've got our provisions.'

Martin handed a bag full of packeted snacks to Colin.

'What, did you go to The Links first?'

'Aye, just hair o' the dog, eh.'

Colin followed Martin back through to the lounge.

'Martin, we need to talk mate, eh!'

'Aye, good can it wait till we're in the car, cos we're kind o' late, eh.'

'Aye, we're late.'

Colin wasn't sure if Martin was taking the piss or not, could he not realise that the reason they were late was that he'd been filling himself in the pub?

'Listen Martin, Lara was in a wee while ago.'

Martin was equipping himself with joint rolling equipment for the journey.

'Oh, right aye, she'll have been on her lunch hour, disnae matter, ah'll se her th' night eh.'

Colin looked at Daniel and grimaced.

'Aye, well that's the thing, eh. She left this for you!'

Colin handed over a white envelope. Martin accepted.

'What is it?'

'Well, ah think ya need to read it!'

Martin opened the letter and began to read.

Martin

I'm really sorry to be doing this to you now but I think that for the good of both of us, I'm leaving the flat and moving in with a workmate.

I think that we both realise that things haven't been working for a while so the best thing would be to end it now.

I'm sorry to end it like this and not face to face but I'm not sure about what your reaction would be. In fact for a little time now I haven't really been able to work out what you've been thinking.

We've both changed and I suppose that happens. For weeks now you've been talking about Manchester and how everything would be great after you've been but I don't think you realise that I don't really want to live with an occasional drug smuggler.

I really hope that you can get over whatever is wrong with you at the moment and I know that a letter like this is not the best way to do this but I really hope you can stop drinking so much. It'll not help.

I'll always remember the good times and hope you can too.

Lara.

Martin walked over to the window and looked at the people outside busily carrying out their daily business in the Bruntsfield sun.

'Did you know about this?'

Colin joined him at the window.

'Ah did have a word with her like, aye.'

'Ach well, suppose that's that, we should get going though, eh.'

Martin was about to turn back into the room but Colin stopped him.

'Martin look, you've just had some pretty bad news and you've had a few.'

Colin just stopped himself from mentioning what happened the last time Martin had tried to make a drug deal after splitting up with a girlfriend.

'Maybe, you should sit this one out, eh. Me and Daniel'll go this time. You can be on the next run.'

Colin stood at the window waiting for the inevitable outburst but to his surprise it didn't come.

Martin wasn't sure of which bit of news to consider first but as he stood there beside Colin in the bright sunshine he could work one decision out quite clearly. Right now would he rather spend a whole day going to Manchester and back or would he prefer a couple of joints and back down to The Links for a few more games of pool with his sponging, student muckers?

'Aye, fair do's Colin. Maybe that's a good idea.'

60

'Colin, we're not able to get the package into the car this time, we know that the police are watching us.'

'What, is this a wasted trip then, could you not have told Lawrie this before we came?'

Parveas motioned with an open hand for Colin to calm down.

'It doesn't have to be a wasted trip, we can get you some product but this time you may have to get your hands a little more dirty than usual.'

Parveas reached into a drawer and pulled out a single A4 sheet of paper. There was a photocopy of a map and a name and address.

'If you go to this address and ask for Peter, he'll be expecting you and he knows what to give you.'

Colin surveyed the sheet of paper.

'A map? X marks the spot, is that it? Do you no' think it would be easier if you got someone to take us?'

Parveas sighed deeply.

'Colin, perhaps you think I'm exaggerating, we *are* under surveillance!'

'Maybe you're being watched now!'

'I fully believe we are Colin, yes, but when you go away from here, you're just another car that drove into our lot and then drove off again. You'll not be followed!'

Colin couldn't help his reaction, turning around to see if he could spot who may be looking at them. Picking up from a flat in Salford just seemed so risky. Introducing himself to someone he didn't know freaked him.

'Well, who is this guy? Peter?'

'He's OK Colin, you know, he's trustworthy.'

'But you can't get involved?'

Parveas pushed away from the table to free his legs from the desk and swivelled to relax in his chair.

'There's a drugs war in Manchester, you know. People are being shot and the police are cracking down.'

'So, it's risky is what you're saying.'

'It's risky, yeah!'

'You're no' getting involved but you expect us tae?'

Parveas got up from his seat, walked around the desk and positioned himself on the ledge.

'Colin, this is where you earn your stripes friend. Sometimes you have to have the balls to do the dangerous things! You just have to take the package from this address, get in the car, take it to the club and hand it over. Once you've done this, you're in the clear.'

Parveas placed his hand on Colin's shoulder.

'You have to face facts Colin. You smuggle drugs. There are risks.'

Colin leant back in his chair and checked over towards Daniel who was silently taking in the conversation.

'Ah know the risks!'

'Believe me, if we thought they were too great, we would not ask you to do this.'

It wasn't doing jail time himself that bothered Colin. He'd done that before and he knew how to handle it. The worst thing about jail was the time away from Carrie and he knew that this affected her as well. Only worse this time it not only meant that he would go to jail, so would her little brother.

'We'll understand if you don't want to do it!'

Colin swivelled in his chair to meet Parveas' eyes head on.

'No Parveas, it's fine. We'll do it.'

**

Colin and Daniel had been driving for around five minutes. Daniel had been pretending to understand the map that they had been given. He began to have his doubts.

'Colin, mate, are you certain you know where you're goin'?'

'Ah know where ah'm going mate, aye!'

Daniel turned the map in a different direction.

'Aye, but it was supposed to be back intae Salford but you're headin' towards the centre o' Manchester.'

'Ah'm no' headin' towards the pickup.'

'Right, well, ah thought you were gonnae dae it!'

Colin momentarily took his eyes off the road to gauge Daniel's reaction.

'Ah'm gonnae do the pickup mate but you're no'.'

Daniel sat straighter in his seat.

'What d'ya mean?'

'Ah mean, it's one thing one of us doin' this but pointless both of us takin' the risk. It's a one-man job.'

'Well, where are we goin' now like?'

'We're goin' to the train station for you. Ah want you to get the first train you can get back to Edinburgh.'

61

Martin had spent the day trawling the pubs around Lothian Road. Spent a bit of time in the show bars on the pubic triangle. Didn't need Lara for a bit of filth but now he had to get to the Citrus Club. The Rhumba was on and he knew that Colin and Daniel would finish there. Martin had to be there when they arrived. Had to show that he was still part of the operation.

Probably a bit stupid going to The Links that morning and not going to Manchester but he could make that right tonight. He stumbled past the queue straight to the door. Two familiar bruiser-type doormen were allowing people in according to their own time schedule.

'Alright boys?'

They looked at him with a little more concentration than normal. Usually they would just usher him in free of charge.

'Aye. Y'alright y'rsel? You look a wee bit ropey!'

Martin looked up at them, quelling the temptation to tell them to away and fuck themselves, he knew that no matter what the circumstances, it never really did to upset doormen. He straightened himself up and concentrated hard on not looking too smashed.

'Naw, ah'm fine!'

The doormen held some eager clubbers away from the door to make the space for Martin.

'OK mate, in you go!'

They were used to letting people in who looked a state.

It was just after ten o'clock and the place was buzzing. The buses from Perth, Fife and Dundee had clearly arrived and a few familiar faces were in the bar area. Clearly none more familiar than his flatmate Scott Henderson though. Scott stood with a gang of eager of people around him, it was quite clear to anyone paying attention what he was doing. To Martin it seemed like he was just getting careless now. Martin bustled his way through the bar to him.

'Scotty, how you doin'?'

'Just fine Martin how's yersel''

'What you got mate?'

Scott winked as he answered.

'Snawbaws Martin, only the best you know that. What y' needin'?'

Martin thought for a moment, could be a long night, might want to sober up a bit and could do with something to take his mind off the whole Lara situation, among other things.

'Aye, gie's 20.'

Scott drew his head back in surprise.

'What ya on about? 20? Ah'm tryin' tae make a profit here!'

Martin thought about it. 20 was a bit much.

'Oh right well, gie's fuckin' ten then!'

'10?'

'Aye mate, for fuck's sake, the amount of stuff ah'm always geein' you!'

Scott reached into his money change bag and started fumbling around.

'OK, OK, calm down man, eh. Tell you what though, you're on the drinks for the rest of the night.'

***

Martin had considered what a reasonable amount of Snowballs to take at one time would be and came to the conclusion that four wouldn't be breaking the bank. Six could be kept as back-up. Stored in his shirt pocket for use as and when needed. Bored with the conversation in the bar – why everybody kept feeling the urge to tell him how they were feeling at every drop of a hat he couldn't imagine – he walked through to the main club.

In the back of his mind he expected that Lara might be there. She had some questions to answer. He looked out across the dance floor to see if he could make out her face but was in fact having trouble making out anybody's faces other than those a matter of feet away from him.

The dance floor was crowded and the music loud. The DJ's name was Andrew Weatherall. Martin didn't generally care too much about that kind of thing. He had no time for those characters that generally walked around with headphones on, knew the names of every tune and had ideas about issues such as the correct BPM but he had heard of Andrew Weatherall. He'd been in right at the start of the scene and had a reputation as being different. The music was different alright! Deeper, darker, dirtier, seemingly slower than the usual Rhumba fare.

At once Martin's focus sharpened and he could make out the faces of the people on the dance floor. Not the stretched out smiles and happy grins as usual but everyone seemed to wear the same sunken expression. Their eyes fixed on the floor, they sulked as they moved unnaturally to the rhythm of the music.

Martin could feel a gloom descend on the whole room. The mood was completely out of kilter from what he was used to. He leaned on one of the scaffolding pole rails as he took in the scene of a club in despair. The music started to shrink back to the DJ console. It was getting quieter and Martin could hear the chatter of people back in the bar. Vague interference of hundreds of people all talking at once, not nearly clear enough to make out the content of any one conversation until one voice came through clear as a bell. The drawl of the South East American accent drilling into Martin's psyche like a shot.

'You dirty Scottish bastard!'

Martin spun back to face the door leading back into the bar. Nobody familiar. The music once again filled the room and Martin turned back to see the whole dance floor populated by people cheering and hugging. Smiling as though they were having the time of their lives. Martin drew a deep breath.

'Shit man, ah need to get out o' here!'

He barged back to the bar, shoving people as he went. Not a great problem in there. People were used to flailing arms. Back in the relative normality of the bar, once again the music disappeared to be replaced by the indecipherable conversation of the crowd. Martin needed a drink. He looked towards the bar and saw the staff, busy as ever. Somebody was being served by an attractive bar girl at the far end. Somebody familiar. Martin's vision focused clearly again and he knew that it was him. The American was there, being handed a tall glass. He looked over and met Martin's eye, lifting his glass and clearly mouthing the word 'Cheers!'.

'Oh, fuckin' hell. This is nuts. What the fuck is he doin' here?'

Martin pushed his way to the other side of the bar bumping into all sorts of people, familiar and unfamiliar as he went. He grabbed the American roughly by the shoulder.

'What'r you doin' here?'

The American turned round, the expression on his face one of complete surprise.

'Whae the fuck are you likes?'

Martin checked himself.

'Wait, you're no' the American.'

'No I'm no' a fuckin' American, I'm fae Gorgie ya daft cunt!'

Martin could feel a tugging on his arm. He turned round to see Colin lightly holding his shirt sleeve.

'Martin, what you up to?'

'Eh?'

The man at the bar was clearly unimpressed.

'Whoah hey, you've spilt mah drink.'

Martin looked completely lost, Colin wasn't even sure Martin recognised him. He reached into his pocket and pulled out a £5 note.

'Right mate, sorry eh, here get yoursel' another, eh.'

Colin cajoled Martin to a quiet part of the bar.

'What was all that about?'

'Colin, where have you been mate?'

Colin drew his head back to survey Martin's face. He was right. Martin was just starting to recognise him.

'Martin, what you talkin' about man? You know fine where ah've been.'

Martin spun back towards the bar and pointed to his new Gorgie associate.

'Colin look that's the fuckin' Amer...'

Martin stopped mid sentence. There was nobody at the bar that he recognised save one vaguely familiar guy staring over at him and Colin with a £5 note raised to attract the barmaid. Martin seemed to be gathering some composure. He smiled and began to giggle.

'Fuckin' hell mate, think ah might have freaked out there though, eh.'

Colin looked behind him. Two girls were sitting almost straight in their seats, their heads pressed to the headrests. Colin asked if they could budge over just a bit to let Martin sit. They didn't look too pleased to be asked. They didn't actually look as if they knew what was going on but they did move sidewards. A synchronised shuffle, without change of facial expression, it was like something they'd been practising. Colin gripped Martin by the shoulders, turned him and placed him into the space they were leaving.

Martin blew out hard, his focus and vision were just about returning to normal and for the first time in around half an hour he felt like he knew what was going on.

'Jesus Col, that was a bit mental that, eh.'

'Must've been aye. What was aw that at the bar, who's he?'

'Ah've no' got a fuckin' clue mate, for a minute there ah thought…'

Martin thought about what he was saying. Admitting that he was experiencing apparitions of the American just seemed that little bit too weird.

'Ah dunno. Don't know the guy. Have you been here long? Is Lara here?'

'Don't know about that mate, ahm just in but ah think she'll be steerin' clear eh.'

Martin drew another deep breath, letting out a 'ya fuckerya' as he exhaled.

Colin patted him on the shoulder shaking his head and laughing quietly.

'You're some fuckin' boy Martin, you needin' a drink?'

'Naw ah'm fine mate, eh. Had plenty th'day likes.'

'You gonnae be OK?'

'Eh, no' sure about that likes. Think ah might head hame, get a bit o' sleep, eh.'

'You want me to come wi' ya?'

'Naw, naw, dinnae be daft, ah'll be fine eh. Actually come to think of it though, have you got the keys to the hire car?'

'Well, aye but…'

Colin reckoned that Martin looked ten times better than he had a few minutes ago but he still looked a bit of a state.

'You be alright to drive like?'

'Oh fuck aye Colin, shit ah've drove in worse nick than this. It's just tae Bruntsfield, eh.'

Colin knew this was true and didn't like the idea of Martin walking around like this in the dark. He fished in his pocket for the key.

'Aye, fair do's mate.'

He just stopped himself from adding 'Straight home now!'

A thought occurred to Martin.

'Aw, hold on though, is the car clean yet?'

Colin handed him the keys.

'The car was never dirty mate. Like ah said, it was a quick down and back today.'

Martin ambled to the doorway of the club. The cold May air provided chill after the heat of the club. The two bouncers looked at Martin then to one another as if to say 'ah seen that comin'.'

The car was in the usual spot. Martin checked the key fob, spotted the "H" Honda logo and, sure enough, the car waiting for him was a blue Honda Accord. Martin shook his head, he always hated the choice of cars for these missions although he had been told the reason. It was an OAP car and, let's face it, senior citizens tend not to be drug smugglers. Martin opened the door and sat in the driver's seat. It was adjusted for Colin's long legs and his feet only just touched the pedals. He reached under the seat and pulled the catch to set the seat forward. Fumbling for a few seconds he located the key into the ignition and turned. The key felt spongy in his hands, seemed like it was going to keep turning in revolutions.

The radio came to life, Pete Tong gibbering some nonsense about some posse or other on their way to Gatecrasher.

'Play some music Pete eh, ya fuckin' blether!'

The engine noise began to drown out Tongy's voice, louder than it should have been really. Martin checked the dash. Three and a half thousand revs. He checked his feet and, sure enough, he was pressing the gas all the way down.

'Whoops!'

He felt under the seat again and thrust himself backwards. The engine noise all but stopped as Tongy raved about the next anthem he was about to play. Martin reached for the steering wheel and was just about able to make contact with his fingertips. His left hand disappeared below the seat again.

'Right, concentrate ya mug!'

Slowly he edged the seat forward until the position at least seemed right. Still a bit strange but it was an unusual car and all, so perfect might not be an option. He depressed the clutch and looked over to the gear stick. Reverse was to the left and there didn't seem to be any catches. He pushed down on the lever and slid it over. Grindlay Street was quiet, wide and bright from the lights of the theatre. Reversing into the open space wasn't difficult. Getting back to Bruntsfield would be manageable. He manoeuvred the car away from Grindlay Street and onto the one-way Cambridge Street, where the bright lights of the theatre faded into the dim casts provided by Edinburgh street lighting.

Somewhere behind, the flashes of photographers, or some festival attraction, were reflecting in the wing mirror. Bright blue beams of light. Martin studied them a little closer in the mirror before swivelling his head to see the unmistakeable display of police car flashing lights some 50 metres behind. Headlights flashing in unison, there was no mistake. He was being pulled over. A wave of panic hit Martin all at once. About to be stopped by the police. Way over the limit for alcohol, loose ecstasy in his top pocket and driving a car that as little as an hour ago had been used for the purpose of smuggling drugs.

It was almost inadvertent. As if his right foot was thinking for itself it started to press down on the pedal. The car accelerated down Cambridge Street, the following police vehicle keeping pace. A thought hit Martin.

'Cambridge Street. One-way street. But not this way ya dozy cunt – of aw the stupid fuckin' things to do ahm about to get caught wi drugs for driving the wrong way down the street.'

Snowballs were making knowing what to do next difficult. Dead ahead were the Kings Stables and the cliffs off Edinburgh Castle. The only options were turning left towards the seedy nightlife of Lothian Road or right along the atmospherically lit Castle Terrace, where the ancient fortress loomed large to the left atop its rocky perch. Martin could easily decide the preferred scenery should there absolutely have to be a police chase.

At the end of Cambridge Street, the Honda still travelling way too fast to negotiate a turn under control, Martin swung the steering wheel towards the right. The back tyres screeched as they struggled for stability on the cobbled road. More blue lights flashed in front. Police cars were already on Castle Terrace and another one was making its way in front of the Honda from Cornwall Street. The correct way to Castle Terrace from Grindlay Street.

'What the fuck's aw this?'

This was way over the top for a car caught driving the wrong way on a one-way street, or had they been there waiting for the Honda? Martin knew he had to get out of there now. This wasn't just a traffic thing now. There were far too many police. At least four sets of flashing lights ahead and the pursuing car now swinging on from behind. The Honda steadied itself and Martin pushed the accelerator all the way to the floor. The car directly in front though had no intention of letting him past as it manoeuvred into the Honda's path. Martin jerked the steering wheel full left. The car juddered over now making its way into the car park elevated above the Kings Stables Road. A violent jolt made its way throughout the car followed by the crumpling noise of the front of the Honda pressing into a cast iron post on the perimeter of the car park.

The car came to an instant halt. Martin flew forward, his chest bouncing off the steering wheel, taking the impact out of his head's contact with the windscreen. His body continued out of the seat and into the other side of the cabin, his shoulder impacting the dashboard on the passenger's side of the steering wheel. All of the wind was knocked out of Martin as he watched a single white pill spin out of his shirt pocket, rattling off the windscreen and coming to rest on the dashboard. He remembered that he had six of them left. One sat on the dashboard, the rest unaccounted for. He knew he'd have to get rid of them. Knew the police would be there any minute. He reached his left hand into the pocket. There were certainly some pills still in there.

The car door swung open. Someone outside had pulled the handle. A hand darted towards the key and killed the engine and he could hear shouting: 'SIR, PLACE BOTH HANDS ON THE STEERING WHEEL!'

62

Lothian and Borders Police headquarters in Fettes Avenue may have been an all-singing, all-dancing modern building. A fitting monument to the sterling work being done by Edinburgh's boys in blue it may have been, but the cells weren't quite so welcoming. Around 15 foot by 12 foot with a strongroom door and a toilet cistern positioned directly beside it. No wash handbasin, which Martin considered disgusting, and at the opposite side of the cell a thin mattress apparently fixed to the floor. The walls were a dirty cream colour with no markings or graffiti.

The only hint of an outlook was provided by a square of 12 small reinforced panelled windows on the ceiling. Martin had been studying the windows with a view to getting up to them and breaking through to make good his escape. Not a particularly feasible, or in fact serious, plan but it was something to do while he was waiting and hair-brained ideas were pretty commonplace when on Snowballs.

He had been held for around an hour and, as yet, had not been charged with anything. He was pretty sure that he would be charged at some point though. Having been caught in a crashed car with seven pills of what the press generally described as dangerously evil ecstasy in his possession. This wasn't how he'd have chosen to spend the early hours of a Saturday morning but the more he thought about it the less he worried about the implications of him being there.

Crashing the hired car. A simple fine for drink driving and a six-month ban. The breathalyser must have just about blown a gasket. Martin smirked to himself. As for the drugs, getting caught with fewer than ten would almost always result in a simple possession charge. When intent to supply was taken out of the equation, the fact that he was registered as unemployed would probably mean that community service would be the worst he'd be facing and, let's face it, he wasn't the busiest of chaps these days.

He had wondered for a while why so many police were involved. When he was dragged out of the car there seemed to be a whole division gathered around, dogs being released into the car and all sorts but Colin had assured him that the car was clean and he was beginning to accept that this was almost certainly the case. With the major worry of having been caught as a major drug smuggler diminishing, Martin lay on the mattress and began to consider the little windows differently. No longer were they portals through which he might escape; rather, they were small and quite fascinating kaleidoscopic screens. They didn't offer a clear view of the night sky outside but the light of the moon was certainly being cast on them and in turn processed into flickers and beams of all sorts of different colours and contrasts. Each window seemed to offer a different perspective of the outside, looking directly up to the heavens. The colours swooped and throbbed and melted together in no certain format other than that decided by themselves.

'God almighty those Snowballs are good.'

'Oi, gimp, get on yir fuckin' feet son!'

Martin's concentration was broken with a sharp pressure to the top of his left arm. He looked left to see the standing figure of an official-looking man in uniform. He might have been in the room for five minutes trying to attract Martin's attention. He certainly looked pissed off.

'C'mon you yi little fuckin' toerag on yir fuckin' feet!'

Charm clearly wasn't something that he felt he needed to work too hard at. Martin got up to stand and noticed another man standing outside the open cell door. This man was not in uniform but rather wore a not overly expensive looking wool suit and an off white shirt with dark tie. The turnkey led Martin out of the room and the suited man introduced himself.

'You alright there Martin? I'm Detective Constable Clover.'

Martin looked at him wondering if it was his looks that were holding him back from promotion. His long face and obvious skin problem made him look like the stereotypical sci-fi geek as opposed to a police detective.

'Ah'm alright aye!'

'OK.'

The turnkey locked the door behind Martin, made his excuses and left Martin and Clover standing there. After around what seemed like five minutes but was probably actually more like a half, Martin was beginning to wonder just how weird this was going to get when the detective spoke.

'You want a fag Martin?'

Martin looked from side to side, clearly wondering if the offer was for real.

'It's fine Martin, you can smoke here.'

Martin took a cigarette from a packet being held up by Clover, who did the same, lighting both Martin's and then his own. The detective took a couple of draws clearly enjoying the break before shaking his head in obvious discontentment.

'Honestly, this job, I sometimes wonder why I bother!'

He looked Martin in the eyes. Martin was starting to wonder if this was all part of the most interesting trip he'd ever experienced but felt awkward enough to consider that he should say something.

'Aye, must be a cunt, eh.'

The detective blew out a sharp plume of smoke.

'You dinnae know the half o' it mate.'

This was really becoming the most bizarre thing ever. Here Martin was having a very early Saturday morning social with the man who was probably going to charge him next and now he was starting to call him mate.

'Honestly though, you work hard at getting your collar. Nae offence likes Martin but you're a no bad wee collar for a Friday night!'

Martin made a gesture to suggest no offence taken.

'And then after aw our hard work, in swans somebody from Greater Manchester Police, who's just got here tonight and he tells you he's taking over the case. Fuckin' typical I tell ya.'

The word 'Manchester' hit Martin like a battering ram. He could feel the tension rise in his chest and his head began to swim with implications that he hadn't considered. Had the car been spotted by police in Manchester? Obviously it had. Was Colin wrong? Had they hidden drugs in it somewhere? The dogs on the scene had certainly drawn a blank but what did that mean? Then again, why were there even dogs there in the first place? Why so many cars? And now there was somebody there from Manchester in charge of the case. Martin knew now that he was involved in something big.

All the way through the corridors and up the stairs of Fettes Avenue Martin had willed his new found police constable ally to tell him some more of what was happening but he didn't speak at all until they were in an interview room with another older man that Martin assumed to be the Manchester connection.

**

'Interview begins zero twenty seven hours Saturday 12th May 1994. Present in the room are suspect, Martin Bridges, Detective Constable Clover and Detective Inspector Horsburgh of Greater Manchester Police CID.'

The statement was for the tape and clearly bona fide. Now Martin knew that the Manchester thing wasn't just some bullshit line that Clover was feeding him.

Horsburgh spoke first. He was sharp and to the point, clearly Mr Nasty to Clover's Nice.

'What were you doing in Manchester today Mr Bridges?'

Martin raised a hand to his face. Obviously being caught in a car that had been to Manchester on drugs business was backfiring badly.

273

'Ah wasnae in Manchester today!'

'You sure about that?'

'Aye, ah'd kind o' know if ah'd been to Manchester or no'.'

The detectives flicked one another a look.

'Strange. The car you were apprehended in, Blue Honda Accord, registration CAM 97J was spotted and indeed recorded today as having been parked outside the lot of Anwar Quality Motors. That lot, Mr Bridges, is in Salford and give or take some argument among the Salford residents, that my friend, is in Manchester.'

The mention of the name Anwar produced an instant shiver in Martin's spine. He had to get out of this. Had to prove that he wasn't in Manchester.

'Naw, the car might have been in Manchester but ah was here aw day. It's a hire car. Ah just borrowed it to get home. Ah swear it.'

Horsburgh frowned.

'So what, somebody let you borrow their hired car? You mind if I ask you the name?'

Martin thought hard. He knew the answer to this. The name on the licence that the car was hired under was Barney Marr. This was the name to use. A name down on all the documentation but a country mile away from anyone who'd actually been using the car that day. Just blurting out the name seemed a bit too convenient though. He had to do it a little more nonchalantly.

'Aye, ah know him, he's name's Bernie or Barnie. Aye, ah think it's Bernie.'

Horsburgh laughed, completely without mirth.

'Oh, yeah, very good, a fella who you don't even really know the name of loaned you his hired car.'

His strong Mancunian accent dripped heavily of sarcasm.

'Look, ah can prove ah wasnae in Manchester today. Ah'll tell you all the places ah was in.'

Martin launched into a list of places he had visited, in the main comprehensive but missing the names of some of the strip joints that he'd forgotten.

Clover stretched over the desk and talked for the first time.

'Anybody in any of these places see you, can verify you were there?'

He actually still seemed as though he was siding with Martin over the Mancunian.

'Well, aye, in The Links bar. A few of the boys in there know me quite well. They'll tell ya!'

'Yeah, I think you'll have to do better than that.'

Horsburgh's tone was now mocking.

274

'Wheelin' in a few of your drinking buddies won't really wash Martin.'

Martin thought hard.

'Wait, what about cameras? Those places on the Pubic Triangle, they've all got cameras.'

Horsburgh and Clover sat back in their seats. Martin was right. The strip clubs did have internal security cameras. They had no idea if Martin was telling the truth or not but these cameras would either nail him or get him off the hook. They'd have to charge him, but with what? Like it or not, all they had for the moment was six pills and a crumpled Honda. They needed Martin to crumble and say something incriminating and for the moment getting hold of tapes to show he wasn't where he was claiming to be would be the best ammunition they could have. He was either a drug smuggler or an unlucky and unwitting friend of one from whom he'd borrowed a car. The tapes would help to find out which.

Horsburgh leaned over the desk towards the tape machine with one eye on his wristwatch.

'Interview suspended at zero thirty five hours.'

'OK Martin, we'll have you back here once we've ascertained that you weren't anywhere near where you say you were and we can start getting down to what you were doin' in Manchester.'

Martin felt pretty good about things. He was confident that he would be on tape somewhere and he knew that the police would definitely look. They would know that they couldn't hide evidence like that from a defence council.

***

Martin and Clover made their way back down the stairs to the cell. Martin knew he wasn't dreaming now. This policeman actually was on his side against the Manchester copper. He thought he could work out why.

'Ah see what you mean about the guy Horsburgh.'

Clover stopped walking.

'What d'ya mean?'

Martin stopped as well.

'Well, what is he like, eh? Comin' up here and spoilin' your drugs bust by tryin' to say ah was somethin' to do wi' somethin' in Manchester.'

Martin was finding his rhythm and keeping it light-hearted.

'Fair do's like. You caught me with a few pills and ah'll hold my hands up tae that nae bother and you get your result and everybody's happy, eh.'

After a few seconds silence Martin noticed Clover's expression change. His mouth contorted into an ugly scowl and his eyes sharpened. He made the distance down the two stairs that he was away from Martin.

'Everybody's happy aye? You're happy are ya? Fuckin' enjoyin' y'rsel are ya?"

His tone was cold and threatening.

'You little fuckin' scumbag!'

He wrapped his right arm around Martin's neck and bent him over, bringing his own head down to position his mouth close to Martin's ear.

'You fuckin' dirty cunt. Whae the fuck do yae think you are likes? Do you no' realise Bridges? We know about you. We know aw about you. Evertyhin'!'

Clover removed his arm from around the neck and quickly replaced it with his left hand on his throat, pushing him against the railings, almost enough to push him over.

'You getting' it ya cunt? We know all about you and you're fuckin' goin' down. The next time you experience freedom you'll be an auld man.'

Clover released his throat and Martin was able to bring himself forward from his precarious position on the ledge.

Clover continued his onslaught.

'D'Ya understand what we're saying ya little prick. We – know – all – about – you!'

'What do you mean? Know about what?'

There was something strange about the way Martin asked this and Clover could see it. Deep etched fear in all of his features. Not just the fear of physical violence. Clover could see that he had hit on something. He didn't know what it was but he had said something that had put complete dread into Martin. He must have had a point when he said that Martin had done something that would land him a long jail term. Clover decided to push his advantage.

'You fuckin' know what! We know what you've done and you and I both know. You're going to rot in the most horrible dungeon our jail network will allow. Do you hear me? You're goin' tae fuckin' rot.'

***

Clover knew he was onto something. Something had freaked Martin Bridges on the stairs. Something that he needed to press out of him. He was now sure that Martin was up to his neck in the smuggling operation and, for some reason, he was close to cracking.

He couldn't let him have any time in the cells. Time to think. Time to recover. They had to get him in now.

He couldn't get him back in his cell quick enough. Clover sprinted back up the stairs. He had to talk to Horsburgh. They had to get Martin Bridges back into the interview room as soon as they could.

* * *

Martin was exhausted. His mind had taken way over its limit for one day. He walked over to the mattress and crumpled into a foetal position. What did they have? How did Clover know? But he knew. Martin could see it in his eyes. The tapes from the Pubic Triangle would prove that he wasn't in Manchester and Horsburgh would be out of the equation. That would be when Clover went to work. If he knew, then no way was he going to let Martin off with murdering a tourist!

What could Clover have though? He knew. Martin was sure of that but what could he prove? What was he going to do? Martin had to clear his head. If he said one wrong thing then he could just give Clover what he wanted. It wasn't just him. Colin, Daniel and Scott had all helped to take the body to London. Would Clover know that? If Horsburgh was going to wait for tapes than that would give him time. Martin lay back on the mattress. He had to get some sleep and get the Snowballs out of his system. They wouldn't help!

Martin could feel the throb of amphetamine in the nape of his neck. His eyelids were like leaden weights. He closed them and started to think. A thousand things on his mind.

Lara, Manchester, Colin, The American, Lawrie Gordon and the Anwars.

Lara, what a cow!

Daniel and Scott, they could be in the shit as well.

The police, fuckin' thousands of them.

Colin and Scott, still in the Citrus. Or was it being raided as well? That was a lot of police.

Horsburgh, big shot from Manchester.

Clover, he'd want to make a name for himself.

The Links, that was a good laugh today. He was a bit pissed though. Just about remembered playing some spotty student at pool. Wanted to make it interesting. Lost the game. Was due him twenty pounds. He was gettin' fuck all. Not really important now.

Manchester. He should have went there. Should have stayed on the ball.

Totteridge. Country park with a little moss covered lake. How did Colin know about that? Little kids going along with their parents, with nets for catching tadpoles. No idea that there was a dead American in the boot of a car just underneath where they were fishing.

Dead American.

Fuckin' idiot.

Fuckin' actin' like Bruce Lee in the pissin' rain.

Who was he tryin' to impress?

Why couldn't he just act like a fuckin' adult and take his money back.

Why the fuck did it have to be a fuckin' pitchfork he'd picked up. What the fuck was he doin' anyway, tryin' to rip somebody off on New Year's Eve?

He was tired as hell but within seconds of closing his eyes, he knew he was not going to sleep. He opened his eyes and looked towards the window panels. The moon was away now, the windows were almost completely dark. Maybe it was behind the clouds. Little glints of light remained. Shapes and shadows. The clouds must have moved as light hit the panels again.

Something was moving on the other side of the panels. Birds perched, maybe. Looked like a couple of feet on the panels though. Was there a walkway above? Definitely somebody standing on the panels.

Was it the turnkey?

Did he have a walkway over the cells?

'Wait, it's probably that fuckin' Clover.

Peering inside to check the state of his prisoner. Seeing if he was going to crack.

'No chance Clover!'

That cunt probably had fuck all anyway. Just sit it out with him. He cannae prove a thing.

Sure enough though, the figure on the windows was peering in. Through the toughened glass panels Martin couldn't make out who it was but he knew it was that cunt Clover. One of the feet started to pound on the windows. What was that all about? The noise of the heel hitting the glass grew louder. Whoever it was was trying to get in. Not Clover then! He'd just come through the door. Whoever it was, shouting something now. It was muffled. Martin couldn't work out what he was saying but the accent was familiar.

'Wait though.'

He knew that accent, how could he not! Southern Eastern American drawl. How could he be here though? Martin pushed himself backwards on the mattress, cowering towards the corner of the cell. The sound of the boots to the window were now deafening.

Martin buried his head in his arms. The American was going to get in. He must have been making good progress on the windows because Martin could now hear clearly what he was shouting.

'YOU DIRTY SCOTTISH BASTARD. HOW COULD I HAVE BEEN SO DUMB?'

Martin sprung out of his crouch when he felt a pressure on his shoulder.

'Shit! He got in.'

'You alright there sonny?'

Martin looked up to see the turnkey bending over him. Clover was standing in his position just outside the door.

'OK Martin, up you get. You're on again!'

***

Martin and DC Clover walked up the first flight of the stairs in silence. No cigarette this time. No idle banter about police rank and internal politics. Martin was tired now. He had absolutely no definite take on the police officer he was climbing the stairs with. Certainly he was no longer an ally. Was he now working with Horsburgh on the whole Manchester connection or did he have his own agenda? Was Horsburgh in on what Clover knew and were they just leading him up a blind alley with all the talk of Manchester? Ready to spring their real allegations at him when he was most vulnerable.

Martin knew that the next interview wouldn't be an easy matter of denying he was in Manchester and getting away with the knuckles rapped over six ecstasy. The fact was he had no idea what was ahead of him up the stairs. He had decided that he needed legal representation and would ask for a brief. He didn't particularly want to go back to the cell but a little more time would be handy and it would certainly be useful to have someone there on his side who was awake.

Clover stopped just outside the interview room and Martin feared another physical assault.

'You know, there is a way out of this for you.'

'What?'

Another ruse by Clover, Martin was sure of it. He wanted to ask him *'Please no more games, I can't take it'* but he knew this would be playing into his hands.

'We know what you've done Martin. You know that don't ya?'

Martin's eyes darted to the left and then back to meet Clover's but he could think of nothing to say.

Clover moved to within inches and Martin could smell stale coffee and cigarette smoke on his breath.

'We can forget about that though.'

Martin's eyes widened.

'Forget about it?'

The tone of Martin's voice made Clover wonder if they were doing the right thing. What was it they were planning to let him off with? No time for doubts now though.

'Aye, Martin, to be honest, the paperwork, the court case, the time, it would actually be a relief to just let you off with what we caught you with tonight.'

'But…'

Martin was a pinhair away from blurting it all out *'Ah murdered someone – Ah've got blood on my hands'* but was able to stop himself when he remembered who he was talking to. Was he seriously being offered to be let away with murder though?

'Just a job to us this Martin. Sometimes it's just like, you know, bit of a pain in the arse to put in the effort.'

Martin couldn't believe what he was hearing. This was another trick, it must be but with nothing better on the horizon he had to cling on to the hope.

'Right.'

'You're alright wi' that then Martin, aye?'

'Aye, aye, ah'm fine aye.'

Martin didn't have the composure to be playing the situation coolly.

'You've got to remember though, we're doin' you a favour here. Ya know what I'm sayin'?'

Clover pulled back slightly to take in Martin's full expression.

'Ah do, aye.'

'Well, that's good Martin. Cos when we get back in to the room, we'll need you to answer some questions and if we think you're no quite telling us what we need to know then we're back to square one and Martin.'

Clover placed his left hand on Martin's right shoulder making him flinch away as he drew within breathing distance again.

'You're fuckin' goin' down.'

Clover reached down to the handle and the interview room door idled open.

Horsburgh was waiting. He picked a cigarette from between his lips and pressed it into a tin ashtray. Blue-grey smoke escaped from his mouth and eased up over his face but his eyes pierced through, sharp as daggers and straight into Martin. This was the business end of the stick and he looked intent on getting what he wanted. Martin walked in first, closely followed by the detective constable.

Horsburgh sat behind the formica desk with the chair nearest the door tilted out.

'Take a seat Martin!'

On top of the desk sat the tape recorder that they had been using to record the interview and on the centre of the table there were four small cards neatly laid out.

Martin approached the desk and sat down. He could see that the cards were in fact A5 sized black and white photos. The top photo was of Tariq Anwar. Martin had no idea where the photo may have been taken. Underneath them and laid in a line were photos of Naz and Parveas Anwar. Nazim was shaking the hand of someone out of shot and Parveas was talking on a mobile phone. In both photos, the brothers were surrounded by cars and Martin assumed that these were taken looking into the car lot.

The bottom photograph was of Lawrie Gordon. He was lighting a cigarette and Martin recognised exactly where he was standing. The doorway of the Earl Of Marchmont pub. The photo looked as if it was taken from one of the flats on the other side of Warrender Park Road directly overlooking Gordon's own flat. Martin looked up at Horsburgh who was keenly studying every reaction.

'Interview resumed at zero one twelve hours on Saturday 12th May 1994. Present in the room are suspect, Martin Bridges, Detective Constable Clover and Detective inspector Horsburgh of Greater Manchester Police CID.'

Horsburgh shuffled slightly in his seat.

'Martin, I want you to listen very carefully to the next question I ask you. Do you understand?'

'Aye.'

'OK, do you recognise any of the men on any of the photographs in front of you?'

Horsburgh's stare was boring through Martin's eyes and deep into his innermost psyche. Martin didn't usually find eye contact difficult but felt that at least a little relief was needed. He flicked a glance over to Clover who was standing in the corner with an equally intense look on his face. He raised his eyebrows in obvious expectation. Martin looked back into the inescapable gaze of the senior officer. He slumped a little in his chair unable in his drug-induced state to gauge the exact enormity of what he was about to say next but deadly certain that it would change everything.

'Ah do, aye!'

JANUARY 1995

DECAYED

63

Martin sat on a Bruntsfield Links park bench in the morning sun. He liked Edinburgh. Really enjoyed living there. Sure it was just brick and mortar buildings. Same as any city? He glanced over towards Edinburgh Castle, visible between the buildings lining either side of Leven Street. Grand and ancient, it imposed itself on its surroundings, a monument to Scotland.

Actually when he thought about it, Edinburgh wasn't just a collection of buildings. He couldn't exactly consider himself particularly cultured or informed on such matters but when he thought about it what a glorious city it was. What was it they called it? Athens Of The North? Auld Greekie? He'd never been to Athens but he could appreciate that.

It wasn't just how well Edinburgh had been put together that Martin liked though. Especially where he lived, with all of the students apparently on a five-year bender, determined to spend all of their university days in virtual wantonness. Not really different from the toffs at St Andrews but with a more international feel and certainly with more opportunity and outlet for the partygoers. For ten months of the year the whole area was one long shindig for anyone with a will to join in.

The remaining two months were the lead up to, presentation of and wind-down to the Edinburgh International Festival. The official festival itself may have flown directly over Martin's head but the Fringe Festival that had now apparently taken over from the high art celebration. The events being held and the people it attracted to the city held deep fascination for someone brought up on an air base when the closest thing to revelry was the occasional organised event in the NAAFI.

Sunny was one thing but the bite of winter cut across the Meadows like a switchblade and was still in the air when a sudden gust sent a shiver down Martin's back. He slipped his hands in his jacket pocket to pull it tighter around him feeling as he did so the pieces of paper in his pockets. In his left pocket, the piece of paper that arrived by post that morning and a piece of paper that Martin hoped would never come. A piece of paper that would almost make certain that Martin could not stay in Edinburgh. Or for that matter anywhere where he had friends or people who knew him. The chill brought ideas of moving abroad to somewhere where protecting yourself against the wind wouldn't be necessary and from where the long arm of Manchester's legal community couldn't force him to come back. In his other pocket he could feel the roll of cash that his life's avoiding organised gainful employment, in preference to ducking and diving, had afforded him.

In one pocket the document forcing him to escape the city and the other pocket the only means he had of making this escape possible. The document was an appointment which he read to mean summons to meet with a representative of the Crown Prosecution Service in Manchester, to discuss how a statement made while in custody in Fettes Avenue might help them build a case against The Anwars and Lawrie Gordon. The other pocket containing just shy of a thousand pounds.

Martin had no idea what sort of escape such a relatively piddling amount of money could achieve. Two hours after finding out that leaving life as he knew it would be necessary, he had absolutely no clue about how or to where his escape would be in the long term. Glancing over his left shoulder though, he was quickly able to work out the short term escape that a minimal percentage of the money in his pocket could achieve.

Gillian, the regular barmaid at The Links, was making herself busy opening the main doors of the bar and positioning the A-frame blackboards with details of meal deals.

Tall, attractive, intelligent and funny, Gillian would provide perfect company for the next few hours of Martin's life and the service she provided via the optics at the bar were usually sufficient to provide the escape that Martin craved. He rose to his feet and turned towards his local.

'Well Gill, looks like you've got yoursel' your first customer!'

64

The lift door opened to reveal a shell-suit-clad figure. Leaning idly against a wall his eyes fixed firmly on the floor. He raised his head slowly to survey the outside of the capsule that had just transported him to the ground floor. Colin cast his gaze away from him. Didn't want to make contact with anybody.

The lift occupant didn't move. Neither exiting nor pressing for a different floor. The door started to close. Colin made his way over to keep the door open. He looked up to see the man inside. No longer leaning on the wall. Swaying from side to side, possibly contemplating an exit. Colin checked the rest of the foyer. He could pull this guy out and be done with it. Nobody else would see but at this time it was just too much like causing a scene.

Tracksuit boy said something. Growled in broad Dundonian. Whatever it was started with 'F'. Probably the word 'fuck'.

He moved forward out of the lift and checked over to look at whoever was holding the door open for him. Colin squeezed past and replaced him in the lift. The doors shuddered, they were doing something but were not yet ready to close.

Tracksuit boy lifted his head and looked into the lift. Colin looked him in the eyes for the first time. He had to gauge what this was guy was thinking. He shuffled back a couple of fairy steps and listlessly raised both hands just above his head, his eyes returning to the floor. The lift door began to close and he decided he needed to make his point again. Possibly he realised that Colin hadn't quite got his point earlier.

'Eh'm fucked!'

The steel shutter had closed completely and Colin quickly pressed on the number 11 button. He couldn't run the risk of the stoned sportsman pressing the open button just to reiterate his point. The lift juddered into movement and Colin could sense it beginning to move upwards.

Colin breathed out heavily. That may have been too close for comfort but the chances of his new and fucked friend remembering the encounter were probably not good. Colin wasn't overly fond of lifts anyway but this one was particularly unpleasant. Small and basic, the only light came from a dull strip light behind wire-enforced glass. The panels may have been futuristic dimpled stainless steel but the smell was purest stale urine.

Colin ran his fingers through his hair, sweeping off sweat as he did so.

The hill climb to get to the multi-storey block had been a bit of an exertion but Colin didn't think that it was this that was making him sweat. He carried out a quick inventory of what he'd need. He pulled out the clothesline from his jacket pocket to inspect it. Quickly putting it away again, not likely it was going to be faulty. He felt his shirt breast pocket. The wrap was there. As close as you could get to pure heroin in Scotland. That's what he'd been told. Pure unadulterated filth is how he would have described it. In his other coat pocket, a clinical pack containing a hypodermic needle and syringe, along with some anti-bacterial wipes. Did junkies use such things? He had no idea.

The lift slowed to a halt and the doors opened. He stepped out onto a landing. The smell changed from urine to a disinfectant and rubber tang. Somebody had at least been keeping this part clean. There were letters on the cream white walls. A-F, with an arrow pointing to the left, and G-J, the arrow pointing right. Colin turned right, he'd been told to go to H. He pushed through a couple of swing fire doors. The clean rubber smell intensified. The door marked H was at the far end of the corridor. There was no name on the door, but a small amount of graffiti. A few people had added their names and there was a drawing of a patch of magic mushrooms that actually really wasn't bad. Pride of place was a rasta coloured sticker of a ganja leaf positioned just below the doorbell.

Colin looked at the doorbell for a few more seconds. He checked back up the hall but he was definitely alone. He knew that if he rang this bell he was crossing a line. If he went into this house he was going to do something that he couldn't come back from. He lifted his finger to the bell, the faint chime from inside was Amazing Grace. 'Not very imaginative.'

Several seconds passed. Nothing happened. Colin bit his top lip. He didn't fancy having to go through the whole process of coming back but couldn't afford to hang around.

'Come on ya cunt!' He hunched his shoulders as he talked in a hushed tone.

Then, movement. He could hear movement from inside. His pulse began to race. This might be it. If this was who it was supposed to be then he knew now that he was going to do it. He could hear footsteps coming downstairs inside. The lock was undone and the door tilted open just as far as the latch would allow. Colin peered inside at the eyes looking outward, just gaining focus.

He recognised the eyes. It was definitely him. Not only that but he could see recognition in the eyes. The face behind the door began to smile and Colin smiled back trying to look as convivial as he could.

Colin took his hands out of his jacket pocket, spread his empty palms, tilted back and slightly cocked his head with his eyebrows raised and a grin across his face.

'Alright Steve? Long time no see, eh?'

65

Martin's vision was blurred. A whole day's drinking could do that to man. This was fair enough, there had to be some small price to pay. He'd completely forgotten about his summons and he was on top of the game, having a great laugh with all the intelligent Links bar punters.

He could have done with seeing straight though because he was sure he recognised the big fat guy at the bar. He'd seen him before. He probably wasn't the size he was now but his face was familiar. Martin pushed through the busy lounge, closer all the better for identifying the fat guy. He knew that face. From St Andrews! From Madras in fact, it was Simon Gorrie. Simple Simon. It was definitely him. Daft Simple Simon, only about double the size. Martin shouted.

'HOI SIMON!'

Simon obviously couldn't hear him. Friday night in The Links, of course he couldn't hear him. He was at the bar apparently deep in discussion with some similarly poorly dressed and just as unattractive mates. Simon Gorrie holding court like he used to do at school, telling all sorts of tales about what other people were doing. Martin drew closer and shouted again.

'HOI, SIMON GORRIE!'

No reaction, Martin would have to get close enough to tap him on the shoulder. Martin pushed through the scrum to the bar.

'Scuse mate, sorry pal, need to get past is that alright?'

It was an effort but Martin made it close enough to put an open hand on Simple Simon's shoulder. Simon pivoted on his bar stool, a little surprised at being interrupted. Martin launched into his drunken greeting.

'Alright there Simon Gorrie, ya fat bastard, what the fuck are you daein' here?'

Simon recognised Martin straight away. Martin could see that but far from the welcome he may have expected, Simon looked shocked. Frightened even.

'What the fuck's up wi' you likes?'

Simon flicked a glance at his friends and then back to Martin. He still looked like a rabbit trapped in headlights.

'Martin?'

'Aye, fuckin' Martin, who the fuck did ya think it was, Pope John Paul?'

Martin couldn't believe Simon's reaction. This was a simple meeting between two people who hadn't seen one another since school but Simon was reacting like he was in the pub with the grim reaper. He slid from his bar stool whimpering as he made to push past the people between himself and the door.

'Martin, ah'm sorry, eh. Eh've got to go, eh. Sorry mate, honestly didnae mean it!'

With this, Simon pushed his way out of the bar leaving Martin there dumbfounded.

'Sorry about what ya stupid fat fuck?'

Martin stood motionless among the bustle of The Links wondering about what had just happened. Any amount of things may have caused Simon to react like that but clarity hit Martin all at once. There could only be one reason, Simon was thick but for some reason, even when they were back at school, he always seemed to know what was happening. He looked over towards the pool tables, his jacket was hanging on a rail. The summons was still in the pocket.

Word was out. Somehow people knew. People were suspicious anyway. He'd fielded plenty of questions from people all who seemed concerned about his impending court case but he could tell they were fishing for information about what he had said in Fettes Avenue. Had he mentioned them?

In the majority of cases the answer was yes but Martin could bullshit his way out of that.

'Ah know the fuckin' scoop, you're safe man, ah told them fuck all!'

Now though, Martin knew the truth was out there. He'd seen it in Simon Gorrie's eyes. Sure as the summons sitting in his jacket pocket, the truth was out and he was no longer safe.

Not safe in The Links. That was his local. He had to get out but he hadn't finished drinking yet. Not by a long way. Wasn't even midnight and this was Edinburgh. No, he still had a bit of drinking to do. He knew where he could go as well. There were clubs off Lothian Road that anybody who knew Martin would know he'd never go anywhere near. Normally they were right but tonight such a place would be ideal. Nobody would look for him in there and if he wanted to admit it to himself he knew there would be loose girls in there. Chewing-gum-swinging sluts that would do most anything for a bottle of lemon Hooch and a few witty one-liners.

Tonight was his last night in Edinburgh. It was about time he tried out one of the city's hingoots.

66

Martin bounced down Lothian Road, crashing into people indiscriminately of whether they were male, female, young or old. A few people were pissed off enough to shout at him but on a Friday night on Lothian Road nobody was going to let some drunk with a hood up, even though it hadn't rained in weeks, spoil their party.

Martin just ignored them, grumbling incomprehensibly.

'Shut yir puss yi dick! What're you gonnae dae about it likes?'

Out of the growing chorus of disconcerted voices Martin heard one that he recognised. A female voice. Not a toff but certainly not an Edinburgher.

'Hey, bloody hell, you want to watch where you're goin' mate!'

Then a male voice. This one was not familiar. Well to do but with a distinct Edinburgh accent.

'No Lara, just leave it, not worth it, you know.'

Martin peered through the gap in his hood at the couple, he could see that Lara had just recognised him. She stood wearing a similar expression to the one Simon Gorrie had earlier. Martin drew back his hood. Taking in the scene he could see that the man standing beside her was a good head bigger than her. His shoulders, also as broad as chest, was bulging; he had wavy blond hair that wasn't long but was way beyond control. He wore brown cords and what looked like Hush Puppies on his feet. Of course he was wearing some rugby top or other. It was freezing and this guy was wearing just a rugby top? People who played rugby in Scotland, regardless of whether they were painting their lounge or out on Friday night on Lothian Road, always seemed to like to advertise the fact.

Lara looked great in a coat and dress that seemed a lot more formal than anything she would have on when out with Martin. She'd lost a bit of weight over the last year or so and it suited her. Martin knew he hadn't complimented her half as much as he should have.

The rugby player spoke first.

'Listen mate, let's not have any bother, you know, you did bump into her, bit rude you know.'

Martin lifted two fingers to his mouth and adopted a camp tone.

'Ooh, bit rude, I do beg your pardon. And I'm soooh sorry Lara, how very careless of me bumping into you like that.'

Lara winced. It was clear that she might have preferred to have made it away from the situation without revealing that she knew the ruffian that they were talking to.

'What's the matter Lara, aren't you going to introduce me to David Campese here? I've always wanted to meet him.'

Rugby player pointed with all the rudeness he could muster at Martin.

'You know this guy?'

The tone of his voice as he asked Lara this question more than suggested that the question he would like to ask would include the words 'how the hell could you?'

Anger was rising in Martin's chest. Who was this? Is he the real reason that Lara had left him?

'Oh yes David!'

Martin knew exactly what to say to get at him. He raised his eyebrows suggestively.

'Intimately!'

Martin could see rugby player rising to the bait, his eyes widening in surprise. If he was shocked that Lara could have been involved with the drunk man on Lothian Road, how would he react to finding out that his squeeze was one of the most notorious female drug dealers in St Andrews recent history. There was scope here to fuck this guy off badly.

Rugby player composed himself.

'The name's not David. It's Geoff.'

'Really?' Martin interjected. 'I almost care.'

Martin was about to ask Lara if she could sort him out with some cocaine 'til he could get her the money next week. That would take a bit of explaining but rugby player butted in.

'C'mon Lara, let's not waste any more time with this loser.'

There weren't many more straws to be broken with Martin.

'Wasting time wi' me? You've got nae idea how much time me and Lara have wasted together. Plenty o' fuckin' time pal.'

Martin hated this guy already. Stuck-up twat that he was. Lara clearly thought she was going up in the world but people like him had no idea. No chance would he be able to keep her happy. Martin had changed his mind. He no longer wanted to taint Lara in his eyes. He wanted to teach rugby player a harsh lesson in life.

Being stuck at the back of a scrummage for 80 minutes and a history of being buggered by prefects at public school did not prepare you for a meeting with a genuine St Andrews tough nut. Martin wanted to smash him. Maybe it was the alcohol. Maybe a release of frustration and Martin didn't have them to want but he decided right there and then that the next word that rugby player said he was going to break some of his perfectly polished teeth.

'One more word mate! Just give me the excuse.'

Rugby player obliged and Martin was right. Was he hell expecting it!

'OK Lara, let's get out…'

He was half turned to leave, wasn't paying attention. Talking when he should have been listening.

Martin's fist collided squarely on his mouth. This guy could've been the incredible hulk but an unexpected hit like that was going to hurt. He stumbled backwards and towards the ground. Six foot five of Edinburgh loose head prop crashing into a shop door railing. He was on the ground, half in shock from the fact that it had happened and more than a little stunned by the impact. Martin thrust a Timberland boot squarely into his nose. He'd kicked people in the head before but usually he would hold back a little. A full-on volley in the face was after all a little bit of a grim thing to do. No such caution tonight though.

Some people who had noticed the initial attack may have been surprised by the suddenness of the violence but were forced to draw gasps that someone would kick someone in the head with such force.

Rugby player's head rifled backwards, colliding with the shop gate and all sign of consciousness was gone. Martin stooped over him and grabbed him by the collar.

'YOU FUCKIN' JUMPED-UP PRICK. I'LL FUCKIN' KILL YA!'

Martin could feel light impacts raining fast on the back of his head. Screaming. He could hear screaming. He turned around and Lara landed a punch on to his face. The impact wasn't hard but Martin could feel jewellery scraping his cheek. Lara continued punching, mainly on his chest, screaming as she went.

'YOU BASTARD, I HATE YOU, I HATE YOU, GET AWAY, I FUCKIN' HATE YOU.'

Martin took a pace back. Room to get away from the onslaught. Room to assess what he was hearing.

'Hate me? Hate me?'

He looked into her eyes. She was still screaming but Martin had tuned out to what she was saying. He could clearly make out the look on her face. She wasn't lying. Complete intense vicious hatred. She made her way forward the better to make another attack but Martin wasn't having that.

'I'll show you fuckin' hatred darlin'.'

Martin drew back his hand. The whole thing went so fast, it could have been slow motion but every detail of what was happening was etched into Martin's consciousness. The momentum of Lara flying forward made it worse. Martin's clenched fist hit Lara just to the left side of her mouth. Her head sprung backwards, her hair cartwheeling, providing a kaleidoscope when combined with the bright street lights. She stumbled a couple of steps backwards and fell onto Lothian Road.

A taxi driver, quite correctly, was not really paying attention for falling women onto the road in front of him. He missed hitting her by less than a foot. A helpful onlooker moved onto the road to flag down the rest of the traffic to ensure it didn't happen again. Martin moved to the side of the pavement to survey what he had done.

Lara wasn't screaming anymore. She was whimpering. Stunned and in shock. The hit was hard but she was still in control of her faculties. She was feeling her face and helpful guy began to help her from the road. Another helpful onlooker who fancied his chances decided it was his turn to get involved.

'Ya prick, that was right oot o' order likesay!'

Martin watched him approach. He was at least six inches smaller than rugby player and no way had he spent a quarter of the amount of time in the gym. Martin had to know that he could take this one as well. Especially in the form he was in tonight. A thought hit Martin though. This guy was right. He was a prick. He was way out of order. Lara was being moved off the road. Not ready to stand up yet though.

Traffic was stopped. Rugby player groaned a little. It would be a while before he worked out what had just happened. Everyone not involved in Lara's recovery was looking at Martin and not one of them showed signs of anything less than complete disgust. Martin turned up Lothian Road and began to walk. After a few steps he pulled up his hood again. There was absolutely no rain from which he needed to protect himself.

67

Martin bundled through the front door of the flat almost falling into the lounge.

Colin was sitting alone in the seat adjacent the window. He hardly seemed to notice the commotion and drama of Martin's entrance.

Martin shuffled over to the window and peered out between the curtains.

'Shit, shit, shit.'

Colin glanced over, nonchalantly as though nothing particularly unusual was happening, his concentration clearly more focused on the joint he was busy preparing.

'You alright there?'

Martin paused. It was difficult to know what to say next. If Simon Gorrie knew that he was a grass then the chances were that so did Colin. Maybe he should come straight out and tell him. This was Colin after all. If anybody was going to understand it would be him. He surveyed Colin's body language. Martin had been making quite a deal about being upset since coming in but Colin didn't seem to be bothered. Maybe he already knew. One problem at a time though, he had to make sense of what he'd just done.

'Colin, mate, ah've fucked up!'

Colin continued with the joint.

''S that a fact?'

He knew! Knew that he was a grass. Martin was sure of that now. Did he think that he'd stuck him in as well though? That could wait. No point in blurting all that out. Deal with tonight.

'Just seen Lara on the Lothian Road. She was wi' some bloke. Ah lost it, eh. Ended up hittin' her. Kind o' a bad one like.'

Colin looked up from what he was doing. This bit of news grabbed his interest.

'Hit her?'

'Aye, mate, this is what ah'm tryin' tae tell ya'. Ah'm losin' it man. Ah've been out aw day. Fuckin' pissed stottin' down Lothian Road and bumped into her wi' this big dick. Couldnae handle it man, just went fuckin' loopy. Totally cannae believe what ah done!'

Colin licked the skins and looked for his roach material.

'Aye that is a bit fucked up!'

Martin was now certain. Colin knew. Too casual. Martin was pouring his heart out about assaulting Lara and he hardly seemed bothered.

He finished the joint and looked for a lighter.

'You know what ah did th'day while you were out enjoying yoursel'?'

'Enjoying mysel'? Ah'm no tryin' to be funny here Colin but ah'm no' kiddin' ah'm… ah'm fuckin' crackin' up here.'

Colin faced his friend and studied his face for reaction while he uttered the next sentence.

'I went over tae Dundee and executed Steve McNaughton.'

Martin shook his head in double take, unsure if he'd heard correctly.

'What?'

'Sit down Martin, mate.'

Martin sat and Colin lit the joint he had been so diligently creating, taking a long draw before continuing.

'It's a long story, but guess who ah bumped intae last week. You'll never guess. Fuckin' Simon Gorrie. He's living in Edinburgh now and you know what he's like, he's probably been hanging around Bruntsfield because he knows we're here.'

'Aye, ah saw him earlier in The Links. Surprise to see him in there eh.'

Martin thought back to his reaction.

'Fuckin' dopey dos' cunt!'

'Aye, well it was The Links where ah saw him. He's probably makin' it his local 'cos of all the young student birds. Anyway, he starts bothering me about Steve McNaughton. Ah've no' really any idea why. Must've thought he was making a connection with me or something.'

Martin thought back to what Colin had said earlier. Something about McNaughton and execution. Had he actually heard properly? An awful lot of weird shit was happening. Suppose that could have been a trip flashback.

'Anyway, Simple Simon's just recently moved tae Edinburgh. He'd been livin' in Dundee amongst the pond life and he's harping on about all the stories he's heard. Thought he'd cheer me up with a story that McNaughton was telling him about you.'

'Stories about me?'

Martin thought back to Simple Simon in the bar and how he had been when he'd seen him. What was the daft cunt on about?

'He was apparently harping on about haein' met you last New Year in Dundee and what a great guy ya are. Telling a story about a couple of years ago how you and him hatched a plot to steal some money off a couple of stupid cunts by giving one another a couple of digs and saying that you're been turned over by Digger Stewart. Long time ago now mind. All very hilarious stuff.'

Martin didn't react to what Colin was saying he was still trying to work out what

Simon Gorrie's reaction at seeing him was all about.

Colin realised that he wasn't quite on the ball yet.

'No' sure he thought it was that funny when ah told him that one of those daft cunts was me!'

All at once Martin realised the enormity of what he was being told. His whole body turned cold.

'Oh, naw, Colin naw.'

'Och, s'pose it was quite funny eh, watching all the colour drain out of his stupid fat puss. Bit like yours now eh!'

Colin placed the joint into an ashtray and pushed it across the table.

'Aw, mate, Colin, it wasnae like that, eh.'

'Well, maybe ah'm no' too clever cos ah cannae really think about what else it could have been like, eh.'

Martin thought back to Simon Gorrie's reaction at seeing him. It was probably nothing to do with knowing that he'd grassed; rather having worked out that he'd let something slip to Colin earlier that he shouldn't have.

'Naw Colin please, it really wasnae. It was fuckin' that dodgy cunt McNaughton.'

Martin looked at the joint in the ashtray. It seemed now to represent almost the last cigarette as always given to the condemned man in the movies but it was now just too tempting. He picked it up and took three hurried tokes before considering.

'He was in a bit of bother and he, well, he convinced me!'

'Nothing to do with the cash then?'

Martin looked into Colin's eyes for the first time since sitting down.

'Naw, naw Colin, he took the money, he needed it, eh. He was intae Digger for a lot more than that likes, eh.'

'What and you took nothin'?'

Martin looked away. He could assure Colin that he took none of the money but would he believe him?

'Thing is Martin.'

Colin encouraged Martin to look him in the eye again. Colin now had a callous smile on his face but his eyes were still pure rage.

'Steve McNaughton'll never get the chance to dae that again!'

'How, wh-what've you done!'

'Ah told ya mate. I executed him.'

Martin took a long draw of the joint, this was getting surreal but he didn't doubt that

Colin was telling him the truth.

'Executed? How?'

Colin motioned to have the joint back. Martin obliged.

'Well, ah found out where the dodgy cunt stayed. You know the multis on the middle o' The Hull. Classy, y'know. So ah went to pay him a visit. Liked what he'd done wi' the place. Sort of seventies retro wallpaper. Tatty secondhand shite for furniture. Rustic effect. Very effective!'

Martin could picture the place.

'Anyway, luckily he was alone at home, Ah'd heard he was a bit of a skag head now so when ah offered him some brown he kind of put aside all the questions and welcomed me in. Ya know what these dirty junkies are like.'

Martin sat listening to what he was being told, he didn't doubt this had actually happened, bizarre as it was and he knew where this was going.

'Anyway, ah knew this was good heroin, I'd been assured o' that but it was clearly better than any shite he was getting in Dundee cos he was out for the fuckin' count, eh. So anyway, ah just whipped out some washing line that ah just happened to have on me. Put in a window above his living room door swung the rope around the beam and then hung the cunt, eh. That woke him up. No' for long though, eh.'

'Nah, ya couldnae have, you're no' serious!'

Colin banged his hand down on the table dropping the joint. He was staring directly at Martin.

'Do ah fuckin' look like ah'm takin' the piss?'

Martin shuddered, he knew it was true. He was surprised that his immediate thought was that Colin was now in big trouble.

'You just cannae go about killin' people Colin, you'll no' get away wi' it!'

Colin made obvious his disappointment at this statement.

'Dinnae see why no' Martin. You fuckin' have.'

'Aye but Colin.'

He was right, Martin had for the moment at least got away with murder. Thanks mainly to Colin. What was it that made him think that Colin would be less careful with himself?

'Have ya just left him hangin' there?'

'Ah have, aye.'

'Well, it's fuckin' different though, eh. That American cunt's now at the bottom o' a lake in fuckin' Totteridge. You've left McNaughton where he'll be found and the police'll…'

'Relax Martin, the police'll be cool about it. Another junkie tops himself, no biggy. Toxicology report says he's full o' skag. How the fuck do they know how much it takes to knock a cunt like that out? So he's depressed about his habit and decides to end it all with a fuckin' clothesline. Happens all the time. Case open. Case shut!'

Martin thought back to St Andrews all those years ago. Colin almost killing Billy Fotheringham, then being so cool afterwards. So calculating. He was right then. Martin didn't doubt he was right now.

Colin picked up the joint stubbed it in the ashtray and then began to build another one. It just seemed so natural. He seemed so unperturbed by the whole situation.

Martin began to think of more pressing matters.

'What does this mean?'

Colin looked up, distracted from the new joint.

'What does this mean what?'

'Well, what does this mean for you and me.'

Colin lay all of the joint paraphernalia down and looked at his friend.

'You and me Martin?' He shrugged. 'Ah'll tell you what it means mate! There's you and there's me. Ah winnae bother you. You winnae bother me.'

Martin slumped back in the chair. He felt no relief that Colin didn't mention any punishment. He knew now that Colin was washing his hands of him. Part of him wished that Colin had stood up and pointed a gun at his head.

Colin leaned forward to be better understood.

'Martin!' He needed to break his distracted attention. 'You're on your own now mate and ah hae to tell ya. Ah dinnae think you're gonna make it!'

Martin placed both palms on his forehead and leaned forwards. This was his worst nightmare and it was coming true.

'Where'll I go?'

'Eh, no really my problem mate, eh.'

Colin returned to his joint.

'Look, obviously don't want to kick a man when he's down, eh but you should know that everybody knows what you done in Fettes Avenue!'

Martin sat bolt upright his eyes now wide with shock.

'What d'ya mean!'

'Ah mean, Lawrie Gordon, the Anwars, they know you stuck them in.'

All at once Martin's ability to stay upright seemed to drain from his body and he slumped back in the chair.

'Ah'm fucked!'

'Aye, you're fucked, fuckin' course you are. What the fuck were you thinking about? How could ya be so fuckin' stupid?'

'Honestly, Colin, ah didnae know what the fuck ah was doin. 'Ah was trippin' in there eh. It was just like. None of it seemed real but the American. It was all they were interested in, ah swear it. They were playin wi' my head.'

'The American?'

Colin was interested now. The American was after all not just Martin's problem.

'Aye Colin, like ah said, ah was trippin' and ah was sure that they had the American. Fuckin' panicked mate. It was the only way out.'

A thought suddenly struck him.

'Colin mate, ah never mentioned your name. Not once. They fuckin' asked like.'

Colin looked at Martin and nodded slightly. The anger was subsiding.

'Ah know that mate, that's the only reason you're still here.'

Colin reached below the coffee table and brought out a small grey address indexer. He opened it and began to write something down on the pad.

'Seriously mate, if those cunts found out ah was doin' this ah'd be in as much trouble as you.'

He tore off the page and put it down in front of Martin.

Martin leant forward to read the note. It was a 071 telephone number, inner London, but it wasn't Bruce Dunne's.

'What's this?'

'It's a telephone number. Ah think ya should use it.'

'Somebody ah know?'

'Aye, it's somebody ya know alright. Somebody ya should have phoned ages ago.'

Martin sat in silence. He didn't want to ask.

'It's Natalie's number.'

Martin's face began to quiver and a tear tumbled down his left cheek.

'You kept in touch?'

'Course we kept in touch. It's fuckin' Natalie man.'

Martin dared to look Colin in the eyes again. The cold calculated killer was gone. It was Colin again, his friend, and he could see genuine concern.

'She's always asking how you're doing. Just lately ah havenae had the heart tae tell her the truth.'

68

Martin woke up in Waverley Station shivering from the intense cold. He looked at his wrist to check the time but his watch had gone. He couldn't remember taking it off. Had no reason to. Had it come off when he was fighting Lara's rugby player? He didn't know.

He looked around the station. He wasn't the only person who had used the place as digs. There didn't seem to be many of the tramps and apparently homeless people that sat on North Bridge and asked for your change during the days. They probably all knew better places to go than the freezing concourse of Waverley Station at nights.

The other benches had smartly enough dressed travellers with rucksacks who had clearly missed their connections. A couple were sharing one of the benches, keeping close. All the better to benefit from each other's body temperatures.

There was a billboard showing all of the times of the trains yet to arrive and when they would depart but nothing to indicate the actual time of morning. Martin felt in his jeans pocket for his mobile. Glancing at the top of the screen he could see that the battery was low. No chance of charging it, he would soon be out of contact with all whom he knew. Not a great problem although there was one number that he planned to use, hopefully before the phone went dead.

The other side of the telephone screen showed the time, twelve minutes past seven. A little early for a Saturday morning he thought. He looked over towards the central area where the ticket office was housed. Doors locked, nothing even looking like activity within.

Martin looked back at the screen. There were five missed calls. He dreaded to think who was trying to contact him as he pressed the button to reveal the identity. All five were listed as 'LARA B'. All of these calls received within the last 20 minutes. Starting even before seven in the morning.

The muddled memories of the previous night came flooding back all at once but sharper clearer and in perfect detail. The noise that Lara had made as the impact of Martin's full power collided with her face. The look of complete shock on her face as she lay flat on the ground. Her perfect teeth tainted red with the flow of blood pouring out of her mouth.

Why was she calling? This couldn't be good news. He placed the phone back into his pocket and began to ready himself. He'd need to have breakfast before his trip and there was no point in paying British Rail prices. Never having been to McDonald's this early on a Saturday morning, he wondered if they would be open. There was only one way to find out.

He could feel the vibration of the phone in his pocket, the way it always did before the tone kicked in. He fished the phone out and looked at the name that he knew it would be displaying. He needed the battery power it had left but had still not worked out how to cancel a call. He was beginning to doubt it was possible. In any case he was now thinking that Lara would keep calling all day until he answered and thought that at least she deserved the courtesy of an answer before the phone became dead once and for all. He pressed the answer button.

'Lara, look, ah'm really, really sorry about what ah did last night, eh.'

There was a pause, long enough for Martin to wonder whether Lara was still on the line.

'Lara?'

'Aye Martin, I cannae believe you did that.'

She talked slowly and purposefully, it was impossible to tell how she was feeling about it.

Why she was calling?

'Honestly, Lara, ah don't know what the fuck ah was thinkin', eh. Just cannae believe ah done that. Are you OK?'

There was another pause.

'Ah'm, well, ah've been better. Ah've no' called about me though Martin. Listen. Ah've just heard something and you're in a lot o' bother. You've got to get out o' Edinburgh.'

Much as Martin knew this, hearing it from Lara, hearing it early Saturday morning with the urgency it was being delivered hit Martin all at once. He walked to the nearest bench, slumped onto it and buried his head in his lap, the phone still pressed to his ear.

'Martin?'

Martin was sobbing quietly into the telephone but loud enough for Lara to hear.

'Lara, ah know, ah've got to go. Ah'm in the train station. Dinnae even know where to go tae.'

'OK, which station are you in?'

'Waverley, why?'

'Ah'll come and pick you up! Get you out of Edinburgh.'

302

Martin thought about it. Taking the train actually seemed more sensible but he didn't want to refuse Lara's help.

'OK, ah'll wait at the taxi rank.'

***

Lara pulled up in the car just next to where Martin was sitting. He didn't notice it was there. His head was buried into his chest and quite apart from the complete despondency of knowing that he had to leave his whole life behind, he felt awful. His two-ply lined Stone Island jacket was usually more than enough to protect its wearer against the winter weather in Edinburgh but was clearly not up to the task of providing comfortable all night sleeping protection from the chill wind blowing through the station. Apart from being freezing, Martin was hungry and on the verge of gaining an almighty hangover. His mouth lacked even a hint of moisture. He would have happily drunk the water out of the taps in the Gents toilets but they were still probably about an hour away from being opened.

Lara used her horn. It echoed around the Victorian station, sending a cascade of pigeons towards the roof.

Martin looked up and with the minimum of movement from the rest of his body he allowed his legs to carry him to the open door of the warm automobile. He removed his hand from his pocket and exerted what seemed like a mountain of effort to close the door before replacing his hand in his pocket and facing Lara. He couldn't remember ever feeling so bad. Physically, emotionally or mentally but if he had thought that he had reached the depth of despair, then looking at Lara proved him wrong, sending him deeper into the depths of shame and self pity. Her usually alabaster textured left cheek was swollen out to double the size, coloured a phase of black and deep purple with a dark red spilt stretching from the edge of her mouth for around a half inch.

'Oh no, Lara. Ah'm so sorry, ah really cannae believe ah did that.'

Lara faced the front to start driving, if anything her injuries looked worse from the side. She seemed distant, unemotional and certainly not interested in Martin's excuses.

'Aye, you shouldnae have done that!'

Martin had no confidence to say anything else. Not so much he couldn't think what to say but more that he was certain that there was nothing he could possibly say that would provide sufficient apology for his actions.

Lara drove out of Waverley and turned right towards Princes Street. Martin had never seen Edinburgh's main street look so deserted. They turned right again towards the Regent Road. This was the main route through Edinburgh South to the A1 before the bypass was built. They were going to England. This made sense. St Andrews would not be safe. Dundee worse. Glasgow, just too close.

Martin wanted to ask Lara where they were going but his level of courage to do this simple and obvious thing amounted to nil. People talked about keeping quiet like a chastised schoolchild and Martin could never really link the two. He must have been chastised once every two days when he was at school but it was hardly enough to keep him quiet. This however must have been exactly what they meant. Having a thorough knowledge that you'd fucked up so badly that you had absolutely no right to talk.

They headed out the usual route of turning right from London Road along Willowbrae Road with the ancient volcanic Arthur's Seat looming ominously to their right, still heading south, still on the A1. The way out. At the Duddingston junction, Lara turned right. In busy times Martin might have done the same thing himself to avoid the bottlenecks ahead but it seemed a little unnecessary at eight o'clock on a Saturday morning.

Still, no need for criticism of her route. She turned left again through the housing scheme at Niddrie, the housing blocks of the scheme providing sharp contrast with the grandeur of the old volcano behind them and the picture postcard scenery of Duddingston Loch, just a short walking distance away.

Niddrie was well known as one of the areas of the city where crime and violence were rife. High unemployment, teenage pregnancy. A community spirit based mainly on survival of the least scrupulous. Such stereotypical views of these schemes may have been wildly inaccurate but the buildings themselves did nothing to encourage people to consider otherwise. These were the stay-away areas of Edinburgh for visitors to the city, or indeed anyone within the city with any sort of wellness of heel, either actual or imaginary. The scheme was known to be riddled with drugs and Martin could be reasonably sure that he had played at least some small part in making it so, but he never had to feel the need to go there. The distribution part of the process had never needed the help of either Martin or Colin. They were smugglers and occasional pushers among the city's trendy drug takers. The chattering class of Edinburgh's drug trade.

There was then no small surprise when Lara diverted into the scheme. She stopped beside a block to announce that she would go and pick up some things for him. It was not as though all his confidence came flooding back at once but the question needed to be asked.

'What, is this where you're livin'?'

'What did you think ah'd moved out of the flat and into the Balmoral?'

She paused outside the car looked back inside at her passenger.

'You shouldnae have hit me Martin.'

She looked completely without any positive emotion and Martin had never seen her like that. She deserved something, even if another pathetic apology. Surely there was something he could say to make her feel better.

'Ah know, ah, of aw the things ah've done, hitting you was the worst, ah'm really sorry.'

Lara looked towards the ground.

'You shouldn't have done it.'

She closed the door.

Deep body heat was beginning to be restored in Martin's bones. It was good to be rid of the chill. The trepidation of what lay ahead was still there and a hangover from hell was probably in the post but for the moment being warm was a definite boon to his morale.

It wasn't like he was about to start cracking jokes when Lara got back but, with a possibly long journey ahead, he thought that a civil tongue would at least be acceptable and he was really now anxious to know where she was taking him.

After around two minutes the driver door opened. Martin faced the person entering the car.

'You were quick…' and then stopped.

Lara wasn't climbing into the car but a large man in an old Barbour jacket was seating himself beside him. The back passenger door opened and the car lulled towards the left as someone of considerable weight climbed into the back. Martin turned to see the piercing eyes and bushy beard of the car's newest passenger.

Blind panic hit him and Martin reached for the door handle but on pushing the door found that another man was standing outside, exerting all of his force to keep the door closed. Martin could feel the hands of the man behind him wrapping themselves around his face, covering his eyes and mouth.

'OK pal, you jist keep yir mooth shut an' sit still.'

69

Colin stood by the window of the flat, looking down on the people below going about their Saturday morning rituals. Shop assistants struggling with the shutters that protected their windows from the high jinks of the Bruntsfield nights but hardly allowed a peek at the goods on parade for sale during this, their busiest day.

The convenience corner store, whose front door was becoming busier and busier. The frequency of people inning and outing increasing as the day grew ever so slightly older. Shoppers in for The Scotsman and the Saturday morning staple of well fired rolls and lean back bacon. Muesli, cereal and oats were consigned to stay in the cupboards. Those were for the weekdays.

Uncomplicated lives being played out below in the street. Or at least that was the assumption. How could he be sure that the unassuming looking gentleman in the cloth cap and cords politely holding the door open for an old dear to leave the shop before he could enter wasn't just as involved in all the shifty dealings, treachery and underhandedness that Edinburgh and life in general had to offer?

Perhaps his casual manner was his way of dealing with the indignity of the deeds that he'd committed. Sordid and malevolent, this man may have been the very embodiment of evil and no amount of holding doors open for the elderly would make up for that. Looking ordinary meant nothing. Villains weren't like they looked like in movies. They didn't walk around with dark leather clothes. Only when they were unhappy did they wear a scowl and hardly ever did they feel the need to laugh in a extroverted fashion while flicking their fingers in front of their faces.

Colin knew villains. He knew the real ones who wouldn't hesitate to harm, maim and, of course, kill should their plans require such a course of action. A hurdle of course that Colin himself knew that he had no trouble negotiating. He wasn't one of them though, *'was he?'*

McNaughton after all was floating in the scum pool anyway. On the way to Dundee Colin wasn't sure he could go through with what he was going to do but on the way back he wasn't sure he hadn't done the guy a favour.

How far would he have to go now though. He thought about Martin the night before.

'What a state.'

'What had happened to him?'

'What was going to happen to him?'

Colin wondered if he would ever see him again and it seemed doubtful. He'd done the right thing the night before though but maybe he should have done more. Telling him to get out of town could still lead Colin into trouble but surely that was the least he could do. He hadn't told him the extent of the trouble he was in and with what he knew he could only give Martin a 50/50 chance of making it out of Edinburgh.

He could have taken him to safety but that was risky. Being caught taking him away would not be understood or forgiven by the Anwars. Gordon maybe. He at least had a human side. He was a friend but the Anwars had little to gain by having any kind of kindred feelings towards Colin. They would punish him in exactly the same way they would punish anybody that they thought would knowingly help Martin against them.

Colin looked over the adjacent buildings as the sun began to wake up the city. Chances were that the polite chap now inside the convenience store wasn't really up to anything particularly sinister but this was a big city. Picture postcards did much to promote the pigeonhole that the city had been slotted into. Edinburgh. Charming, friendly, cultured and welcoming.

Colin knew a different city though. He knew the worst side of it. Criminals, chancers, deviants and those previously normal people who would do most anything for another hit. Those people and there were many. Those people had just as dark thoughts as the ones racing through Colin's mind. Those people were fully aware of the iniquity around them and, like Colin, those people had been forced to make their peace with that fact. In Colin's case, quite some time ago. The almost certain thought that he wasn't alone with such thoughts however did nothing to relieve the weight of them from his shoulders.

Carrie and Daniel sat on the main sofa behind him. They were fully aware of his pain. They could feel it. Carrie in particular wanted to help. She'd asked him about it of course. His explanation that there was no way in the world he would want her to know. That he would always do everything he could to make sure she was protected from such things had made her feel all at once so safe in his presence but so sorry at the undoubted fact that she couldn't help. The fact was that he would much prefer she stayed safe from such troubles rather than take the easier route of allowing her to be a confidante.

Colin's mobile phone rang in his pocket. He looked at the display and after a few seconds shared a look both with Carrie and Daniel before seemingly without proclivity lifting the phone to his ear and pressing to receive the call. Colin listened on the line for around 30 seconds, saying nothing, and then hung up with the briefest remark.

'Alright!'

He looked into the room. Daniel was making much of not looking directly at him. The body language clearly meant to signal that it was OK, none of his business.

Carrie looked directly at him. She willed him to open up. Wanted him to share the trouble. She could see a change in his expression. He was ready to say something. Ready to share at least something of what was troubling him.

He breathed deeply, closed his eyes for a short pause before looking again directly at the woman he loved.

'That's Martin away. We'll no' see him again.'

70

Martin could still feel the impact of the hits as they contacted with his body. Or, not so much feel as hear. Dull thuds in an uneven rhythm. The pain had gone. He was over that. Past it. Just like he was past the whole situation. Had it up to here with it.

'Fuckin' deadbeat small town Scots! Fuckin' wankers. Mancunian twats! Wannabe gangsters the whole fuckin' lot of them. Ah don't need this! Don't need them! Ah'm outta here!'

***

Martin looked around. He was now in an unfamiliar place. Not Edinburgh, he knew that. It was a glorious day and he was clearly in an upmarket part of town. Which town though?

'Martin!'

He turned to face the direction of the voice but he already knew who it was.

'Natalie, how'ya doin?'

She was standing outside the gate of a whitewashed mansion, trees hanging over the perimeter walls, their greenery contrasting with the brilliant white.

'Ah'm OK Martin. So you made it then.'

She looked great. Just like she did when he left her all those years earlier, although just that bit older. Reasonable, he supposed. She was wearing a white loose fitting summer dress with a flowery design down one side, her hair hanging just over her shoulders. Martin looked around, he still had no idea exactly where he was but he was sure he was meant to be there.

'Aye, looks awfy like it Natalie!'

Martin walked over and they embraced there at the gate.

'Ah've missed you Martin!'

'Aw Natalie, you dinnae know the half o' it.'

'Are ya coming inside then?'

Martin took a second look at the house.

'What, is this where you're living like?'

Natalie's expression was one that Martin was familiar with. Like every time before when he used to compliment her. Shy and embarrassed but obviously pleased.

'Aye, it's no' bad is it?'

'Oh aye, lush. So what's the story, you live here with your man?'

Natalie stopped, looked at the ground and blinked a couple of times. Picture perfect, she smiled.

'Nah, there's nae man. Hasnae been since ah got here.'

Martin started to feel chilly. He looked up into the sky and the sun was beaming. *'Strange,'* he thought.

Natalie was now opening the front doors. Huge panelled oak double doors with ornate brass handles.

Martin followed her into the foyer. The walls were all white and clear, the carpets deep red and plush. There was a looping double flight of stairs in front of him starting together, branching off and meeting together at the top, leading up to the first floor rooms with a water feature ornament of some Greek god or other in between.

'Holy shit Natalie, this is like Tony Montana's house!' A reference to one of his favourite films.

'Tony who?'

'Nah, dinnae worry about it, you dinnae know him.'

He knew she didn't watch too many movies.

'You want to come up the stairs, ah'll fix you a drink.'

'Oh Jeez aye, ah could do wi' a drink right enough.'

Martin struggled up the stairs. Something not quite right with his legs. Must've been something to do with that beating he took in Edinburgh.

He couldn't really remember much about that now though but he didn't really want to either. Martin could hear muffled shouting from some of the downstairs rooms. Scottish accents, he was sure he recognised them.

'Who's that down there?'

'Where?'

Natalie was just a few steps higher than Martin.

'In the rooms down there.'

Natalie held out her hand.

'Dinnae worry about them. If we go upstairs we'll be away fae them.'

Martin reached out to take her hand but his arms were heavy. He struggled to reach up towards her. Natalie seemed to realise this and came down level with him and took his hand.

'Just as well,' thought Martin, as he wasn't sure he was going to make it up the stairs by himself and he was really looking forward to that drink now.

Natalie led him into the room directly across from where the staircases met again at the top. It was a huge bedroom, decorated in the same style as the foyer, with large bay windows which looked like it led on to a balcony. A four-poster bed was situated against the wall. Natalie led Martin to the bed and he took the opportunity to take the weight off his feet. Natalie looked down at him and smiled.

'What do ya want to drink?'

A can of Tennent's hardly seemed apt.

'Natalie, if it's wet and even vaguely alcoholic ah'll be happy.'

'Nae bother.'

Natalie walked over to a cabinet by the door. Martin looked out of the huge windows. It was almost perfectly dark outside.

'That's strange, sun was splitting the pavement when I come in here.'

'What's that you're saying?'

Martin turned back to face Natalie. She was now holding a couple of drinks in her hand and had shed the white dress. She was wearing black underwear. Martin always liked black underwear. He could feel himself slumping on the bed. He just hadn't the energy to stay sitting upright.

'Aw Martin, you're tired.'

She placed the drinks back on the cabinet and reached towards the light switch.

Martin wanted to tell her not to turn them off. He wanted to look at her longer and had a terrible feeling that if she turned the light off she would leave him there but by now he didn't even have the energy to speak.

Natalie just looked over and smiled. Then she turned the light off.

ACKNOWLEDGEMENTS

First of all, my most heartfelt thanks go to Lesley. Understanding, time and love. You name it, she gave it.

Thanks also to Craig & Lou and Vince & Katie. Reading this in its original format must've been hard work. To Greivesy and Billy for their input as well, I'm grateful.

Decade is, of course, a complete work of fiction. None of the main characters are real and any likeness to people or actual events is entirely coincidental. Some of the places and organisations do exist but it is with genuine affection that I include them in the tale.

Beez Neez, Fever, Fat Sams, Caskies Bars, Houlihan's, The Cosmos Centre, The Links and, of course, the Rhumba Club. A place of infinite inspiration, I include it with great admiration, thanks and good wishes for the future.

Reference is also made to actual persons but I think I managed to keep to the truth about them. Jacqui Morrison was wonderful, Alistair Cooke was a genius and Andrew Weatherall was very different.

A fair amount of artistic licence has been employed and in particular I would hope that the actual DJs at the Rhumba's opening night in Edinburgh would understand and forgive their own demotion and inclusion of the late, great Alistair Cooke. For the record, Paul Wain was also a rather splendid spinner of discs.

Also available from Phoenix Publishing

ALL CREWS

Jungle / Drum & Bass is amongst the most exciting music to have come out of the UK. This underground sound now receives international attention and is fronted by stars like Goldie, Grooverider, DJ Rap and Roni Size. *All Crews* is over ten years of journeys through the music and features interviews with the music's top artists. However, it also delves deeper and looks at the pirate radio stations, labels, crews, promoters and ravers that form the backbone of the scene. Initially printed in 1999 as *All Crew Muss Big Up*, it was considered the definitive snapshot of jungle's earliest years but quickly went out of print and became cult reading. *All Crews* not only features a reprint of the original but also an extensive update on the many developments in the last five years.

Time Out: "As well as evoking the passion and energy of the music, the book is strong on the politics of jungle and the way it has interacted with racial issues over the years."

Grooverider: "The definitive book on Jungle."

DJ Fresh: "As colourful and vibrant as the scene it's about."

Bailey: "All Crews is the REAL source for tales from the drum & bass side - the D&B bible."

www.kmag.co.uk/allcrews

UK £10
ISBN: 0-9548897-0-3